KT-195-651

Quantum of Solace

The Complete James Bond Short Stories

Ian Fleming

TOWER HAMLETS LIBRARIES	
WFHOWES	£17.95
1 0 FEB 2010	
LOCN. THRET	CLASS F
ACC. No. C1823359	

W F HOWES LTD

This large print edition published in 2010 by
W F Howes Ltd
Unit 4, Rearsby Business Park, Gaddesby Lane,
Rearsby, Leicester LE7 4YH

1 3 5 7 9 10 8 6 4 2

For Your Eyes Only first published in Great Britain by
Jonathan Cape Ltd 1960
'Octopussy' and 'The Living Daylights' first published in Great
Britain by Jonathan Cape Ltd 1966
'The Property of a Lady' first published in Great Britain by
Pan Books Ltd 1967
'007 in New York' first published in Penguin Books (UK) 2002

For Your Eyes Only copyright © Glidrose Productions Ltd, 1960
'Octopussy' copyright © The Literary Executors of Ian Fleming, 1965,
1966
'The Property of a Lady' copyright © Ian Fleming, 1962
'007 in New York' © Ian Fleming, 1963

The right of Ian Fleming to be identified as
the author of these works has been asserted by him
in accordance with the Copyright, Designs and
Patents Act, 1988.

All rights reserved

A CIP catalogue record for this book is available
from the British Library

ISBN 978 1 40745 396 5

Typeset by Palimpsest Book Production Limited,
Grangemouth, Stirlingshire
Printed and bound in Great Britain
by MPG Books Ltd, Bodmin, Cornwall

FSC

Mixed Sources
Product group from well-managed
forests, controlled sources and
recycled wood or fiber
SA-COC-1565
www.fsc.org
© 1996 Forest Stewardship Council

CONTENTS

CHAPTER 1

FROM A VIEW TO A KILL

The eyes behind the wide black rubber goggles were cold as flint. In the howling speed-turmoil of a BSA M20 doing seventy, they were the only quiet things in the hurtling flesh and metal. Protected by the glass of the goggles, they stared fixedly ahead from just above the centre of the handlebars, and their dark unwavering focus was that of gun muzzles. Below the goggles, the wind had got into the face through the mouth and had wrenched the lips back into a square grin that showed big tombstone teeth and strips of whitish gum. On both sides of the grin the cheeks had been blown out by the wind into pouches that fluttered slightly. To right and left of the hurtling face under the crash helmet, the black gauntlets, broken-wristed at the controls, looked like the attacking paws of a big animal.

The man was dressed in the uniform of a dispatch-rider in the Royal Corps of Signals, and his machine, painted olive green, was, with certain modifications to the valves and the carburettor and the removal of some of the silencer baffles to give more speed, identical with a standard British

1

Army machine. There was nothing in the man or his equipment to suggest that he was not what he appeared to be, except a fully loaded Luger held by a clip to the top of the petrol tank.

It was seven o'clock on a May morning and the dead straight road through the forest glittered with the tiny luminous mist of spring. On both sides of the road the moss- and flower-carpeted depths between the great oak trees held the theatrical enchantment of the royal forests of Versailles and St Germain. The road was D98, a secondary road serving local traffic in the St Germain area, and the motor-cyclist had just passed beneath the Paris-Mantes autoroute already thundering with commuter traffic for Paris. He was heading north towards St Germain and there was no one else in sight in either direction, except, perhaps half a mile ahead, an almost identical figure – another Royal Corps dispatch-rider. He was a younger, slimmer man and he sat comfortably back on his machine, enjoying the morning and keeping his speed to around forty. He was well on time and it was a beautiful day. He wondered whether to have his eggs fried or scrambled when he got back to HQ around eight.

Five hundred yards, four hundred, three, two, one. The man coming up from behind slowed to fifty. He put his right gauntlet up to his teeth and pulled it off. He stuffed the gauntlet between the buttons of his tunic and reached down and unclipped the gun.

2

By now he must have been big in the driving-mirror of the young man ahead, for suddenly the young man jerked his head round, surprised to find another dispatch-rider on his run at that time of the morning. He expected that it would be an American or perhaps French military police. It might be anyone from the eight NATO nations that made up the staff of SHAPE, but when he recognized the uniform of the Corps he was astonished and delighted. Who the hell could it be? He raised a cheerful right thumb in recognition and cut his speed to thirty, waiting for the other man to drift up alongside. With one eye on the road ahead and the other on the approaching silhouette in the mirror, he ran through the names of the British riders in the Special Service Transportation Unit at Headquarters Command. Albert, Sid, Wally – might be Wally, same thick build. Good show! He'd be able to pull his leg about that little frog bit in the canteen – Louise, Elise, Lise – what the hell was her name.

The man with the gun had slowed. Now he was fifty yards away. His face, undistorted by the wind, had set into blunt, hard, perhaps Slav lines. A red spark burned behind the black, aimed muzzles of the eyes. Forty yards, thirty. A single magpie flew out of the forest ahead of the young dispatch-rider. It fled clumsily across the road into the bushes behind a Michelin sign that said that St Germain was one kilometre to go. The young man grinned and raised an ironical finger in salute and self-protection – 'One magpie is sorrow'.

Twenty yards behind him the man with the gun took both hands off the handlebars, lifted the Luger, rested it carefully on his left forearm and fired one shot.

The young man's hands whipped off his controls and met across the centre of his backward-arching spine. His machine veered across the road, jumped a narrow ditch and ploughed into a patch of grass and lilies of the valley. There it rose up on its screaming back wheel and slowly crashed backwards on top of its dead rider. The BSA coughed and kicked and tore at the young man's clothes and at the flowers, and then lay quiet.

The killer executed a narrow turn and stopped with his machine pointing back the way he had come. He stamped down the wheel-rest, pulled his machine up on to it and walked in among the wild flowers under the trees. He knelt down beside the dead man and brusquely pulled back an eyelid. Just as roughly he tore the black leather dispatch-case off the corpse and ripped open the buttons of the tunic and removed a battered leather wallet. He wrenched a cheap wristwatch so sharply off the left wrist that the chrome expanding bracelet snapped in half. He stood up and slung the dispatch-case over his shoulder. While he stowed the wallet and the watch away in his tunic pocket he listened. There were only forest sounds and the slow tick of hot metal from the crashed BSA.

4

The killer retraced his steps to the road. He walked slowly, scuffing leaves over the tyre marks in the soft earth and moss. He took extra trouble over the deep scars in the ditch and the grass verge, and then stood beside his motor-cycle and looked back towards the lily of the valley patch. Not bad! Probably only the police dogs would get it, and, with ten miles of road to cover, they would be hours, perhaps days – plenty long enough. The main thing in these jobs was to have enough safety margin. He could have shot the man at forty yards, but he had preferred to get to twenty. And taking the watch and the wallet had been nice touches – pro touches.

Pleased with himself, the man heaved his machine off its rest, vaulted smartly into the saddle and kicked down on the starter. Slowly, so as not to show skid marks, he accelerated away back down the road and in a minute or so he was doing seventy again and the wind had redrawn the empty turnip grin across his face.

Around the scene of the killing, the forest, which had held its breath while it was done, slowly began to breathe again.

James Bond had his first drink of the evening at Fouquet's. It was not a solid drink. One cannot drink seriously in French cafés. Out of doors on a pavement in the sun is no place for vodka or whisky or gin. A *fine à l'eau* is fairly serious, but it intoxicates without tasting very good. A *quart de champagne* or a *champagne à l'orange* is all right before luncheon, but in the evening one *quart* leads to another *quart* and a bottle of indifferent champagne is a bad foundation for the night. Pernod is possible, but it should be drunk in company, and anyway Bond had never liked the stuff because its liquorice taste reminded him of his childhood. No, in cafés you have to drink the least offensive of the musical comedy drinks that go with them, and Bond always had the same thing – an Americano – Bitter Campari, Cinzano, a large slice of lemon peel and soda. For the soda he always stipulated Perrier, for in his opinion expensive soda water was the cheapest way to improve a poor drink.

When Bond was in Paris he invariably stuck to the same addresses. He stayed at the Terminus Nord, because he liked station hotels and because this was the least pretentious and most anonymous of them. He had luncheon at the Café de la Paix, the Rotonde or the Dôme, because the food was good enough and it amused him to watch the people. If he wanted a solid drink he had it at Harry's Bar, both because of the solidity of the drinks and because, on his first ignorant visit to Paris at the age of sixteen, he had done what Harry's advertisement in the *Continental Daily Mail* had told him to do and had said to his taxi-driver 'Sank Roo Doe Noo'. That had started one of the memorable evenings of his life, culminating in the loss, almost simultaneous, of his virginity and his notecase. For dinner, Bond went to one of the great restaurants – Véfour, the Caneton, Lucas-Carton or the Cochon d'Or. These he considered, whatever Michelin might say about the Tour d'Argent, Maxims and the like, to have somehow avoided the tarnish of the expense account and the dollar. Anyway, he preferred their cooking. After dinner he generally went to the Place Pigalle to see what would happen to him. When, as usual, nothing did, he would walk home across Paris to the Gare du Nord and go to bed.

Tonight Bond decided to tear up this dusty address-book and have himself an old-fashioned ball. He was on his way through Paris after a dismally failed assignment on the Austro-Hungarian border. It had been a question of getting a certain Hungarian out. Bond had been sent from London specially to direct the operation over the head of Station V. This had been unpopular with the Vienna Station. There had been misunderstandings – wilful ones. The man had been killed in the frontier minefield. There would have to be a court of inquiry. Bond was due back at his London headquarters on the following day to make his report, and the thought of it all depressed him. Today had been so beautiful – one of those days when you almost believe that Paris is beautiful and gay – and Bond had decided to give the town just one more chance. He would somehow find himself a girl who was a real girl, and he would take her to dinner at some make-believe place in the Bois like the Armenonville. To clean the money-look out of her eyes – for it would certainly be there – he would as soon as possible give her fifty thousand francs. He would say to her: 'I propose to call you Donatienne, or possibly Solange, because these are names that suit my mood and the evening. We knew each other before and you lent me this money because I was in a jam. Here it is, and now we will tell each other what we have been doing since we last met in St Tropez just a year ago. In the meantime, here is the menu and the wine list and you must choose what will make you happy and fat.' And she would look relieved at not having to try any more, and she would laugh and say: 'But, James, I do not want to be fat.' And there they would be, started on the myth of 'Paris in the Spring', and Bond would stay sober and be interested in her and everything she said. And, by God, by the end of the evening it would not be his fault if it transpired that there was in fact no shred of stuffing left in the hoary old fairytale of 'A good time in Paris'.

Sitting in Fouquet's, waiting for his Americano, Bond smiled at his vehemence. He knew that he was only playing at this fantasy for the satisfaction of launching a last kick at a town he had cordially disliked since the War. Since 1945, he had not had a happy day in Paris. It was not that the town had sold its body. Many towns have done that. It was its heart that was gone – pawned to the tourists, pawned to the Russians and Roumanians and Bulgars, pawned to the scum of the world who had gradually taken the town over. And, of course, pawned to the Germans. You could see it in the people's eyes – sullen, envious, ashamed. Architecture? Bond glanced across the pavement at the shiny black ribbons of cars off which the sun glinted painfully. Everywhere it was the same as in the Champs-Elysées. There were only two hours in which you could even see the town – between five and seven in the morning. After seven it was engulfed in a thundering stream of black metal with which no beautiful buildings, no spacious, tree-lined boulevards, could compete.

The waiter's tray clattered down on the marble-topped table. With a slick one-handed jerk that Bond had never been able to copy, the waiter's bottle-opener prised the cap off the Perricr. The man slipped the tab under the ice-bucket, said a mechanical 'Voilà, M'sieur' and darted away. Bond put ice into his drink, filled it to the top with soda and took a long pull at it. He sat back and lit a Laurens jaune. Of course the evening would be a disaster. Even supposing he found the girl in the next hour or so, the contents would certainly not stand up to the wrapping. On closer examination she would turn out to have the heavy, dank, wide-pored skin of the bourgeois French. The blonde hair under the rakish velvet beret would be brown at the roots and as coarse as piano wire. The peppermint on the breath would not conceal the midday garlic. The alluring figure would be intricately scaffolded with wire and rubber. She would be from Lille and she would ask him if he was American. And, Bond smiled to himself, she or her *maquereau* would probably steal his notecase. La ronde! He would be back where he came in. More or less, that was. Well, to hell with it!

A battered black Peugeot 403 broke out of the centre stream of traffic, cut across the inside line of cars and pulled in to double park at the kerb. There was the usual screaming of brakes, hooting and yelling. Quite unmoved, a girl got out of the car and, leaving the traffic to sort itself out, walked purposefully across the sidewalk. Bond sat up. She had everything, but absolutely everything that belonged in his fantasy. She was tall and, although her figure was hidden by a light raincoat, the way she moved and the way she held herself promised that it would be beautiful. The face had the gaiety and bravado that went with her driving, but now there was impatience in the compressed lips and the eyes fretted as she pushed diagonally through the moving crowd on the pavement.

Bond watched her narrowly as she reached the edge of the tables and came up the aisle. Of course it was hopeless. She was coming to meet someone – her lover. She was the sort of woman who always belongs to somebody else. She was late for him. That's why she was in such a hurry. What damnable luck – right down to the long blonde hair under the rakish beret! And she was looking straight at him. She was smiling . . . !

Before Bond could pull himself together, the girl

had come up to his table and had drawn out a chair and sat down.

She smiled rather tautly into his startled eyes. 'I'm sorry I'm late, and I'm afraid we've got to get moving at once. You're wanted at the office.' She added under her breath: 'Crash dive.'

Bond jerked himself back to reality. Whoever she was, she was certainly from 'the firm'. 'Crash dive' was a slang expression the Secret Service had borrowed from the Submarine Service. It meant bad news – the worst. Bond dug into his pocket and slid some coins over the table. He said 'Right. Let's go,' and got up and followed her down through the tables and across to her car. It was still obstructing the inner lane of traffic. Any minute now there would be a policeman. Angry faces glared at them as they climbed in. The girl had left the engine running. She banged the gears into second and slid out into the traffic.

Bond looked sideways at her. The pale skin was velvet. The blonde hair was silk – to the roots. He said: 'Where are you from and what's it all about?'

She said, concentrating on the traffic: 'From the Station. Grade two assistant. Number 765 on duty, Mary Ann Russell off. I've no idea what it's all about. I just saw the signal from HQ – personal from M to Head of Station. Most Immediate and all that. He was to find you at once and if necessary use the Deuxième to help. Head of F said you always went to the same places when you were in Paris, and I and another girl were given a list.'

11

She smiled. 'I'd only tried Harry's Bar, and after Fouquet's I was going to start on the restaurants. It was marvellous picking you up like that.' She gave him a quick glance. 'I hope I wasn't very clumsy.'

Bond said: 'You were fine. How were you going to handle it if I'd had a girl with me?'

She laughed. 'I was going to do much the same except call you "sir". I was only worried about how you'd dispose of the girl. If she started a scene I was going to offer to take her home in my car and for you to take a taxi.'

'You sound pretty resourceful. How long have you been in the Service?'

'Five years. This is my first time with a Station.'

'How do you like it?'

'I like the work all right. The evenings and days off drag a bit. It's not easy to make friends in Paris without' – her mouth turned down with irony – 'without all the rest. I mean,' she hastened to add, 'I'm not a prude and all that, but somehow the French make the whole business such a bore. I mean I've had to give up taking the Metro or buses. Whatever time of day it is, you end up with your behind black and blue.' She laughed. 'Apart from the boredom of it and not knowing what to say to the man, some of the pinches really hurt. It's the limit. So to get around I bought this car cheap, and other cars seem to keep out of my way. As long as you don't catch the other driver's eye, you can take on even the meanest of them. They're

12

afraid you haven't seen them. And they're worried by the bashed-about look of the car. They give you a wide berth.'

They had come to the Rond Point. As if to demonstrate her theory, she tore round it and went straight at the line of traffic coming up from the Place de la Concorde. Miraculously it divided and let her through into the Avenue Matignon.

Bond said: 'Pretty good. But don't make it a habit. There may be some French Mary Anns about.'

She laughed. She turned into the Avenue Gabrielle and pulled up outside the Paris head-quarters of the Secret Service: 'I only try that sort of manoeuvre in the line of duty.'

Bond got out and came round to her side of the car. He said: 'Well, thanks for picking me up. When this whirl is over, can I pick you up in exchange? I don't get the pinches, but I'm just as bored in Paris as you are.'

Her eyes were blue and wide apart. They searched his. She said seriously: 'I'd like that. The switchboard here can always find me.'

Bond reached in through the window and pressed the hand on the wheel. He said 'Good,' and turned and walked quickly in through the archway.

Wing Commander Rattray, Head of Station F, was a fattish man with pink cheeks and fair hair brushed straight back. He dressed in a mannered fashion with turned-back cuffs and double slits to his coat, bow-ties and fancy waistcoats. He made a good-living, wine-and-food-society impression in which only the slow, rather cunning blue eyes struck a false note. He chain-smoked Gauloises and his office stank of them. He greeted Bond with relief. 'Who found you?'

'Russell. At Fouquet's. Is she new?'

'Six months. She's a good one. But take a pew. There's the hell of a flap on and I've got to brief you and get you going.' He bent to his intercom and pressed down a switch. 'Signal to M, please. Personal from Head of Station. "Located 007 briefing now." Okay?' He let go the switch.

Bond pulled a chair over by the open window to keep away from the fog of Gauloises. The traffic on the Champs-Elysées was a soft roar in the background. Half an hour before he had been fed up with Paris, glad to be going. Now he hoped he would be staying.

Head of F said: 'Somebody got our dawn dispatch-rider from SHAPE to the St Germain Station yesterday morning. The weekly run from the SHAPE Intelligence Division with the Summaries, Joint Intelligence papers, Iron Curtain Order of Battle – all the top gen. One shot in the back. Took his dispatch-case and his wallet and watch.'

Bond said: 'That's bad. No chance that it was an ordinary hold-up? Or do they think the wallet and watch were cover?'

'SHAPE Security can't make up their minds. On the whole they guess it was cover. Seven o'clock in the morning's a rum time for a hold-up. But you can argue it out with them when you get down there. M's sending you as his personal representative. He's worried as hell. Apart from the loss of the Intelligence dope, their I. people have never liked having one of our Stations outside the Reservation so to speak. For years they've been trying to get the St Germain unit incorporated in the SHAPE Intelligence set-up. But you know what M is, independent old devil. He's never been happy about NATO Security. Why, right in the SHAPE Intelligence Division there are not only a couple of Frenchmen and an Italian, but the head of their Counter Intelligence and Security section is a German!'

Bond whistled.

'The trouble is that this damnable business is all SHAPE needs to bring M to heel. Anyway, he says you're to get down there right away. I've fixed up clearance for you. Got the passes. You're to report to Colonel Schreiber, Headquarters Command Security Branch. American. Efficient chap. He's been handling the thing from the beginning. As far as I can gather, he's already done just about all there was to be done.'

'What's he done? What actually happened?'

Head of F picked up a map from his desk and walked over with it. It was the big-scale Michelin *Environs de Paris*. He pointed with a pencil. 'Here's Versailles, and here, just north of the park, is the big junction of the Paris-Mantes and the Versailles autoroutes. A couple of hundred yards north of that, on N184, is SHAPE. Every Wednesday, at seven in

15

the morning, a Special Services dispatch-rider leaves SHAPE with the weekly Intelligence stuff I told you about. He has to get to this little village called Fourqueux, just outside St Germain, deliver his stuff to the duty officer at our HQ, and report back to SHAPE by seven-thirty. Rather than go through all this built-up area, for security reasons his orders are to take this N307 to St Nom, turn right-handed on to D98 and go under the autoroute and through the forest of St Germain. The distance is about twelve kilometres, and taking it easy he'll do the trip in under a quarter of an hour. Well, yesterday it was a corporal from the Corps of Signals, good solid man called Bates, and when he hadn't reported back to SHAPE by seven-forty-five they sent another rider to look for him. Not a trace, and he hadn't reported at our HQ. By eight-fifteen the Security Branch was on the job, and by nine the roadblocks were up. The police and the Deuxième were told and search parties got under way. The dogs found him, but not till the evening around six, and by that time if there had been any clues on the road they'd have been wiped out by the traffic.' Head of F handed the map to Bond and walked back to his desk. 'And that's about the lot, except that all the usual steps have been taken – frontiers, ports, aerodromes and so forth. But that sort of thing won't help. If it was a professional job, whoever did it could have had the stuff out of the country by midday or into an embassy in Paris inside an hour.'

Bond said impatiently: 'Exactly! And so what

the hell does M expect me to do? Tell SHAPE Security to do it all over again, but better? This sort of thing isn't my line at all. Bloody waste of time.'

Head of F smiled sympathetically. 'Matter of fact I put much the same point of view to M over the scrambler. Tactfully. The old man was quite reasonable. Said he wanted to show SHAPE he was taking the business just as seriously as they were. You happened to be available and more or less on the spot, and he said you had the sort of mind that might pick up the invisible factor. I asked him what he meant, and he said that at all closely guarded headquarters there's bound to be an invisible man – a man everyone takes so much for granted that he just isn't noticed – gardener, window cleaner, postman. I said that SHAPE had thought of that, and that all those sort of jobs were done by enlisted men. M told me not to be so literal-minded and hung up.'

Bond laughed. He could see M's frown and hear the crusty voice. He said: 'All right, then. I'll see what I can do. Who do I report back to?'

'Here. M doesn't want the St Germain unit to get involved. Anything you have to say I'll put straight on the printer to London. But I may not be available when you call up. I'll make someone your duty officer and you'll be able to get them any time in the twenty-four hours. Russell can do it. She picked you up. She might as well carry you. Suit you?'

'Yes,' said Bond. 'That'll be all right.'

The battered Peugeot, commandeered by Rattray, smelled of her. There were bits of her in the glove compartment – half a packet of Suchard milk chocolate, a twist of paper containing bobby pins, a paperback John O'Hara, a single black suede glove. Bond thought about her as far as the Etoile and then closed his mind to her and pushed the car along fast through the Bois. Rattray had said it would take about fifteen minutes at fifty. Bond said to halve the speed and double the time and to tell Colonel Schreiber that he would be with him by nine-thirty. After the Porte de St Cloud there was little traffic, and Bond held seventy on the autoroute until the second exit road came up on his right and there was the red arrow for SHAPE. Bond turned up the slope and on to N184. Two hundred yards farther, in the centre of the road, was the traffic policeman Bond had been told to look out for. The policeman waved him in through the big gates on the left and he pulled up at the first checkpoint. A grey-uniformed American policeman hung out of his cabin and glanced at his pass. He was told to pull inside and hold it. Now a French policeman took his pass, noted the details on a printed form clipped to a board, gave him a large plastic windscreen number and waved him on. As Bond pulled in to the car park, with theatrical suddenness a hundred arc-lights blazed and lit up the acre of low-lying hutments in front of him as if it was day. Feeling

18

naked, Bond walked across the open gravel beneath the flags of the NATO countries and ran up the four shallow steps to the wide glass doors that gave entrance to the Supreme Headquarters Allied Forces Europe. Now there was the main Security desk. American and French military police checked his pass and noted the details. He was handed over to a red-capped British MP and led off down the main corridor past endless office doors. They bore no names but the usual alphabetical abracadabra of all headquarters. One said COMSTRIKFLTLANT AND SACLANT LIAISON TO SACEUR. Bond asked what it meant. The military policeman, either ignorant or, more probably, security-minded, said stolidly: 'Couldn't rightly say, sir.'

Behind a door that said *Colonel G. A. Schreiber, Chief of Security, Headquarters Command,* was a ramrod-straight, middle-aged American with greying hair and the politely negative manner of a bank manager. There were several family photographs in silver frames on his desk and a vase containing one white rose. There was no smell of tobacco smoke in the room. After cautiously amiable preliminaries, Bond congratulated the Colonel on his security. He said: 'All these checks and double checks don't make it easy for the opposition. Have you ever lost anything before, or have you ever found signs of a serious attempt at a coup?'

'No to both questions, Commander. I'm quite satisfied about Headquarters. It's only the outlying

19

units that worry me. Apart from this section of your Secret Service, we have various detached signal units. Then, of course, there are the Home Ministries of fourteen different nations. I can't answer for what may leak from those quarters.'

'It can't be an easy job,' agreed Bond. 'Now, about this mess. Has anything else come up since Wing Commander Rattray spoke to you last?'

'Got the bullet. Luger. Severed the spinal cord. Probably fired at around thirty yards, give or take ten yards. Assuming our man was riding a straight course, the bullet must have been fired from dead astern on a level trajectory. Since it can't have been a man standing in the road, the killer must have been moving in or on some vehicle.'

'So your man would have seen him in the driving-mirror?'

'Probably.'

'If your riders find themselves being followed, do they have any instructions about taking evasive action?'

The Colonel smiled slightly. 'Sure. They're told to go like hell.'

'And at what speed did your man crash?'

'Not fast, they think. Between twenty and forty. What are you getting at, Commander?'

'I was wondering if you'd decided whether it was a pro or an amateur job. If your man wasn't trying to get away, and assuming he saw the killer in his mirror, which I agree is only a probability, that suggests that he accepted the man on his tail as

20

friend rather than foe. That could mean some sort of disguise that would fit in with the set-up here – something your man would accept even at that hour of the morning.'

A small frown had been gathering across Colonel Schreiber's smooth forehead. 'Commander,' there was an edge of tension in the voice, 'we have, of course, been considering every angle of this case, including the one you mention. At midday yesterday the Commanding General declared emergency in this matter, standing security and security ops committees were set up, and from that moment on every angle, every hint of a clue, has been systematically run to earth. And I can tell you, Commander,' the Colonel raised one well-manicured hand and let it descend in soft emphasis on his blotting-pad, 'any man who can come up with an even remotely original idea on this case will have to be closely related to Einstein. There is nothing, repeat nothing, to go on in this case whatsoever.'

Bond smiled sympathetically. He got to his feet. 'In that case, Colonel, I won't waste any more of your time this evening. If I could just have the minutes of the various meetings to bring myself up to date, and if one of your men could show me the way to the canteen and my quarters . . .'

'Sure, sure.' The Colonel pressed a bell. A young crew-cutted aide came in. 'Proctor, show the Commander to his room in the VIP wing, would you, and then take him along to the bar and the canteen.' He turned to Bond. 'I'll have those papers

21

ready for you after you've had a meal and a drink. They'll be in my office. They can't be taken out, of course, but you'll find everything to hand next door, and Proctor will be able to fill you in on anything that's missing.' He held out his hand. 'Okay? Then we'll meet again in the morning.'

Bond said goodnight and followed the aide out. As he walked along the neutral-painted, neutral-smelling corridors, he reflected that this was probably the most hopeless assignment he had ever been on. If the top security brains of fourteen countries were stumped, what hope had he got? By the time he was in bed that night, in the Spartan luxury of the visitors' overnight quarters, Bond had decided he would give it a couple more days – largely for the sake of keeping in touch with Mary Ann Russell for as long as possible – and then chuck it. On this decision he fell immediately into a deep and untroubled sleep.

Not two, but four days later, as the dawn came up over the Forest of St Germain, James Bond was lying along the thick branch of an oak tree keeping watch over a small empty glade that lay deep among the trees bordering D98, the road of the murder.

He was dressed from head to foot in parachutists' camouflage – green, brown and black. Even his hands were covered with the stuff, and there was a hood over his head with slits cut for the eyes and mouth. It was good camouflage which would be still better when the sun was higher and the shadows blacker, and from anywhere on the ground, even directly below the high branch, he could not be seen.

It had come about like this. The first two days at SHAPE had been the expected waste of time. Bond had achieved nothing except to make himself mildly unpopular with the persistence of his double-checking questions. On the morning of the third day he was about to go and say his goodbyes when he had a telephone call from the Colonel. 'Oh, Commander, thought I'd let you know that the last team of police dogs got in late last night – your idea that it might be worth while covering the whole forest. Sorry' – the voice sounded un-sorry – 'but negative, absolutely negative.'

'Oh. My fault for the wasted time.' As much to annoy the Colonel as anything, Bond said: 'Mind if I have a talk with the handler?'

'Sure, sure. Anything you want. By the way, Commander, how long are you planning to be around? Glad to have you with us for as long as you like. But it's a question of your room. Seems there's a big party coming in from Holland in a few days' time. Top level staff course or something of the kind, and Admin says they're a bit pushed for space.'

Bond had not expected to get on well with Colonel Schreiber and he had not done so. He said amiably: 'I'll see what my Chief has to say and call you back, Colonel.'

'Do that, would you.' The Colonel's voice was equally polite, but the manners of both men were running out and the two receivers broke the line simultaneously.

The chief handler was a Frenchman from the Landes. He had the quick sly eyes of a poacher. Bond met him at the kennels, but the handler's proximity was too much for the Alsatians and, to get away from the noise, he took Bond into the duty-room, a tiny office with binoculars hanging from pegs, and waterproofs, gumboots, dog-harness and other gear stacked round the walls. There were a couple of deal chairs and a table covered with a large-scale map of the Forest of St Germain. This had been marked off into pencilled squares. The handler made a gesture over the map. 'Our dogs covered it all, Monsieur. There is nothing there.'

'Do you mean to say they didn't check once?'

The handler scratched his head. 'We had trouble with a bit of game, Monsieur. There was a hare or two. A couple of foxes' earths. We had quite a time getting them away from a clearing near the Carrefour Royal. They probably still smelled the gipsies.'

'Oh.' Bond was only mildly interested. 'Show me. Who were these gipsies?'

The handler pointed daintily with a grimy little finger. 'These are the names from the old days. Here is the Etoile Parfaite, and here, where the killing took place, is the Carrefour des Curieux. And here, forming the bottom of the triangle, is the Carrefour Royal. It makes,' he added dramatically, 'a cross with the road of death.' He took a pencil out of his pocket and made a dot just off the crossroads. 'And this is the clearing, Monsieur. There was a gipsy caravan there for most of the winter. They left last month. Cleaned the place up all right, but, for the dogs, their scent will hang about there for months.'

Bond thanked him, and after inspecting and admiring the dogs and making some small talk about the handler's profession, he got into the Peugeot and went off to the gendarmerie in St Germain. 'Yes, certainly they had known the gipsies. Real Romany-looking fellows. Hardly spoke a word of French, but they had behaved themselves. There had been no complaints. Six men and two women. No. No one had seen them go. One morning they just weren't there any more. Might have been gone a week for all one knew. They had chosen an isolated spot.'

Bond took the D98 through the forest. When the great autoroute bridge showed up a quarter of a mile ahead over the road, Bond accelerated and then switched off the engine and coasted silently until he came to the Carrefour Royal. He stopped and got out of the car without a sound, and, feeling rather foolish, softly entered the forest and walked with great circumspection towards where the clearing would be. Twenty yards inside the trees he came to it. He stood in the fringe of bushes and trees and examined it carefully. Then he walked in and went over it from end to end.

The clearing was about as big as two tennis

courts and floored in thick grass and moss. There was one large patch of lilies of the valley and, under the bordering trees, a scattering of bluebells. To one side there was a low mound, perhaps a tumulus, completely surrounded and covered with brambles and brier roses now thickly in bloom. Bond walked round this and gazed in among the roots, but there was nothing to see except the earthy shape of the mound.

Bond took one last look round and then went to the corner of the clearing that would be nearest to the road. Here there was easy access through the trees. Were there traces of a path, a slight flattening of the leaves? Not more than would have been left by the gipsies or last year's picnickers. On the edge of the road there was a narrow passage between two trees. Casually Bond bent to examine the trunks. He stiffened and dropped to a crouch. With a fingernail, he delicately scraped away a narrow sliver of caked mud. It hid a deep scratch in the tree-trunk. He caught the scraps of mud in his free hand. He now spat and moistened the mud and carefully filled up the scratch again. There were three camouflaged scratches on one tree and four on the other. Bond walked quickly out of the trees on to the road. His car had stopped on a slight slope leading down under the autoroute bridge. Although there was some protection from the boom of the traffic on the autoroute, Bond pushed the car, jumped in and only engaged the gears when he was well under the bridge.

And now Bond was back in the clearing, above it, and he still did not know if his hunch had been right. It had been M's dictum that had put him on the scent – if it was a scent – and the mention of the gipsies. 'It was the gipsies the dogs smelled . . . Most of the winter . . . they went last month. No complaints . . . One morning they just weren't there any more.' The invisible factor. The invisible man. The people who are so much part of the background that you don't know if they're there or not. Six men and two girls and they hardly spoke a word of French. Good cover, gipsies. You could be a foreigner and yet not a foreigner, because you were only a gipsy. Some of them had gone off in the caravan. Had some of them stayed, built themselves a hide-out during the winter, a secret place from which the hijacking of the top secret dispatches had been the first sortie? Bond had thought he was building fantasies until he found the scratches, the carefully camouflaged scratches, on the two trees. They were just at the height where, if one was carrying any kind of a cycle, the pedals might catch against the bark. It could all be a pipedream, but it was good enough for Bond. The only question in his mind was whether these people had made a one-time-only coup or whether they were so confident of their security that they would try again. He confided only in Station F. Mary Ann Russell told him to be careful. Head of F, more constructively, ordered his unit at St Germain to cooperate. Bond said goodbye to Colonel Schreiber and moved to a camp bed in the unit's HQ – an anonymous house in an anonymous village back street. The unit had provided the camouflage outfit and the four Secret Service men who ran the unit had happily put themselves under Bond's orders. They realized as well as Bond did that if Bond managed to wipe the eye of the whole security machine of SHAPE, the Secret Service would have won a priceless feather in its cap *vis-à-vis* the SHAPE High Command, and M's worries over the independence of his unit would be gone for ever.

Bond, lying along the oak branch, smiled to himself. Private armies, private wars. How much energy they siphoned off from the common cause, how much fire they directed away from the common enemy!

Six-thirty. Time for breakfast. Cautiously Bond's right hand fumbled in his clothing and came up to the slit of his mouth. Bond made the glucose tablet last as long as possible and then sucked another. His eyes never left the glade. The red squirrel that had appeared at first light and had been steadily eating away at young beech shoots ever since, ran a few feet nearer to the rose-bushes on the mound, picked up something and began turning it in his paws and nibbling at it. Two wood pigeons that had been noisily courting among the thick grass started to make clumsy, fluttering love. A pair of hedge sparrows went busily on collecting bits and pieces for a nest they were tardily building in a thorn-bush. The fat thrush finally located its worm and began pulling at it, its legs braced. Bees clustered thick among the roses on the mound, and from where he was, perhaps twenty yards away from and above the mound, Bond could just hear their summery sound. It was a scene from a fairytale – the roses, the lilies of the valley, the birds and the great shafts of sunlight lancing down through the tall trees into the pool of glistening green. Bond had climbed to his hide-out at four in the morning and he had never examined so closely or for so long the transition from night to a glorious day. He suddenly felt rather foolish. Any moment now and some damned bird would come and sit on his head!

It was the pigeons that gave the first alarm. With a loud clatter they took off and dashed into the trees. All the birds followed, and the squirrel. Now the glade was quiet except for the soft hum of the bees. What had sounded the alarm? Bond's heart began to thump. His eyes hunted, quartering the glade for a clue. Something was moving among the roses. It was a tiny movement, but an extraordinary one. Slowly, inch by inch, a single thorny stem, an unnaturally straight and rather thick one, was rising through the upper branches. It went on rising until it was a clear foot above the bush. Then it stopped. There was a solitary pink rose at the tip of the stem. Separated from the bush, it looked unnatural, but only if one happened to have watched the whole process. At a casual glance it was a stray stem and nothing else. Now, silently, the petals of the rose seemed to swivel and expand, the yellow pistils drew

29

aside and sun glinted on a glass lens the size of a shilling. The lens seemed to be looking straight at Bond, but then very, very slowly, the rose-eye began to turn on its stem and continued to turn until the lens was again looking at Bond and the whole glade had been minutely surveyed. As if satisfied, the petals softly swivelled to cover the eye and very slowly the single rose descended to join the others.

Bond's breath came out with a rush. He momentarily closed his eyes to rest them. Gipsies! If that piece of machinery was any evidence, inside the mound, deep down in the earth, was certainly the most professional left-behind spy unit that had ever been devised – far more brilliant than anything England had prepared to operate in the wake of a successful German invasion, far better than what the Germans themselves had left behind in the Ardennes. A shiver of excitement and anticipation – almost of fear – ran down Bond's spine. So he had been right! But what was to be the next act?

Now, from the direction of the mound, came a thin high-pitched whine – the sound of an electric motor at very high revs. The rose bush trembled slightly. The bees took off, hovered, and settled again. Slowly, a jagged fissure formed down the centre of the big bush and smoothly widened. Now the two halves of the bush were opening like double doors. The dark aperture broadened until Bond could see the roots of the bush running into the earth on both sides of the opening doorway.

The whine of machinery was louder and there was a glint of metal from the edges of the curved doors. It was like the opening of a hinged Easter egg. In a moment the two segments stood apart and the two halves of the rose bush, still alive with bees, were splayed widely open. Now the inside of the metal caisson that supported the earth and the roots of the bush were naked to the sun. There was a glint of pale electric light from the dark aperture between the curved doors. The whine of the motor had stopped. A head and shoulders appeared, and then the rest of the man. He climbed softly out and crouched, looking sharply round the glade. There was a gun – a Luger – in his hand. Satisfied, he turned and gestured into the shaft. The head and shoulders of a second man appeared. He handed up three pairs of what looked like snow-shoes and ducked out of sight. The first man selected a pair and knelt and strapped them over his boots. Now he moved about more freely, leaving no footprints, for the grass flattened only momen-tarily under the wide mesh and then rose slowly again. Bond smiled to himself. Clever bastards!

The second man emerged. He was followed by a third. Between them they manhandled a motor-cycle out of the shaft and stood holding it slung between them by harness webbing while the first man, who was clearly the leader, knelt and strapped the snowshoes under their boots. Then, in single file, they moved off through the trees towards the road. There was something extraordinarily sinister

31

about the way they softly high-stepped along through the shadows, lifting and carefully placing each big webbed foot in turn.

Bond let out a long sigh of released tension and laid his head softly down on the branch to relax the strain in his neck muscles. So that was the score! Even the last small detail could now be added to the file. While the two underlings were dressed in grey overalls, the leader was wearing the uniform of the Royal Corps of Signals and his motor-cycle was an olive green BSA M20 with a British Army registration number on its petrol tank. No wonder the SHAPE dispatch-rider had let him get within range. And what did the unit do with its top secret booty? Probably radioed the cream of it out at night. Instead of the periscope, a rose-stalk aerial would rise up from the bush, the pedal generator would get going deep down under the earth and off would go the high-speed cipher groups. Ciphers? There would be many good enemy secrets down that shaft if Bond could round up the unit when it was outside the hide-out. And what a chance to feed back phoney intelligence to GRU, the Soviet Military Intelligence Apparat which was presumably the control! Bond's thoughts raced.

The two underlings were coming back. They went into the shaft and the rose bush closed over it. The leader with his machine would be among the bushes on the verge of the road. Bond glanced at his watch. Six-fifty-five. Of course! He would be waiting to see if a dispatch-rider came along. Either he did

32

not know the man he had killed was doing a weekly run, which was unlikely, or he was assuming that SHAPE would now change the routine for additional security. These were careful people. Probably their orders were to clean up as much as possible before the summer came and there were too many holidaymakers about in the forest. Then the unit might be pulled out and put back again in the winter. Who could say what the long-term plans were? Sufficient that the leader was preparing for another kill.

The minutes ticked by. At seven-ten the leader reappeared. He stood in the shadow of a big tree at the edge of the clearing and whistled once on a brief, high, birdlike note. Immediately the rose bush began to open and the two underlings came out and followed the leader back into the trees. In two minutes they were back with the motor-cycle slung between them. The leader, after a careful look round to see that they had left no traces, followed them down into the shaft and the two halves of the rose bush closed swiftly behind him.

Half an hour later life had started up in the glade again. An hour later still, when the high sun had darkened the shadows, James Bond silently edged backwards along his branch, dropped softly on to a patch of moss behind some brambles and melted carefully back into the forest.

That evening Bond's routine call with Mary Ann Russell was a stormy one. She said: 'You're crazy.

I'm not going to let you do it. I'm going to get Head of F to ring up Colonel Schreiber and tell him the whole story. This is SHAPE's job. Not yours.'

Bond said sharply: 'You'll do nothing of the sort. Colonel Schreiber says he's perfectly happy to let me make a dummy run tomorrow morning instead of the duty dispatch-rider. That's all he needs to know at this stage. Reconstruction of the crime sort of thing. He couldn't care less. He's practically closed the file on this business. Now, be a good girl and do as you're told. Just put my report on the printer to M. He'll see the point of me cleaning this thing up. He won't object.'

'Damn M! Damn you! Damn the whole silly Service!' There were angry tears in the voice. 'You're just a lot of children playing at Red Indians. Taking these people on by yourself! It's – it's showing off. That's all it is. Showing off.'

Bond was beginning to get annoyed. He said: 'That's enough, Mary Ann. Put that report on the printer. I'm sorry, but it's an order.'

There was resignation in the voice. 'Oh, all right. You don't have to pull your rank on me. But don't get hurt. At least you'll have the boys from the local Station to pick up the bits. Good luck.'

'Thanks, Mary Ann. And will you have dinner with me tomorrow night? Some place like Armenonville. Pink champagne and gipsy violins. Paris in the spring routine.'

'Yes,' she said seriously. 'I'd like that. But then take care all the more, would you? Please?'

34

'Of course I will. Don't worry. Goodnight.'

''Night.'

Bond spent the rest of the evening putting a last high polish on his plans and giving a final briefing to the four men from the Station.

It was another beautiful day. Bond, sitting comfortably astride the throbbing BSA waiting for the off, could hardly believe in the ambush that would now be waiting for him just beyond the Carrefour Royal. The corporal from the Signal Corps who had handed him his empty dispatch-case and was about to give him the signal to go said: 'You look as if you'd been in the Royal Corps all your life, sir. Time for a haircut soon, I'd say, but the uniform's bang on. How d'you like the bike, sir?'

'Goes like a dream. I'd forgotten what fun these damned things are.'

'Give me a nice little Austin A40 any day, sir.' The corporal looked at his watch. 'Seven o'clock just coming up.' He held up his thumb. 'Okay.'

Bond pulled the goggles down over his eyes, lifted a hand to the corporal, kicked the machine into gear and wheeled off across the gravel and through the main gates.

Off 184 and on to 307, through Bailly and Noisy-le-Roi and there was the straggle of St Nom. Here he would be turning sharp right on to D98 – the 'route de la mort', as the handler had called it. Bond pulled into the grass verge and once more looked to the long-barrel .45 Colt. He put the warm gun back against his stomach and left the jacket button undone. On your marks! Get set . . . !

Bond took the sharp corner and accelerated up to fifty. The viaduct carrying the Paris autoroute loomed up ahead. The dark mouth of the tunnel beneath it opened and swallowed him. The noise of his exhaust was gigantic, and for an instant there was a tunnel smell of cold and damp. Then he was out in the sunshine again and immediately across the Carrefour Royal. Ahead the oily tarmac glittered dead straight for two miles through the enchanted forest and there was a sweet smell of leaves and dew. Bond cut his speed to forty. The driving-mirror by his left hand shivered slightly with his speed. It showed nothing but an empty unfurling vista of road between lines of trees that curled away behind him like a green wake. No sign of the killer. Had he taken fright? Had there been some hitch? But then there was a tiny black speck in the centre of the convex glass – a midge that became a fly and then a bee and then a beetle. Now it was a crash helmet bent low over handlebars between two big black paws. God, he was coming fast! Bond's eyes flickered from the mirror to the road ahead and back to the mirror. When the killer's right hand went for his gun . . . !

Bond slowed – thirty-five, thirty, twenty. Ahead the tarmac was smooth as metal. A last quick look in the mirror. The right hand had left the handlebars. The sun on the man's goggles made huge fiery eyes below the rim of the crash helmet. Now! Bond braked fiercely and skidded the BSA through forty-five degrees, killing the engine. He was not quite quick enough on the draw. The killer's gun flared twice and a bullet tore into the saddle-springs beside Bond's thigh. But then the Colt spoke its single word, and the killer and his BSA, as if lassoed from within the forest, veered crazily off the road, leapt the ditch and crashed head-on into the trunk of a beech. For a moment the tangle of man and machinery clung to the broad trunk and then, with a metallic death-rattle, toppled backwards into the grass.

Bond got off his machine and walked over to the ugly twist of khaki and smoking steel. There was no need to feel for a pulse. Wherever the bullet had struck, the crash helmet had smashed like an eggshell. Bond turned away and thrust his gun back into the front of his tunic. He had been lucky. It would not do to press his luck. He got on the BSA and accelerated back down the road.

He leant the BSA up against one of the scarred trees just inside the forest and walked softly through to the edge of the clearing. He took up his stand in the shadow of the big beech. He moistened his lips and gave, as near as he could, the killer's bird-whistle. He waited. Had he got the whistle wrong? But then the bush trembled and the high thin whine began. Bond hooked his right thumb through his belt within inches of his gun-butt. He hoped he would not have to do any more killing. The two underlings had not seemed to be armed. With any luck they would come quietly.

Now the curved doors were open. From where he was, Bond could not see down the shaft, but within seconds the first man was out and putting on his snowshoes and the second followed. Snowshoes! Bond's heart missed a beat. He had forgotten them! They must be hidden back there in the bushes. Blasted fool! Would they notice?

The two men came slowly towards him, delicately placing their feet. When he was about twenty feet away, the leading man said something softly in what sounded like Russian. When Bond did not reply, the two men stopped in their tracks. They stared at him in astonishment, waiting perhaps for the answer to a password. Bond sensed trouble. He whipped out his gun and moved towards them, crouching. 'Hands up.' He gestured with the muzzle of the Colt. The leading man shouted an order and threw himself forward. At the same time the second man made a dash back towards the hideout. A rifle boomed from among the trees and the man's right leg buckled under him. The men from the Station broke cover and came running. Bond fell to one knee and clubbed upwards with his gun-barrel at the hurtling body. It made contact, but then the man was on him. Bond saw fingernails flashing towards his eyes, ducked and ran into an uppercut. Now a hand was at his right wrist and his gun was being slowly turned on him. Not wanting to kill, he had kept the safety catch up. He tried to get his thumb to it. A boot hit him in the side of the head and he let the gun go and fell back. Through a red mist he saw the muzzle of the gun pointing at his face. The thought flashed through his mind that he was going to die – die for showing mercy . . . !

Suddenly the gun muzzle had gone and the weight of the man was off him. Bond got to his knees and then to his feet. The body, spreadeagled in the grass beside him, gave a last kick. There were bloody rents in the back of the dungarees. Bond looked round. The four men from the Station were in a group. Bond undid the strap of his crash helmet and rubbed the side of his head. He said: 'Well, thanks. Who did it?'

Nobody answered. The men looked embarrassed.

Bond walked towards them, puzzled. 'What's up?'

Suddenly Bond caught a trace of movement behind the men. An extra leg showed – a woman's leg. Bond laughed out loud. The men grinned sheepishly and looked behind them. Mary Ann Russell, in a brown shirt and black jeans, came out from behind them with her hands up. One of the hands held what looked like a .22 target pistol. She brought her hands down and tucked the pistol into the top of her jeans. She came up to Bond. She said anxiously: 'You won't blame anybody, will you? I just wouldn't let them leave this morning without me.' Her eyes pleaded. 'Rather lucky I did come, really. I mean, I just happened to get to you first. No one wanted to shoot for fear of hitting you.'

Bond smiled into her eyes. He said: 'If you hadn't come, I'd have had to break that dinner date.' He turned back to the men, his voice businesslike. 'All right. One of you take the motor-bike and report the gist of this to Colonel Schreiber. Say we're waiting for his team before we take a look at the hideout. And would he include a couple of anti-sabotage men. That shaft may be booby-trapped. All right?'

Bond took the girl by the arm. He said: 'Come over here. I want to show you a bird's nest.'

'Is that an order?'

'Yes.'

CHAPTER 2

FOR YOUR EYES ONLY

The most beautiful bird in Jamaica, and some say the most beautiful bird in the world, is the streamertail or doctor humming-bird. The cock bird is about nine inches long, but seven inches of it are tail – two long black feathers that curve and cross each other and whose inner edges are in a form of scalloped design. The head and crest are black, the wings dark green, the long bill is scarlet, and the eyes, bright and confiding, are black. The body is emerald green, so dazzling that when the sun is on the breast you see the brightest green thing in nature. In Jamaica, birds that are loved are given nicknames. *Trochilus polytmus* is called 'doctor bird' because his two black streamers remind people of the black tail-coat of the old-time physician.

Mrs Havelock was particularly devoted to two families of these birds because she had been watching them sipping honey, fighting, nesting and making love since she married and came to Content. She was now over fifty, so many generations of these two families had come and gone since the original two pairs had been nicknamed

41

Pyramus and Thisbe and Daphnis and Chloe by her mother-in-law. But successive couples had kept the names, and Mrs Havelock now sat at her elegant tea service on the broad cool veranda and watched Pyramus, with a fierce 'tee-tee-tee' dive-bomb Daphnis who had finished up the honey on his own huge bush of Japanese Hat and had sneaked in among the neighbouring Monkey-fiddle that was Pyramus's preserve. The two tiny black and green comets swirled away across the fine acres of lawn, dotted with brilliant clumps of hibiscus and bougainvillaea, until they were lost to slight in the citrus groves. They would soon be back. The running battle between the two families was a game. In this big finely planted garden there was enough honey for all.

Mrs Havelock put down her teacup and took a Patum Peperium sandwich. She said: 'They really are the most dreadful show-offs.'

Colonel Havelock looked over the top of his *Daily Gleaner*. 'Who?'

'Pyramus and Daphnis.'

'Oh, yes.' Colonel Havelock thought the names idiotic. He said: 'It looks to me as if Batista will be on the run soon. Castro's keeping up the pressure pretty well. Chap at Barclay's told me this morning that there's a lot of funk money coming over here already. Said that Belair's been sold to nominees. One hundred and fifty thousand pounds for a thousand acres of cattle-tick and a house the red ants'll have down by Christmas!

42

Somebody's suddenly gone and bought that ghastly Blue Harbour hotel, and there's even talk that Jimmy Farquharson has found a buyer for his place – leaf-spot and Panama disease thrown in for good measure, I suppose.'

'That'll be nice for Ursula. The poor dear can't stand it out here. But I can't say I like the idea of the whole island being bought up by these Cubans. But Tim, where do they get all the money from, anyway?'

'Rackets, union funds, Government money – God knows. The place is riddled with crooks and gangsters. They must want to get their money out of Cuba and into something else quick. Jamaica's as good as anywhere else now we've got this convertibility with the dollar. Apparently the man who bought Belair just shovelled the money on to the floor of Aschenheim's office out of a suitcase. I suppose he'll keep the place for a year or two, and when the trouble's blown over or when Castro's got in and finished cleaning up he'll put it on the market again, take a reasonable loss and move off somewhere else. Pity, in a way. Belair used to be a fine property. It could have been brought back if anyone in the family had cared.'

'It was ten thousand acres in Bill's grandfather's day. It used to take the busher three days to ride the boundary.'

'Fat lot Bill cares. I bet he's booked his passage to London already. That's one more of the old families gone. Soon won't be anyone left of that lot but us. Thank God Judy likes the place.'

Mrs Havelock said 'Yes, dear' calmingly and pinged the bell for the tea things to be cleared away. Agatha, a huge blue-black Negress wearing the old-fashioned white headcloth that has gone out in Jamaica except in the hinterland, came out through the white and rose drawing-room followed by Fayprince, a pretty young quadroon from Port Maria whom she was training as second house-maid. Mrs Havelock said: 'It's time we started bottling, Agatha. The guavas are early this year.'

Agatha's face was impassive. She said: 'Yes'm. But we done need more bottles.'

'Why? It was only last year I got you two dozen of the best I could find at Henriques.'

'Yes'm. Someone done mash five, six of dose.'

'Oh dear. How did that happen?'

'Couldn't say'm.' Agatha picked up the big silver tray and waited, watching Mrs Havelock's face.

Mrs Havelock had not lived most of her life in Jamaica without learning that a mash is a mash and that one would not get anywhere hunting for a culprit. So she just said cheerfully:

'Oh, all right, Agatha. I'll get some more when I go into Kingston.'

'Yes'm.' Agatha, followed by the young girl, went back into the house.

Mrs Havelock picked up a piece of petit-point and began stitching, her fingers moving automatically.

44

Her eyes went back to the big bushes of Japanese Hat and Monkeyfiddle. Yes, the two male birds were back. With gracefully cocked tails they moved among the flowers. The sun was low on the horizon and every now and then there was a flash of almost piercingly beautiful green. A mocking-bird, on the topmost branch of a frangipani, started on its evening repertoire. The tinkle of an early tree-frog announced the beginning of the short violet dusk.

Content, twenty thousand acres in the foothills of Candlefly Peak, one of the most easterly of the Blue Mountains in the county of Portland, had been given to an carly Havelock by Oliver Cromwell as a reward for having been one of the signatories to King Charles's death warrant. Unlike so many other settlers of those and later times the Havelocks had maintained the planta-tion through three centuries, through earthquakes and hurricanes and through the boom and bust of cocoa, sugar, citrus and copra. Now it was in bananas and cattle, and it was one of the richest and best run of all the private estates in the island. The house, patched up or rebuilt after earthquake or hurricane, was a hybrid – a mahogany-pillared, two-storeyed central block on the old stone foun-dations flanked by two single-storeyed wings with widely overhung, flat-pitched Jamaican roofs of silver cedar shingles. The Havelocks were now sitting on the deep veranda of the central block facing the gently sloping garden beyond which a vast tumbling jungle vista stretched away twenty miles to the sea.

Colonel Havelock put down his *Gleaner*. 'I thought I heard a car.'

Mrs Havelock said firmly: 'If it's those ghastly Feddens from Port Antonio, you've simply got to get rid of them. I can't stand any more of their moans about England. And last time they were both quite drunk when they left and dinner was cold.' She got up quickly. 'I'm going to tell Agatha to say I've got a migraine.'

Agatha came out through the drawing-room door. She looked fussed. She was followed closely by three men. She said hurriedly: 'Gemmun from Kingston'm. To see de Colonel.'

The leading man slid past the housekeeper. He was still wearing his hat, a panama with a short very upcurled brim. He took this off with his left hand and held it against his stomach. The rays of the sun glittered on hair-grease and on a mouthful of smiling white teeth. He went up to Colonel Havelock, his outstretched hand held straight in front of him. 'Major Gonzales. From Havana. Pleased to meet you, Colonel.'

The accent was the sham American of a Jamaican taxi-driver. Colonel Havelock had got to his feet. He touched the outstretched hand briefly. He looked over the Major's shoulder at the other two men who had stationed themselves on either side of the door. They were both carrying that new holdall of the tropics – a Pan American overnight bag. The bags looked heavy. Now the two men bent down together and placed them beside their yellowish shoes. They straightened themselves. They wore flat white caps with transparent green visors that cast green shadows down to their cheekbones. Through the green shadows their intelligent animal eyes fixed themselves on the Major, reading his behaviour.

'They are my secretaries.'

Colonel Havelock took a pipe out of his pocket and began to fill it. His direct blue eyes took in the sharp clothes, the natty shoes, the glistening fingernails of the Major and the blue jeans and calypso shirts of the other two. He wondered how he could get these men into his study and near the revolver in the top drawer of his desk. He said: 'What can I do for you?' As he lit his pipe he watched the Major's eyes and mouth through the smoke.

Major Gonzales spread his hands. The width of his smile remained constant. The liquid, almost golden eyes were amused, friendly. 'It is a matter of business, Colonel. I represent a certain gentleman in Havana' – he made a throw-away gesture with his right hand. 'A powerful gentleman. A very fine guy.' Major Gonzales assumed an expression of sincerity. 'You would like him, Colonel. He asked me to present his compliments and to inquire the price of your property.'

Mrs Havelock, who had been watching the scene with a polite half-smile on her lips, moved to stand

47

beside her husband. She said kindly, so as not to embarrass the poor man: 'What a shame, Major. All this way on these dusty roads! Your friend really should have written first, or asked anyone in Kingston or at Government House. You see, my husband's family have lived here for nearly three hundred years.' She looked at him sweetly, apologetically. 'I'm afraid there just isn't any question of selling Content. There never has been. I wonder where your important friend can possibly have got the idea from.'

Major Gonzales bowed briefly. His smiling face turned back to Colonel Havelock. He said, as if Mrs Havelock had not opened her mouth: 'My gentleman is told this is one of the finest estancias in Jamaica. He is a most generous man. You may mention any sum that is reasonable.'

Colonel Havelock said firmly: 'You heard what Mrs Havelock said. The property is not for sale.'

Major Gonzales laughed. It sounded quite genuine laughter. He shook his head as if he was explaining something to a rather dense child. 'You misunderstand me, Colonel. My gentleman desires this property and no other property in Jamaica. He has some funds, some extra funds, to invest. These funds are seeking a home in Jamaica. My gentleman wishes this to be their home.'

Colonel Havelock said patiently: 'I quite understand, Major. And I am so sorry you have wasted your time. Content will never be for sale in my lifetime. And now, if you'll forgive me. My wife and I always dine early, and you have a long way to go.' He made a gesture to the left, along the veranda. 'I think you'll find this is the quickest way to your car. Let me show you.'

Colonel Havelock moved invitingly, but when Major Gonzales stayed where he was, he stopped. The blue eyes began to freeze.

There was perhaps one less tooth in Major Gonzales's smile and his eyes had become watchful. But his manner was still jolly. He said cheerfully, 'Just one moment, Colonel.' He issued a curt order over his shoulder. Both the Havelocks noticed the jolly mask slip with the few sharp words through the teeth. For the first time Mrs Havelock looked slightly uncertain. She moved still closer to her husband. The two men picked up their blue Pan American bags and stepped forward. Major Gonzales reached for the zipper on each of them in turn and pulled. The taut mouths sprang open. The bags were full to the brim with neat solid wads of American money. Major Gonzales spread his arms. 'All hundred dollar bills. All genuine. Half a million dollars. That is, in your money, let us say, one hundred and eighty thousand pounds. A small fortune. There are many other good places to live in the world, Colonel. And perhaps my gentleman would add a further twenty thousand pounds to make the round sum. You would know in a week. All I need is half a sheet of paper with your signature. The lawyers can do the rest. Now, Colonel,' the

49

smile was winning, 'shall we say yes and shake hands on it? Then the bags stay here and we leave you to your dinner.'

The Havelocks now looked at the Major with the same expression – a mixture of anger and disgust. One could imagine Mrs Havelock telling the story next day. 'Such a common, greasy little man. And those filthy plastic bags full of money! Timmy was wonderful. He just told him to get out and take the dirty stuff away with him.'

Colonel Havelock's mouth turned down with distaste. He said: 'I thought I had made myself clear, Major. The property is not for sale at any price. And I do not share the popular thirst for American dollars. I must now ask you to leave.' Colonel Havelock laid his cold pipe on the table as if he was preparing to roll up his sleeves.

For the first time Major Gonzales's smile lost its warmth. The mouth continued to grin but it was now shaped in an angry grimace. The liquid golden eyes were suddenly brassy and hard. He said softly: 'Colonel. It is I who have not made myself clear. Not you. My gentleman has instructed me to say that if you will not accept his most generous terms we must proceed to other measures.'

Mrs Havelock was suddenly afraid. She put her hand on Colonel Havelock's arm and pressed it hard. He put his hand over hers in reassurance. He said through tight lips: 'Please leave us alone and go, Major. Otherwise I shall communicate with the police.'

The pink tip of Major Gonzales's tongue came out and slowly licked along his lips. All the light had gone out of his face and it had become taut and hard. He said harshly. 'So the property is not for sale in your lifetime, Colonel. Is that your last word?' His right hand went behind his back and he clicked his fingers softly, once. Behind him the gun-hands of the two men slid through the opening of their gay shirts above the waistbands. The sharp animal eyes watched the Major's fingers behind his back.

Mrs Havelock's hand went up to her mouth. Colonel Havelock tried to say yes, but his mouth was dry. He swallowed noisily. He could not believe it. This mangy Cuban crook must be bluffing. He managed to say thickly: 'Yes, it is.'

Major Gonzales nodded curtly. 'In that case, Colonel, my gentleman will carry on the negotiations with the next owner – with your daughter.'

The fingers clicked. Major Gonzales stepped to one side to give a clear field of fire. The brown monkey-hands came out from under the gay shirts. The ugly sausage-shaped hunks of metal spat and thudded – again and again, even when the two bodies were on their way to the ground.

Major Gonzales bent down and verified where the bullets had hit. Then the three small men walked quickly back through the rose and white drawing-room and across the dark carved mahogany hall and out through the elegant front door. They climbed unhurriedly into a black Ford Consul

51

Sedan with Jamaican number plates and, with Major Gonzales driving and the two gunmen sitting upright in the back seat, they drove off at an easy pace down the long avenue of Royal Palms. At the junction of the drive and the road to Port Antonio the cut telephone wires hung down through the trees like bright lianas. Major Gonzales slalomed the car carefully and expertly down the rough parochial road until he was on the metalled strip near the coast. Then he put on speed. Twenty minutes after the killing he came to the outer sprawl of the little banana port. There he ran the stolen car on to the grass verge beside the road and the three men got out and walked the quarter of a mile through the sparsely lit main street to the banana wharves. The speedboat was waiting, its exhaust bubbling. The three men got in and the boat zoomed off across the still waters of what an American poetess has called the most beautiful harbour in the world. The anchor chain was already half up on the glittering fifty-ton Chriscraft. She was flying the Stars and Stripes. The two graceful antennae of the deep-sea rods explained that these were tourists – from Kingston, perhaps, or from Montego Bay. The three men went on board and the speedboat was swung in. Two canoes were circling, begging. Major Gonzales tossed a fifty-cent piece to each of them and the stripped men dived. The twin diesels awoke to a stuttering roar and the Chriscraft settled her stern down a fraction and made for the deep channel below the

Titchfield hotel. By dawn she would be back in Havana. The fishermen and wharfingers ashore watched her go, and went on with their argument as to which of the filmstars holidaying in Jamaica this could have been.

Up on the broad veranda of Content the last rays of the sun glittered on the red stains. One of the doctor birds whirred over the balustrade and hovered close above Mrs Havelock's heart, looking down. No, this was not for him. He flirted gaily off to his roosting-perch among the closing hibiscus.

There came the sound of someone in a small sports car making a racing change at the bend of the drive.

If Mrs Havelock had been alive she would have been getting ready to say: 'Judy, I'm always telling you not to do that on the corner. It scatters gravel all over the lawn and you know how it ruins Joshua's lawnmower.'

It was a month later. In London, October had begun with a week of brilliant Indian summer, and the noise of the mowers came up from Regent's Park and in through the wide open windows of M's office. They were motor-mowers and James Bond reflected that one of the most beautiful noises of summer, the drowsy iron song of the old machines, was going for ever from the world. Perhaps today children felt the same about the puff and chatter of the little two-stroke engines. At least the cut grass would smell the same.

Bond had time for these reflections because M seemed to be having difficulty in coming to the point. Bond had been asked if he had anything on at the moment, and he had replied happily that he hadn't and had waited for Pandora's box to be opened for him. He was mildly intrigued because M had addressed him as James and not by his number – 007. This was unusual during duty hours. It sounded as if there might be some personal angle to this assignment – as if it might be put to him more as a request than as an order. And it seemed to Bond that there was an extra small cleft of worry between the frosty, damnably clear, grey eyes. And three minutes was certainly too long to spend getting a pipe going.

M swivelled his chair round square with the desk and flung the box of matches down so that it skidded across the red leather top towards Bond. Bond fielded it and skidded it politely back to the middle of the desk. M smiled briefly. He seemed to make up his mind. He said mildly: 'James, has it ever occurred to you that every man in the fleet knows what to do except the commanding admiral?'

Bond frowned. He said: 'It hadn't occurred to me, sir. But I see what you mean. The rest only have to carry out orders. The admiral has to decide on the orders. I suppose it's the same as saying that Supreme Command is the loneliest post there is.'

M jerked his pipe sideways. 'Same sort of idea. Someone's got to be tough. Someone's got to decide in the end. If you send a havering signal to the Admiralty you deserve to be put on the beach. Some people are religious – pass the decision on to God.' M's eyes were defensive. 'I used to try that sometimes in the Service, but He always passed the buck back again – told me to get on and make up my own mind. Good for one, I suppose, but tough. Trouble is, very few people keep tough after about forty. They've been knocked about by life – had troubles, tragedies, illnesses. These things soften you up.' M looked sharply at Bond. 'How's your coefficient of toughness, James? You haven't got to the dangerous age yet.'

Bond didn't like personal questions. He didn't know what to answer, nor what the truth was. He had not got a wife or children – had never suffered the tragedy of a personal loss. He had not had to stand up to blindness or a mortal disease. He had absolutely no idea how he would face these things that needed so much more toughness than he had ever had to show. He said hesitantly: 'I suppose I can stand most things if I have to and if I think it's right, sir. I mean' – he did not like using such words – 'if the cause is – er – sort of just, sir.' He went on, feeling ashamed at himself for throwing the ball back at M: 'Of course it's not easy to know what is just and what isn't. I suppose I assume that when I'm given an unpleasant job in the Service the cause is a just one.'

'Dammit,' M's eyes glittered impatiently. 'That's just what I mean! You rely on *me*. You won't take any damned responsibility yourself.' He thrust the stem of his pipe towards his chest. 'I'm the one who has to do that. I'm the one who has to decide if a thing is right or not.' The anger died out of the eyes. The grim mouth bent sourly. He said gloomily: 'Oh well, I suppose it's what I'm paid for. Somebody's got to drive the bloody train.' M put his pipe back in his mouth and drew on it deeply to relieve his feelings.

Now Bond felt sorry for M. He had never before heard M use as strong a word as 'bloody'. Nor had M ever given a member of his staff any hint that he felt the weight of the burden he was carrying and had carried ever since he had thrown up the certain prospect of becoming Fifth Sea Lord in order to take over the Secret Service. M had got himself a problem. Bond wondered what it was. It would not be concerned with danger. If M could get the odds more or less right he would risk anything, anywhere in the world. It would not be political. M did not give a damn for the suscep-tibilities of any Ministry and thought nothing of going behind their backs to get a personal ruling from the Prime Minister. It might be moral. It might be personal. Bond said: 'Is there anything I can help over, sir?'

M looked briefly, thoughtfully at Bond, and then swivelled his chair so that he could look out of the window at the high summery clouds. He said abruptly: 'Do you remember the Havelock case?'

'Only what I read in the papers, sir. Elderly couple

56

in Jamaica. The daughter came home one night and found them full of bullets. There was some talk of gangsters from Havana. The housekeeper said three men had called in a car. She thought they might have been Cubans. It turned out the car had been stolen. A yacht had sailed from the local harbour that night. But as far as I remember the police didn't get anywhere. That's all, sir. I haven't seen any signals passing on the case.'

M said gruffly: 'You wouldn't have. They've been personal to me. We weren't asked to handle the case. Just happens,' M cleared his throat: this private use of the Service was on his conscience, 'I knew the Havelocks. Matter of fact I was best man at their wedding. Malta. Nineteen-twenty-five.'

'I see, sir. That's bad.'

M said shortly: 'Nice people. Anyway, I told Station C to look into it. They didn't get anywhere with the Batista people, but we've got a good man with the other side – with this chap Castro. And Castro's Intelligence people seem to have the Government pretty well penetrated. I got the whole story a couple of weeks ago. It boils down to the fact that a man called Hammerstein, or von Hammerstein, had the couple killed. There are a lot of Germans well dug in in these banana republics. They're Nazis who got out of the net at the end of the War. This one's ex-Gestapo. He got a job as head of Batista's Counter Intelligence. Made a packet of money out of extortion and blackmail and protection. He was set up for life until Castro's lot began to make headway. He was one of the first to start easing himself out. He cut one of his officers in on his loot, a man called Gonzales, and this man travelled around the Caribbean with a couple of gunmen to protect him and began salting away Hammerstein's money outside Cuba – put it in real estate and suchlike under nominees. Only bought the best, but at top prices. Hammerstein could afford them. When money didn't work he'd use force – kidnap a child, burn down a few acres, anything to make the owner see reason. Well, this man Hammerstein heard of the Havelocks' property, one of the best in Jamaica, and he told Gonzales to go and get it. I suppose his orders were to kill the Havelocks if they wouldn't sell and then put pressure on the daughter. There's a daughter, by the way. Should be about twenty-five by now. Never seen her myself. Anyway, that's what happened. They killed the Havelocks. Then two weeks ago Batista sacked Hammerstein. May have got to hear about one of these jobs. I don't know. But, anyway, Hammerstein cleared out and took his little team of three with him. Timed things pretty well, I should say. It looks as if Castro may get in this winter if he keeps the pressure up.'

Bond said softly: 'Where have they gone to?'

'America. Right up in the North of Vermont. Up against the Canadian border. Those sort of men like being close to frontiers. Place called Echo

Lake. It's some kind of a millionaire's ranch he's rented. Looks pretty from the photographs. Tucked away in the mountains with this little lake in the grounds. He's certainly chosen himself somewhere where he won't be troubled with visitors.'

'How did you get on to this, sir?'

'I sent a report of the whole case to Edgar Hoover. He knew of the man. I guessed he would. He's had a lot of trouble with this gun-running from Miami to Castro. And he's been interested in Havana ever since the big American gangster money started following the casinos there. He said that Hammerstein and his party had come into the States on six months visitors' visas. He was very helpful. Wanted to know if I'd got enough to build up a case on. Did I want these men extradited for trial in Jamaica? I talked it over here with the Attorney General and he said there wasn't a hope unless we could get the witnesses from Havana. There's no chance of that. It was only through Castro's Intelligence that we even know as much as we do. Officially the Cubans won't raise a finger. Next, Hoover offered to have their visas revoked and get them on the move again. I thanked him and said no, and we left it at that.'

M sat for a moment in silence. His pipe had died and he relit it. He went on: 'I decided to have a talk with our friends the Mounties. I got on to the Commissioner on the scrambler. He's never let me down yet. He strayed one of his frontier patrol

59

planes over the border and took a full aerial survey of this Echo Lake place. Said that if I wanted any other cooperation he'd provide it. And now,' M slowly swivelled his chair back square with the desk, 'I've got to decide what to do next.'

Now Bond realized why M was troubled, why he wanted someone else to make the decision. Because these had been friends of M. Because a personal element was involved, M had worked on the case by himself. And now it had come to the point when justice ought to be done and these people brought to book. But M was thinking: is this justice, or is it revenge? No judge would take a murder case in which he had personally known the murdered person. M wanted someone else, Bond, to deliver judgement. There were no doubts in Bond's mind. He didn't know the Havelocks or care who they were. Hammerstein had operated the law of the jungle on two defenceless old people. Since no other law was available, the law of the jungle should be visited upon Hammerstein. In no other way could justice be done. If it was revenge, it was the revenge of the community.

Bond said: 'I wouldn't hesitate for a minute, sir. If foreign gangsters find they can get away with this kind of thing they'll decide the English are as soft as some other people seem to think we are. This is a case for rough justice – an eye for an eye.'

M went on looking at Bond. He gave no encouragement, made no comment.

Bond said: 'These people can't be hung, sir. But they ought to be killed.'

M's eyes ceased to focus on Bond. For a moment they were blank, looking inward. Then he slowly reached for the top drawer of his desk on the left-hand side, pulled it open and extracted a thin file without the usual title across it and without the top-secret red star. He placed the file squarely in front of him and his hand rummaged again in the open drawer. The hand brought out a rubber stamp and a red-ink pad. M opened the pad, tamped the rubber stamp on it and then carefully, so that it was properly aligned with the top right-hand corner of the docket, pressed it down on the grey cover.

M replaced the stamp and the ink pad in the drawer and closed the drawer. He turned the docket round and pushed it gently across the desk to Bond.

The red sanserif letters, still damp, said: FOR YOUR EYES ONLY.

Bond said nothing. He nodded and picked up the docket and walked out of the room.

Two days later, Bond took the Friday Comet to Montreal. He did not care for it. It flew too high and too fast and there were too many passengers. He regretted the days of the old Stratocruiser – that fine lumbering old plane that took ten hours to cross the Atlantic. Then one had been able to have dinner in peace, sleep for seven hours in a comfortable bunk, and get up in time to wander down to the lower deck and have that ridiculous BOAC 'country house' breakfast while the dawn came up and flooded the cabin with the first bright gold of the Western hemisphere. Now it was all too quick. The stewards had to serve everything almost at the double, and then one had a bare two hours snooze before the hundred-mile-long descent from forty thousand feet. Only eight hours after leaving London, Bond was driving a Hertz U-drive Plymouth saloon along the broad Route 17 from Montreal to Ottawa and trying to remember to keep on the right of the road.

The Headquarters of the Royal Canadian Mounted police are in the Department of Justice alongside Parliament Buildings in Ottawa. Like most Canadian public buildings, the Department of Justice is a massive block of grey masonry built to look stodgily important and to withstand the long and hard winters. Bond had been told to ask at the front desk for the Commissioner and to give his name as 'Mr James'. He did so, and a young fresh-faced RCMP corporal, who looked as if he did not like being kept indoors on a warm sunny day, took him up in the lift to the third floor and handed him over to a sergeant in a large tidy office which contained two girl secretaries and a lot of heavy furniture. The sergeant spoke on an intercom and there was a ten minutes' delay during which Bond smoked and read a recruiting pamphlet which made the Mounties sound like a mixture between a dude ranch, Dick Tracy and

Rose Marie. When he was shown in through the connecting door a tall youngish man in a dark blue suit, white shirt and black tie turned away from the window and came towards him. 'Mr James?' the man smiled thinly. 'I'm Colonel, let's say – er – Johns.'

They shook hands. 'Come along and sit down. The Commissioner's very sorry not to be here to welcome you himself. He has a bad cold – you know, one of those diplomatic ones.' Colonel 'Johns' looked amused. 'Thought it might be best to take the day off. I'm just one of the help. I've been on one or two hunting trips myself and the Commissioner fixed on me to handle this little holiday of yours,' the Colonel paused, 'on me only. Right?'

Bond smiled. The Commissioner was glad to help but he was going to handle this with kid gloves. There would be no come-back on his office. Bond thought he must be a careful and very sensible man. He said: 'I quite understand. My friends in London didn't want the Commissioner to bother himself personally with any of this. And I haven't seen the Commissioner or been anywhere near his headquarters. That being so, can we talk English for ten minutes or so – just between the two of us?'

Colonel Johns laughed. 'Sure. I was told to make that little speech and then get down to business. You understand, Commander, that you and I are about to connive at various felonies, starting with

63

obtaining a Canadian hunting licence under false pretences and being an accessory to a breach of the frontier laws, and going on down from there to more serious things. It wouldn't do anyone one bit of good to have any ricochets from this little lot. Get me?'

'That's how my friends feel too. When I go out of here, we'll forget each other, and if I end up in Sing-Sing that's my worry. Well, now?'

Colonel Johns opened a drawer in the desk and took out a bulging file and opened it. The top document was a list. He put his pencil on the first item and looked across at Bond. He ran his eye over Bond's old black and white hound's-tooth tweed suit and white shirt and thin black tie. He said: 'Clothes.' He unclipped a plain sheet of paper from the file and slid it across the desk. 'This is a list of what I reckon you'll need and the address of a big second-hand clothing store here in the city. Nothing fancy, nothing conspicuous – khaki shirt, dark brown jeans, good climbing boots or shoes. See they're comfortable. And there's the address of a chemist for walnut stain. Buy a gallon and give yourself a bath in the stuff. There are plenty of browns in the hills at this time and you won't want to be wearing parachute cloth or anything that smells of camouflage. Right? If you're picked up, you're an Englishman on a hunting trip in Canada who's lost his way and got across the border by mistake. Rifle. Went down myself and put it in the boot of your Plymouth while you were waiting. One of the new Savage 99Fs, Weatherby 6 x 62 'scope, five-shot repeater with twenty rounds of high-velocity .250–3.000. Lightest big game lever action on the market. Only six and a half pounds. Belongs to a friend. Glad to have it back one day, but he won't miss it if it doesn't turn up. It's been tested and it's okay up to five hundred. Gun licence,' Colonel Johns slid it over, 'issued here in the city in your real name as that fits with your passport. Hunting licence ditto, but small game only, vermin, as it isn't quite the deer season yet, also driving licence to replace the provisional one I had waiting for you with the Hertz people. Haversack, compass – used ones, in the boot of your car. Oh, by the way,' Colonel Johns looked up from his list, 'you carrying a personal gun?'

'Yes. Walther PPK in a Burns Martin holster.'

'Right, give me the number. I've got a blank licence here. If that gets back to me it's quite okay. I've got a story for it.'

Bond took out his gun and read off the number. Colonel Johns filled in the form and pushed it over.

'Now then, maps. Here's a local Esso map that's all you need to get you to the area.' Colonel Johns got up and walked round with the map to Bond and spread it out. 'You take this route 17 back to Montreal, get on to 37 over the bridge at St Anne's and then over the river again on to 7. Follow 7 on down to Pike River. Get on 52 at Stanbridge.

65

Turn right in Stanbridge for Frelighsburg and leave the car in a garage there. Good roads all the way. Whole trip shouldn't take you more than five hours including stops. Okay? Now this is where you've got to get things right. Make it that you get to Frelighsburg around three a.m. Garage-hand'll be half asleep and you'll be able to get the gear out of the boot and move off without him noticing even if you were a double-headed Chinaman.' Colonel Johns went back to his chair and took two more pieces of paper off the file. The first was a scrap of pencilled map, the other a section of aerial photograph. He said, looking seriously at Bond: 'Now, here are the only inflammable things you'll be carrying and I've got to rely on you getting rid of them just as soon as they've been used, or at once if there's a chance of you getting into trouble. This,' he pushed the paper over, 'is a rough sketch of an old smuggling route from Prohibition days. It's not used now or I wouldn't recommend it.' Colonel Johns smiled sourly. 'You might find some rough customers coming over in the opposite direction, and they're apt to shoot and not even ask questions afterwards – crooks, druggers, white-slavers – but nowadays they mostly travel up by Viscount. This route was used for runners between Franklin, just over the Derby Line, and Frelighsburg. You follow this path through the foothills, and you detour Franklin and get into the start of the Green Mountains. There it's all Vermont spruce and pine with a bit of maple, and you can stay inside that stuff for months and not see a soul. You get across country here, over a couple of highways, and you leave Enosburg Falls to the west. Then you're over a steep range and down into the top of the valley you want. The cross is Echo Lake and, judging from the photographs, I'd be inclined to come down on top of it from the east. Got it?'

'What's the distance? About ten miles?'

'Ten and a half. Take you about three hours from Frelighsburg if you don't lose your way, so you'll be in sight of the place around six and have about an hour's light to help you over the last stretch.' Colonel Johns pushed over the square of aerial photograph. It was a central cut from the one Bond had seen in London. It showed a long low range of well-kept buildings made of cut stone. The roofs were of slate, and there was a glimpse of graceful bow windows and a covered patio. A dust road ran past the front door and on this side were garages and what appeared to be kennels. On the garden side was a stone flagged terrace with a flowered border, and beyond this two or three acres of trim lawn stretched down to the edge of the small lake. The lake appeared to have been artificially created with a deep stone dam. There was a group of wrought-iron garden furniture where the dam wall left the bank and, halfway along the wall, a diving-board and a ladder to climb out of the lake. Beyond the lake the forest rose steeply up. It was from this side that Colonel

67

Johns suggested an approach. There were no people in the photograph, but on the stone flags in front of the patio was a quantity of expensive-looking aluminium garden furniture and a central glass table with drinks. Bond remembered that the larger photograph had shown a tennis court in the garden and on the other side of the road the trim white fences and grazing horses of a stud farm. Echo Lake looked what it was – the luxurious retreat, in deep country, well away from atom bomb targets, of a millionaire who liked privacy and could probably offset a lot of his running expenses against the stud farm and an occasional good let. It would be an admirable refuge for a man who had had ten steamy years of Caribbean politics and who needed a rest to recharge his batteries. The lake was also convenient for washing blood off hands.

Colonel Johns closed his now empty file and tore the type-written list into small fragments and dropped them in the wastepaper basket. The two men got to their feet. Colonel Johns took Bond to the door and held out his hand. He said: 'Well, I guess that's all. I'd give a lot to come with you. Talking about all this has reminded me of one or two sniping jobs at the end of the War. I was in the Army then. We were under Monty in Eighth Corps. On the left of the line in the Ardennes. It was much the same sort of country as you'll be using, only different trees. But you know how it is in these police jobs. Plenty of paper work and keep your nose clean for the pension. Well, so long and the best of luck. No doubt I'll read all about it in the papers,' he smiled, 'whichever way it goes.'

Bond thanked him and shook him by the hand. A last question occurred to him. He said: 'By the way, is the Savage single pull or double? I won't have a chance of finding out and there may not be much time for experimenting when the target shows.'

'Single pull and it's a hair-trigger. Keep your finger off until you're sure you've got him. And keep outside three hundred if you can. I guess these men are pretty good themselves. Don't get too close.' He reached for the door handle. His other hand went to Bond's shoulder. 'Our Commissioner's got a motto: "Never send a man where you can send a bullet." You might remember that. So long, Commander.'

Bond spent the night and most of the next day at the KO-ZEE Motor Court outside Montreal. He paid in advance for three nights. He passed the day looking to his equipment and wearing in the soft ripple rubber climbing boots he had bought in Ottawa. He bought glucose tablets and some smoked ham and bread from which he made himself sandwiches. He also bought a large aluminium flask and filled this with three-quarters Bourbon and a quarter coffee. When darkness came he had dinner and a short sleep and then diluted the walnut stain and washed himself all over with the stuff even to the roots of his hair. He came out looking like a Red Indian with blue-grey eyes. Just before midnight he quietly opened the side door into the automobile bay, got into the Plymouth and drove off on the last lap south to Frelighsburg.

The man at the all-night garage was not as sleepy as Colonel Johns had said he would be.

'Goin' huntin', mister?'

You can get far in North America with laconic grunts. Huh, hun and hi! in their various modulations, together with sure, guess so, that so? and nuts! will meet almost any contingency.

Bond, slinging the strap of his rifle over his shoulder, said 'Hun.'

'Man got a fine beaver over by Highgate Springs Saturday.'

Bond said indifferently 'That so?', paid for two nights and walked out of the garage. He had stopped on the far side of the town, and now he only had to follow the highway for a hundred yards before he found the dirt track running off into the woods on his right. After half an hour the track petered out at a broken-down farmhouse. A chained dog set up a frenzied barking, but no light showed in the farmhouse and Bond skirted it and at once found the path by the stream. He was to follow this for three miles. He lengthened his stride to get away from the dog. When the barking stopped there was silence, the deep velvet silence of woods on a still night. It was a warm night with

70

a full yellow moon that threw enough light down through the thick spruce for Bond to follow the path without difficulty. The springy, cushioned soles of the climbing boots were wonderful to walk on, and Bond got his second wind and knew he was making good time. At around four o'clock the trees began to thin and he was soon walking through open fields with the scattered lights of Franklin on his right. He crossed a secondary, tarred road, and now there was a wider track through the woods and on his right the pale glitter of a lake. By five o'clock he had crossed the black rivers of US highways 108 and 120. On the latter was a sign saying ENOSBURG FALLS 1 MI. Now he was on the last lap – a small hunting trail that climbed steeply. Well away from the highway, he stopped and shifted his rifle and knapsack round, had a cigarette and burned the sketch-map. Already there was a faint paling in the sky and small noises in the forest – the harsh, melancholy cry of a bird he did not know and the rustlings of small animals. Bond visualized the house deep down in the little valley on the other side of the mountain ahead of him. He saw the blank curtained windows, the crumpled sleeping faces of the four men, the dew on the lawn and the widening rings of the early rise on the gunmetal surface of the lake. And here, on the other side of the mountain, was the execu-tioner coming up through the trees. Bond closed his mind to the picture, trod the remains of his cigarette into the ground and got going.

Was this a hill or a mountain? At what height does a hill become a mountain? Why don't they manufacture something out of the silver bark of birch trees? It looks so useful and valuable. The best things in America are chipmunks, and oyster stew. In the evening darkness doesn't really fall, it rises. When you sit on top of a mountain and watch the sun go down behind the mountain opposite, the darkness rises up to you out of the valley. Will the birds one day lose their fear of man? It must be centuries since man has killed a small bird for food in these woods, yet they are still afraid. Who was this Ethan Allen who commanded the Green Mountain Boys of Vermont? Now, in American motels, they advertise Ethan Allen furniture as an attraction. Why? Did he make furniture? Army boots should have rubber soles like these.

With these and other random thoughts Bond steadily climbed upwards and obstinately pushed away from him the thought of the four faces asleep on the white pillows.

The round peak was below the tree-line and Bond could see nothing of the valley below. He rested and then chose an oak tree, and climbed up and out along a thick bough. Now he could see everything – the endless vista of the Green Mountains stretching in every direction as far as he could see, away to the east the golden ball of the sun just coming up in glory, and below, two thousand feet down a long easy slope of treetops broken once by a wide band of meadow, through a thin veil of mist, the lake, the lawns and the house.

Bond lay along the branch and watched the band of pale early morning sunshine creeping down into the valley. It took a quarter of an hour to reach the lake, and then seemed to flood at once over the glittering lawn and over the wet slate tiles of the roofs. Then the mist went quickly from the lake and the target area, washed and bright and new, lay waiting like an empty stage.

Bond slipped the telescopic sight out of his pocket and went over the scene inch by inch. Then he examined the sloping ground below him and estimated ranges. From the edge of the meadow, which would be his only open field of fire unless he went down through the last belt of trees to the edge of the lake, it would be about five hundred yards to the terrace and the patio, and about three hundred to the diving-board and the edge of the lake. What did these people do with their time? What was their routine? Did they ever bathe? It was still warm enough. Well, there was all day. If by the end of it they had not come down to the lake, he would just have to take his chance at the patio and five hundred yards. But it would not be a good chance with a strange rifle. Ought he to get on down straight away to the edge of the meadow? It was a wide meadow, perhaps five hundred yards of going without cover. It would be as well to get that behind him before the house awoke. What time did these people get up in the morning?

As if to answer him, a white blind rolled up in one of the smaller windows to the left of the main block. Bond could distinctly hear the final snap of the spring roller. Echo Lake! Of course. Did the echo work both ways? Would he have to be careful of breaking branches and twigs? Probably not. The sounds in the valley would bounce upwards off the surface of the water. But there must be no chances taken.

A thin column of smoke began to trickle up straight into the air from one of the left-hand chimneys. Bond thought of the bacon and eggs that would soon be frying. And the hot coffee. He eased himself back along the branch and down to the ground. He would have something to eat, smoke his last safe cigarette and get on down to the firing point.

The bread stuck in Bond's throat. Tension was building up in him. In his imagination he could already hear the deep bark of the Savage. He could see the black bullet lazily, like a slow flying bee, homing down into the valley towards a square of pink skin. There was a light smack as it hit. The skin dented, broke and then closed up again leaving a small hole with bruised edges. The bullet ploughed on, unhurriedly, towards the pulsing heart – the tissues, the blood-vessels, parting obediently to let it through. Who was this man he was going to do this to? What had he ever done to Bond? Bond looked thoughtfully down at his trigger finger. He crooked it slowly, feeling in his imagination the cool curve of metal. Almost automatically, his left hand reached out for the flask. He held it to his lips and tilted his head back. The coffee and whisky burned a small fire down his throat. He put the top back on the flask and waited for the warmth of the whisky to reach his stomach. Then he got slowly to his feet, stretched and yawned deeply and picked up the rifle and slung it over his shoulder. He looked round carefully to mark the place when he came back up the hill and started slowly off down through the trees.

Now there was no trail and he had to pick his way slowly, watching the ground for dead branches. The trees were more mixed. Among the spruce and silver birch there was an occasional oak and beech and sycamore and, here and there, the blazing Bengal fire of a maple in autumn dress. Under the trees was a sparse undergrowth of their saplings and much dead wood from old hurricanes. Bond went carefully down, his feet making little sound among the leaves and moss-covered rocks, but soon the forest was aware of him and began to pass on the news. A large doe, with two Bambi-like young, saw him first and galloped off with an appalling clatter. A brilliant woodpecker with a scarlet head flew down ahead of him, screeching each time Bond caught up with it, and always there were the chipmunks, craning up on their hind feet, lifting their small muzzles from their teeth as they tried to catch his scent, and then scampering off to their rock holes with chatterings that seemed to fill the woods with fright. Bond willed them to have no fear, that the gun he carried was not meant for them, but with each alarm he wondered if, when he got to the edge of the meadow, he would see down on the lawn a man with glasses who had been watching the frightened birds fleeing the treetops.

But when he stopped behind a last broad oak and looked down across the long meadow to the final belt of trees and the lake and the house, nothing had changed. All the other blinds were still down and the only movement was the thin plume of smoke.

It was eight o'clock. Bond gazed down across the meadow to the trees, looking for one which would suit his purpose. He found it – a big maple, blazing with russet and crimson. This would be right for his clothes, its trunk was thick enough and it stood slightly back from the wall of spruce. From there, standing, he would be able to see all he needed of the lake and the house. Bond stood for a while, plotting his route down through the thick grass and golden-rod of the meadow. He would have to do it on his stomach, and slowly. A small breeze got up and combed the meadow. If only it would keep blowing and cover his passage!

Somewhere not far off, up to the left on the edge of the trees, a branch snapped. It snapped once decisively and there was no further noise. Bond dropped to one knee, his ears pricked and his senses questing. He stayed like that for a full ten minutes, a motionless brown shadow against the wide trunk of the oak.

Animals and birds do not break twigs. Dead wood must carry a special danger signal for them. Birds never alight on twigs that will break under them, and even a large animal like a deer with antlers and four hooves to manipulate moves quite silently in a forest unless he is in flight. Had these people after all got guards out? Gently Bond eased the rifle off his shoulder and put his thumb on the safe. Perhaps, if the people were still sleeping, a single shot, from high up in the woods, would pass for a hunter or a poacher. But then, between him and approximately where the twig had snapped, two deer broke cover and cantered unhurriedly across the meadow to the left. It was true that they stopped twice to look back, but each time they cropped a few mouthfuls of grass before moving on and into the distant fringe of the lower woods. They showed no fright and no haste. It was certainly they who had been the cause of the snapped branch. Bond breathed a sigh. So much for that. And now to get on across the meadow.

A five-hundred-yard crawl through tall concealing grass is a long and wearisome business. It is hard on knees and hands and elbows, there is a vista of nothing but grass and flower stalks, and the dust and small insects get into your eyes and nose and down your neck. Bond focused on placing his hands right and maintaining a slow, even speed. The breeze had kept up and his wake through the grass would certainly not be noticeable from the house.

From above, it looked as if a big ground animal – a beaver perhaps, or a woodchuck – was on its way down the meadow. No, it would not be a beaver. They always move in pairs. And yet perhaps it might be a beaver – for now, from higher up on the meadow, something, somebody else had entered the tall grass, and behind and above Bond a second wake was being cut in the deep sea of grass. It looked as if whatever it was would slowly catch up on Bond and that the two wakes would converge just at the next tree-line.

Bond crawled and slithered steadily on, stopping only to wipe the sweat and dust off his face and, from time to time, to make sure that he was on course for the maple. But when he was close enough for the treeline to hide him from the house, perhaps twenty feet from the maple, he stopped and lay for a while, massaging his knees and loosening his wrists for the last lap.

He had heard nothing to warn him, and when the soft threatening whisper came from only feet away in the thick grass on his left, his head swivelled so sharply that the vertebrae of his neck made a cracking sound.

'Move an inch and I'll kill you.' It had been a girl's voice, but a voice that fiercely meant what it said.

Bond, his heart thumping, stared up the shaft of the steel arrow whose blue-tempered triangular tip parted the grass stalks perhaps eighteen inches from his head.

The bow was held sideways, flat in the grass. The knuckles of the brown fingers that held the binding of the bow below the arrow-tip were white. Then there was the length of glinting steel and, behind the metal feathers, partly obscured by waving strands of grass, were grimly clamped lips below two fierce grey eyes against a background of sunburned skin damp with sweat. That was all Bond could make out through the grass. Who the hell was this? One of the guards? Bond gathered saliva back into his dry mouth and began slowly to edge his right hand, his out-of-sight hand, round and up towards his waistband and his gun. He said softly: 'Who the hell are you?'

The arrow-tip gestured threateningly. 'Stop that right hand or I'll put this through your shoulder. Are you one of the guards?'

'No. Are you?'

'Don't be a fool. What are you doing here?' The tension in the voice had slackened, but it was still hard, suspicious. There was a trace of accent – what was it, Scots? Welsh?

It was time to get to level terms. There was something particularly deadly about the blue arrow-tip. Bond said easily: 'Put away your bow and arrow, Robina. Then I'll tell you.'

'You swear not to go for your gun?'

'All right. But for God's sake let's get out of the middle of this field.' Without waiting, Bond rose on hands and knees and started to crawl again. Now he must get the initiative and hold it. Whoever this damned girl was, she would have to be disposed of quickly and discreetly before the shooting match

79

began. God, as if there wasn't enough to think of already!

Bond reached the trunk of the tree. He got carefully to his feet and took a quick look through the blazing leaves. Most of the blinds had gone up. Two slow-moving coloured maids were laying a large breakfast table on the patio. He had been right. The field of vision over the tops of the trees that now fell sharply to the lake was perfect. Bond unslung his rifle and knapsack and sat down with his back against the trunk of the tree. The girl came out of the edge of the grass and stood up under the maple. She kept her distance. The arrow was still held in the bow but the bow was unpulled. They looked warily at each other.

The girl looked like a beautiful unkempt dryad in ragged shirt and trousers. The shirt and trousers were olive green, crumpled and splashed with mud and stains and torn in places, and she had bound her pale blonde hair with goldenrod to conceal its brightness for her crawl through the meadow. The beauty of her face was wild and rather animal, with a wide sensuous mouth, high cheekbones and silvery grey, disdainful eyes. There was the blood of scratches on her forearms and down one cheek, and a bruise had puffed and slightly blackened the same cheekbone. The metal feathers of a quiver full of arrows showed above her left shoulder. Apart from the bow, she carried nothing but a hunting knife at her belt and, at her other hip, a small brown canvas bag that presumably carried her food. She looked

80

like a beautiful, dangerous customer who knew wild country and forests and was not afraid of them. She would walk alone through life and have little use for civilization.

Bond thought she was wonderful. He smiled at her. He said softly, reassuringly: 'I suppose you're Robina Hood. My name's James Bond.' He reached for his flask and unscrewed the top and held it out. 'Sit down and have a drink of this – firewater and coffee. And I've got some biltong. Or do you live on dew and berries?'

She came a little closer and sat down a yard from him. She sat like a Red Indian, her knees splayed wide and her ankles tucked up high under her thighs. She reached for the flask and drank deeply with her head thrown back. She handed it back without comment. She did not smile. She said 'Thanks' grudgingly, and took her arrow and thrust it over her back to join the others in the quiver. She said, watching him closely: 'I suppose you're a poacher. The deer-hunting season doesn't open for another three weeks. But you won't find any deer down here. They only come so low at night. You ought to be higher up during the day, much higher. If you like, I'll tell you where there are some. Quite a big herd. It's a bit late in the day, but you could still get to them. They're up-wind from here and you seem to know about stalking. You don't make much noise.'

'Is that what you're doing here – hunting? Let's see your licence.'

Her shirt had buttoned-down breast pockets. Without protest she took out from one of them the white paper and handed it over.

The licence had been issued in Bennington, Vermont. It had been issued in the name of Judy Havelock. There was a list of types of permit. 'Non-resident hunting' and 'Non-resident bow and arrow' had been ticked. The cost had been $18.50, payable to the Fish and Game Service, Montpelier, Vermont. Judy Havelock had given her age as twenty-five and her place of birth as Jamaica.

Bond thought: 'God Almighty!' He handed the paper back. So that was the score! He said with sympathy and respect: 'You're quite a girl, Judy. It's a long walk from Jamaica. And you were going to take him on with your bow and arrow. You know what they say in China: "Before you set out on revenge, dig two graves." Have you done that, or did you expect to get away with it?'

The girl was staring at him. 'Who are you? What are you doing here? What do you know about it?'

Bond reflected. There was only one way out of this mess and that was to join forces with the girl. What a hell of a business! He said resignedly: 'I've told you my name. I've been sent out from London by, er, Scotland Yard. I know all about your troubles and I've come out here to pay off some of the score and see you're not bothered by these people. In London we think that the man in that house might start putting pressure on you, about your property, and there's no other way of stopping him.'

The girl said bitterly: 'I had a favourite pony, a Palomino. Three weeks ago they poisoned it. Then they shot my Alsatian. I'd raised it from a puppy. Then came a letter. It said, "Death has many hands. One of these hands is now raised over you." I was to put a notice in the paper, in the personal column, on a particular day. I was just to say, "I will obey. Judy." I went to the police. All they did was to offer me protection. It was people in Cuba, they thought. There was nothing else they could do about it. So I went to Cuba and stayed in the best hotel and gambled big in the casinos.' She gave a little smile. 'I wasn't dressed like this. I wore my best dresses and the family jewels. And people made up to me. I was nice to them. I had to be. And all the while I asked questions. I pretended I was out for thrills – that I wanted to see the underworld and some real gangsters, and so on. And in the end I found out about this man.' She gestured down towards the house. 'He had left Cuba. Batista had found out about him or something. And he had a lot of enemies. I was told plenty about him and in the end I met a man, a sort of high-up policeman, who told me the rest after I had,' she hesitated and avoided Bond's eyes, 'after I had made up to him.' She paused. She went on: 'I left and went to America. I had read somewhere about Pinkerton's, the detective people. I went to them and paid to have them find this man's address.' She turned her hands palm upwards on her lap. Now her eyes were defiant. 'That's all.'

83

'How did you get here?'

'I flew up to Bennington. Then I walked. Four days. Up through the Green Mountains. I kept out of the way of people. I'm used to this sort of thing. Our house is in the mountains in Jamaica. They're much more difficult than these. And there are more people, peasants, about in them. Here no one ever seems to walk. They go by car.'

'And what were you going to do then?'

'I'm going to shoot von Hammerstein and walk back to Bennington.' The voice was as casual as if she had said she was going to pick a wild flower.

From down in the valley came the sound of voices. Bond got to his feet and took a quick look through the branches. Three men and two girls had come on to the patio. There was talk and laughter as they pulled out chairs and sat down at the table. One place was left empty at the head of the table between the two girls. Bond took out his telescopic sight and looked through it. The three men were very small and dark. One of them, who smiled all the time and whose clothes looked the cleanest and smartest, would be Gonzales. The other two were low peasant types. They sat together at the foot of the oblong table and took no part in the talk. The girls were swarthy brunettes. They looked like cheap Cuban whores. They wore bright bathing dresses and a lot of gold jewellery, and laughed and chattered like pretty monkeys. The voices were almost clear enough to understand, but they were talking Spanish.

Bond felt the girl near him. She stood a yard behind him. Bond handed her the glass. He said: 'The neat little man is called Major Gonzales. The two at the bottom of the table are gunmen. I don't know who the girls are. Von Hammerstein isn't there yet.' She took a quick look through the glass and handed it back without comment. Bond wondered if she realized that she had been looking at the murderers of her father and mother.

The two girls had turned and were looking towards the door into the house. One of them called out something that might have been a greeting. A short, square, almost naked man came out into the sunshine. He walked silently past the table to the edge of the flagged terrace facing the lawn and proceeded to go through a five-minute programme of physical drill.

Bond examined the man minutely. He was about five feet four with a boxer's shoulders and hips, but a stomach that was going to fat. A mat of black hair covered his breasts and shoulder blades, and his arms and legs were thick with it. By contrast, there was not a hair on his face or head and his skull was a glittering whitish yellow with a deep dent at the back that might have been a wound or the scar of a trepanning. The bone structure of the face was that of the conventional Prussian officer – square, hard and thrusting – but the eyes under the naked brows were close-set and piggish, and the large mouth had hideous lips – thick and wet and crimson. He wore nothing but a strip of black material, hardly

85

larger than an athletic support-belt, round his stomach, and a large gold wristwatch on a gold bracelet. Bond handed the glass to the girl. He was relieved. Von Hammerstein looked just about as unpleasant as M's dossier said he was.

Bond watched the girl's face. The mouth looked grim, almost cruel, as she looked down on the man she had come to kill. What was he to do about her? He could see nothing but a vista of troubles from her presence. She might even interfere with his own plans and insist on playing some silly rôle with her bow and arrow. Bond made up his mind. He just could not afford to take chances. One short tap at the base of the skull and he would gag her and tie her up until it was all over. Bond reached softly for the butt of his automatic.

Nonchalantly the girl moved a few steps back. Just as nonchalantly she bent down, put the glass on the ground and picked up her bow. She reached behind her for an arrow, and fitted it casually into the bow. Then she looked up at Bond and said quietly: 'Don't get any silly ideas. And keep your distance. I've got what's called wide-angled vision. I haven't come all the way here to be knocked on the head by a flat-footed London bobby. I can't miss with this at fifty yards, and I've killed birds on the wing at a hundred. I don't want to put an arrow through your leg, but I shall if you interfere.'

Bond cursed his previous indecision. He said fiercely: 'Don't be a silly bitch. Put that damned thing down. This is man's work. How in hell do you think you can take on four men with a bow and arrow?'

The girl's eyes blazed obstinately. She moved her right foot back into the shooting stance. She said through compressed, angry lips: 'You go to hell. And keep out of this. It was my mother and father they killed. Not yours. I've already been here a day and a night. I know what they do and I know how to get Hammerstein. I don't care about the others. They're nothing without him. Now then.' She pulled the bow half taut. The arrow pointed at Bond's feet. 'Either you do what I say or you're going to be sorry. And don't think I don't mean it. This is a private thing I've sworn to do and nobody's going to stop me.' She tossed her head imperiously. 'Well?'

Bond gloomily measured the situation. He looked the ridiculously beautiful wild girl up and down. This was good hard English stock spiced with the hot peppers of a tropical childhood. Dangerous mixture. She had keyed herself up to a state of controlled hysteria. He was quite certain that she would think nothing of putting him out of action. And he had absolutely no defence. Her weapon was silent, his would alert the whole neighbourhood. Now the only hope would be to work with her. Give her part of the job and he would do the rest. He said quietly: 'Now listen, Judy. If you insist on coming in on this thing we'd better do it together. Then perhaps we can bring it off and stay alive. This sort of thing is my profession. I was ordered to do it – by a close friend of your family, if you want to know. And I've got the right weapon. It's got at least five times the range of yours. I could take a good chance of killing him now, on the patio. But the odds aren't quite good enough. Some of them have got bathing things on. They'll be coming down to the lake. Then I'm going to do it. You can give supporting fire.' He ended lamely: 'It'll be a great help.'

'No.' She shook her head decisively. 'I'm sorry. You can give what you call supporting fire if you like. I don't care one way or the other. You're right about the swimming. Yesterday they were all down at the lake around eleven. It's just as warm today and they'll be there again. I shall get him from the edge of the trees by the lake. I found a perfect place last night. The bodyguard men bring their guns with them – sort of tommygun things. They don't bathe. They sit around and keep guard. I know the moment to get von Hammerstein and I'll be well away from the lake before they take in what's happened. I tell you I've got it all planned. Now then. I can't hang around any more. I ought to have been in my place already. I'm sorry, but unless you say yes straight away there's no alternative.' She raised the bow a few inches.

Bond thought: 'Damn this girl to hell.' He said angrily: 'All right then. But I can tell you that if we get out of this you're going to get such a spanking you won't be able to sit down for a week.' He shrugged. He said with resignation: 'Go ahead.

88

I'll look after the others. If you get away all right, meet me here. If you don't, I'll come down and pick up the pieces.'

The girl unstrung her bow. She said indifferently: 'I'm glad you're seeing sense. These arrows are difficult to pull out. Don't worry about me. But keep out of sight and mind the sun doesn't catch that glass of yours.' She gave Bond the brief, pitying, self-congratulatory smile of the woman who has had the last word, and turned and made off down through the trees.

Bond watched the lithe dark green figure until it had vanished among the tree-trunks, then he impatiently picked up the glass and went back to his vantage-point. To hell with her! It was time to clear the silly bitch out of his mind and concentrate on the job. Was there anything else he could have done – any other way of handling it? Now he was committed to wait for her to fire the first shot. That was bad. But if he fired first there was no way of knowing what the hot-headed bitch would do. Bond's mind luxuriated briefly in the thought of what he would do to the girl once all this was over. Then there was movement in front of the house, and he put the exciting thoughts aside and lifted his glass.

The breakfast things were being cleared away by the two maids. There was no sign of the girls or the gunmen. Von Hammerstein was lying back among the cushions of an outdoor couch reading a newspaper and occasionally commenting to

Major Gonzales, who sat astride an iron garden chair near his feet. Gonzales was smoking a cigar and from time to time he delicately raised a hand in front of his mouth, leant sideways and spat a bit of leaf out on the ground. Bond could not hear what von Hammerstein was saying, but his comments were in English and Gonzales answered in English. Bond glanced at his watch. It was ten-thirty. Since the scene seemed to be static, Bond sat down with his back to the tree and went over the Savage with minute care. At the same time he thought of what would shortly have to be done with it.

Bond did not like what he was going to do, and all the way from England he had had to keep on reminding himself what sort of men these were. The killing of the Havelocks had been a particularly dreadful killing. Von Hammerstein and his gunmen were particularly dreadful men whom many people around the world would probably be very glad to destroy, as this girl proposed to do, out of private revenge. But for Bond it was different. He had no personal motives against them. This was merely his job – as it was the job of a pest control officer to kill rats. He was the public executioner appointed by M to represent the community. In a way, Bond argued to himself, these men were as much enemies of his country as were the agents of SMERSH or of other enemy Secret Services. They had declared and waged war against British people on British soil and they were currently planning another attack. Bond's mind hunted round for more arguments to bolster his resolve. They had killed the girl's pony and her dog with two casual sideswipes of the hand as if they had been flies. They . . .

A burst of automatic fire from the valley brought Bond to his feet. His rifle was up and taking aim as the second burst came. The harsh racket of noise was followed by laughter and hand-clapping. The kingfisher, a handful of tattered blue and grey feathers, thudded to the lawn and lay fluttering. Von Hammerstein, smoke still dribbling from the snout of his tommy-gun, walked a few steps and put the heel of his naked foot down and pivoted sharply. He took his heel away and wiped it on the grass beside the heap of feathers. The others stood round, laughing and applauding obsequiously. Von Hammerstein's red lips grinned with pleasure. He said something which included the word 'crackshot'. He handed the gun to one of the gunmen and wiped his hands down his fat backsides. He gave a sharp order to the two girls, who ran off into the house, then, with the others following, he turned and ambled down the sloping lawn towards the lake. Now the girls came running back out of the house. Each one carried an empty champagne bottle. Chattering and laughing they skipped down after the men.

Bond got himself ready. He clipped the telescopic sight on to the barrel of the Savage and took his stance against the trunk of the tree. He found a bump in the wood as a rest for his left

91

hand, put his sights at 300, and took broad aim at the group of people by the lake. Then, holding the rifle loosely, he leaned against the trunk and watched the scene.

It was going to be some kind of a shooting contest between the two gunmen. They snapped fresh magazines on to their guns and at Gonzales's orders stationed themselves on the flat stone wall of the dam some twenty feet apart on either side of the diving-board. They stood with their backs to the lake and their guns at the ready.

Von Hammerstein took up his place on the grass verge, a champagne bottle swinging in each hand. The girls stood behind him, their hands over their ears. There was excited jabbering in Spanish, and laughter in which the two gunmen did not join. Through the telescopic sight their faces looked sharp with concentration.

Von Hammerstein barked an order and there was silence. He swung both arms back and counted 'Un . . . Dos . . . Tres.' With the 'tres' he hurled the champagne bottles high into the air over the lake.

The two men turned like marionettes, the guns clamped to their hips. As they completed the turn they fired. The thunder of the guns split the peaceful scene and racketed up from the water. Birds fled away from the trees screeching and some small branches cut by the bullets pattered down into the lake. The left-hand bottle disintegrated into dust, the right-hand one, hit by only a single bullet, split in two a fraction of a second later. The fragments of glass made small splashes over the middle of the lake. The gunman on the left had won. The smoke-clouds over the two of them joined and drifted away over the lawn. The echoes boomed softly into silence. The two gunmen walked along the wall to the grass, the rear one looking sullen, the leading one with a sly grin on his face. Von Hammerstein beckoned the two girls forward. They came reluctantly, dragging their feet and pouting. Von Hammerstein said something, asked a question of the winner. The man nodded at the girl on the left. She looked sullenly back at him. Gonzales and Hammerstein laughed. Hammerstein reached out and patted the girl on the rump as if she had been a cow. He said something in which Bond caught the words 'una noche'. The girl looked up at him and nodded obediently. The group broke up. The prize girl took a quick run and dived into the lake, perhaps to get away from the man who had won her favours, and the other girl followed her. They swam away across the lake calling angrily to each other. Major Gonzales took off his coat and laid it on the grass and sat down on it. He was wearing a shoulder holster which showed the butt of a medium-calibre automatic. He watched von Hammerstein take off his watch and walk along the dam wall to the diving-board. The gunmen stood back from the lake and also watched von Hammerstein and the two girls, who were now out in the middle of the little lake and were making for the far shore. The gunmen stood with their guns cradled in their arms and occasionally one of them would glance round the garden or towards the house. Bond thought there was every reason why von Hammerstein had managed to stay alive so long. He was a man who took trouble to do so.

Von Hammerstein had reached the diving-board. He walked along to the end and stood looking down at the water. Bond tensed himself and put up the safe. His eyes were fierce slits. It would be any minute now. His finger itched on the trigger-guard. What in hell was the girl waiting for?

Von Hammerstein had made up his mind. He flexed his knees slightly. The arms came back. Through the telescopic sight Bond could see the thick hair over his shoulder blades tremble in a breeze that came to give a quick shiver to the surface of the lake. Now his arms were coming forward and there was a fraction of a second when his feet had left the board and he was still almost upright. In that fraction of a second there was a flash of silver against his back and then von Hammerstein's body hit the water in a neat dive.

Gonzales was on his feet, looking uncertainly at the turbulence caused by the dive. His mouth was open, waiting. He did not know if he had seen something or not. The two gunmen were more certain. They had their guns at the ready. They crouched, looking from Gonzales to the trees behind the dam, waiting for an order.

Slowly the turbulence subsided and the ripples spread across the lake. The dive had gone deep.

Bond's mouth was dry. He licked his lips, searching the lake with his glass. There was a pink shimmer deep down. It wobbled slowly up. Von Hammerstein's body broke the surface. It lay head down, wallowing softly. A foot or so of steel shaft stuck up from below the left shoulder blade and the sun winked on the aluminium feathers.

Major Gonzales yelled an order and the two tommy-guns roared and flamed. Bond could hear the crash of the bullets among the trees below him. The Savage shuddered against his shoulder and the right-hand man fell slowly forward on his face. Now the other man was running for the lake, his gun still firing from the hip in short bursts. Bond fired and missed and fired again. The man's legs buckled, but his momentum still carried him forward. He crashed into the water. The clenched finger went on firing the gun aimlessly up towards the blue sky until the water throttled the mechanism.

The seconds wasted on the extra shot had given Major Gonzales a chance. He had got behind the body of the first gunman and now he opened up on Bond with the tommy-gun. Whether he had seen Bond or was only firing at the flashes from the Savage he was doing well. Bullets zipped into the maple and slivers of wood spattered into Bond's face. Bond fired twice. The dead body of the gunman jerked. Too low! Bond reloaded and took fresh aim. A snapped branch fell across his rifle. He shook it free, but now Gonzales was up and running forward to the group of garden furniture.

He hurled the iron table on its side and got behind it as two snap shots from Bond kicked chunks out of the lawn at his heels. With this solid cover his shooting became more accurate, and burst after burst, now from the right of the table and now from the left, crashed into the maple tree while Bond's single shots clanged against the white iron or whined off across the lawn. It was not easy to traverse the telescopic sight quickly from one side of the table to the other and Gonzales was cunning with his changes. Again and again his bullets thudded into the trunk beside and above Bond. Bond ducked and ran swiftly to the right. He would fire, standing, from the open meadow and catch Gonzales off guard. But even as he ran, he saw Gonzales dart from behind the iron table. He also had decided to end the stalemate. He was running for the dam to get across and into the woods and come up after Bond. Bond stood and threw up his rifle. As he did so, Gonzales also saw him. He went down on one knee on the dam wall and sprayed a burst at Bond. Bond stood icily, hearing the bullets.

The crossed hairs centred on Gonzales's chest. Bond squeezed the trigger. Gonzales rocked. He half got to his feet. He raised his arms and, with his gun still pumping bullets into the sky, dived clumsily face forward into the water.

Bond watched to see if the face would rise. It did not. Slowly he lowered his rifle and wiped the back of his arm across his face.

The echoes, the echoes of much death, rolled to

and fro across the valley. Away to the right, in the trees beyond the lake, he caught a glimpse of the two girls running up towards the house. Soon they, if the maids had not already done so, would be on to the state troopers. It was time to get moving.

Bond walked back through the meadow to the lone maple. The girl was there. She stood up against the trunk of the tree with her back to him. Her head was cradled in her arms against the tree. Blood was running down the right arm and dripping to the ground, and there was a black stain high up on the sleeve of the dark green shirt. The bow and quiver of arrows lay at her feet. Her shoulders were shaking.

Bond came up behind her and put a protective arm across her shoulders. He said softly: 'Take it easy, Judy. It's all over now. How bad's the arm?'

She said in a muffled voice: 'It's nothing. Something hit me. But that was awful. I didn't – I didn't know it would be like that.'

Bond pressed her arm reassuringly. 'It had to be done. They'd have got you otherwise. Those were pro killers – the worst. But I told you this sort of thing was man's work. Now then, let's have a look at your arm. We've got to get going – over the border. The troopers'll be here before long.'

She turned. The beautiful wild face was streaked with sweat and tears. Now the grey eyes were soft and obedient. She said: 'It's nice of you to be like that. After the way I was. I was sort of – sort of wound up.'

She held out her arm. Bond reached for the hunting-knife at her belt and cut off her shirtsleeve at the shoulder. There was the bruised, bleeding gash of a bullet wound across the muscle. Bond took out his own khaki handkerchief, cut it into three lengths and joined them together. He washed the wound clean with the coffee and whisky, and then took a thick slice of bread from his haversack and bound it over the wound. He cut her shirtsleeve into a sling and reached behind her neck to tie the knot. Her mouth was inches from his. The scent of her body had a warm animal tang. Bond kissed her once softly on the lips and once again, hard. He tied the knot. He looked into the grey eyes close to his. They looked surprised and happy. He kissed her again at each corner of the mouth and the mouth slowly smiled. Bond stood away from her and smiled back. He softly picked up her right hand and slipped the wrist into the sling. She said docilely: 'Where are you taking me?'

Bond said: 'I'm taking you to London. There's this old man who will want to see you. But first we've got to get over into Canada, and I'll talk to a friend in Ottawa and get your passport straightened out. You'll have to get some clothes and things. It'll take a few days. We'll be staying in a place called the KO-ZEE Motel.'

She looked at him. She was a different girl. She said softly: 'That'll be nice. I've never stayed in a motel.'

Bond bent down and picked up his rifle and

knapsack and slung them over one shoulder. Then he hung her bow and quiver over the other, and turned and started up through the meadow.

She fell in behind and followed him, and as she walked she pulled the tired bits of golden-rod out of her hair and undid a ribbon and let the pale gold hair fall down to her shoulders.

CHAPTER 3

QUANTUM OF SOLACE

James Bond said: 'I've always thought that if I ever married I would marry an air hostess.'

The dinner party had been rather sticky, and now that the other two guests had left accompanied by the ADC to catch their plane, the Governor and Bond were sitting together on a chintzy sofa in the large Office of Works furnished drawing-room, trying to make conversation. Bond had a sharp sense of the ridiculous. He was never comfortable sitting deep in soft cushions. He preferred to sit up in a solidly upholstered armed chair with his feet firmly on the ground. And he felt foolish sitting with an elderly bachelor on his bed of rose chintz gazing at the coffee and liqueurs on the low table between their outstretched feet. There was something clubable, intimate, even rather feminine, about the scene and none of these atmospheres was appropriate.

Bond didn't like Nassau. Everyone was too rich. The winter visitors and the residents who had houses on the island talked of nothing but their money, their diseases and their servant problems. They didn't even gossip well. There was nothing to gossip about. The winter crowd were all too old to have love affairs and, like most rich people, too cautious to say anything malicious about their neighbours. The Harvey Millers, the couple that had just left, were typical – a pleasant rather dull Canadian millionaire who had got into Natural Gas early on and stayed with it, and his pretty chatterbox of a wife. It seemed that she was English. She had sat next to Bond and chattered vivaciously about 'what shows he had recently seen in town' and 'didn't he think the Savoy Grill was the nicest place for supper. One saw so many interesting people – actresses and people like that'. Bond had done his best, but since he had not seen a play for two years, and then only because the man he was following in Vienna had gone to it, he had had to rely on rather dusty memories of London night life which somehow failed to marry up with the experiences of Mrs Harvey Miller.

Bond knew that the Governor had asked him to dinner only as a duty, and perhaps to help out with the Harvey Millers. Bond had been in the Colony for a week and was leaving for Miami the next day. It had been a routine investigation job. Arms were getting to the Castro rebels in Cuba from all the neighbouring territories. They had been coming principally from Miami and the Gulf of Mexico, but when the US Coast Guard had seized two big shipments, the Castro supporters had turned to Jamaica and the Bahamas as possible bases, and Bond had been sent out from London to put a stop to it. He hadn't wanted to do the job. If anything, his sympathies were with the rebels, but the Government had a big export programme with Cuba in exchange for taking more Cuban sugar than they wanted, and a minor condition of the deal was that Britain should not give aid or comfort to the Cuban rebels. Bond had found out about the two big cabin cruisers that were being fitted out for the job, and rather than make arrests when they were about to sail, thus causing an incident, he had chosen a very dark night and crept up on the boats in a police launch. From the deck of the unlighted launch he had tossed a thermite bomb through an open port of each of them. He had then made off at high speed and watched the bonfire from a distance. Bad luck on the insurance companies, of course, but there were no casualties and he had achieved quickly and neatly what M had told him to do.

So far as Bond was aware, no one in the Colony, except the Chief of Police and two of his officers, knew who had caused the two spectacular, and – to those in the know – timely fires in the roadstead. Bond had reported only to M in London. He had not wished to embarrass the Governor, who seemed to him an easily embarrassable man, and it could in fact have been unwise to give him knowledge of a felony which might easily be the subject of a question in the Legislative Council. But the Governor was no fool. He had known the purpose of Bond's visit to the Colony, and that evening, when Bond had shaken him by the hand, the dislike of a peaceable man for violent action had been communicated to Bond by something constrained and defensive in the Governor's manner.

This had been no help to the dinner party, and it had needed all the chatter and gush of a hard-working ADC to give the evening the small semblance of life it had achieved.

And now it was only nine-thirty, and the Governor and Bond were faced with one more polite hour before they could go gratefully to their beds, each relieved that he would never have to see the other again. Not that Bond had anything against the Governor. He belonged to a routine type that Bond had often encountered round the world – solid, loyal, competent, sober and just: the best type of Colonial Civil Servant. Solidly, competently, loyally he would have filled the minor posts for thirty years while the Empire crumbled around him; and now, just in time, by sticking to the ladders and avoiding the snakes, he had got to the top. In a year or two it would be the GCB and out – out to Godalming, or Cheltenham or Tunbridge Wells with a pension and a small packet of memories of places like the Trucial Oman, the Leeward Islands, British Guiana, that no one at the local golf club would have heard of or would care about. And yet, Bond had reflected that evening, how many small dramas such as the affair of the Castro rebels must the Governor have witnessed or been privy to! How much he would know about the chequerboard of the small-power politics, the scandalous side of life in small communities abroad, the secrets of people that lie in the files of Government Houses round the world. But how could one strike a spark off this rigid, discreet mind? How could he, James Bond, whom the Governor obviously regarded as a dangerous man and as a possible source of danger to his own career, extract one ounce of interesting fact or comment to save the evening from being a futile waste of time?

Bond's careless and slightly mendacious remark about marrying an air hostess had come at the end of some desultory conversation about air travel that had followed dully, inevitably, on the departure of the Harvey Millers to catch their plane for Montreal. The Governor had said that BOAC were getting the lion's share of the American traffic to Nassau because, though their planes might be half an hour slower from Idlewild, the service was superb. Bond had said, boring himself with his own banality, that he would rather fly slowly and comfortably than fast and uncosseted. It was then that he had made the remark about air hostesses.

'Indeed,' said the Governor in the polite, controlled voice that Bond prayed might relax and become human. 'Why?'

'Oh, I don't know. It would be fine to have a pretty girl always tucking you up and bringing you drinks and hot meals and asking if you had everything you wanted. And they're always smiling and wanting to please. If I don't marry an air hostess, there'll be nothing for it but marry a Japanese. They seem to have the right ideas too.' Bond had no intention of marrying anyone. If he did, it would certainly not be an insipid slave. He only hoped to amuse or outrage the Governor into a discussion of some human topic.

'I don't know about the Japanese, but I suppose it has occurred to you that these air hostesses are only *trained* to please, that they might be quite different when they're not on the job, so to speak.' The Governor's voice was reasonable, judicious.

'Since I'm not really very interested in getting married, I've never taken the trouble to investigate.'

There was a pause. The Governor's cigar had gone out. He spent a moment or two getting it going again. When he spoke it seemed to Bond that the even tone had gained a spark of life, of interest. The Governor said: 'There was a man I knew once who must have had the same ideas as you. He fell in love with an air hostess and married her. Rather an interesting story, as a matter of fact. I suppose,' the Governor looked sideways at Bond and gave a short self-deprecatory laugh, 'you see quite a lot of the seamy side of life. This story may seem to you on the dull side. But would you care to hear it?'

'Very much.' Bond put enthusiasm into his voice. He doubted if the Governor's idea of what was seamy was the same as his own, but at least it would save him from making any more asinine conversation. Now to get away from this damnably cloying sofa. He said: 'Could I have some more brandy?' He got up, dashed an inch of brandy into his glass and, instead of going back to the sofa, pulled up a chair and sat down at an angle from the Governor on the other side of the drink tray.

The Governor examined the end of his cigar, took a quick pull and held the cigar upright so that the long ash would not fall off. He watched the ash warily throughout his story and spoke as if to the thin trickle of blue smoke that rose and quickly disappeared in the hot, moist air.

He said carefully: 'This man – I'll call him Masters, Philip Masters – was almost a contemporary of mine in the Service. I was a year ahead of him. He went to Fettes and took a scholarship for Oxford – the name of the college doesn't matter – and then he applied for the Colonial Service. He wasn't a particularly clever chap, but he was hard working and capable and the sort of man who makes a good solid impression on interview boards. They took him into the Service. His first post was Nigeria. He did well in it. He liked the natives and he got on well with them. He was a man of liberal ideas and while he didn't actually fraternize, which,' the Governor smiled sourly, 'would have got him into trouble with his superiors in those days, he was lenient and humane towards the Nigerians. It came as quite a surprise

106

to them.' The Governor paused and took a pull at his cigar. The ash was about to fall and he bent carefully over towards the drink tray and let the ash hiss into his coffee cup. He sat back and for the first time looked across at Bond. He said: 'I daresay the affection this young man had for the natives took the place of the affection young men of that age in other walks of life have for the opposite sex. Unfortunately Philip Masters was a shy and rather uncouth young man who had never had any kind of success in that direction. When he hadn't been working to pass his various exams he had played hockey for his college and rowed in the third eight. In the holidays he had stayed with an aunt in Wales and climbed with the local mountaineering club. His parents, by the way, had separated when he was at his public school and, though he was an only child, had not bothered with him once he was safe at Oxford with his scholarship and a small allowance to see him through. So he had very little time for girls and very little to recommend him to those he did come across. His emotional life ran along the frustrated and unhealthy lines that were part of our inheritance from our Victorian grandfathers. Knowing how it was with him, I am therefore suggesting that his friendly relations with the coloured people of Nigeria were what is known as a compensation seized on by a basically warm and full-blooded nature that had been starved of affection and now found it in their simple kindly natures.'

Bond interrupted the rather solemn narrative. 'The only trouble with beautiful Negresses is that they don't know anything about birth control. I hope he managed to stay out of that sort of trouble.'

The Governor held up his hand. His voice held an undertone of distaste for Bond's earthiness. 'No, no. You misunderstand me. I am not talking about sex. It would never have occurred to this young man to have relations with a coloured girl. In fact he was sadly ignorant of sexual matters. Not a rare thing even today among young people in England, but very common in those days, and the cause, as I expect you will agree, of many – very many – disastrous marriages and other tragedies.' Bond nodded. 'No. I am only explaining this young man at some length to show you that what was to come fell upon a frustrated young innocent with a warm but unawakened heart and body, and a social clumsiness which made him seek companionship and affection amongst the Negroes instead of in his own world. He was, in short, a sensitive misfit, physically uninteresting, but in all other respects healthy and able and a perfectly adequate citizen.'

Bond took a sip of his brandy and stretched out his legs. He was enjoying the story. The Governor was telling it in a rather elderly narrative style which gave it a ring of truth.

The Governor continued: 'Young Masters's service in Nigeria coincided with the first Labour Government. If you remember, one of the first things they got down to was a reform of the foreign services. Nigeria got a new Governor with advanced views on the native problem who was surprised and pleased to find that he had a junior member of his staff who was already, in his modest sphere, putting something like the Governor's own views into practice. He encouraged Philip Masters, gave him duties which were above his rank, and in due course, when Masters was due for a move, he wrote such a glowing report that Masters jumped a grade and was transferred to Bermuda as Assistant Secretary to Government.'

The Governor looked through his cigar smoke at Bond. He said apologetically: 'I hope you aren't being too bored by all this. I shan't be long in coming to the point.'

'I'm very interested indeed. I think I've got a picture of the man. You must have known him well.'

The Governor hesitated. He said: 'I got to know him still better in Bermuda. I was just his senior and he worked directly under me. However, we haven't quite got to Bermuda yet. It was the early days of the air services to Africa and, for one reason or another, Philip Masters decided to fly home to London and so have a longer home leave than if he had taken ship from Freetown. He went by train to Nairobi and caught the weekly service of Imperial Airways – the forerunner of BOAC. He had never flown before and he was interested but slightly nervous when they took off, after the air hostess, whom he noticed was very pretty, had given him a sweet to suck and shown him how to fasten his seat-belt. When the plane had levelled out and he found that flying seemed a more peaceful business than he had expected, the hostess came back down the almost empty plane. She smiled at him. "You can undo the belt now." When Masters fumbled with the buckle she leant down and undid it for him. It was an intimate little gesture. Masters had never been so close to a woman of about his own age in his life. He blushed and felt an extraordinary confusion. He thanked her. She smiled rather saucily at his embarrassment and sat on the arm of the empty seat across the aisle and asked him where he had come from and where he was going. He told her. In his turn, he asked her about the plane and how fast they were flying and where they would stop, and so forth. He found her very easy to talk to and almost dazzlingly pretty to look at. He was surprised at her easy way with him and her apparent interest in what he had to say about Africa. She seemed to think he led a far more exciting and glamorous life than, to his mind, he did. She made him feel important. When she went away to help the two stewards prepare lunch, he sat and thought about her and thrilled to his thoughts. When he tried to read he could not focus on the page. He had to be looking up the plane to catch a glimpse of her. Once she caught his gaze and gave him what seemed to him a secret smile. We are the only young people on the plane, it seemed to say.

110

We understand each other. We're interested in the same sort of things.

'Philip Masters gazed out of the window, seeing her in the sea of white clouds below. In his mind's eye he examined her minutely, marvelling at her perfection. She was small and trim with a milk-and-roses complexion and fair hair tied in a neat bun. (He particularly liked the bun. It suggested that she wasn't "fast".) She had cherry red smiling lips and blue eyes that sparkled with mischievous fun. Knowing Wales, he guessed that she had Welsh blood in her, and this was confirmed by her name, Rhoda Llewellyn, which, when he went to wash his hands before luncheon, he found printed at the bottom of the crew list above the magazine rack beside the lavatory door. He speculated deeply about her. She would be near him now for nearly two days, but how could he get to see her again? She must have hundreds of admirers. She might even be married. Did she fly all the time? How many days off did she get between trips? Would she laugh at him if he asked her out to dinner and a theatre? Might she even complain to the captain of the aircraft that one of the passengers was getting fresh? A sudden vision came to Masters of being turned off the plane at Aden, a complaint to the Colonial Office, his career ruined.

'Luncheon came, and reassurance. When she fitted the little tray across his knees, her hair brushed his cheek. Masters felt that he had been

111

touched by a live electric wire. She showed him how to deal with the complicated little cellophane packages, how to get the plastic lid off the salad dressing. She told him that the sweet was particularly good – a rich layer cake. In short she made a fuss of him, and Masters couldn't remember when it had ever happened before, even when his mother had looked after him as a child.

'At the end of the trip, when the sweating Masters had screwed up his courage to ask her out to dinner, it was almost an anticlimax when she readily agreed. A month later she resigned from Imperial Airways and they were married. A month after that, Masters's leave was up and they took ship for Bermuda.'

Bond said: 'I fear the worst. She married him because his life sounded exciting and "grand". She liked the idea of being the belle of the tea parties at Government House. I suppose Masters had to murder her in the end?'

'No,' said the Governor mildly. 'But I daresay you're right about why she married him, that and being tired of the grind and danger of flying. Perhaps she really meant to make a go of it, and certainly when the young couple arrived and settled into their bungalow on the outskirts of Hamilton we were all favourably impressed by her vivacity and her pretty face and by the way she made herself pleasant to everyone. And, of course, Masters was a changed man. Life had become a fairy-tale for him. Looking back, it was almost

112

pitiful to watch him try to spruce himself up so that he could live up to her. He took trouble about his clothes, put some dreadful brilliantine on his hair and even grew a military-type moustache, presumably because she thought it looked distinguished. At the end of the day, he would hurry back to the bungalow, and it was always Rhoda this and Rhoda that and when do you think Lady Burford – who was the Governor's wife – is going to ask Rhoda to lunch?

'But he worked hard and everyone liked the young couple, and things went along like a marriage bell for six months or so. Then, and now I'm only guessing, the occasional word began to drop like acid in the happy little bungalow. You can imagine the sort of thing: "Why doesn't the Colonial Secretary's wife ever take me out shopping with her? How long must we wait before we can give another cocktail party? You know we can't afford to have a baby. When are you due for promotion? It's awfully dull here all day with nothing to do. You'll have to get the dinner tonight. I simply can't be bothered. You have such an interesting time. It's all right for you . . ." and so on and so forth. And of course the cosseting quickly went by the board. Now it was Masters, and of course he was delighted to do it, who brought the air hostess breakfast in bed before he went off to work. It was Masters who tidied up the house when he came back in the evening and found cigarette ash and chocolate papers all over the

113

place. It was Masters who had to give up smoking and his occasional drink to buy her new clothes so that she could live up to the other wives. Some of this showed, at any rate to me who knew Masters well, in the Secretariat. The preoccupied frown, the occasional enigmatic, over-solicitous telephone call in office hours, the ten minutes stolen at the end of the day so that he could take Rhoda to the cinema, and, of course, the occasional half joking questions about marriage in general: What do other wives do all day long? Do most women find it a bit hot out here? I suppose women (he almost added "God bless 'em") are much more easily upset than men. And so forth. The trouble, or at least most of it, was that Masters was besotted. She was his sun and his moon and if she was unhappy or restless it was all his fault. He cast about desperately for something that would occupy her and make her happy, and finally, of all things, he settled – or rather they settled together – on golf. Golf is very much the thing in Bermuda. There are several fine links – including the famous Mid-Ocean Club where all the quality play and get together at the club afterwards for gossip and drinks. It was just what she wanted – a smart occupation and high society. God knows how Masters saved up enough to join and buy her the clubs and the lessons and all the rest, but somehow he did it and it was a roaring success. She took to spending all day at the Mid-Ocean. She worked hard at her lessons and got a handicap and met people through the little competitions and the monthly medals, and in six months she was not only playing a respectable game but had become quite the darling of the men members. I wasn't surprised. I remember seeing her there from time to time, a delicious, sunburned little figure in the shortest of shorts with a white eyeshade with a green lining, and a trim compact swing that flattered her figure, and I can tell you,' the Governor twinkled briefly, 'she was the prettiest thing I've ever seen on a golf course. Of course the next step didn't take long. There was a mixed-foursome competition. She was partnered with the oldest Tattersall boy – they're the leading Hamilton merchants and more or less the ruling clique in Bermudan society. He was a young hellion – handsome as be damned, a beautiful swimmer and a scratch golfer, with an open MG and a speedboat and all the trimmings. You know the type. Got all the girls he wanted, and, if they didn't sleep with him pretty quickly, they didn't get the rides in the MG or the Chriscraft or the evenings in the local night clubs. The couple won the competition after a hard fight in the final and Philip Masters was in the fashionable crowd round the eighteenth green to cheer them home. That was the last time he cheered for many a long day, perhaps for all his life. Almost at once she started "going" with young Tattersall, and once started she went like the wind. And believe me, Mr Bond' – the Governor closed a fist

115

and brought it softly down on the edge of the drinks table – 'it was ghastly to see. She didn't make the smallest attempt to soften the blow or hide the affair in any way. She just took young Tattersall and hit Masters in the face with him, and went on hitting. She would come home at any hour of the night – she had insisted that Masters should move into the spare room, some pretext about it being too hot to sleep together – and if she ever tidied the house or cooked him a meal it was only makeshift and to keep up some kind of appearance. Of course, in a month, the whole thing was public property and poor Masters was wearing the biggest pair of horns that had ever been seen in the Colony. Lady Burford finally stepped in and gave Rhoda Masters a talking to – said she was ruining her husband's career and so forth. But the trouble was that Lady Burford found Masters a pretty dull dog, and having perhaps had one or two escapades in her own youth – she was still a handsome woman with a twinkle in her eye – she was probably a bit too lenient with the girl. Of course Masters himself, as he was to tell me later, went through the usual dreary sequence – remonstrance, bitter quarrel, furious rage, violence (he told me he damned nearly throttled her one night) and, finally, icy withdrawal and sullen misery.' The Governor paused.' I don't know if you've ever seen a heart being broken, Mr Bond, broken slowly and delib- erately. Well, that's what I saw happening to Philip

Masters, and it was a dreadful thing to watch. There he had been, a man with Paradise in his face, and, within a year of his arrival in Bermuda, Hell was written all over it. Of course I did my best, we all did in one way or another, but once it had happened, on that eighteenth green at the Mid-Ocean, there was really nothing to do but try and pick up the bits. But Masters was like a wounded dog. He just drew away from us into a corner and snarled when anyone tried to come near him. I even went to the length of writing him one or two letters. He later told me he had torn them up without reading them. One day, several of us got together and asked him to a stag party in my bungalow. We tried to get him drunk. We got him drunk all right. The next thing that happened was a crash from the bathroom. Masters had tried to cut his wrists with my razor. That broke our nerve and I was deputed to go and see the Governor about the whole business. The Governor knew about it, of course, but had hoped he wouldn't have to interfere. Now the question was whether Masters could even stay on in the Service. His work had gone to pieces. His wife was a public scandal. He was a broken man. Could we stick the bits together again? The Governor was a fine man. Once action had been forced on him, he was determined to make a last effort to stave off the almost inevitable report to Whitehall which would finally smash what remained of Masters. And Providence stepped in to lend a hand. The very next day after my inter-view with the Governor, there was a dispatch from the Colonial Office saying there was to be a meeting in Washington to delineate off-shore fishing rights, and that Bermuda and the Bahamas had been invited to send representatives of their Governments. The Governor sent for Masters, spoke to him like a Dutch uncle, told him that he was being sent to Washington and that he had better have his domestic affairs settled one way or the other in the next six months, and packed him off. Masters left in a week and sat in Washington talking fish for five months, and we all heaved a sigh of relief and cut Rhoda Masters whenever we could find an opportunity to do it.'

The Governor stopped speaking and it was silent in the big, brightly lit drawing-room. He took out a handkerchief and wiped it over his face. His memories had excited him and his eyes were bright in the flushed face. He got to his feet and poured a whisky and soda for Bond, and one for himself.

Bond said: 'What a mess. I suppose something like that was bound to happen sooner or later, but it was bad luck on Masters that it had to happen so soon. She must have been a hard-hearted little bitch. Did she show any signs of being sorry for what she'd done?'

The Governor had finished lighting a fresh cigar. He looked at the glowing tip and blew on it. He said: 'Oh no. She was having a wonderful time. She probably knew it wouldn't last for ever, but it

118

was what she had dreamed about – what the readers of women's magazines dream about, and she was pretty typical of that sort of mentality. She had everything – the best catch on the island, love on the sands under the palm trees, gay times in the town and at the Mid-Ocean, fast drives in the car and the speedboat – all the trappings of cheap romance. And, to fall back on, a slave of a husband well out of the way, and a house to have a bath in and change her clothes and get some sleep. And she knew she could get Philip Masters back. He was so abject. There would be no difficulty. And then she could go round and apologize to everyone and turn on the charm again and everyone would forgive her. It would be all right. If it wasn't all right, there were plenty of other men in the world besides Philip Masters – and more attractive ones at that. Why, look at all the men at the golf club! She could have her pick of them at the drop of a hat. No, life was good, and if one was being a bit naughty it was after all only the way plenty of other people behaved. Look at the way the filmstars went on in Hollywood.

'Well, she was soon put to the test. Tattersall got a bit tired of her and, thanks to the Governor's wife, the Tattersall parents were making the hell of a fuss. That gave Tattersall a good excuse to get out of it all without too much of a scene. And it was summer and the island was flooded with pretty American girls. It was time for some fresh blood. So he chucked Rhoda Masters. Like that.

Just told her they were through. That his parents had insisted or they would cut off his allowance. It was a fortnight before Philip Masters was due back from Washington, and I will say she took it well. She was tough and she had known it would have to come some time or other. She didn't squeal. For that matter there was no one to squeal to. She just went and told Lady Burford that she was sorry and that she was now going to be a good wife to Philip Masters, and she started on the house and cleaned it up and got everything shipshape ready for the big reconciliation scene. The necessity for bringing about this reconciliation was made clear to her by the attitude of her former cronies at the Mid-Ocean. She had suddenly become bad news there. You know how these things can happen, even in an open-handed place like a country club in the tropics. Now not only the Government House set but also the Hamilton merchants clique frowned on her. She was suddenly shoddy goods, used and discarded. She tried to be the same gay little flirt, but it didn't work any more. She got sharply snubbed once or twice and stopped going. Now it was vital to get back to a secure base and start slowly working her way up again. She stayed at home and set to with a will, rehearsing over and over again the act she would put on – the tears, the air hostess cosseting, the lengthy, sincere excuses and explanations, the double bed.

'And then Philip Masters came home.'

The Governor paused and looked reflectively over at Bond. He said: 'You're not married, but I think it's the same with all relationships between a man and a woman. They can survive anything so long as some kind of basic humanity exists between the two people. When all kindness has gone, when one person obviously and sincerely doesn't care if the other is alive or dead, then it's just no good. That particular insult to the ego – worse, to the instinct of self-preservation – can never be forgiven. I've noticed this in hundreds of marriages. I've seen flagrant infidelities patched up, I've seen crimes and even murder forgiven by the other party, let alone bankruptcy and every other form of social crime. Incurable disease, blindness, disaster – all these can be overcome. But never the death of common humanity in one of the partners. I've thought about this and I've invented a rather high-sounding title for this basic factor in human relations. I have called it the Law of the Quantum of Solace.'

Bond said: 'That's a splendid name for it. It's certainly impressive enough. And of course I see what you mean. I should say you're absolutely right. Quantum of Solace – the amount of comfort. Yes, I suppose you could say that all love and friendship is based in the end on that. Human beings are very insecure. When the other person not only makes you feel insecure but actually seems to want to destroy you, it's obviously the end. The Quantum of Solace stands at zero. You've got to get away to save yourself. Did Masters see that?'

The Governor didn't answer the question. He said: 'Rhoda Masters should have been warned when her husband walked through the bungalow door. It wasn't so much what she saw on the surface – though the moustache had gone and Masters's hair was once again the untidy mop of their first meeting – it was the eyes and the mouth and the set of the chin. Rhoda Masters had put on her quietest frock. She had taken off most of her make-up and had arranged herself in a chair where the light from the window left her face in half shadow and illuminated the pages of a book on her lap. She had decided that, when he came through the door, she would look up from her book, docilely, submissively, and wait for him to speak. Then she would get up and come quietly to him and stand in front of him with her head bowed. She would tell him all and let the tears come and he would take her in his arms and she would promise and promise. She had practised the scene many times until she was satisfied.

'She duly glanced up from her book. Masters quietly put down his suitcase and walked slowly over to the mantelpiece and stood looking vaguely down at her. His eyes were cold and impersonal and without interest. He put his hand in his inside pocket and took out a piece of paper. He said in the matter-of-fact voice of a house agent: "Here is a plan of the house. I have divided the house in two. Your rooms are the kitchen and your bedroom. Mine are this room and the spare bedroom. You may use the bathroom when I am not in it." He leant over and dropped the paper on the open pages of her book. "You are never to enter my rooms except when we have friends in.' Rhoda Masters opened her mouth to speak. He held up his hand. "This is the last time I shall speak to you in private. If you speak to me, I shall not answer. If you wish to communicate, you may leave a note in the bathroom. I shall expect my meals to be prepared punctually and placed in the dining-room, which you may use when I have finished. I shall give you twenty pounds a month to cover the housekeeping, and this amount will be sent to you by my lawyers on the first of each month. My lawyers are preparing the divorce papers. I am divorcing you, and you will not fight the action because you cannot. A private detective has provided full evidence against you. The action will take place in one year from now when my time in Bermuda is up. In the meantime, in public, we shall behave as a normal married couples.'

'Masters put his hands in his pockets and looked politely down at her. By this time tears were pouring down her face. She looked terrified – as if someone had hit her. Masters said indifferently: "Is there anything else you'd like to know? If not, you had better collect your belongings from here and move into the kitchen." He looked at his watch. "I would like dinner every evening at eight. It is now seven-thirty."'

The Governor paused and sipped his whisky. He said: 'I've put all this together from the little that Masters told me and from fuller details Rhoda Masters gave to Lady Burford. Apparently Rhoda Masters tried every way to shake him – arguments, pleadings, hysterics. He was unmoved. She simply couldn't reach him. It was as if he had gone away and had sent someone else to the house to represent him at this extraordinary interview. And in the end she had to agree. She had no money. She couldn't possibly afford the passage to England. To have a bed and food she had to do what he told her. And so it was. For a year they lived like that, polite to each other in public, but utterly silent and separate when they were alone. Of course, we were all astonished by the change. Neither of them told anyone of the arrangement. She would have been ashamed to do so and there was no reason why Masters should. He seemed to us a bit more withdrawn than before, but his work was first-class and everyone heaved a sigh of relief and agreed that by some miracle the marriage had been saved. Both of them gained great credit from the fact, and they became a popular couple with everything forgiven and forgotten.

'The year passed and it was time for Masters to go. He announced that Rhoda would stay behind to close the house, and they went through the usual round of farewell parties. We were a bit surprised that she didn't come to see him off in the ship, but he said she wasn't feeling well. So that was that until, in a couple of weeks, news of the divorce case began leaking back from England. Then Rhoda Masters turned up at Government House and had a long interview with Lady Burford, and gradually the whole story, including its really terrible next chapter, leaked out.'

The Governor swallowed the last of his whisky. The ice made a hollow rattle as he put the glass softly down. He said: 'Apparently on the day before Masters left he found a note from his wife in the bathroom. It said that she simply must see him for one last talk before he left her for ever. There had been notes like this before and Masters had always torn them up and left the bits on the shelf above the basin. This time he scribbled a note giving her an appointment in the sitting-room at six o'clock that evening. When the time arrived, Rhoda Masters came meekly in from the kitchen. She had long since given up making emotional scenes or trying to throw herself on his mercy. Now she just quietly stood and said that she had only ten pounds left from that month's house-keeping money and nothing else in the world. When he left she would be destitute.

'"You have the jewels I gave you, and the fur cape."

'"I'd be lucky if I got fifty pounds for them."

'"You'll have to get some work."

'"It'll take time to find something. I've got to

live somewhere. I have to be out of the house in a fortnight. Won't you give me anything at all? I shall starve."

'Masters looked at her dispassionately. "You're pretty. You'll never starve."

'"You must help me, Philip. You must. It won't help your career having me begging at Government House."

'Nothing in the house belonged to them except a few odds and ends. They had taken it furnished. The owner had come the week before and agreed the inventory. There only remained their car, a Morris that Masters had bought second hand, and a radiogramophone he had bought as a last resort to try and keep his wife amused before she took up golf.

'Philip Masters looked at her for the last time. He was never to see her again. He said: "All right. You can have the car and the radiogram. Now that's all. I've got to pack. Goodbye." And he walked out of the door and up to his room.'

The Governor looked across at Bond. 'At least one last little gesture. Yes?' The Governor smiled grimly. 'When he had gone and Rhoda Masters was left alone, she took the car and her engagement ring and her few trinkets and the fox fur tippet and went into Hamilton and drove round the pawn-brokers. In the end she collected forty pounds for the jewellery and seven pounds for the bit of fur. Then she went to the car dealers whose nameplate was on the dashboard of the car and asked to see the manager. When she asked how much he would give her for the Morris he thought she was pulling his leg. "But, madam, Mr Masters bought the car by hire purchase and he's very badly behind on his payments. Surely he told you that we had to send him a solicitor's letter about it only a week ago. We heard he was leaving. He wrote back that you would be coming in to make the necessary arrangements. Let me see" – he reached for a file and leafed through it. "Yes, there's exactly two hundred pounds owing on the car."

'Well, of course, Rhoda Masters burst into tears and in the end the manager agreed to take back the car, although it wasn't worth two hundred pounds by then, but he insisted that she should leave it with him then and there, petrol in the tank and all. Rhoda Masters could only accept and be grateful not to be sued, and she walked out of the garage and along the hot street and already she knew what she was going to find when she got to the radio shop. And she was right. It was the same story, only this time she had to pay ten pounds to persuade the man to take back the radiogram. She got a lift back to within walking distance of the bungalow and went and threw herself down on the bed and cried for the rest of the day. She had already been a beaten woman. Now Philip Masters had kicked her when she was down.'

The Governor paused. 'Pretty extraordinary,

really. A man like Masters, kindly, sensitive, who wouldn't normally hurt a fly. And here he was performing one of the cruellest actions I can recall in all my experience. It was my law operating.' The Governor smiled thinly. 'Whatever her sins, if she had given him that Quantum of Solace he could never have behaved to her as he did. As it was, she had awakened in him a bestial cruelty – a cruelty that perhaps lies deeply hidden in all of us and that only a threat to our existence can bring to the surface. Masters wanted to make the girl suffer, not as much as he had suffered because that was impossible, but as much as he could possibly contrive. And that false gesture with the motor car and the radiogramophone was a fiendishly brilliant bit of delayed action to remind her, even when he was gone, how much he hated her, how much he wanted still to hurt her.'

Bond said: 'It must have been a shattering experience. It's extraordinary how much people can hurt each other. I'm beginning to feel rather sorry for the girl. What happened to her in the end – and to him, for the matter of that?'

The Governor got to his feet and looked at his watch. 'Good heavens, it's nearly midnight. And I've been keeping the staff up all this time,' he smiled, 'as well as you.' He walked across to the fireplace and rang a bell. A Negro butler appeared. The Governor apologized for keeping him up and told him to lock up and turn the light out. Bond was on his feet. The Governor turned to him.

'Come along and I'll tell you the rest. I'll walk through the garden with you and see that the sentry lets you out.'

They walked slowly through the long rooms and down the broad steps to the garden. It was a beautiful night under a full moon that raced over their heads through the thin high clouds.

The Governor said: 'Masters went on in the Service, but somehow he never lived up to his good start. After the Bermuda business something seemed to go out of him. Part of him had been killed by the experience. He was a maimed man. Mostly her fault, of course, but I guess that what he did to her lived on with him and perhaps haunted him. He was good at his work, but he had somehow lost the human touch and he gradually dried up. Of course he never married again and in the end he got shunted off into the ground nuts scheme, and when that was a failure he retired and went to live in Nigeria – back to the only people in the world who had shown him any kindness – back to where it had all started from. Bit tragic, really, when I remember what he was like when we were young.'

'And the girl?'

'Oh, she went through a pretty bad time. We handed round the hat for her and she pottered in and out of various jobs that were more or less charity. She tried to go back to being an air hostess, but the way she had broken her contract with Imperial Airways put her out of the running for that. There weren't so many airlines in those days and there was no shortage of applicants for the few hostess jobs that were going. The Burfords got transferred to Jamaica later in that same year and that removed her main prop. As I said, Lady Burford had always had a soft spot for her. Rhoda Masters was pretty nearly destitute. She still had her looks and various men had kept her for a while; but you can't make the rounds for very long in a small place like Bermuda, and she was very near to becoming a harlot and getting into trouble with the police when Providence again stepped in and decided she had been punished enough. A letter came from Lady Burford enclosing her fare to Jamaica and saying she had got her a job as receptionist at the Blue Hills Hotel, one of the best of the Kingston hotels. So she left, and I expect – I'd been transferred to Rhodesia by then – that Bermuda was heartily relieved to see the last of her.'

The Governor and Bond had come to the wide entrance gates to the grounds of Government House. Beyond them shone, white and black and pink under the moon, the huddle of narrow streets and pretty clapboard houses with ginger-bread gables and balconies that is Nassau. With a terrific clatter the sentry came to attention and presented arms. The Governor raised a hand: 'All right. Stand at ease.' Again the clockwork sentry rattled briefly into life and there was silence.

The Governor said: 'And that's the end of the

story except for one final quirk of fate. One day a Canadian millionaire turned up at the Blue Hills Hotel and stayed for the winter. At the end of the time he took Rhoda Masters back to Canada and married her. She's lived in clover ever since.'

'Good heavens. That was a stroke of luck. Hardly deserved it.'

'I suppose not. One can't tell. Life's a devious business. Perhaps, for all the harm she'd done to Masters, Fate decided that she had paid back enough. Perhaps Masters's father and mother were the true guilty people. They turned Masters into an accident-prone man. Inevitably he was involved in the emotional crash that was due to him and that they had conditioned him for. Fate had chosen Rhoda for its instrument. Now Fate reimbursed her for her services. Difficult to judge these things. Anyway, she made her Canadian very happy. I thought they both seemed happy tonight.'

Bond laughed. Suddenly the violent dramatics of his own life seemed very hollow. The affair of the Castro rebels and the burned out yachts was the stuff of an adventure-strip in a cheap newspaper. He had sat next to a dull woman at a dull dinner party and a chance remark had opened for him the book of real violence – of the Comédie Humaine where human passions are raw and real, where Fate plays a more authentic game than any Secret Service conspiracy devised by Governments.

Bond faced the Governor and held out his hand. He said: 'Thank you for the story. And I owe you an apology. I found Mrs Harvey Miller a bore. Thanks to you I shall never forget her. I must pay more attention to people. You've taught me a lesson.'

They shook hands. The Governor smiled. 'I'm glad the story interested you. I was afraid you might be bored. You lead a very exciting life. To tell you the truth, I was at my wit's end to know what we could talk about after dinner. Life in the Colonial Service is very humdrum.'

They said goodnight. Bond walked off down the quiet street towards the harbour and the British Colonial Hotel. He reflected on the conference he would be having in the morning with the Coast Guard and the FBI in Miami. The prospect, which had previously interested, even excited him, was now edged with boredom and futility.

CHAPTER 4

RISICO

'In this pizniss is much risico.'

The words came softly through the thick brown moustache. The hard black eyes moved slowly over Bond's face and down to Bond's hands which were carefully shredding a paper match on which was printed *Albergo Colombo d'Oro*.

James Bond felt the inspection. The same surreptitious examination had been going on since he had met the man two hours before at the rendezvous in the Excelsior bar. Bond had been told to look for a man with a heavy moustache who would be sitting by himself drinking an Alexandra. Bond had been amused by this secret recognition signal. The creamy, feminine drink was so much cleverer than the folded newspaper, the flower in the buttonhole, the yellow gloves that were the hoary, slipshod callsigns between agents. It had also the great merit of being able to operate alone, without its owner. And Kristatos had started off with a little test. When Bond had come into the bar and looked round there had been perhaps twenty people in the room. None of them had a moustache. But on a corner table at the far side of the tall, discreet room, flanked by a saucer of olives and another of cashew nuts, stood the tall-stemmed glass of cream and vodka. Bond went straight over to the table, pulled out a chair and sat down.

The waiter came. 'Good evening, sir. Signor Kristatos is at the telephone.'

Bond nodded. 'A Negroni. With Gordon's, please.'

The waiter walked back to the bar. 'Negroni. Uno. Gordon's.'

'I am so sorry.' The big hairy hand picked up the small chair as if it had been as light as a matchbox and swept it under the heavy hips. 'I had to have a word with Alfredo.'

There had been no handshake. These were old acquaintances. In the same line of business, probably. Something like import and export. The younger one looked American. No. Not with those clothes. English.

Bond returned the fast serve. 'How's his little boy?'

The black eyes of Signor Kristatos narrowed. Yes, they had said this man was a professional. He spread his hands. 'Much the same. What can you expect?'

'Polio is a terrible thing.'

The Negroni came. The two men sat back comfortably, each one satisfied that he had to do with a man in the same league. This was rare in 'The Game'. So many times, before one had even started on a tandem assignment like this, one had lost confidence in the outcome. There was so often, at least in Bond's imagination, a faint smell of burning in the air at such a rendezvous. He knew it for the sign that the fringe of his cover had already started to smoulder. In due course the smouldering fabric would burst into flames and he would be *brûlé*. Then the game would be up and he would have to decide whether to pull out or wait and get shot at by someone. But at this meeting there had been no fumbling.

Later that evening, at the little restaurant off the Piazza di Spagna called the Colomba d'Oro, Bond was amused to find that he was still on probation. Kristatos was still watching and weighing him, wondering if he could be trusted. This remark about the risky business was as near as Kristatos had so far got to admitting that there existed any business between the two of them. Bond was encouraged. He had not really believed in Kristatos. But surely all these precautions could only mean that M's intuition had paid off – that Kristatos knew something big.

Bond dropped the last shred of match into the ashtray. He said mildly: 'I was once taught that any business that pays more than ten per cent or is conducted after nine o'clock at night is a dangerous business. The business which brings us together pays up to one thousand per cent and is conducted almost exclusively at night. On both counts it is obviously a risky business.' Bond lowered his voice. 'Funds are available. Dollars,

Swiss francs, Venezuelan bolivars – anything convenient.'

'That makes me glad. I have already too much lire.' Signor Kristatos picked up the folio menu. 'But let us feed on something. One should not decide important pizniss on a hollow stomach.'

A week earlier M had sent for Bond. M was in a bad temper. 'Got anything on, 007?'

'Only paper work, sir.'

'What do you mean, only paper work?' M jerked his pipe towards his loaded in-tray. 'Who hasn't got paper work?'

'I meant nothing active, sir.'

'Well, say so.' M picked up a bundle of dark red files tied together with tape and slid them so sharply across the desk that Bond had to catch them. 'And here's some more paper work. Scotland Yard stuff mostly – their narcotics people. Wads from the Home Office and the Ministry of Health, and some nice thick reports from the International Opium Control people in Geneva. Take it away and read it. You'll need today and most of tonight. Tomorrow you fly to Rome and get after the big men. Is that clear?'

Bond said that it was. The state of M's temper was also explained. There was nothing that made him more angry than having to divert his staff from their primary duty. This duty was espionage, and when necessary sabotage and subversion. Anything else was a misuse of the Service and of

Secret Funds which, God knows, were meagre enough.

'Any questions?' M's jaw stuck out like the prow of a ship. The jaw seemed to tell Bond to pick up the files and get the hell out of the office and let M move on to something important.

Bond knew that a part of all this – if only a small part – was an act. M had certain bees in his bonnet. They were famous in the Service, and M knew they were. But that did not mean that he would allow them to stop buzzing. There were queen bees, like the misuse of the Service, and the search for true as distinct from wishful intelligence, and there were worker bees. These included such idiosyncrasies as not employing men with beards, or those who were completely bilingual, instantly dismissing men who tried to bring pressure to bear on him through family relationships with members of the Cabinet, mistrusting men or women who were too 'dressy', and those who called him 'sir' off-duty; and having an exaggerated faith in Scotsmen. But M was iron-ically conscious of his obsessions, as, thought Bond, a Churchill or a Montgomery were about theirs. He never minded his bluff, as it partly was, being called on any of them. Moreover, he would never have dreamed of sending Bond out on an assignment without proper briefing.

Bond knew all this. He said mildly: 'Two things, sir. Why are we taking this thing on, and what lead, if any, have Station I got towards the people involved in it?'

M gave Bond a hard, sour look. He swivelled his chair sideways so that he could watch the high, scudding October clouds through the broad window. He reached out for his pipe, blew through it sharply, and then, as if this action had let off the small head of steam, replaced it gently on the desk. When he spoke, his voice was patient, reasonable. 'As you can imagine, 007, I do not wish the Service to become involved in this drug business. Earlier this year I had to take you off other duties for a fortnight so that you could go to Mexico and chase off that Mexican grower. You nearly got yourself killed. I sent you as a favour to the Special Branch. When they asked for you again to tackle this Italian gang I refused. Ronnie Vallance went behind my back to the Home Office and the Ministry of Health. The Ministers pressed me. I said that you were needed here and that I had no one else to spare. Then the two Ministers went to the PM.' M paused. 'And that was that. I must say the PM was very persuasive. Took the line that heroin, in the quantities that have been coming in, is an instrument of psychological warfare – that it saps a country's strength. He said he wouldn't be surprised to find that this wasn't just a gang of Italians out to make big money – that subversion and not money was at the back of it.' M smiled sourly. 'I expect Ronnie Vallance thought up that line of argument. Apparently his narcotics people have been having the devil of a time with the traffic – trying to stop it getting a hold on the teenagers as it has in America. Seems the dance halls and the amusement arcades are full of pedlars. Vallance's Ghost Squad have managed to penetrate back up the line to one of the middle-men, and there's no doubt it's all coming from Italy, hidden in Italian tourists' cars. Vallance has done what he can through the Italian police and Interpol, and got nowhere. They get so far back up the pipeline, arrest a few little people, and then, when they seem to be getting near the centre, there's a blank wall. The inner ring of distributors are too frightened or too well paid.'

Bond interrupted. 'Perhaps there's protection somewhere, sir. That Montesi business didn't look so good.'

M shrugged impatiently. 'Maybe, maybe. And you'll have to watch out for that too, but my impression is that the Montesi case resulted in a pretty extensive clean-up. Anyway, when the PM gave me the order to get on with it, it occurred to me to have a talk with Washington. CIA were very helpful. You know the Narcotics Bureau have a team in Italy. Have had ever since the War. They're nothing to do with CIA – run by the American Treasury Department, of all people. The American Treasury control a so-called Secret Service that looks after drug smuggling and counterfeiting. Pretty crazy arrangement. Often wonder what the FBI must think of it. However,' M slowly swivelled his chair away from the window. He linked his hands behind his head and leaned back, looking across the desk at Bond. 'The point is that the CIA Rome Station works pretty closely with this little narcotics team. Has to, to prevent crossed lines and so on. And CIA – Alan Dulles himself, as a matter of fact – gave me the name of the top narcotics agent used by the Bureau. Apparently he's a double. Does a little smuggling as cover. Chap called Kristatos. Dulles said that of course he couldn't involve his people in any way and he was pretty certain the Treasury Department wouldn't welcome their Rome Bureau playing too closely with us. But he said that, if I wished, he would get word to this Kristatos that one of our, er, best men would like to make contact with a view to doing business. I said I would much appreciate that, and yesterday I got word that the rendezvous is fixed for the day after tomorrow.' M gestured towards the files in front of Bond. 'You'll find all the details in there.'

There was a brief silence in the room. Bond was thinking that the whole affair sounded unpleasant, probably dangerous and certainly dirty. With the last quality in mind, Bond got to his feet and picked up the files. 'All right, sir. It looks like money. How much will we pay for the traffic to stop?'

M let his chair tip forward. He put his hands flat down on the desk, side by side. He said roughly: 'A hundred thousand pounds. In any currency. That's the PM's figure. But I don't want you to get hurt. Certainly not picking other people's coals out of the fire. So you can go up to another hundred thousand if there's bad trouble. Drugs are the biggest and tightest ring in crime.' M reached for his in-basket and took out a file of signals. Without looking up he said: 'Look after yourself.'

Signor Kristatos picked up the menu. He said: 'I do not beat about bushes, Mr Bond. How much?'

'Fifty thousand pounds for one hundred per cent results.'

Kristatos said indifferently: 'Yes. Those are important funds. I shall have melon with prosciutto ham and a chocolate ice-cream. I do not eat greatly at night. These people have their own Chianti. I commend it.'

The waiter came and there was a brisk rattle of Italian. Bond ordered Tagliatelli Verdi with a Genoese sauce which Kristatos said was improbably concocted of basil, garlic and fir cones.

When the waiter had gone, Kristatos sat and chewed silently on a wooden toothpick. His face gradually became dark and glum as if bad weather had come to his mind. The black, hard eyes that glanced restlessly at everything in the restaurant except Bond, glittered. Bond guessed that Kristatos was wondering whether or not to betray somebody. Bond said encouragingly: 'In certain circumstances, there might be more.'

Kristatos seemed to make up his mind. He said:

'So?' He pushed back his chair and got up. 'Forgive me. I must visit the toiletta.' He turned and walked swiftly towards the back of the restaurant.

Bond was suddenly hungry and thirsty. He poured out a large glass of Chianti and swallowed half of it. He broke a roll and began eating, smothering each mouthful with deep yellow butter. He wondered why rolls and butter are delicious only in France and Italy. There was nothing else on his mind. It was just a question of waiting. He had confidence in Kristatos. He was a big, solid man who was trusted by the Americans. He was probably making some telephone call that would be decisive. Bond felt in good spirits. He watched the passers-by through the plate-glass window. A man selling one of the Party papers went by on a bicycle. Flying from the basket in front of the handlebars was a pennant. In red on white it said: PROGRESSO? – SI! – AVVENTURI? – NO! Bond smiled. That was how it was. Let it so remain for the rest of the assignment.

On the far side of the square, rather plain room, at the corner table by the *caisse*, the plump fair-haired girl with the dramatic mouth said to the jovial good-living man with the thick rope of spaghetti joining his face to the plate: 'He has a rather cruel smile. But he is very handsome. Spies aren't usually so good-looking. Are you sure you are right, mein Täubchen?'

The man's teeth cut through the rope. He wiped his mouth on a napkin already streaked with tomato sauce, belched sonorously and said: 'Santos is never wrong about these things. He has a nose for spies. That is why I chose him as the permanent tail for that bastard Kristatos. And who else but a spy would think of spending an evening with the pig? But we will make sure.' The man took out of his pocket one of those cheap tin snappers that are sometimes given out, with paper hats and whistles, on carnival nights. It gave one sharp click. The maître d'hôtel on the far side of the room stopped whatever he was doing and hurried over.

'Si, padrone.'

The man beckoned. The maître d'hôtel went over and received the whispered instructions. He nodded briefly, walked over to a door near the kitchens marked UFFICIO, and went in and closed the door behind him.

Phase by phase, in a series of minute moves, an exercise that had long been perfected was then smoothly put into effect. The man near the *caisse* munched his spaghetti and critically observed each step in the operation as if it had been a fast game of chess.

The maître d'hôtel came out of the door marked UFFICIO, hurried across the restaurant and said loudly to his No. 2: 'An extra table for four. Immediately.' The No. 2 gave him a direct look and nodded. He followed the maître d'hôtel over

143

to a space adjoining Bond's table, clicked his fingers for help, borrowed a chair from one table, a chair from another table and, with a bow and an apology, the spare chair from Bond's table. The fourth chair was being carried over from the direction of the door marked UFFICIO by the maître d'hôtel. He placed it square with the others, a table was lowered into the middle and glass and cutlery were deftly laid. The maître d'hôtel frowned. 'But you have laid a table for four. I said three – for three people.' He casually took the chair he had himself brought to the table and switched it to Bond's table. He gave a wave of the hand to dismiss his helpers and everyone dispersed about their business.

The innocent little flurry of restaurant movement had taken about a minute. An innocuous trio of Italians came into the restaurant. The maître d'hôtel greeted them personally and bowed them to the new table, and the gambit was completed.

Bond had hardly been conscious of it. Kristatos returned from whatever business he had been about, their food came and they got on with the meal.

While they ate they talked about nothing – the election chances in Italy, the latest Alfa Romeo, Italian shoes compared with English. Kristatos talked well. He seemed to know the inside story of everything. He gave information so casually that it did not sound like bluff. He spoke his own kind of English with an occasional phrase borrowed from other languages. It made a lively mixture. Bond was interested and amused. Kristatos was a tough insider – a useful man. Bond was not surprised that the American Intelligence people found him good value.

Coffee came, Kristatos lit a thin black cigar and talked through it, the cigar jumping up and down between the thin straight lips. He put both hands flat on the table in front of him. He looked at the tablecloth between them and said softly: 'This pizniss. I will play with you. To now I have only played with the Americans. I have not told them what I am about to tell you. There was no requirement. This machina does not operate with America. These things are closely regulated. This machina operates only with England. Yes? Capito?'

'I understand. Everyone has his own territory. It's the usual way in these things.'

'Exact. Now, before I give you the informations, like good commercials we make the terms. Yes?'

'Of course.'

Signor Kristatos examined the tablecloth more closely. 'I wish for ten thousand dollars American, in paper of small sizes, by tomorrow lunchtime. When you have destroyed the machina I wish for a further twenty thousand.' Signor Kristatos briefly raised his eyes and surveyed Bond's face. 'I am not greedy. I do not take all your funds, isn't it?'

'The price is satisfactory.'

'Bueno. Second term. There is no telling where

you get these informations from. Even if you are beaten.'

'Fair enough.'

'Third term. The head of this machina is a bad man.' Signor Kristatos paused and looked up. The black eyes held a red glint. The clenched dry lips pulled away from the cigar to let the words out. 'He is to be destrutto – killed.'

Bond sat back. He gazed quizzically at the other man who now leaned slightly forward over the table, waiting. So the wheels had now shown within the wheels! This was a private vendetta of some sort. Kristatos wanted to get himself a gunman. And he was not paying the gunman, the gunman was paying him for the privilege of disposing of an enemy. Not bad! The fixer was certainly working on a big fix this time – using the Secret Service to pay off his private scores. Bond said softly: 'Why?'

Signor Kristatos said indifferently: 'No questions catch no lies.'

Bond drank down his coffee. It was the usual story of big syndicate crime. You never saw more than the tip of the iceberg. But what did that matter to him? He had been sent to do one specific job. If his success benefited others, nobody, least of all M, could care less. Bond had been told to destroy the machine. If this unnamed man was the machine, it would be merely carrying out orders to destroy the man. Bond said: 'I cannot promise that. You must see that. All I can

146

say is that if the man tries to destroy me, I will destroy him.'

Signor Kristatos took a toothpick out of the holder, stripped off the paper and set about cleaning his fingernails. When he had finished one hand he looked up. He said: 'I do not often gamble on incertitudes. This time I will do so because it is you who are paying me, and not me you. Is all right? So now I will give you the informations. Then you are alone – solo. Tomorrow night I fly to Karachi. I have important pizniss there. I can only give you the informations. After that you run with the ball and—' he threw the dirty toothpick down on the table – 'Che sera, sera.'

'All right.'

Signor Kristatos edged his chair nearer to Bond. He spoke softly and quickly. He gave specimen dates and names to document his narrative. He never hesitated for a fact and he did not waste time on irrelevant detail. It was a short story and a pithy one. There were two thousand American gangsters in the country – Italian-Americans who had been convicted and expelled from the United States. These men were in a bad way. They were on the blackest of all police lists and, because of their records, their own people were wary of employing them. A hundred of the toughest among them had pooled their funds and small groups from this elite had moved to Beirut, Istanbul, Tangier and Macao – the great smuggling centres of the world. A further large section

147

acted as couriers, and the bosses had acquired, through nominees, a small and respectable pharmaceutical business in Milan. To this centre the outlying groups smuggled opium and its derivatives. They used small craft across the Mediterranean, a group of stewards in an Italian charter airline and, as a regular weekly source of supply, the through carriage of the Orient Express in which whole sections of bogus upholstery were fitted by bribed members of the train cleaners in Istanbul. The Milan firm – Pharmacia Colomba SA – acted as a clearing-house and as a convenient centre for breaking down the raw opium into heroin. Thence the couriers, using innocent motor cars of various makes, ran a delivery service to the middlemen in England.

Bond interrupted. 'Our Customs are pretty good at spotting that sort of traffic. There aren't many hiding-places in a car they don't know about. Where do these men carry the stuff?'

'Always in the spare wheel. You can carry twenty thousand pounds worth of heroin in one spare wheel.'

'Don't they ever get caught – either bringing the stuff in to Milan or taking it on?'

'Certainly. Many times. But these are well-trained men. And they are tough. They never talk. If they are convicted, they receive ten thousand dollars for each year spent in prison. If they have families, they are cared for. And when all goes well they make good money. It is a cooperative.

Each man receives his *tranche* of the *brutto*. Only the chief gets a special *tranche*.'

'All right. Well, who is this man?'

Signor Kristatos put his hand up to the cheroot in his mouth. He kept the hand there and spoke softly from behind it. 'Is a man they call "The Dove", Enrico Colombo. Is the padrone of this restaurant. That is why I bring you here, so that you may see him. Is the fat man who sits with a blonde woman. At the table by the cassa. She is from Vienna. Her name is Lisl Baum. A luxus whore.'

Bond said reflectively: 'She is, is she?' He did not need to look. He had noticed the girl, as soon as he had sat down at the table. Every man in the restaurant would have noticed her. She had the gay, bold, forthcoming looks the Viennese are supposed to have and seldom do. There was a vivacity and a charm about her that lit up her corner of the room. She had the wildest possible urchin cut in ash blonde, a pert nose, a wide laughing mouth and a black ribbon round her throat. James Bond knew that her eyes had been on him at intervals throughout the evening. Her companion had seemed just the type of rich, cheerful, good-living man she would be glad to have as her lover for a while. He would give her a good time. He would be generous. There would be no regrets on either side. On the whole, Bond had vaguely approved of him. He liked cheerful, expansive people with a zest for life. Since he, Bond, could not have the girl, it was at least something that she was in good hands. But now? Bond glanced across the room. The couple were laughing about something. The man patted her cheek and got up and went to the door marked UFFICIO and went through and shut the door. So this was the man who ran the great pipeline into England. The man with M's price of a hundred thousand pounds on his head. The man Kristatos wanted Bond to kill. Well, he had better get on with the job. Bond stared rudely across the room at the girl. When she lifted her head and looked at him, he smiled at her. Her eyes swept past him, but there was a half smile, as if for herself, on her lips, and when she took a cigarette out of her case and lit it and blew the smoke straight up towards the ceiling there was an offering of the throat and the profile that Bond knew were for him.

It was nearing the time for the after-cinema trade. The maître d'hôtel was supervising the clearing of the unoccupied tables and the setting up of new ones. There was the usual bustle and slapping of napkins across chair-seats and tinkle of glass and cutlery being laid. Vaguely Bond noticed the spare chair at his table being whisked away to help build up a nearby table for six. He began asking Kristatos specific questions – the personal habits of Enrico Colombo, where he lived, the address of his firm in Milan, what other business interests he had. He did not notice the casual progress of the spare chair from its fresh table to another, and then to another,

150

and finally through the door marked UFFICIO. There was no reason why he should.

When the chair was brought into his office, Enrico Colombo waved the maître d'hôtel away and locked the door behind him. Then he went to the chair and lifted off the squab cushion and put it on his desk. He unzipped one side of the cushion and withdrew a Grundig tape-recorder, stopped the machine, ran the tape back, took it off the recorder and put it on a playback and adjusted the speed and volume. Then he sat down at his desk and lit a cigarette and listened, occasionally making further adjustments and occasionally repeating passages. At the end, when Bond's tinny voice said 'She is, is she?' and there was a long silence interspersed with background noises from the restaurant, Enrico Colombo switched off the machine and sat looking at it. He looked at it for a full minute. His face showed nothing but acute concentration on his thoughts. Then he looked away from the machine and into nothing and said softly, out loud: 'Son-a-beech.' He got slowly to his feet and went to the door and unlocked it. He looked back once more at the Grundig, said 'Son-a-beech' again with more emphasis and went out and back to his table.

Enrico Colombo spoke swiftly and urgently to the girl. She nodded and glanced across the room at Bond. He and Kristatos were getting up from the table. She said to Colombo in a low, angry voice: 'You are a disgusting man. Everybody said so and warned me against you. They were right. Just because you give me dinner in your lousy restaurant you think you have the right to insult me with your filthy propositions' – the girl's voice had got louder. Now she had snatched up her handbag and had got to her feet. She stood beside the table directly in the line of Bond's approach on his way to the exit.

Enrico Colombo's face was black with rage. Now he, too, was on his feet. 'You goddam Austrian beech—'

'Don't dare insult my country, you Italian toad.' She reached for a half-full glass of wine and hurled it accurately in the man's face. When he came at her it was easy for her to back the few steps into Bond who was standing with Kristatos politely waiting to get by.

Enrico Colombo stood panting, wiping the wine off his face with a napkin.' He said furiously to the girl: 'Don't *ever show* your face inside my restaurant again.' He made the gesture of spitting on the floor between them, turned and strode off through the door marked UFFICIO.

The maître d'hôtel had hurried up. Everyone in the restaurant had stopped eating. Bond took the girl by the elbow. 'May I help you find a taxi?'

She jerked herself free. She said, still angry: 'All men are pigs.' She remembered her manners. She said stiffly: 'You are very kind.' She moved haughtily towards the door with the men in her wake.

There was a buzz in the restaurant and a renewed clatter of knives and forks. Everyone was delighted with the scene. The maître d'hôtel, looking solemn, held open the door. He said to Bond: 'I apologize, Monsieur. And you are very kind to be of assistance.' A cruising taxi slowed. He beckoned it to the pavement and held open the door.

The girl got in. Bond firmly followed and closed the door. He said to Kristatos through the window: 'I'll telephone you in the morning. All right?' Without waiting for the man's reply he sat back in the seat. The girl had drawn herself away into the farthest corner. Bond said: 'Where shall I tell him?'

'Hotel Ambassadori.'

They drove a short way in silence. Bond said: 'Would you like to go somewhere first for a drink?'

'No thank you.' She hesitated. 'You are very kind, but tonight I am tired.'

'Perhaps another night.'

'Perhaps, but I go to Venice tomorrow.'

'I shall also be there. Will you have dinner with me tomorrow night?'

The girl smiled. She said: 'I thought Englishmen were supposed to be shy. You are English, aren't you? What is your name? What do you do?'

'Yes, I'm English – My name's Bond – James Bond. I write books – adventure stories. I'm writing one now about drug smuggling. It's set in Rome and Venice. The trouble is that I don't know enough about the trade. I am going round picking up stories about it. Do you know any?'

'So that is why you were having dinner with that Kristatos. I know of him. He has a bad reputation. No. I don't know any stories. I only know what everybody knows.'

Bond said enthusiastically: 'But that's exactly what I want. When I said "stories" I didn't mean fiction. I meant the sort of high-level gossip that's probably pretty near the truth. That sort of thing's worth diamonds to a writer.'

She laughed. 'You mean that . . . diamonds?'

Bond said: 'Well, I don't earn all that as a writer, but I've already sold an option on this story for a film, and if I can make it authentic enough I dare say they'll actually buy the film.' He reached out and put his hand over hers in her lap. She did not take her hand away. 'Yes, diamonds. A diamond clip from Van Cleef. Is it a deal?'

Now she took her hand away. They were arriving at the Ambassadori. She picked up her bag from the seat beside her. She turned on the seat so that she faced him. The commissionaire opened the door and the light from the street turned her eyes into stars. She examined his face with a certain seriousness. She said: 'All men are pigs, but some are lesser pigs than others. All right. I will meet you. But not for dinner. What I may tell you is not for public places. I bathe every afternoon at the Lido. But not at the fashionable plage. I bathe at the Bagni Alberoni, where the English poet

Byron used to ride his horse. It is at the tip of the peninsula. The Vaporetto will take you there. You will find me there the day after tomorrow – at three in the afternoon. I shall be getting my last sunburn before the winter. Among the sand-dunes. You will see a pale yellow umbrella. Underneath it will be me.' She smiled. 'Knock on the umbrella and ask for Fräulein Lisl Baum.'

She got out of the taxi. Bond followed. She held out her hand. 'Thank you for coming to my rescue. Goodnight.'

Bond said: 'Three o'clock then. I shall be there. Goodnight.'

She turned and walked up the curved steps of the hotel. Bond looked after her thoughtfully, and then turned and got back into the taxi and told the man to take him to the Nazionale. He sat back and watched the neon signs ribbon past the window. Things, including the taxi, were going almost too fast for comfort. The only one over which he had any control was the taxi. He leant forward and told the man to drive more slowly.

The best train from Rome to Venice is the Laguna express that leaves every day at midday. Bond, after a morning that was chiefly occupied with difficult talks with his London Headquarters on Station I's scrambler, caught it by the skin of his teeth. The Laguna is a smart, streamlined affair that looks and sounds more luxurious than it is. The seats are made for small Italians and the

155

restaurant car staff suffer from the disease that afflicts their brethren in the great trains all over the world – a genuine loathing for the modern traveller and particularly for the foreigner. Bond had a gangway seat over the axle in the rear aluminium coach. If the seven heavens had been flowing by outside the window he would not have cared. He kept his eyes inside the train, read a jerking book, spilled Chianti over the tablecloth and shifted his long, aching legs and cursed the Ferrovie Italiane dello Stato.

But at last there was Mestre and the dead straight finger of rail across the eighteenth century aquatint into Venice. Then came the unfailing shock of the beauty that never betrays and the soft swaying progress down the Grand Canal into a blood-red sunset, and the extreme pleasure – so it seemed – of the Gritti Palace that Bond should have ordered the best double room on the first floor.

That evening, scattering thousand-lira notes like leaves in Vallombrosa, James Bond sought, at Harry's Bar, at Florian's, and finally upstairs in the admirable Quadri, to establish to anyone who might be interested that he was what he had wished to appear to the girl – a prosperous writer who lived high and well. Then, in the temporary state of euphoria that a first night in Venice engenders, however high and serious the purpose of the visitor, James Bond walked back to the Gritti and had eight hours dreamless sleep.

May and October are the best months in Venice. The sun is soft and the nights are cool. The glittering scene is kinder to the eyes and there is a freshness in the air that helps one to hammer out those long miles of stone and terrazza and marble that are intolerable to the feet in summer. And there are fewer people. Although Venice is the one town in the world that can swallow up a hundred thousand tourists as easily as it can a thousand – hiding them down its side-streets, using them for crowd scenes on the piazzas, stuffing them into the vaporetti – it is still better to share Venice with the minimum number of packaged tours and Lederhosen.

Bond spent the next morning strolling the back-streets in the hope that he would be able to uncover a tail. He visited a couple of churches – not to admire their interiors but to discover if anyone came in after him through the main entrance before he left by the side door. No one was following him. Bond went to Florian's and had an Americano and listened to a couple of French culture-snobs discussing the imbalance of the containing façade of St Mark's Square. On an impulse, he bought a postcard and sent it off to his secretary who had once been with the Georgian Group to Italy and had never allowed Bond to forget it. He wrote: "Venice is wonderful. Have so far inspected the railway station and the Stock Exchange. Very aesthetically satisfying. To the Municipal Waterworks this afternoon and then

157

an old Brigitte Bardot at the Scala Cinema. Do you know a wonderful tune called 'O Sole Mio?' It's v. romantic like everything here. JB.'

Pleased with his inspiration, Bond had an early luncheon and went back to his hotel. He locked the door of his room and took off his coat and ran over the Walther PPK. He put up the safe and practised one or two quick draws and put the gun back in the holster. It was time to go. He went along to the landing-stage and boarded the twelve-forty vaporetto to Alberoni, out of sight across the mirrored lagoons. Then he settled down in a seat in the bows and wondered what was going to happen to him.

From the jetty at Alberoni, on the Venice side of the Lido peninsula, there is a half mile dusty walk across the neck of land to the Bagni Alberoni facing the Adriatic. It is a curiously deserted world, this tip of the famous peninsula. A mile down the thin neck of land the luxury real estate development has petered out in a scattering of cracked stucco villas and bankrupt housing projects, and here there is nothing but the tiny fishing village of Alberoni, a sanatorium for students, a derelict experimental station belonging to the Italian Navy and some massive weed-choked gun emplacements from the last war. In the no man's land in the centre of this thin tongue of land is the Golf du Lido, whose brownish undulating fairways meander around the ruins of ancient fortifications. Not many people come to Venice to play golf, and the project is kept alive for its snob appeal by the grand hotels of the Lido. The golf course is surrounded by a high wire fence hung at intervals, as if it protected something of great value or secrecy, with threatening Vietatos and Prohibitos. Around this wired enclave, the scrub and sandhills have not even been cleared of mines, and amongst the rusting barbed wire are signs saying MINAS. PERICOLO DI MORTE beneath a roughly stencilled skull and crossbones. The whole area is strange and melancholy and in extra-ordinary contrast to the gay carnival world of Venice less than an hour away across the lagoons.

Bond was sweating slightly by the time he had walked the half mile across the peninsula to the plage, and he stood for a moment under the last of the acacia trees that had bordered the dusty road to cool off while he got his bearings. In front of him was a rickety wooden archway whose central span said BAGNI ALBERONI in faded blue paint. Beyond were the lines of equally dilapidated wooden cabins, and then a hundred yards of sand and then the quiet blue glass of the sea. There were no bathers and the place seemed to be closed, but when he walked through the archway he heard the tinny sound of a radio playing Neapolitan music. It came from a ramshackle hut that adver-tised Coca-Cola and various Italian soft drinks. Deck-chairs were stacked against its walls and there were two pedallos and a child's half inflated seahorse. The whole establishment looked so derelict that Bond could not imagine it doing business even at the height of the summer season. He stepped off the narrow duckboards into the soft, burned sand and moved round behind the huts to the beach. He walked down to the edge of the sea. To the left, until it disappeared in the autumn heat haze, the wide empty sand swept away in a slight curve towards the Lido proper. To the right was half a mile of beach terminating in the seawall at the tip of the peninsula. The seawall stretched like a finger out into the silent mirrored sea, and at intervals along its top were the flimsy derricks of the octopus fishermen. Behind the beach were the sandhills and a section of the wire fence surrounding the golf course. On the edge of the sandhills, perhaps five hundred yards away, there was a speck of bright yellow.

Bond set off towards it along the tide-line.

'Ahem.'

The hands flew to the top scrap of bikini and pulled it up. Bond walked into her line of vision and stood looking down. The bright shadow of the umbrella covered only her face. The rest of her – a burned cream body in a black bikini on a black and white striped bath-towel – lay offered to the sun.

She looked up at him through half closed eyelashes. 'You are five minutes early and I told you to knock.'

Bond sat down close to her in the shade of the

big umbrella. He took out a handkerchief and wiped his face. 'You happen to own the only palm tree in the whole of this desert. I had to get underneath it as soon as I could. This is the hell of a place for a rendezvous.'

She laughed. 'I am like Greta Garbo. I like to be alone.'

'Are we alone?'

She opened her eyes wide. 'Why not? You think I have brought a chaperone?'

'Since you think all men are pigs . . .'

'Ah, but you are a gentleman pig,' she giggled. 'A milord pig. And anyway, it is too hot for that kind of thing. And there is too much sand. And besides this is a business meeting, no? I tell you stories about drugs and you give me a diamond clip. From Van Cleef. Or have you changed your mind?'

'No. That's how it is. Where shall we begin?'

'You ask the questions. What is it you want to know?' She sat up and pulled her knees to her between her arms. Flirtation had gone out of her eyes and they had become attentive, and perhaps a little careful.

Bond noticed the change. He said casually, watching her: 'They say your friend Colombo is a big man in the game. Tell me about him. He would make a good character for my book – disguised, of course. But it's the detail I need. How does he operate, and so on? That's not the sort of thing a writer can invent.'

She veiled her eyes. She said: 'Enrico would be very angry if he knew that I had told any of his secrets. I don't know what he would do to me.'

'He will never know.'

She looked at him seriously. 'Lieber Mr Bond, there is very little that he does not know. And he is also quite capable of acting on a guess. I would not be surprised' – Bond caught her quick glance at his watch – 'if it had crossed his mind to have me followed here. He is a very suspicious man.' She put her hand out and touched his sleeve. Now she looked nervous. She said urgently: 'I think you had better go now. This has been a great mistake.'

Bond openly looked at his watch. It was three-thirty. He moved his head so that he could look behind the umbrella and back down the beach. Far down by the bathing huts, their outlines dancing slightly in the heat haze, were three men in dark clothes. They were walking purposefully up the beach, their feet keeping step as if they were a squad.

Bond got to his feet. He looked down at the bent head. He said drily: 'I see what you mean. Just tell Colombo that from now on I'm writing his life-story. And I'm a very persistent writer. So long.' Bond started running up the sand towards the tip of the peninsula. From there he could double back down the other shore to the village and the safety of people.

Down the beach the three men broke into a fast jog-trot, elbows and legs pounding in time with each other as if they were long-distance runners out for a training spin. As they jogged past the girl, one of the men raised a hand. She raised hers in answer and then lay down on the sand and turned over – perhaps so that her back could now get its toasting, or perhaps because she did not want to watch the man-hunt.

Bond took off his tie as he ran and put it in his pocket. It was very hot and he was already sweating profusely. But so would the three men be. It was a question who was in better training. At the tip of the peninsula, Bond clambered up on to the seawall and looked back. The men had hardly gained, but now two of them were fanning out to cut round the edge of the golf course boundary. They did not seem to mind the danger notices with the skull and crossbones. Bond, running fast down the wide seawall, measured angles and distances. The two men were cutting across the base of the triangle. It was going to be a close call.

Bond's shirt was already soaked and his feet were beginning to hurt. He had run perhaps a mile. How much farther to safety? At intervals along the seawall the breeches of antique cannon had been sunk in the concrete. They would be mooring posts for the fishing fleets sheltering in the protection of the lagoons before taking to the Adriatic. Bond counted his steps between two of them. Fifty yards. How many black knobs to the end of the wall – to the first houses of the village? Bond counted up to thirty before the line vanished into the heat haze. Probably another mile to go. Could he do it, and fast enough to beat the two flankers? Bond's breath was already rasping in his throat. Now even his suit was soaked with sweat and the cloth of his trousers was chafing his legs. Behind him, three hundred yards back, was one pursuer. To his right, dodging among the sand-dunes and converging fast, were the other two. To his left was a twenty-foot slope of masonry to the green tide ripping out into the Adriatic.

Bond was planning to slow down to a walk and keep enough breath to try and shoot it out with the three men, when two things happened in quick succession. First he saw through the haze ahead a group of spear-fishermen. There were about half a dozen of them, some in the water and some sunning themselves on the seawall. Then, from the sand-dunes came the deep roar of an explosion. Earth and scrub and what might have been bits of a man fountained briefly into the air, and a small shock-wave hit him. Bond slowed. The other man in the dunes had stopped. He was standing stock-still. His mouth was open and a frightened jabber came from it. Suddenly he collapsed on the ground with his arms wapped round his head. Bond knew the signs. He would not move again until someone came and carried him away from there. Bond's heart lifted. Now he had only about two hundred yards to go to the fishermen. They were already gathering into a group, looking towards him. Bond summoned a few words of Italian and rehearsed them. 'Mi Ingles. Prego, dove il carabinieri.' Bond glanced over his shoulder. Odd, but despite the witnessing spear-fishers, the man was still coming on. He had gained and was only about a hundred yards behind. There was a gun in his hand. Now, ahead, the fishermen had fanned out across Bond's path. They had harpoon guns held at the ready. In the centre was a big man with a tiny red bathing-slip hanging beneath his stomach. A green mask was slipped back on to the crown of his head. He stood with his blue swim-fins pointing out and his arms akimbo. He looked like Mr Toad of Toad Hall in Technicolor. Bond's amused thought died in him stillborn. Panting, he slowed to a walk. Automatically his sweaty hand felt under his coat for the gun and drew it out. The man in the centre of the arc of pointing harpoons was Enrico Colombo.

Colombo watched him approach. When he was twenty yards away, Colombo said quietly: 'Put away your toy, Mr Bond of the Secret Service. These are CO_2 harpoon guns. And stay where you are. Unless you wish to make a copy of Mantegna's St Sebastian.' He turned to the man on his right. He spoke in English. 'At what range was that Albanian last week?'

'Twenty yards, padrone. And the harpoon went right through. But he was a fat man – perhaps twice as thick as this one.'

Bond stopped. One of the iron bollards was beside him. He sat down and rested the gun on his knee. It pointed at the centre of Colombo's big stomach. He said: 'Five harpoons in me won't stop one bullet in you, Colombo.'

Colombo smiled and nodded, and the man who had been coming softly up behind Bond hit him once hard in the base of the skull with the butt of his Luger.

When you come to from being hit on the head the first reaction is a fit of vomiting. Even in his wretchedness Bond was aware of two sensations – he was in a ship at sea, and someone, a man, was wiping his forehead with a cool wet towel and murmuring encouragement in bad English. 'Is okay, amigo. Take him easy. Take him easy.'

Bond fell back on his bunk, exhausted. It was a comfortable small cabin with a feminine smell and dainty curtains and colours. A sailor in a tattered vest and trousers – Bond thought he recognized him as one of the spear-fishermen – was bending over him. He smiled when Bond opened his eyes. 'Is better, yes? Subito okay.' He rubbed the back of his neck in sympathy. 'It hurts for a little. Soon it will only be a black. Beneath the hair. The girls will see nothing.'

Bond smiled feebly and nodded. The pain of the nod made him screw up his eyes. When he opened them the sailor shook his head in admonition. He brought his wrist-watch close up to Bond's eyes.

It said seven o'clock. He pointed with his little finger at the figure nine. 'Mangiare con Padrone, Si?'

Bond said: 'Si.'

The man put his hand to his cheek and laid his head on one side. 'Dormire.'

Bond said 'Si' again and the sailor went out of the cabin and closed the door without locking it.

Bond got gingerly off the bunk and went over to the wash basin and set about cleaning himself. On top of the chest of drawers was a neat pile of his personal belongings. Everything was there except his gun. Bond stowed the things away in his pockets, and sat down again on the bunk and smoked and thought. His thoughts were totally inconclusive. He was being taken for a ride, or rather a sail, but from the behaviour of the sailor it did not seem that he was regarded as an enemy. Yet a great deal of trouble had been taken to make him prisoner and one of Colombo's men had even, though inadvertently, died in the process. It did not seem to be just a question of killing him. Perhaps this soft treatment was the preliminary to trying to make a deal with him. What was the deal – and what was the alternative?

At nine o'clock the same sailor came for Bond and led him down a short passage to a small, blowzy saloon, and left him. There was a table and two chairs in the middle of the room, and beside the table a nickel-plated trolley laden with food and drinks. Bond tried the hatchway at the end of the saloon. It was bolted. He unlatched one of the portholes and looked out. There was just enough light to see that the ship was about two hundred tons and might once have been a large fishing-vessel. The engine sounded like a single diesel and they were carrying sail. Bond estimated the ship's speed at six or seven knots. On the dark horizon there was a tiny cluster of yellow lights. It seemed probable that they were sailing down the Adriatic coast.

The hatchway bolt rattled back. Bond pulled in his head. Colombo came down the steps. He was dressed in a sweat-shirt, dungarees and scuffed sandals. There was a wicked, amused gleam in his eyes. He sat down in one chair and waved to the other. 'Come, my friend. Food and drink and plenty of talk. We will now stop behaving like little boys and be grown-up. Yes? What will you have – gin, whisky, champagne? And this is the finest sausage in the whole of Bologna. Olives from my own estate. Bread, butter, Provelone – that is smoked cheese – and fresh figs. Peasant food, but good. Come. All that running must have given you an appetite.'

His laugh was infectious. Bond poured himself a stiff whisky and soda, and sat down. He said: 'Why did you have to go to so much trouble? We could have met without all these dramatics. As it is you have prepared a lot of grief for yourself. I warned my chief that something like this might happen – the way the girl picked me up in your restaurant was too childish for words. I said that

168

I would walk into the trap to see what it was all about. If I am not out of it again by tomorrow midday, you'll have Interpol as well as Italian police on top of you like a load of bricks.'

Colombo looked puzzled. He said: 'If you were ready to walk into the trap, why did you try and escape from my men this afternoon? I had sent them to fetch you and bring you to my ship, and it would all have been much more friendly. Now I have lost a good man and you might easily have had your skull broken. I do not understand.'

'I didn't like the look of those three men. I know killers when I see them. I thought you might be thinking of doing something stupid. You should have used the girl. The men were unnecessary.'

Colombo shook his head. 'Lisl was willing to find out more about you, but nothing else. She will now be just as angry with me as you are. Life is very difficult. I like to be friends with everyone, and now I have made two enemies in one afternoon. It is too bad.' Colombo looked genuinely sorry for himself. He cut a thick slice of sausage, impatiently tore the rind off it with his teeth and began to eat. While his mouth was still full he took a glass of champagne and washed the sausage down with it. He said, shaking his head reproachfully at Bond: 'It is always the same, when I am worried I have to eat. But the food that I eat when I am worried I cannot digest. And now you have worried me. You say that we could have met and talked things over – that I need not have taken all

169

this trouble.' He spread his hands helplessly. 'How was I to know that? By saying that, you put the blood of Mario on my hands. I did not tell him to take a short cut through that place.' Colombo pounded the table. Now he shouted angrily at Bond. 'I do not agree that this was all my fault. It was your fault. Yours only. You had agreed to kill me. How does one arrange a friendly meeting with one's murderer? Eh? Just tell me that.' Colombo snatched up a long roll of bread and stuffed it into his mouth, his eyes furious.

'What the hell are you talking about?'

Colombo threw the remains of the roll on the table and got to his feet, holding Bond's eyes locked in his. He walked sideways, still gazing fixedly at Bond, to a chest of drawers, felt for the knob of the top drawer, opened it, groped and lifted out what Bond recognized as a tape-recorder playback machine. Still looking accusingly at Bond, he brought the machine over to the table. He sat down and pressed a switch.

When Bond heard the voice he picked up his glass of whisky and looked into it. The tinny voice said: 'Exact, Now, before I give you the informations, like good commercials we make the terms. Yes?' The voice went on: 'Ten thousand dollars American . . . There is no telling where you get these informations from. Even if you are beaten . . . The head of this machina is a bad man. He is to be destrutto – killed.' Bond waited for his own voice to break through the restaurant noises. There had been a long pause while he thought about the last condition. What was it he had said? His voice came out of the machine, answering him. 'I cannot promise that. You must see that. All I can say is that if the man tries to destroy me, I will destroy him.'

Colombo switched off the machine. Bond swallowed down his whisky. Now he could look up at Colombo. He said defensively: 'That doesn't make me a murderer.'

Colombo looked at him sorrowfully. 'To me it does. Coming from an Englishman. I worked for the English during the War. In the Resistance. I have the King's Medal.' He put his hand in his pocket and threw the silver Freedom medal with the red, white and blue striped ribbon on to the table. 'You see?'

Bond obstinately held Colombo's eyes. He said: 'And the rest of the stuff on that tape? You long ago stopped working for the English. Now you work against them, for money.'

Colombo grunted. He tapped the machine with his forefinger. He said impassively: 'I have heard it all. It is lies.' He banged his fist on the table so that the glasses jumped. He bellowed furiously: 'It is lies, lies. Every word of it.' He jumped to his feet. His chair crashed down behind him. He slowly bent and picked it up. He reached for the whisky bottle and walked round and poured four fingers into Bond's glass. He went back to his chair and sat down and put the champagne bottle

171

on the table in front of him. Now his face was composed, serious. He said quietly: 'It is not all lies. There is a grain of truth in what that bastard told you. That is why I decided not to argue with you. You might not have believed me. You would have dragged in the police. There would have been much trouble for me and my comrades. Even if you or someone else had not found reason to kill me, there would have been scandal, ruin. Instead I decided to show you the truth – the truth you were sent to Italy to find out. Within a matter of hours, tomorrow at dawn, your mission will have been completed.' Colombo clicked his fingers. 'Presto – like that.'

Bond said: 'What part of Kristatos's story is not lies?'

Colombo's eyes looked into Bond's calculating. Finally he said: 'My friend, I am a smuggler. That part is true. I am probably the most successful smuggler in the Mediterranean. Half the American cigarettes in Italy are brought in by me from Tangier. Gold? I am the sole supplier of the black valuta market. Diamonds? I have my own purveyor in Beirut with direct lines to Sierra Leone and South Africa. In the old days, when these things were scarce, I also handled aureomycin and peni-cillin and such medicines. Bribery at the American base hospitals. And there have been many other things – even beautiful girls from Syria and Persia for the houses of Naples. I have also smuggled out escaped convicts. But,' Colombo's fist crashed

172

on the table, 'drugs, heroin, opium, hemp – no! Never! I will have nothing to do with these things. These things are evil. There is no sin in the others.' Colombo held up his right hand. 'My friend, this I swear to you on the head of my mother.'

Bond was beginning to see daylight. He was prepared to believe Colombo. He even felt a curious liking for this greedy, boisterous pirate who had so nearly been put on the spot by Kristatos. Bond said: 'But why did Kristatos put the finger on you? What's he got to gain?'

Colombo slowly shook a finger to and fro in front of his nose. He said: 'My friend, Kristatos is Kristatos. Hc is playing the biggest double game it is possible to conceive. To keep it up – to keep the protection of American Intelligence and thcir Narcotics people – he must now and then throw them a victim – some small man on the fringe of the big game. But with this English problem it is different. That is a huge traffic. To protect it, a big victim was required. I was chosen – by Kristatos, or by his employers. And it is true that if you had been vigorous in your investigations and had spent enough hard currency on buying information, you might have discovered the story of my operations. But each trail towards *me* would have led you further away from the truth. In the end, for I do not underestimate your Service, I would have gone to prison. But the big fox you are after would only be laughing at the sound of the hunt dying away in the distance.'

'Why did Kristatos want you killed?'

Colombo looked cunning. 'My friend, I know too much. In the fraternity of smugglers, we occasionally stumble on a corner of the next man's business. Not long ago, in this ship, I had a running fight with a small gunboat from Albania. A lucky shot set fire to their fuel. There was only one survivor. He was persuaded to talk. I learnt much, but like a fool I took a chance with the minefields and set him ashore on the coast north of Tirana. It was a mistake. Ever since then I have had this bastard Kristatos after me. Fortunately,' Colombo grinned wolfishly, 'I have one piece of information he does not know of. And we have a rendezvous with this piece of information at first light tomorrow – at a small fishing-port just north of Ancona, Santa Maria. And there,' Colombo gave a harsh, cruel laugh, 'we shall see what we shall see.'

Bond said mildly, 'What's your price for all this? You say my mission will have been completed tomorrow morning. How much?'

Colombo shook his head. He said indifferently: 'Nothing. It just happens that our interests coincide. But I shall need your promise that what I have told you this evening is between you and me and, if necessary, your Chief in London. It must never come back to Italy. Is that agreed?'

'Yes. I agree to that.'

Colombo got to his feet. He went to the chest of drawers and took out Bond's gun. He handed it to Bond. 'In that case, my friend, you had better have this, because you are going to need it. And you had better get some sleep. There will be rum and coffee for everyone at five in the morning.' He held out his hand. Bond took it. Suddenly the two men were friends. Bond felt the fact. He said awkwardly 'All right, Colombo,' and went out of the saloon and along to his cabin.

The *Colombina* had a crew of twelve. They were youngish, tough-looking men. They talked softly among themselves as the mugs of hot coffee and rum were dished out by Colombo in the saloon. A storm lantern was the only light – the ship had been darkened – and Bond smiled to himself at the Treasure Island atmosphere of excitement and conspiracy. Colombo went from man to man on a weapon inspection. They all had Lugers, carried under the jersey inside the trouser-band, and flick-knives in the pocket. Colombo had a word of approval or criticism for each weapon. It struck Bond that Colombo had made a good life for himself – a life of adventure and thrill and risk. It was a criminal life – a running fight with the currency laws, the State tobacco monopoly, the Customs, the police – but there was a whiff of adolescent rascality in the air which somehow changed the colour of the crime from black to white – or at least to grey.

Colombo looked at his watch. He dismissed the men to their posts. He dowsed the lantern and, in the oyster light of dawn, Bond followed him up to the bridge. He found the ship was close to a black, rocky shore which they were following at reduced speed. Colombo pointed ahead. 'Round that headland is the harbour. Our approach will not have been observed. In the harbour, against the jetty, I expect to find a ship of about this size unloading innocent rolls of newsprint down a ramp into a warehouse. Round the headland, we will put on full speed and come alongside this ship and board her. There will be resistance. Heads will be broken. I hope it is not shooting. We shall not shoot unless they do. But it will be an Albanian ship manned by a crew of Albanian toughs. If there is shooting, you must shoot well with the rest of us. These people are enemies of your country as well as mine. If you get killed, you get killed. Okay?'

'That's all right.'

As Bond said the words, there came a ting on the engine-room telegraph and the deck began to tremble under his feet. Making ten knots, the small ship rounded the headland into the harbour.

It was as Colombo had said. Alongside a stone jetty lay the ship, its sails flapping idly. From her stern a ramp of wood planks sloped down towards the dark mouth of a ramshackle corrugated iron warehouse, inside which burned feeble electric lights. The ship carried a deck cargo of what appeared to be rolls of newsprint, and these were being hoisted one by one on to the ramp whence they rolled down under their own momentum through the mouth of the warehouse. There were about twenty men in sight. Only surprise would straighten out these odds. Now Colombo's craft was fifty yards away from the other ship, and one or two of the men had stopped working and were looking in their direction. One man ran off into the warehouse. Simultaneously Colombo issued a sharp order. The engines stopped and went into reverse. A big searchlight on the bridge came on and lit the whole scene brightly as the ship drifted up alongside the Albanian trawler. At the first hard contact, grappling-irons were tossed over the Albanian's rail fore and aft, and Colombo's men swarmed over the side with Colombo in the lead.

Bond had made his own plans. As soon as his feet landed on the enemy deck, he ran straight across the ship, climbed the far rail and jumped. It was about twelve feet to the jetty and he landed like a cat, on his hands and toes, and stayed for a moment, crouching, planning his next move. Shooting had already started on deck. An early shot killed the searchlight and now there was only the grey, luminous light of dawn. A body, one of the enemy, crunched to the stone in front of him and lay spread-eagled, motionless. At the same time, from the mouth of the warehouse, a light machine gun started up, firing short bursts with a highly professional touch. Bond ran towards it in the dark shadow of the ship. The machine-gunner saw him and gave him a burst. The bullets zipped round Bond, clanged against the iron hull of the ship and whined off into the night. Bond got to the cover of the sloping ramp of boards and dived forward on his stomach. The bullets crashed into the wood above his head. Bond crept forward into the narrowing space. When he had got as close as he could, he would have a choice of breaking cover either to right or left of the boards. There came a series of heavy thuds and a swift rumble above his head. One of Colombo's men must have cut the ropes and sent the whole pile of newsprint rolls down the ramp. Now was Bond's chance. He leapt out from under cover – to the left. If the machine-gunner was waiting for him, he would expect Bond to come out firing on the right. The machine-gunner was there, crouching up against the wall of the warehouse. Bond fired twice in the split second before the bright muzzle of the enemy weapon had swung through its small arc. The dead man's finger clenched on the trigger and, as he slumped, his gun made a brief Catherine-wheel of flashes before it shook itself free from his hand and clattered to the ground.

Bond was running forward towards the warehouse door when he slipped and fell headlong. He lay for a moment, stunned, his face in a pool of black treacle. He cursed and got to his hands and knees and made a dash for cover behind a jumble of the big newsprint rolls that had crashed into the wall of the warehouse. One of them, sliced by a burst from the machine gun, was leaking black treacle. Bond wiped as much of the stuff off his hands and face as he could. It had the musty sweet smell that Bond had once smelled in Mexico. It was raw opium.

A bullet whanged into the wall of the warehouse not far from his head. Bond gave his gun-hand a last wipe on the seat of his trousers and leapt for the warehouse door. He was surprised not to be shot at from the interior as soon as he was silhouetted against the entrance. It was quiet and cool inside the place. The lights had been turned out, but it was now getting brighter outside. The pale newsprint rolls were stacked in orderly ranks with a space to make a passageway down the centre. At the far end of the passageway was a door. The whole arrangement leered at him, daring him. Bond smelled death. He edged back to the entrance and out into the open. The shooting had become spasmodic. Colombo came running swiftly towards him, his feet close to the ground as fat men run. Bond said peremptorily: 'Stay at this door. Don't go in or let any of your men in. I'm going round to the back.' Without waiting for an answer he sprinted round the corner of the building and down along its side.

The warehouse was about fifty feet long. Bond slowed and walked softly to the far corner. He flattened himself against the corrugated iron wall and took a swift look round. He immediately drew back. A man was standing up against the back

179

entrance. His eyes were at some kind of spyhole. In his hand was a plunger from which wires ran under the bottom of the door. A car, a black Lancia Granturismo convertible with the hood down, stood beside him, its engine ticking over softly. It pointed inland along a deeply tracked dust road.

The man was Kristatos.

Bond knelt. He held his gun in both hands for steadiness, inched swiftly round the corner of the building and fired one shot at the man's feet. He missed. Almost as he saw the dust kick up inches off the target, there was the rumbling crack of an explosion and the tin wall hit him and sent him flying.

Bond scrambled to his feet. The warehouse had buckled crazily out of shape. Now it started to collapse noisily like a pack of tin cards. Kristatos was in the car. It was already twenty yards away, dust fountaining up from the traction on the rear wheels. Bond stood in the classic pistol-shooting pose and took careful aim. The Walther roared and kicked three times. At the last shot, at fifty yards, the figure crouched over the wheel jerked backwards. The hands flew sideways off the wheel. The head craned briefly into the air and slumped forward. The right hand remained sticking out as if the dead man was signalling a right-hand turn. Bond started to run up the road, expecting the car to stop, but the wheels were held in the ruts and, with the weight of the dead right foot still on the accelerator, the Lancia tore onwards in its screaming third gear. Bond stopped and watched it. It hurried on along the flat road across the burned-up plain and the cloud of white dust blew gaily up behind. At any moment Bond expected it to veer off the road, but it did not, and Bond stood and saw it out of sight into the early morning mist that promised a beautiful day.

Bond put his gun on safe and tucked it away in the belt of his trousers. He turned to find Colombo approaching him. The fat man was grinning delightedly. He came up with Bond and, to Bond's horror, threw open his arms, clutched Bond to him and kissed him on both cheeks.

Bond said: 'For God's sake, Colombo.'

Colombo roared with laughter. 'Ah, the quiet Englishman! He fears nothing save the emotions. But me,' he hit himself in the chest, 'me, Enrico Colombo, loves this man and he is not ashamed to say so. If you had not got the machine-gunner, not one of us would have survived. As it is, I lost two of my men and others have wounds. But only half a dozen Albanians remain on their feet and they have escaped into the village. No doubt the police will round them up. And now you have sent that bastard Kristatos motoring down to hell. What a splendid finish to him! What will happen when the little racing-hearse meets the main road? He is already signalling for the right-hand turn on to the autostrada, I hope he will remember to drive on the right.' Colombo clapped Bond boisterously on the shoulder. 'But come, my friend. It is time we got out of here. The cocks are open in the Albanian ship and she will soon be on the bottom. There are no telephones in this little place. We will have a good start on the police. It will take them some time to get sense out of the fishermen. I have spoken to the head man. No one here has any love for Albanians. But we must be on our way. We have a stiff sail into the wind and there is no doctor I can trust this side of Venice.'

Flames were beginning to lick out of the shattered warehouse, and there was billowing smoke that smelled of sweet vegetables. Bond and Colombo walked round to windward. The Albanian ship had settled on the bottom and her decks were awash. They waded across her and climbed on board the *Colombina*, where Bond had to go through some more handshaking and backslapping. They cast off at once and made for the headland guarding the harbour. There was a small group of fishermen standing by their boats that lay drawn up on the beach below a huddle of stone cottages. They made a surly impression, but when Colombo waved and shouted something in Italian most of them raised a hand in farewell, and one of them called back something that made the crew of the *Colombina* laugh. Colombo explained: 'They say we were better than the cinema at Ancona and we must come again soon.'

Bond suddenly felt the excitement drain out of

him. He felt dirty and unshaven, and he could smell his own sweat. He went below and borrowed a razor and a clean shirt from one of the crew, and stripped in his cabin and cleansed himself. When he took out his gun and threw it on the bunk he caught a whiff of cordite from the barrel. It brought back the fear and violence and death of the grey dawn. He opened the porthole. Outside, the sea was dancing and gay, and the receding coastline, that had been black and mysterious, was now green and beautiful. A sudden delicious scent of frying bacon came downwind from the galley. Abruptly Bond pulled the porthole to and dressed and went along to the saloon.

Over a mound of fried eggs and bacon washed down with hot sweet coffee laced with rum, Colombo dotted the i's and crossed the t's.

'This we have done, my friend,' he said through crunching toast. 'That was a year's supply of raw opium on its way to Kristatos's chemical works in Naples. It is true that I have such a business in Milan and that it is a convenient depot for some of my wares. But it fabricates nothing more deadly than cascara and aspirin. For all that part of Kristatos's story, read Kristatos instead of Colombo. It is he who breaks the stuff down into heroin and it is he who employs the couriers to take it to London. That huge shipment was worth perhaps a million pounds to Kristatos and his men. But do you know something, my dear James? It cost him not one solitary cent. Why? Because it is a gift from Russia. The gift of a massive and deadly projectile to be fired into the bowels of England. The Russians can supply unlimited quantities of the charge for the projectile. It comes from their poppy fields in the Caucasus, and Albania is a convenient entrepôt. But they have not the apparatus to fire this projectile. The man Kristatos created the necessary apparatus, and it is he, on behalf of his masters in Russia, who pulls the trigger. Today, between us, we have destroyed, in half an hour, the entire conspiracy. You can now go back and tell your people in England that the traffic will cease. You can also tell them the truth – that Italy was not the origin of this terrible underground weapon of war. That it is our old friends the Russians. No doubt it is some psychological warfare section of their Intelligence apparatus. That I cannot tell you. Perhaps, my dear James,' Colombo smiled encouragingly, 'they will send you to Moscow to find out. If that should happen, let us hope you will find some girl as charming as your friend Fräulein Lisl Baum to put you on the right road to the truth.'

'What do you mean "my friend"? She's yours.'

Colombo shook his head. 'My dear James, I have many friends. You will be spending a few more days in Italy writing your report, and no doubt,' he chuckled, 'checking on some of the things I have told you. Perhaps you will also have an enjoyable half an hour explaining the facts of life to your colleagues in American Intelligence. In between these duties you will need companionship – someone to show you the beauties of my beloved homeland. In uncivilized countries, it is the polite custom to offer one of your wives to a man whom you love and wish to honour. I also am uncivilized. I have no wives, but I have many such friends as Lisl Baum. She will not need to receive any instructions in this matter. I have good reason to believe that she is awaiting your return this evening.' Colombo fished in his trousers pocket and tossed something down with a clang on the table in front of Bond. 'Here is the good reason.' Colombo put his hand to his heart and looked seriously into Bond's eyes. 'I give it to you from my heart. Perhaps also from hers.'

Bond picked the thing up. It was a key with a heavy metal tag attached. The metal tag was inscribed *Albergo Danielli. Room 68.*

CHAPTER 5

THE HILDEBRAND RARITY

The sting-ray was about six feet from wing-tip to wing-tip, and perhaps ten feet long from the blunt wedge of its nose to the end of its deadly tail. It was dark grey with that violet tinge that is so often a danger signal in the underwater world. When it rose up from the pale golden sand and swam a little distance it was as if a black towel was being waved through the water.

James Bond, his hands along his flanks and swimming with only a soft trudge of his fins, followed the black shadow across the wide palm-fringed lagoon, waiting for a shot. He rarely killed fish except to eat, but there were exceptions – big moray eels and all the members of the scorpion-fish family. Now he proposed to kill the sting-ray because it looked so extraordinarily evil.

It was ten o'clock in the morning of a day in April, and the lagoon, Belle Anse near the south-ernmost tip of Mahe, the largest island in the Seychelles group, was glassy calm. The north-west monsoon had blown itself out months before and it would be May before the south-east monsoon

186

brought refreshment. Now the temperature was eighty in the shade and the humidity ninety, and in the enclosed waters of the lagoon the water was near blood heat. Even the fish seemed to be sluggish. A ten-pound green parrot-fish, nibbling algae from a lump of coral, paused only to roll its eyes as Bond passed overhead, and then went back to its meal. A school of fat grey chub, swimming busily, broke courteously in half to let Bond's shadow by, and then joined up and continued on their opposite course. A chorus line of six small squids, normally as shy as birds, did not even bother to change their camouflage at his passage.

Bond trudged lazily on, keeping the sting-ray just in sight. Soon it would get tired or else be reassured when Bond, the big fish on the surface, did not attack. Then it would settle on to a patch of flat sand, change its camouflage down to the palest, almost translucent grey, and, with soft undulations of its wing-tips, bury itself in the sand.

The reef was coming nearer and now there were outcrops of coral niggerheads and meadows of sea-grass. It was like arriving in a town from open country. Everywhere the jewelled reef fish twinkled and glowed and the giant anemones of the Indian Ocean burned like flames in the shadows. Colonies of spined sea-eggs made sepia splashes as if someone had thrown ink against the rock, and the brilliant blue and yellow feelers of langoustes quested and waved from their crevices like small dragons. Now and then, among the

187

seaweed on the brilliant floor, there was the speckled glitter of a cowrie bigger than a golf ball – the leopard cowrie – and once Bond saw the beautiful splayed fingers of a Venus's harp. But all these things were now commonplace to him and he drove steadily on, interested in the reef only as cover through which he could get to seaward of the ray and then pursue it back towards the shore. The tactic worked, and soon the black shadow with its pursuing brown torpedo were moving back across the great blue mirror. In about twelve feet of water the ray stopped for the hundredth time. Bond stopped also, treading water softly. Cautiously he lifted his head and emptied water out of his goggles. By the time he looked again the ray had disappeared.

Bond had a Champion harpoon-gun with double rubbers. The harpoon was tipped with a needle-sharp trident – a short-range weapon, but the best for reef work. Bond pushed up the safe and moved slowly forward, his fins pulsing softly just below the surface so as to make no sound. He looked around him, trying to pierce the misty horizons of the great hall of the lagoon. He was looking for any big lurking shape. It would not do to have a shark or a large barracuda as witness of the kill. Fish sometimes scream when they are hurt, and even when they do not the turbulence and blood caused by a sharp struggle bring the scavengers. But there was not a living thing in sight and the sand stretched away into the smoky wings like the bare boards of a stage. Now Bond could see the faint outline on the bottom. He swam directly over it and lay motionless on the surface looking down. There was a tiny movement in the sand. Two minute fountains of sand were dancing above the nostril-like holes of the spiracles. Behind the holes was the slight swelling of the thing's body. That was the target. An inch behind the holes. Bond estimated the possible upward lash of the tail and slowly reached his gun down and pulled the trigger.

Below him the sand erupted and for an anxious moment Bond could see nothing. Then the harpoon line came taut and the ray showed, pulling away from him while its tail, in reflex aggression, lashed again and again over the body. At the base of the tail Bond could see the jagged poison-spines standing up from the trunk. These were the spines that were supposed to have killed Ulysses, that Pliny said would destroy a tree. In the Indian Ocean, where the sea poisons are at their most virulent, one scratch from the ray's sting would mean certain death. Cautiously, keeping the ray on a taut line, Bond trudged after the furiously wrestling fish. He swam to one side to keep the line away from the lashing tail which could easily sever it. This tail was the old slave-drivers' whip of the Indian Ocean. Today it is illegal even to possess one in the Seychelles, but they are handed down in the families for use on faithless wives, and if the word goes round that this or that woman

189

a eu la crapule, the Provençal name for the sting ray, it is as good as saying that that woman will not be about again for at least a week. Now the lashes of the tail were getting weaker and Bond swam round and ahead of the ray, pulling it after him towards the shore. In the shallows the ray went limp and Bond pulled it out of the water and well up on the beach. But he still kept away from it. It was as well he did so. Suddenly, at some move from Bond and perhaps in the hope of catching its enemy unawares, the giant ray leapt clean into the air. Bond sprang aside and the ray fell on its back and lay with its white underbelly to the sun and the great ugly sickle of the mouth sucking and panting.

Bond stood and looked at the sting-ray and wondered what to do next.

A short, fat white man in khaki shirt and trousers came out from under the palm trees and walked towards Bond through the scattering of sea-grape and sun-dried wrack above high-water mark. When he was near enough he called out in a laughing voice: 'The Old Man and the Sea! Who caught who?'

Bond turned. 'It *would* be the only man on the island who doesn't carry a machete. Fidele, be a good chap and call one of your men. This animal won't die, and he's got my spear stuck in him.'

Fidele Barbey, the youngest of the innumerable Barbeys who own nearly everything in the Seychelles, came up and stood looking down at the ray. 'That's a good one. Lucky you hit the right spot or he'd have towed you over the reef and you'd have had to let go your gun. They take the hell of a time to die. But come on. I've got to get you back to Victoria. Something's come up. Something good. I'll send one of my men for the gun. Do you want the tail?'

Bond smiled. 'I haven't got a wife. But what about some *raie au beurre noir* tonight?'

'Not tonight, my friend. Come. Where are your clothes?'

On their way down the coast road in the station wagon Fidele said: 'Ever hear of an American called Milton Krest? Well, apparently he owns the Krest hotels and a thing called the Krest Foundation. One thing I can tell you for sure. He owns the finest damned yacht in the Indian Ocean. Put in yesterday. The *Wavekrest*. Nearly two hundred tons. Hundred feet long. Everything in her from a beautiful wife down to a big transistor gramophone on gimbals so the waves won't jerk the needle. Wall-to-wall carpeting an inch deep. Airconditioned throughout. The only dry cigarettes this side of the African continent, and the best after-breakfast bottle of champagne, since the last time I saw Paris.' Fidele Barbey laughed delightedly. 'My friend, that is one hell of a bloody fine ship, and if Mr Krest is a grand slam redoubled in bastards, who the hell cares?'

'Who cares anyway? What's it got to do with you – or me for the matter of that?'

'Just this, my friend. We are going to spend a

191

few days sailing with Mr Krest – and Mrs Krest, the beautiful Mrs Krest. I have agreed to take the ship to Chagrin – the island I have spoken to you about. It is bloody miles from here – off the African Banks, and my family have never found any use for it except for collecting boobies' eggs. It's only about three feet above sea-level. I haven't been to the damned place for five years. Anyway, this man Krest wants to go there. He's collecting marine specimens, something to do with his Foundation, and there's some blasted little fish that's supposed to exist only around Chagrin Island. At least Krest says the only specimen in the world came from there.'

'Sounds rather fun. Where do I come in?'

'I knew you were bored and that you'd got a week before you sail, so I said that you were the local underwater ace and that you'd soon find the fish if it was there, and anyway that I wouldn't go without you. Mr Krest was willing. And that's that. I knew you'd be fooling around somewhere down the coast, so I just drove along until one of the fishermen told me there was a crazy white man trying to commit suicide alone at Belle Anse and I knew that would be you.'

Bond laughed. 'Extraordinary the way these island people are afraid of the sea. You'd think they'd have got on terms with it by now. Damned few of the Seychellois can even swim.'

'Roman Catholic Church. Doesn't like them taking their clothes off. Bloody nonsense, but there it is. And as for being afraid, don't forget you've only been here for a month. Shark, barracuda – you just haven't met a hungry one. And stone-fish. Ever seen a man that's stepped on a stone-fish? His body bends backwards like a bow with the pain. Sometimes it's so frightful his eyes literally fall out of their sockets. They very seldom live.'

Bond said unsympathetically: 'They ought to wear shoes or bind their feet up when they go on the reef. They've got these fish in the Pacific and the giant clam into the bargain. It's damned silly. Everybody moans about how poor they are here, although the sea's absolutely paved with fish. And there are fifty varieties of cowrie under those rocks. They could make another good living selling those round the world.'

Fidele Barbey laughed boisterously. 'Bond for Governor! That's the ticket. Next meeting of LegCo I'll put the idea up. You're just the man for the job – far-sighted, full of ideas, plenty of drive. Cowries! That's splendid. They'll balance the budget for the first time since the patchouli boom after the War. "We sell sea-shells from the Seychelles." That'll be our slogan. I'll see you get the credit. You'll be Sir James in no time.'

'Make more money that way than trying to grow vanilla at a loss.' They continued to wrangle with light-hearted violence until the palm groves gave way to the giant sangdragon trees on the outskirts of the ramshackle capital of Mahe.

It had been nearly a month before when M had

told Bond he was sending him to the Seychelles. 'Admiralty are having trouble with their new fleet base in the Maldives. Communists creeping in from Ceylon. Strikes, sabotage – the usual picture. May have to cut their losses and fall back on the Seychelles. A thousand miles farther south, but at least they look pretty secure. But they don't want to be caught again. Colonial Office say it's safe as houses. All the same I've agreed to send someone to give an independent view. When Makarios was locked up there a few years ago there were quite a few Security scares. Japanese fishing-boats hanging about, one or two refugee crooks from England, strong ties with France. Just go and have a good look.' M glanced out of the window at the driving March sleet. 'Don't get sunstroke.'

Bond's report, which concluded that the only conceivable security hazard in the Seychelles lay in the beauty and ready availability of the Seychelloises, had been finished a week before and then he had nothing to do but wait for the SS *Kampala* to take him to Mombasa. He was thoroughly sick of the heat and the drooping palm trees and the plaintive cry of the terns and the interminable conversations about copra. The prospect of a change delighted him.

Bond was spending his last week in the Barbey house, and after calling there to pick up their bags, they drove out to the end of Long Pier and left the car in the Customs shed. The gleaming white yacht lay half a mile out in the roadstead. They took a pirogue with an outboard motor across the glassy bay and through the opening in the reef. The *Wavekrest* was not beautiful – the breadth of beam and cluttered superstructure stunted her lines – but Bond could see at once that she was a real ship, built to cruise the world and not just the Florida Keys. She seemed deserted, but as they came alongside two smart-looking sailors in white shorts and singlets appeared and stood by the ladder with boathooks ready to fend the shabby pirogue off the yacht's gleaming paint. They took the two bags and one of them slid back an aluminium hatch and gestured for them to go down. A breath of what seemed to Bond to be almost freezing air struck him as he went through and down a few steps into the lounge.

The lounge was empty. It was not a cabin. It was a room of solid richness and comfort with nothing to associate it with the interior of a ship. The windows behind the half-closed venetian blinds were full size, as were the deep armchairs round the low central table. The carpet was the deepest pile in pale blue. The walls were panelled in a silvery wood and the ceiling was off-white. There was a desk with the usual writing-materials and a telephone. Next to the big gramophone was a sideboard laden with drinks. Above the sideboard was what looked like an extremely good Renoir – the head and shoulders of a pretty dark-haired girl in a black and white striped blouse. The impression of a luxurious living-room in a

195

town house was completed by a large bowl of white and blue hyacinths on the central table and by the tidy range of magazines to one side of the desk.

'What did I tell you, James?'

Bond shook his head admiringly. 'This is certainly the way to treat the sea – as if it damned well didn't exist.' He breathed in deeply. 'What a relief to get a mouthful of fresh air. I'd almost forgotten what it tastes like.'

'It's the stuff outside that's fresh, feller. This is canned.' Mr Milton Krest had come quietly into the room and was standing looking at them. He was a tough, leathery man in his early fifties. He looked hard and fit, and the faded blue jeans, military-cut shirt and wide leather belt suggested that he made a fetish of doing so – looking tough. The pale brown eyes in the weather-beaten face were slightly hooded and their gaze was sleepy and contemptuous. The mouth had a downward twist that might be humorous or disdainful – probably the latter – and the words he had tossed into the room, innocuous in themselves except for the patronizing 'feller' had been tossed like small coin to a couple of coolies. To Bond the oddest thing about Mr Krest was his voice. It was a soft, most attractive lisping through the teeth. It was exactly the voice of the late Humphrey Bogart. Bond ran his eyes down the man from the sparse close-cropped black and grey hair, like iron filings sprinkled over the bullet head, to the tattooed eagle above a fouled anchor on the right forearm, and then down to the naked leathery feet that stood nautically square on the carpet. He thought: this man likes to be thought a Hemingway hero. I'm not going to get on with him.

Mr Krest came across the carpet and held out his hand. 'You Bond? Glad to have you aboard, sir.'

Bond was expecting the bone-crushing grip and parried it with stiffened muscles.

'Free-diving or aqualung?'

'Free, and I don't go deep. It's only a hobby.'

'Whadya do the rest of the time?'

'Civil Servant.'

Mr Krest gave a short barking laugh. 'Civility and Servitude. You English make the best goddam butlers and valets in the world. Civil Servant, you say? I reckon we're likely to get along fine. Civil Servants are just what I like to have around me.'

The click of the deck hatch sliding back saved Bond's temper. Mr Krest was swept from his mind as a naked sunburned girl came down the steps into the saloon. No, she wasn't quite naked after all, but the pale brown satin scraps of bikini were designed to make one think she was.

''Lo, treasure. Where have you been hiding? Long time no see. Meet Mr Barbey and Mr Bond, the fellers who are coming along.' Mr Krest raised a hand in the direction of the girl. 'Fellers, this is Mrs Krest. The fifth Mrs Krest. And just in case anybody should get any ideas, she loves Mr Krest. Don't you, treasure?'

'Oh don't be silly, Milt, you know I do.' Mrs Krest smiled prettily. 'How do you do, Mr Barbey. And Mr Bond. It's nice to have you with us. What about a drink?'

'Now just a minute, treas. Suppose you let me fix things aboard my own ship, hein?' Mr Krest's voice was soft and pleasant.

The woman blushed. 'Oh yes, Milt, of course.'

'Okay then, just so we know who's skipper aboard the good ship *Wavekrest*.' The amused smile embraced them all. 'Now then, Mr Barbey. What's your first name, by the way? Fidele, eh? That's quite a name. Old Faithful,' Mr Krest chuckled bonhomously. 'Well now, Fido, how's about you and me go up on the bridge and get this little old skiff moving, hein? Mebbe you better take her out into the open sea and then you can set a course and hand over to Fritz. I'm the captain. He's the mate, and there are two for the engine-room and pantry. All three Germans. Only darned sailors left in Europe. And Mr Bond. First name? James, eh? Well, Jim, what say you practise a bit of that civility and servitude on Mrs Krest. Call her Liz, by the way. Help her fix the canapés and so on for drinks before lunch. She was once a Limey too. You can swap yarns about Piccadilly Circus and the Dooks you both know. Okay? Move, Fido.' He sprang boyishly up the steps. 'Let's get the hell outa here.'

When the hatch closed, Bond let out a deep breath. Mrs Krest said apologetically: 'Please don't mind his jokes. It's just his sense of humour.

And he's a bit contrary. He likes to see if he can rile people. It's very naughty of him. But it's really all in fun.'

Bond smiled reassuringly. How often did she have to make this speech to people, try and calm the tempers of the people Mr Krest had practised his 'sense of humour' on? He said: 'I expect your husband needs a bit of knowing. Does he go on the same way back in America?'

She said without bitterness: 'Only with me. He loves Americans. It's when he's abroad. You see, his father was a German, a Prussian really. He's got that silly German thing of thinking Europeans and so on are decadent, that they aren't any good any more. It's no use arguing with him. It's just a thing he's got.'

So that was it! The old Hun again. Always at your feet or at your throat. Sense of humour indeed! And what must this woman have to put up with, this beautiful girl he had got hold of to be his slave – his English slave? Bond said: 'How long have you been married?'

'Two years. I was working as a receptionist in one of his hotels. He owns the Krest Group, you know. It was wonderful. Like a fairy story. I still have to pinch myself sometimes to make sure I'm not dreaming. This, for instance,' she waved a hand at the luxurious room, 'and he's terribly good to me. Always giving me presents. He's a very important man in America, you know. It's fun being treated like royalty wherever you go.'

'It must be. He likes that sort of thing, I suppose?'

'Oh yes.' There was resignation in the laugh. 'There's a lot of the sultan in him. He gets quite impatient if he doesn't get proper service. He says that when one's worked very hard to get to the top of the tree one has a right to the best fruit that grows there.' Mrs Krest found she was talking too freely. She said quickly: 'But really, what am I saying? Anyone would think we had known each other for years.' She smiled shyly. 'I suppose it's meeting someone from England. But I really must go and get some more clothes on. I was sunbathing on deck.' There came a deep rumble from below-deck amidships. 'There. We're off. Why don't you watch us leave harbour from the afterdeck, and I'll come and join you in a minute. There's so much I want to hear about London. This way.' She moved past him and slid open a door. 'As a matter of fact, if you're sensible, you'll stake a claim to this for the nights. There are plenty of cushions, and the cabins are apt to get a bit stuffy in spite of the air-conditioning.'

Bond thanked her, and walked out and shut the door behind him. It was a big well-deck with hemp flooring and a cream-coloured semicircular foam rubber settee in the stern. Rattan chairs were scattered about and there was a serving-bar in one corner. It crossed Bond's mind that Mr Krest might be a heavy drinker. Was it his imagination, or was Mrs Krest terrified of him?

There was something painfully slavish in her attitude towards him. No doubt she had to pay heavily for her 'fairy story'. Bond watched the green flanks of Mahe slowly slip away astern. He guessed that their speed was about ten knots. They would soon be at North Point and heading for the open sea. Bond listened to the glutinous bubble of the exhaust and idly thought about the beautiful Mrs Elizabeth Krest.

She could have been a model – probably had been before she became a hotel receptionist – that respectable female calling that yet has a whiff of the high demi-monde about it – and she still moved her beautiful body with the unselfconsciousness of someone who is used to going about with nothing, or practically nothing, on. But there was none of the chill of the model about her – it was a warm body and a friendly, confiding face. She might be thirty, certainly not more, and her prettiness, for it was not more than that, was still immature. Her best feature was the ash-blonde hair that hung heavily to the base of her neck, but she seemed pleasantly lacking in vanity about it. She didn't toss it about or fiddle with it, and it occurred to Bond that she didn't in fact show any signs of coquetry. She had stood quietly, almost docilely, with her large, clear blue eyes fixed almost the whole time on her husband. There was no lipstick on her mouth and no lacquer on her fingernails or toenails, and her eyebrows were natural. Did Mr Krest perhaps order that it should be so – that she should be a Germanic child of nature? Probably. Bond shrugged his shoulders. They were certainly a curiously assorted couple – the middle-aged Hemingway with the Bogart voice and the pretty, artless girl. And there was tension in the air – in the way she had cringed as he brought her to heel when she had offered them drinks, in the forced maleness of the man. Bond toyed idly with the notion that the man was impotent and that all the tough, rude act was nothing more than exaggerated virility-play. It certainly wasn't going to be easy to live with for four or five days. Bond watched the beautiful Silhouette Island slip away to starboard and made a vow not to lose his temper. What was that American expression? 'Eating crow'. It would be an interesting mental exercise for him. He would eat crow for five days and not let this damnable man interfere with what should be a good trip.

'Well, feller. Taking it easy?' Mr Krest was standing on the boat-deck looking down into the well. 'What have you done with that woman I live with? Left her to do all the work, I guess. Well, and why not? That's what they're for, ain't it? Care to look over the ship? Fido's doin' a spell at the wheel and I've got time on my hands.' Without waiting for an answer, Mr Krest bent and lowered himself down into the well-deck, dropping the last four feet.

'Mrs Krest's putting on some clothes. Yes, I'd like to see over the ship.'

Mr Krest fixed Bond with his hard, disdainful stare. "Kay. Well now, facts first. It's built by the Bronson Shipbuilding Corporation. I happen to own ninety per cent of the stock, so I got what I wanted. Designed by Rosenblatts – the top naval architects. Hundred feet long, twenty-one broad, and draws six. Two five-hundred-horsepower Superior diesels. Top speed, fourteen knots. Cruises two thousand five hundred miles at eight. Air-conditioned throughout. Carrier Corporation designed two special five-ton units. Carries enough frozen food and liquor for a month. All we need is fresh water for the baths and showers. Right? Now let's go up front and you can see the crew's quarters, and we'll work back. And one thing, Jim,' Mr Krest stamped on the deck. 'This is the floor, see? And the head's the can. And if I want someone to stop doing whatever they're doing I don't shout "belay" I shout "hold it". Get me, Jim?'

Bond nodded amiably. 'I've got no objection. She's your ship.'

'It's my ship,' corrected Mr Krest. 'That's another bit of damned nonsense, making a hunk of steel and wood a female. Anyway, let's go. You don't need to mind your head. Everything's a six-foot-two clearance.'

Bond followed Mr Krest down the narrow passage that ran the length of the ship, and for half an hour made appropriate comments on what was certainly the finest and most luxuriously designed yacht he had ever seen. In every detail the margin was for extra comfort. Even the crew's bath and shower was full size, and the stainless steel galley, or kitchen as Mr Krest called it, was as big as the Krest stateroom. Mr Krest opened the door of the latter without knocking. Liz Krest was at the dressing-table. 'Why, treasure,' said Mr Krest in his soft voice, 'I reckoned you'd be out there fixing the drink tray. You've sure been one heck of a time dressing up. Puttin' on a little extra Ritz for Jim, eh?'

'I'm sorry, Milt. I was just coming. A zip got stuck.' The girl hurriedly picked up a compact and made for the door. She gave them both a nervous half-smile and went out.

'Vermont birch panelling, Corning glass lamps, Mexican tuft rugs. That sailing-ship picture's a genuine Montague Dawson, by the way . . .' Mr Krest's catalogue ran smoothly on. But Bond was looking at something that hung down almost out of sight by the bedside table on what was obviously Mr Krest's side of the huge double bed. It was a thin whip about three feet long with a leather-thonged handle. It was the tail of a sting-ray.

Casually Bond walked over to the side of the bed and picked it up. He ran a finger down its spiny gristle. It hurt his finger even to do that. He said: 'Where did you pick that up? I was hunting one of these animals this morning.'

'Bahrein. The Arabs use them on their wives.' Mr Krest chuckled easily. 'Haven't had to use more than one stroke at a time on Liz so far. Wonderful results. We call it my "Corrector".'

Bond put the thing back. He looked hard at Mr Krest and said: 'Is that so? In the Seychelles, where the creoles are pretty tough, it's illegal even to own one of those, let alone use it.' Mr Krest moved towards the door. He said indifferently: 'Feller, this ship happens to be United States territory. Let's go get ourselves something to drink.'

Mr Krest drank three double bullshots – vodka in iced consommé – before luncheon, and beer with the meal. The pale eyes darkened a little and acquired a watery glitter, but the sibilant voice remained soft and unemphatic as, with a complete monopoly of the conversation, he explained the object of the voyage. 'Ya see, fellers, it's like this. In the States we have this Foundation system for the lucky guys that got plenty dough and don't happen to want to pay it into Uncle Sam's Treasury. You make a Foundation – like this one, the Krest Foundation – for charitable purposes – charitable to anyone, to kids, sick folk, the cause of science – you just give the money away to anyone or anything except yourself or your dependants and you escape tax on it. So I put a matter of ten million dollars into the Krest Foundation, and since I happen to like yachting and seeing the world I built this yacht with two million of the money and told the Smithsonian – that's our big natural history institution – that I would go to any part of the world and collect specimens for them.

So that makes me a scientific expedition, see? For three months of every year I have a fine holiday that costs me just sweet Fatty Arbuckle!' Mr Krest looked to his guests for applause. 'Get me?'

Fidele Barbey shook his head doubtfully. 'That sounds fine, Mr Krest. But these rare specimens. They are easy to find? The Smithsonian it wants a giant panda, a sea-shell. You can get hold of these things where they have failed?'

Mr Krest slowly shook his head. He said sorrowfully: 'Feller, you sure were born yesterday. Money, that's all it takes. You want a panda? You buy it from some goddam zoo that can't afford central heating for its reptile house or wants to build a new block for its tigers or something. The sea-shell? You find a man that's got one and you offer him so much goddam money that even if he cries for a week he sells it to you. Sometimes you have a little trouble with Governments. Some goddam animal is protected or something. All right. Give you an example. I arrive at your island yesterday. I want a black parrot from Praslin Island. I want a giant tortoise from Aldabra. I want the complete range of your local cowries and I want this fish we're after. The first two are protected by law. Last evening I pay a call on your Governor after making certain inquiries in the town. Excellency, I says, I understand you want to build a public swimming-pool to teach the local kids to swim. Okay. The Krest Foundation will put up the money. How much? Five thousand, ten thousand? Okay, so it's ten thousand. Here's my cheque. And I write it out there and then. Just one little thing, Excellency, I says, holding on to the cheque. It happens I want a specimen of this black parrot you have here and one of these Aldabra tortoises. I understand they're protected by law. Mind if I take one of each back to America for the Smithsonian? Well, there's a bit of a palaver, but seeing it's the Smithsonian and seeing I've still got hold of the cheque, in the end we shake hands on the deal and everyone's happy. Right? Well, on the way back I stop in the town to arrange with your nice Mr Abendana, the merchant feller, to have the parrot and tortoise collected and held for me, and I get talking about the cowries. Well, it so happens that this Mr Abendana has been collecting the dam' things since he was a child. He shows them to me. Beautifully kept – each one in its bit of cotton wool. Fine condition and several of those Isabella and Mappa ones I was asked particularly to watch out for. Sorry, he couldn't think of selling. They meant so much to him and so on. Crap! I just look at Mr Abendana and I say, how much? No no. He couldn't think of it. Crap again! I take out my chequebook and write a cheque for five thousand dollars and push it under his nose. He looks at it. Five thousand dollars! He can't stand it. He folds the cheque and puts it in his pocket and then the dam' sissy breaks down and weeps! Would you believe it?' Mr Krest opened his palms in disbelief. 'Over a few goddam sea-shells. So I just tell him to take it easy, and I pick up the trays of sea-shells and get the hell out of there before the crazy so-and-so shoots himself from remorse.'

Mr Krest sat back, well pleased with himself. 'Well, what d'you say to that, fellers? Twenty-four hours in the island and I've already knocked off three-quarters of my list. Pretty smart, eh, Jim?'

Bond said: 'You'll probably get a medal when you get home. What about this fish?'

Mr Krest got up from the table and rummaged in a drawer of his desk. He brought back a type-written sheet. 'Here you are.' He read out: '"Hildebrand Rarity. Caught by Professor Hildebrand of the University of the Witwatersrand in a net off Chagrin Island in the Seychelles group, April 1925".' Mr Krest looked up. 'And then there's a lot of scientific crap. I got them to put it into plain English, and here's the translation.' He turned back to the paper. '"This appears to be a unique member of the squirrel-fish family. The only specimen known, named the 'Hildebrand Rarity' after its discoverer, is six inches long. The colour is a bright pink with black transverse stripes. The anal, ventral and dorsal fins are pink. The tail fin is black. Eyes, large and dark blue. If found, care should be taken in handling this fish because all fins are even more sharply spiked than is usual with the rest of this family. Professor Hildebrand records that he found the specimen in three feet of water on the edge of the south-western reef".'

Mr Krest threw the paper down on the table. 'Well, there you are, fellers. We're travelling about a thousand miles at a cost of several thousand dollars to try and find a goddam six-inch fish. And two years ago the Revenue people had the gall to suggest that my Foundation was a phoney!'

Liz Krest broke in eagerly: 'But that's just it, Milt, isn't it? It's really rather important to bring back plenty of specimens and things this time. Weren't those horrible tax people talking about disallowing the yacht and the expenses and so on for the last five years if we didn't show an outstanding scientific achievement? Wasn't that the way they put it?'

'Treasure,' Mr Krest's voice was soft as velvet. 'Just supposin' you keep that flippin' trap shut about my personal affairs. Yes?' The voice was amiable, nonchalant. 'You know what you just done, treas? You just earned yourself a little meeting with the Corrector this evening. That's what you've gone and done.'

The girl's hand flew to her mouth. Her eyes were wide. She said in a whisper: 'Oh no, Milt. Oh no, please.'

On the second day out, at dawn, they came up with Chagrin Island. It was first picked up by the radar – a small bump in the dead level line on the scanner – and then a minute blur on the great curved horizon grew with infinite slowness into half a mile of green fringed with white. It was extraordinary to come upon land after two days

209

in which the yacht had seemed to be the only moving, the only living thing in an empty world. Bond had never seen or even clearly imagined the doldrums before. Now he realized what a terrible hazard they must have been in the days of sail – the sea of glass under a brazen sun, the foul, heavy air, the trail of small clouds along the rim of the world that never came closer, never brought wind or blessed rain. How must centuries of mariners have blessed this tiny dot in the Indian Ocean as they bent to the oars that moved the heavy ship perhaps a mile a day! Bond stood in the bows and watched the flying-fish squirt from beneath the hull as the blue-black of the sea slowly mottled into the brown and white and green of deep shoal. How wonderful that he would soon be walking and swimming again instead of just sitting and lying down. How wonderful to have a few hours' solitude – a few hours away from Mr Milton Krest!

They anchored outside the reef in ten fathoms and Fidele Barbey took them through the opening in the speedboat. In every detail Chagrin was the prototype coral island. It was about twenty acres of sand and dead coral and low scrub surrounded, after fifty yards of shallow lagoon, by a necklace of reef on which the quiet, long swell broke with a soft hiss. Clouds of birds rose when they landed – terns, boobies, men-of-war, frigates – but quickly settled again. There was a strong ammoniac smell of guano, and the scrub was white with it. The only other living things were the land-crabs that scuttled and scraped among the *liane sans fin* and the fiddler-crabs that lived in the sand.

The glare from the white sand was dazzling and there was no shade. Mr Krest ordered a tent to be erected and sat in it smoking a cigar while gear of various kinds was ferried ashore. Mrs Krest swam and picked up seashells while Bond and Fidele Barbey put on masks and, swimming in opposite directions, began systematically to comb the reef all the way round the island.

When you are looking for one particular species underwater – shell or fish or seaweed or coral formation – you have to keep your brain and your eyes focused for that one individual pattern. The riot of colour and movement and the endless variety of light and shadow fight your concentration all the time. Bond trudged slowly along through the wonderland with only one picture in his mind – a six-inch pink fish with black stripes and big eyes – the second such fish man had ever seen. 'If you see it,' Mr Krest had enjoined, 'just you let out a yell and stay with it. I'll do the rest. I got a little something in the tent that's just the dandiest thing for catching fish you ever saw.'

Bond paused to rest his eyes. The water was so buoyant that he could lie face downwards on the surface without moving. Idly he broke up a sea-egg with the tip of his spear and watched the horde of glittering reef-fish darting for the shreds of yellow flesh among the needle-sharp black spine. How infernal that if he did find the Rarity it would

211

benefit only Mr Krest! Should he say nothing if he found it? Rather childish, and anyway he was under contract, so to speak. Bond moved slowly on, his eyes automatically taking up the search again while his mind turned to considering the girl. She had spent the previous day in bed. Mr Krest had said it was a headache. Would she one day turn on him? Would she get herself a knife or a gun and one night, when he reached for that damnable whip, would she kill him? No. She was too soft, too malleable. Mr Krest had chosen well. She was the stuff of slaves. And the trappings of her 'fairytale' were too precious. Didn't she realize that a jury would certainly acquit her if the sting-ray whip was produced in court? She could have the trappings without this dreadful, damnable man. Should Bond tell her that? Don't be ridiculous! How could he put it? 'Oh Liz, if you want to murder your husband, it'll be quite all right.' Bond smiled inside his mask. To hell with it! Don't interfere with other people's lives. She probably likes it – masochist. But Bond knew that that was too easy an answer. This was a girl who lived in fear. Perhaps she also lived in loathing. One couldn't read much in those soft blue eyes, but the windows had opened once or twice and a flash of something like a childish hate had shown through. Had it been hate? It had probably been indigestion. Bond put the Krests out of his mind and looked up to see how far round the island he had got. Fidele Barbey's snorkel was only a hundred yards away. They had nearly completed the circuit.

They came up with each other and swam to the shore and lay on the hot sand. Fidele Barbey said: 'Nothing on my side of the property except every fish in the world bar one. But I've had a stroke of luck. Ran into a big colony of green snail. That's the pearl shell as big as a small football. Worth quite a lot of money. I'll send one of my boats after them one of these days. Saw a blue parrotfish that must have been a good thirty pounds. Tame as a dog, like all the fish round here. Hadn't got the heart to kill it. And if I had, there might have been trouble. Saw two or three leopard sharks cruising around over the reef. Blood in the water might have brought them through. Now I'm ready for a drink and something to eat. After that we can swap sides and have another go.'

They got up and walked along the beach to the tent. Mr Krest heard their voices and came out to meet them. 'No dice, eh?' He scratched angrily at an armpit. 'Goddam sandfly bit me. This is one hell of a godawful island. Liz couldn't stand the smell. Gone back to the ship. Guess we'd better give it one more going-over and then get the hell out of here. Help yourselves to some chow and you'll find cold beer in the icepack. Here, gimme one of those masks. How do you use the dam' things? I guess I might as well take a peek at the sea's bottom while I'm about it.'

They sat in the hot tent and ate the chicken salad

and drank beer, and moodily watched Mr Krest poking and peering about in the shallows. Fidele Barbey said: 'He's right, of course. These little islands are bloody awful places. Nothing but crabs and bird dung surrounded by too dam' much sea. It's only the poor bloody frozen Europeans that dream of coral islands. East of Suez, you won't find any sane man who gives a damn for them. My family owns about ten of them – decent-sized ones too, with small villages on them and a good income from copra and turtle. Well, you can have the whole bloody lot in exchange for a flat in Paris or London.'

Bond laughed. He began: 'Put an advertisement in *The Times* and you'd get sackloads . . .' when, fifty yards away, Mr Krest began to make frantic signals. Bond said: 'Either the bastard's found it or he's trodden on a guitar-fish,' and picked up his mask and ran down to the sea.

Mr Krest was standing up to his waist among the shallow beginnings of the reef. He jabbed his finger excitedly at the surface. Bond swam softly forward. A carpet of sea-grass ended in broken coral and an occasional niggerhead. A dozen varieties of butterfly and other reef-fish flirted among the rocks, and a small langouste quested towards Bond with its feelers. The head of a large green moray protruded from a hole, its half-open jaws showing the rows of needle teeth. Its golden eyes watched Bond carefully. Bond was amused to note that Mr Krest's hairy legs, magnified into pale

214

tree-trunks by the glass, were not more than a foot away from the moray's jaws. He gave an encouraging poke at the moray with his spear, but the eel only snapped at the metal points and slid back out of sight. Bond stopped and floated, his eyes scanning the brilliant jungle. A red blur materialized through the far mist and came towards him. It circled closely beneath him as if showing itself off. The dark blue eyes examined him without fear. The small fish busied itself rather self-consciously with some algae on the underside of a niggerhead, made a dart at a speck of something suspended in the water, and then, as if leaving the stage after showing its paces, swam languidly off back into the mist.

Bond backed away from the moray's hole and put his feet to the ground. He took off his mask. He said to Mr Krest, who was standing gazing impatiently at him through his goggles: 'Yes, that's it all right. Better move quietly away from here. He won't go away unless he's frightened. These reef-fish stick pretty well to the same pastures.'

Mr Krest pulled off his mask. 'Goddam, I found it!' he said reverently. 'Well, goddam I did.' He slowly followed Bond to the shore.

Fidele Barbey was waiting for them. Mr Krest said boisterously: 'Fido, I found that goddam fish. Me – Milton Krest. Whadya know about that? After you two goddam experts had been at it all morning. I just took that mask of yours – first time I ever put one on, mark you – and I walked out and found the goddam fish in fifteen minutes flat. Whadya say to that eh, Fido?'

'That's good, Mr Krest. That's fine. Now how do we catch it?'

'Aha.' Mr Krest winked slowly. 'I got just the ticket for that. Got it from a chemist friend of mine. Stuff called Rotenone. Made from derris root. What the natives fish with in Brazil. Just pour it in the water, where it'll float over what you're after, and it'll get him as sure as eggs is eggs. Sort of poison. Constricts the blood vessels in their gills. Suffocates them. No effect on humans because no gills, see?' Mr Krest turned to Bond. 'Here, Jim. You go on out and keep watch. See the darned fish don't vamoose. Fido and I'll bring the stuff out there' – he pointed up-current from the vital area. 'I'll let go the Rotenone when you say the word. It'll drift down towards you. Right? But for lands sakes get the timing right. I've only got a five-gallon tin of this stuff. 'Kay?'

Bond said 'All right,' and walked slowly down and into the water. He swam lazily out to where he had stood before. Yes, everyone was still there, going about his business. The moray's pointed head was back again at the edge of its hole, the langouste again queried him. In a minute, as if it had a rendezvous with Bond, the Hildebrand Rarity appeared. This time it swam up quite close to his face. It looked through the glass at his eyes and then, as if disturbed by what it had seen there, darted out of range. It played around among the rocks for a while and then went off into a mist.

Slowly the little underwater world within Bond's vision began to take him for granted. A small octopus that had been camouflaged as a piece of coral revealed its presence and groped carefully down towards the sand. The blue and yellow langouste came a few steps out from under the rock, wondering about him. Some very small fish like minnows nibbled at his legs and toes, tickling. Bond broke a sea-egg for them and they darted to the better meal. Bond lifted his head. Mr Krest, holding the flat can, was twenty yards away to Bond's right. He would soon begin pouring, when Bond gave the sign, so that the liquid would get a good wide spread over the surface.

'Okay?' called Mr Krest.

Bond shook his head. 'I'll raise my thumb when he's back here. Then you'll have to pour fast.'

'Okay, Jim. You're at the bomb-sight.'

Bond put his head down. There was the little community, everyone busied with his affairs. Soon, to get one fish that someone vaguely wanted in a museum five thousand miles away, a hundred, perhaps a thousand small people were going to die. When Bond gave the signal, the shadow of death would come down on the stream. How long would the poison last? How far would it travel on down the reef? Perhaps it would not be thousands but tens of thousands that would die.

A small trunk-fish appeared, its tiny fins whirring

like propellers. A rock beauty, gorgeous in gold and red and black, pecked at the sand, and a pair of the inevitable black and yellow striped sergeant-majors materialized from nowhere, attracted by the scent of the broken sea-egg.

Inside the reef, who was the predator in the world of small fishes? Who did they fear? Small barracuda? An occasional bill-fish? Now, a big, a fully grown predator, a man called Krest, was standing in the wings, waiting. And this one wasn't even hungry. He was just going to kill – almost for fun.

Two brown legs appeared in Bond's vision. He looked up. It was Fidele Barbey with a big creel strapped to his chest, and a long-handled landing-net.

Bond lifted his mask. 'I feel like the bomb-aimer at Nagasaki.'

'Fish are cold-blooded. They don't feel anything.'

'How do you know? I've heard them scream when they're hurt.'

Barbey said indifferently: 'They won't be able to scream with this stuff. It strangles them. What's eating you? They're only fish.'

'I know, I know.' Fidele Barbey had spent his life killing animals and fish. While he, Bond, had some-times not hesitated to kill men. What was he fussing about? He hadn't minded killing the sting-ray. Yes, but that was an enemy fish. These down here were friendly people. People? The pathetic fallacy!

'Hey!' came the voice of Mr Krest. 'What's goin' on over there? This ain't no time for chewing the fat. Get that head down, Jim.'

Bond pulled down his mask and lay again on the surface. At once he saw the beautiful red shadow coming out of the far mists. The fish swam fast up to him as if it now took him for granted. It lay below him, looking up. Bond said into his mask: 'Get away from here, damn you.' He gave a sharp jab at the fish with his harpoon. The fish fled back into the mist. Bond lifted his head and angrily raised his thumb. It was a ridiculous and petty act of sabotage of which he was already ashamed. The dark brown oily liquid was pouring out on to the surface of the lagoon. There was time to stop Mr Krest before it was all gone – time to give him another chance at the Hildebrand Rarity. Bond stood and watched until the last drop was tilted out. To hell with Mr Krest!

Now the stuff was creeping slowly down on the current – a shiny, spreading stain which reflected the blue sky with a metallic glint. Mr Krest, the giant reaper, was wading down with it. 'Get set, fellers,' he called cheerfully. 'It's right up with you now.'

Bond put his head back under the surface. Everything was as before in the little community. And then, with stupefying suddenness, everyone went mad. It was as if they had all been seized with St Vitus's dance. Several fish looped the loop crazily and then fell like heavy leaves to the sand.

The moray eel came slowly out of the hole in the coral, its jaws wide. It stood carefully upright on its tail and gently toppled sideways. The small langouste gave three kicks of its tail and turned over on its back, and the octopus let go its hold of the coral and drifted to the bottom upside-down. And then into the arena drifted the corpses from up-stream – white-bellied fish, shrimps, worms, hermit crabs, spotted and green morays, langoustes of all sizes. As if blown by some light breeze of death the clumsy bodies, their colours already fading, swept slowly past. A five-pound bill-fish struggled by with snapping beak, fighting death. Down-reef there were splashes on the surface as still bigger fish tried to make for safety. One by one, before Bond's eyes, the sea-urchins dropped off the rocks to make black ink-blots on the sand.

Bond felt a touch on his shoulder. Mr Krest's eyes were bloodshot with the sun and glare. He had put white sunburn paste on his lips. He shouted impatiently at Bond's mask, 'Where in hell's our goddam fish?'

Bond lifted his mask. 'Looks as if it managed to get away just before the stuff came down. I'm still watching for it.'

He didn't wait to hear Mr Krest's reply but got his head quickly under water again. Still more carnage, still more dead bodies. But surely the stuff had passed by now. Surely the area was safe just in case the fish, his fish because he had saved it, came back again! He stiffened. In the far mists there was a pink flash. It had gone. Now it was back again. Idly the Hildebrand Rarity swam towards him through the maze of channels between the broken outposts of the reef.

Not caring about Mr Krest, Bond raised his free hand out of the water and brought it down with a sharp slap. Still the fish came. Bond shifted the safe on his harpoon-gun and fired it in the direction of the fish. No effect. Bond put his feet down and began to walk towards the fish through the scattering of corpses. The beautiful red and black fish seemed to pause and quiver. Then it shot straight through the water towards Bond and dived down to the sand at his feet and lay still. Bond only had to bend to pick it up. There was not even a last flap from the tail. It just filled Bond's hand, lightly pricking the palm with the spiny black dorsal fin. Bond carried it back underwater so as to preserve its colours. When he got to Mr Krest he said 'Here,' and handed him the small fish. Then he swam away towards the shore.

That evening, with the *Wavekrest* heading for home down the path of a huge yellow moon, Mr Krest gave orders for what he called a 'wingding'. 'Gotta celebrate, Liz. This is terrific, a terrific day. Cleaned up the last target and we can get the hell out of these goddam *Seychelles* and get on back to civilization. What say we make it to Mombasa when we've taken on board the tortoise and that goddam parrot? Fly to Nairobi and pick up a big plane for Rome, Venice, Paris – anywheres you care for. What say, treasure?' He squeezed her chin and cheeks in his big hand and made the pale lips pout. He kissed them drily. Bond watched the girl's eyes. They had shut tight. Mr Krest let go. The girl massaged her face. It was still white with his finger-marks.

'Gee, Milt,' she said half laughing, 'you nearly squashed me. You don't know your strength. But do let's celebrate. I think that would be lots of fun. And that Paris idea sounds grand. Let's do that, shall we? What shall I order for dinner?'

'Hell – caviare of course.' Mr Krest held his hands apart. 'One of those two-pound tins from Hammacher Schlemmer – the grade ten shot size, and all the trimmings. And that pink champagne.' He turned to Bond. 'That suit you, feller?'

'Sounds like a square meal.' Bond changed the subject. 'What have you done with the prize?'

'Formalin. Up on the boat-deck with some other jars of stuff we've picked up here and there – fish, shells. All safe in our home morgue. That's how we were told to keep the specimens. We'll airmail that damned fish when we get back to civilization. Give a Press conference first. Should make a big play in the papers back home. I've already radioed the Smithsonian and the news agencies. My accountants'll sure be glad of some Press cuttings to show those darned revenue boys.'

Mr Krest got very drunk that night. It did not show greatly. The soft Bogart voice became softer and slower. The round, hard head turned more deliberately on the shoulders. The lighter's flame took increasingly long to relight the cigar, and one glass was swept off the table. But it showed in the things Mr Krest said. There was a violent cruelty, a pathological desire to wound, quite near the surface in the man. That night, after dinner, the first target was James Bond. He was treated to a soft-spoken explanation as to why Europe, with England and France in the van, was a rapidly diminishing asset to the world. Nowadays, said Mr Krest, there were only three powers – America, Russia and China. That was the big poker game and no other country had either the chips or the cards to come into it. Occasionally some pleasant little country – and he admitted they'd been pretty big league in the past – like England would be lent some money so that they could take a hand with the grown-ups. But that was just being polite like one sometimes had to be – to a chum in one's club who'd gone broke. No. England – nice people, mind you, good sports – was a place to see the old buildings and the Queen and so on. France? They only counted for good food and easy women. Italy? Sunshine and spaghetti. Sanatorium, sort of. Germany? Well, they still had some spunk, but two lost wars had knocked the heart out of them. Mr Krest dismissed the rest of the world with a few similar tags and then asked Bond for his comments.

Bond was thoroughly tired of Mr Krest. He said

he found Mr Krest's point of view oversimplified – he might even say naïve. He said: 'Your argument reminds me of a rather sharp aphorism I once heard about America. Care to hear it?'

'Sure, sure.'

'It's to the effect that America has progressed from infancy to senility without having passed through a period of maturity.'

Mr Krest looked thoughtfully at Bond. Finally he said: 'Why, say, Jim, that's pretty neat.' His eyes hooded slightly as they turned towards his wife. 'Guess you'd kinda go along with that remark of Jim's, eh, treasure? I recall you saying once you reckoned there was something pretty childish about the Americans. Remember?'

'Oh Milt.' Liz Krest's eyes were anxious. She had read the signs. 'How can you bring that up? You know it was only something casual I said about the comic sections of the papers. Of course I don't agree with what James says. Anyway, it was only a joke, wasn't it, James?'

'That's right,' said Bond. 'Like when Mr Krest said England had nothing but ruins and a queen.'

Mr Krest's eyes were still on the girl. He said softly: 'Shucks, treasure. Why are you looking so nervous? 'Course it was a joke.' He paused. 'And one I'll remember, treasure. One I'll sure remember.'

Bond estimated that by now Mr Krest had just about one whole bottle of various alcohols, mostly whisky, inside him. It looked to Bond as if, unless Mr Krest passed out, the time was not far off when Bond would have to hit Mr Krest just once very hard on the jaw. Fidele Barbey was now being given the treatment. 'These islands of yours, Fido. When I first looked them up on the map I thought it was just some specks of fly-dirt on the page.' Mr Krest chuckled. 'Even tried to brush them off with the back of my hand. Then I read a bit about them and it seemed to me my first thoughts had just about hit the nail on the head. Not much good for anything, are they, Fido? I wonder an intelligent guy like you doesn't get the hell out of there. Beachcombing ain't any kind of a life. Though I did hear one of your family had logged over a hundred illegitimate children. Mebbe that's the attraction, eh, feller?' Mr Krest grinned knowingly.

Fidele Barbey said equably: 'That's my uncle, Gaston. The rest of the family doesn't approve. It's made quite a hole in the family fortune.'

'Family fortune, eh?' Mr Krest winked at Bond. 'What's it in? Cowrie-shells?'

'Not exactly.' Fidele Barbey was not used to Mr Krest's brand of rudeness. He looked mildly embarrassed. 'Though we made quite a lot out of tortoiseshell and mother-of-pearl about a hundred years ago when there was a rage for these things. Copra's always been our main business.'

'Using the family bastards as labour, I guess. Good idea. Wish I could fix something like that in my home circle.' He looked across at his wife. The rubber lips turned still further down.

Before the next gibe could be uttered, Bond had pushed his chair back and had gone out into the well-deck and pulled the door shut behind him.

Ten minutes later, Bond heard feet coming softly down the ladder from the boat-deck. He turned. It was Liz Krest. She came over to where he was standing in the stern. She said in a strained voice: 'I said I'd go to bed. But then I thought I'd come back here and see if you'd got everything you want. I'm not a very good hostess, I'm afraid. Are you sure you don't mind sleeping out here?'

'I like it. I like this kind of air better than the canned stuff inside. And it's rather wonderful to have all those stars to look at. I've never seen so many before.'

She said eagerly, grasping at a friendly topic: 'I like Orion's Belt and the Southern Cross the best. You know, when I was young, I used to think the stars were really holes in the sky. I thought the world was surrounded by a great big black sort of envelope, and that outside it the universe was full of bright light. The stars were just holes in the envelope that let little sparks of light through. One gets terribly silly ideas when one's young.' She looked up at him, wanting him not to snub her.

Bond said: 'You're probably quite right. One shouldn't believe all the scientists say. They want to make everything dull. Where did you live then?'

'At Ringwood in the New Forest. It was a good place to be brought up. A good place for children. I'd like to go there again one day.'

Bond said: 'You've certainly come a long way since then. You'd probably find it pretty dull.'

She reached out and touched his sleeve. 'Please don't say that. You don't understand—' there was an edge of desperation in the soft voice – 'I can't bear to go on missing what other people have – ordinary people. I mean,' she laughed nervously, 'you won't believe me, but just to talk like this for a few minutes, to have someone like you to talk to, is something I'd almost forgotten.' She suddenly reached for his hand and held it hard. 'I'm sorry. I just wanted to do that. Now I'll go to bed.'

The soft voice came from behind them. The speech had slurred, but each word was carefully separated from the next. 'Well, well. Whadya know? Necking with the underwater help!'

Mr Krest stood framed in the hatch to the saloon. He stood with his legs apart and his arms upstretched to the lintel above his head. With the light behind him he had the silhouette of a baboon. The cold, imprisoned breath of the saloon rushed out past him and for a moment chilled the warm night air in the well-deck. Mr Krest stepped out and softly pulled the door to behind him.

Bond took a step towards him, his hands held loosely at his sides. He measured the distance to Mr Krest's solar plexus. He said: 'Don't jump to conclusions, Mr Krest. And watch your tongue. You're lucky not to have got hurt so far tonight. Don't press your luck. You're drunk. Go to bed.'

'Oho! Listen to the cheeky feller.' Mr Krest's moon-burned face turned slowly from Bond to his wife. He made a contemptuous, Hapsburg-lip grimace. He took a silver whistle out of his pocket and whirled it round on its string. 'He sure don't get the picture, does he, treasure? You ain't told him that those Heinies up front ain't just for ornament?' He turned back to Bond. 'Feller, you move any closer and I blow this – just once. And you know what? It'll be the old heave-ho for Mr goddam Bond' – he made a gesture towards the sea – 'over the side. Man overboard. Too bad. We back up to make a search and you know what, feller? Just by chance we back up into you with those twin screws. Would you believe it! What lousy bad luck for that nice feller Jim we were all getting so fond of!' Mr Krest swayed on his feet. 'Dya get the photo, Jim? Okay, so let's all be friends again and get some shut-eye.' He reached for the lintel of the hatch and turned to his wife. He lifted his free hand and slowly crooked a finger. 'Move, treasure. Time for bed.'

'Yes, Milt.' The wide, frightened eyes turned sideways. 'Goodnight, James.' Without waiting for an answer, she ducked under Mr Krest's arm and almost ran through the saloon.

Mr Krest lifted a hand. 'Take it easy, feller. No hard feelings, eh?'

Bond said nothing. He went on looking hard at Mr Krest.

Mr Krest laughed uncertainly. He said: 'Okay

228

then.' He stepped into the saloon and slid the door shut. Through the window Bond watched him walk unsteadily across the saloon and turn out the lights. He went into the corridor and there was a momentary gleam from the stateroom door, and then that too went dark.

Bond shrugged his shoulders. God, what a man! He leant against the stern rail and watched the stars and the flashes of phosphorescence in the creaming wake, and set about washing his mind clear and relaxing the coiled tensions in his body.

Half an hour later, after taking a shower in the crew's bathroom forrard, Bond was making a bed for himself among the piled Dunlopillo cushions when he heard a single, heart-rending scream. It tore briefly into the night and was smothered. It was the girl. Bond ran through the saloon and down the passage. With his hand on the stateroom door, he stopped. He could hear her sobs and, above them, the soft even drone of Mr Krest's voice. He took his hand away from the latch. Hell! What was it to do with him? They were man and wife. If she was prepared to stand this sort of thing and not kill her husband, or leave him, it was no good Bond playing Sir Galahad. Bond walked slowly back down the passage. As he was crossing the saloon the scream, this time less piercing, rang out again. Bond cursed fluently and went out and lay down on his bed and tried to focus his mind on the soft thud of the diesels. How could a girl have so little guts? Or was it that women could take almost anything from a man? Anything except indifference? Bond's mind refused to unwind. Sleep got further and further away.

An hour later Bond had reached the edge of unconsciousness when, up above him on the boat-deck, Mr Krest began to snore. On the second night out from Port Victoria, Mr Krest had left his cabin in the middle of the night and had gone up to the hammock that was kept slung for him between the speedboat and the dinghy. But that night he had not snored. Now he was snoring with those deep, rattling, utterly lost snores that come from big blue sleeping-pills on top of too much alcohol.

This was too damned much. Bond looked at his watch. One-thirty. If the snoring didn't stop in ten minutes, Bond would go down to Fidele Barbey's cabin and sleep on the floor, even if he did wake up stiff and frozen in the morning.

Bond watched the gleaming minute-hand slowly creep round the dial. Now! He had got to his feet and was gathering up his shirt and shorts when, from up on the boat-deck, there came a heavy crash. The crash was immediately followed by scrabbling sounds and a dreadful choking and gurgling. Had Mr Krest fallen out of his hammock? Reluctantly Bond dropped his things back on the deck and walked over and climbed the ladder. As his eyes came level with the boat-deck, the choking stopped. Instead there was another, a more dreadful sound – the quick drumming of heels. Bond knew that sound. He leapt up the last steps and ran towards the figure lying spreadeagled on its back in the bright moonlight. He stopped and knelt slowly down, aghast. The horror of the strangled face was bad enough, but it was not Mr Krest's tongue that protruded from his gaping mouth. It was the tail of a fish. The colours were pink and black. It was the Hildebrand Rarity!

The man was dead – horribly dead. When the fish had been crammed into his mouth, he must have reached up and desperately tried to tug it out. But the spines of the dorsal and anal fins had caught inside the cheeks and some of the spiny tips now protruded through the blood-flecked skin round the obscene mouth. Bond shuddered. Death must have come inside a minute. But what a minute!

Bond slowly got to his feet. He walked over to the racks of glass specimen jars and peered under the protective awning. The plastic cover of the end jar lay on the deck beside it. Bond wiped it carefully on the tarpaulin, and then, holding it by the tips of his fingernails, laid it loosely back over the mouth of the jar.

He went back and stood over the corpse. Which of the two had done this? There was a touch of fiendish spite in using the treasured prize as a weapon. That suggested the woman. She certainly had her reasons. But Fidele Barbey, with his creole blood, would have had the cruelty and at the same time the macabre humour. '*Je lui ai foutu son sacré*

231

poisson dans la gueule.' Bond could hear him say the words. If, after Bond had left the saloon, Mr Krest had needled the Seychellois just a little bit further – particularly about his family or his beloved islands – Fidele Barbey would not have hit him then and there, or used a knife, he would have waited and plotted.

Bond looked round the deck. The snoring of the man could have been a signal for either of them. There were ladders to the boat-deck from both sides of the cabin-deck amidships. The man at the wheel in the pilot-house forrard would have heard nothing above the noise from the engine-room. To pick the small fish out of its formalin bath and slip it into Mr Krest's gaping mouth would have only needed seconds. Bond shrugged. Whichever had done it had not thought of the consequences – of the inevitable inquest, perhaps of a trial in which he, Bond, would be an additional suspect. They were certainly all going to be in one hell of a mess unless he could tidy things up.

Bond glanced over the edge of the boat-deck. Below was the three-foot-wide strip of deck that ran the length of the ship. Between this and the sea there was a two-foot-high rail. Supposing the hammock had broken, and Mr Krest had fallen and rolled under the speedboat and over the edge of the upper deck, could he have reached the sea? Hardly, in this dead calm but that was what he was going to have done.

Bond got moving. With a table-knife from the

saloon, he carefully frayed and then broke one of the main cords of the hammock so that the hammock trailed realistically on the deck. Next, with a damp cloth, he cleaned up the specks of blood on the woodwork and the drops of formalin that led from the specimen jar. Then came the hardest part – handling the corpse. Carefully Bond pulled it to the very edge of the deck and himself went down the ladder and, bracing himself, reached up. The corpse came down on top of him in a heavy, drunken embrace. Bond staggered under it to the low rail and eased it over. There was a last hideous glimpse of the obscenely bulging face, a sickening fume of stale whisky, a heavy splash, and it was gone and rolling sluggishly away in the small waves of the wake. Bond flattened himself back against the saloon hatchway, ready to slip through if the helmsman came aft to investigate. But there was no movement forrard and the iron tramp of the diesels held steady.

Bond sighed deeply. It would be a very troublesome coroner who brought in anything but misadventure. He went back to the boat-deck, gave it a final look over, disposed of the knife and the wet cloth, and went down the ladder to his bed in the well. It was two-fifteen. Bond was asleep inside ten minutes.

By pushing the speed up to twelve knots they made North Point by six o'clock that evening.

Behind them the sky was ablaze with red and gold streaked across aquamarine. The two men, with the woman between them, stood at the rail of the well-deck and watched the brilliant shore slip by across the mother-of-pearl mirror of the sea. Liz Krest was wearing a white linen frock with a black belt and a black and white handkerchief round her neck. The mourning colours went well with the golden skin. The three people stood stiffly and rather self-consciously, each one nursing his own piece of secret knowledge, each one anxious to convey to the other two that their particular secrets were safe with him.

That morning there had seemed to be a conspiracy among the three to sleep late. Even Bond had not been awakened by the sun until ten o'clock. He showered in the crew's quarters and chatted with the helmsman before going below to see what had happened to Fidele Barbey. He was still in bed. He said he had a hangover. Had he been very rude to Mr Krest? He couldn't remember much about it except that he seemed to recall Mr Krest being very rude to him. 'You remember what I said about him from the beginning, James? A grand slam re-doubled in bastards. Now do you agree with me? One of these days someone's going to shut that soft ugly mouth of his for ever.'

Inconclusive. Bond had fixed himself some breakfast in the galley and was eating it there when Liz Krest had come in to do the same. She was dressed in a pale blue shantung kimono to her knees. There were dark rings under her eyes and she ate her breakfast standing. But she seemed perfectly calm and at ease. She whispered conspiratorially: 'I do apologize about last night. I suppose I'd had a bit too much to drink too. But do forgive Milt. He's really awfully nice. It's only when he's had a bit too much that he gets sort of difficult. He's always sorry the next morning. You'll see.'

When eleven o'clock came and neither of the other two showed any signs of, so to speak, blowing the gaff, Bond decided to force the pace. He looked very hard at Liz Krest who was lying on her stomach in the well-deck reading a magazine. He said: 'By the way, where's your husband? Still sleeping it off?'

She frowned. 'I suppose so. He went up to his hammock on the boat-deck. I've no idea what time. I took a sleeping-pill and went straight off.'

Fidele Barbey had a line out for amberjack. Without looking round he said: 'He's probably in the pilot-house.'

Bond said: 'If he's still asleep on the boat-deck, he'll be getting the hell of a sunburn.'

Liz Krest said: 'Oh, poor Milt! I hadn't thought of that. I'll go and see.'

She climbed the ladder. When her head was above the level of the boat-deck she stopped. She called down, anxiously: 'Jim. He's not here. And the hammock's broken.'

Bond said: 'Fidele's probably right. I'll have a look forrard.'

He went to the pilot-house. Fritz, the mate and the engineer were there. Bond said: 'Anyone seen Mr Krest?'

Fritz looked puzzled. 'No, sir. Why? Is anything wrong?'

Bond flooded his face with anxiety. 'He's not aft. Here, come on! Look round everywhere. He was sleeping on the boat-deck. He's not there and his hammock's broken. He was rather the worse for wear last night. Come on! Get cracking!'

When the inevitable conclusion had been reached, Liz Krest had a short but credible fit of hysterics. Bond took her to her cabin and left her there in tears. 'It's all right, Liz,' he said. 'You stay out of this. I'll look after everything. We'll have to radio Port Victoria and so on. I'll tell Fritz to put on speed. I'm afraid it's hopeless turning back to look. There've been six hours of daylight when he couldn't have fallen overboard without being heard or seen. It must have been in the night. I'm afraid anything like six hours in these seas is just not on.'

She stared at him, her eyes wide. 'You mean – you mean sharks and things?'

Bond nodded.

'Oh Milt! Poor darling Milt! Oh, why did this have to happen?'

Bond went out and softly shut the door.

★　★　★

The yacht rounded Cannon Point and reduced speed. Keeping well away from the broken reef, it slid quietly across the broad bay, now lemon and gunmetal in the last light, towards the anchorage. The small township beneath the mountains was already dark with indigo shadow in which a sprinkling of yellow lights showed. Bond saw the Customs and Immigration launch move off from Long Pier to meet them. The little community would already be buzzing with the news that would have quickly leaked from the radio station to the Seychelles Club and then, through the members' chauffeurs and staffs, into the town.

Liz Krest turned to him. 'I'm beginning to get nervous. Will you help me through the rest of this – these awful formalities and things?'

'Of course.'

Fidele Barbey said: 'Don't worry too much. All these people are my friends. And the Chief Justice is my uncle. We shall all have to make a statement. They'll probably have the inquest tomorrow. You'll be able to leave the day after.'

'You really think so?' A dew of sweat had sprung below her eyes. 'The trouble is, I don't really know where to leave for, or what to do next. I suppose,' she hesitated, not looking at Bond. 'I suppose, James, you wouldn't like to come on to Mombasa? I mean, you're going there, anyway, and I'd be able to get you there a day earlier than this ship of yours, this Camp something.'

'*Kampala*.' Bond lit a cigarette to cover his hesitation. Four days in a beautiful yacht with this girl! But the tail of that fish sticking out of the mouth! Had she done it? Or had Fidele, who would know that his uncles and cousins on Mahe would somehow see that he came to no harm? If only one of them would make a slip. Bond said easily: 'That's terribly nice of you, Liz. Of course I'd love to come.'

Fidele Barbey chuckled. 'Bravo, my friend. And I would love to be in your shoes, but for one thing. That damned fish. It is a great responsibility. I like to think of you both being deluged with cables from the Smithsonian about it. Don't forget that you are now both trustees of a scientific Koh-i-noor. And you know what these Americans are. They'll worry the life out of you until they've got their hands on it.'

Bond's eyes were hard as flint as he watched the girl. Surely that put the finger on her. Now he would make some excuse – get out of the trip. There had been something about that particular way of killing a man . . .

But the beautiful, candid eyes did not flicker. She looked up into Fidele Barbey's face and said, easily, charmingly: 'That won't be a problem. I've decided to give it to the British Museum.'

James Bond noticed that the sweat dew had now gathered at her temples. But, after all, it was a desperately hot evening . . .

The thud of the engines stopped and the anchor chain roared down into the quiet bay.

CHAPTER 6

OCTOPUSSY

'You know what?' said Major Dexter Smythe to the octopus. 'You're going to have a real treat today if I can manage it.'

He had spoken aloud and his breath had steamed up the glass of his Pirelli mask. He put his feet down to the sand beside the nigger-head and stood up. The water reached to his armpits. He took off the mask and spat into it, rubbed the spit round the glass, rinsed it clean and pulled the rubber band of the mask back over his head. He bent down again.

The eye in the mottled brown sack was still watching him carefully from the hole in the coral, but now the tip of a single small tentacle wavered hesitatingly an inch or two out of the shadows and quested vaguely with its pink suckers uppermost. Dexter Smythe smiled with satisfaction. Given time, perhaps one more month on top of the two during which he had been chumming up with the octopus, and he would have tamed the darling. But he wasn't going to have that month. Should he take a chance today and reach down and offer his hand, instead of the expected lump of raw meat on the end of his spear, to the tentacle – shake it by the hand, so to speak? No, Pussy, he thought. I can't quite trust you yet. Almost certainly other tentacles would whip out of the hole and up his arm. He only needed to be dragged down less than two feet, the cork valve on his mask would automatically close and he would be suffocated inside it or, if he tore it off, drowned. He might get in a quick lucky jab with his spear, but it would take more than that to kill Pussy. No. Perhaps later in the day. It would be rather like playing Russian roulette, and at about the same five-to-one-odds. It might be a quick, a whimsical way out of his troubles! But not now. It would leave the interesting question unsolved. And he had promised that nice Professor Bengry at the Institute. Dexter Smythe swam leisurely off towards the reef, his eyes questing for one shape only, the squat sinister wedge of a scorpion fish, or, as Bengry would put it, *Scorpaena Plumieri.*

Major Dexter Smythe, OBE, Royal Marines (Retd), was the remains of a once brave and resourceful officer and of a handsome man who had made easy sexual conquests all his military life and particularly among the Wrens and Wracs and ATS who manned the communications and secretariat of the very special task force to which he had been attached at the end of his service career. Now he was fifty-four, slightly bald and his belly sagged in the Jantzen trunks. And he had had two coronary thromboses. His doctor, Jimmy

240

Greaves (who had been one of their high poker game at Queen's Club when Dexter Smythe had first come to Jamaica), had half-jocularly described the later one, only a month before, as 'the second warning'. But, in his well-chosen clothes, his varicose veins out of sight and his stomach flattened by a discreet support belt behind an immaculate cummerbund, he was still a fine figure of a man at a cocktail party or dinner on the North Shore, and it was a mystery to his friends and neighbours why, in defiance of the two ounces of whisky and ten cigarettes a day to which his doctor had rationed him, he persisted in smoking like a chimney and going to bed drunk, if amiably drunk, every night.

The truth of the matter was that Dexter Smythe had arrived at the frontier of the death-wish. The origins of this state of mind were many and not all that complex. He was irretrievably tied to Jamaica, and tropical sloth had gradually riddled him so that while outwardly he appeared a piece of fairly solid hardwood, under the varnished surface the termites of sloth, self-indulgence, guilt over an ancient sin and general disgust with himself had eroded his once hard core into dust. Since the death of Mary two years before, he had loved no one. He wasn't even sure that he had really loved her, but he knew that, every hour of the day, he missed her love of him and her gay, untidy, chiding and often irritating presence, and though he ate their canapés and drank their

241

martinis, he had nothing but contempt for the international riff-raff with whom he consorted on the North Shore. He could perhaps have made friends with the soldier elements, the gentleman-farmers inland, or the plantation owners on the coast, the professional men and the politicians, but that would mean regaining some serious purpose in life which his sloth, his spiritual accidie, prevented, and cutting down on the bottle, which he was definitely unwilling to do. So Major Smythe was bored, bored to death, and, but for one factor in his life, he would long ago have swallowed the bottle of barbiturates he had easily acquired from a local doctor. The lifeline that kept him clinging to the edge of the cliff was a tenuous one. Heavy drinkers veer towards an exaggeration of their basic temperaments, the classic four – Sanguine, Phlegmatic, Choleric and Melancholic. The Sanguine drunk goes gay to the point of hysteria and idiocy. The Phlegmatic sinks into a morass of sullen gloom. The Choleric is the fighting drunk of the cartoonists who spends much of his life in prison for smashing people and things, and the Melancholic succumbs to self-pity, mawkishness and tears. Major Smythe was a Melancholic who had slid into a drooling fantasy woven around the birds and insects and fish that inhabited the five acres of Wavelets (the name he had given his small villa is symptomatic), its beach and the coral reef beyond. The fish were his particular favourites. He referred to them as 'people' and, since reef fish stick to their territories as closely as do most small birds, after two years he knew them all intimately, 'loved' them and believed that they loved him in return.

They certainly knew him, as the denizens of zoos know their keepers, because he was a daily and a regular provider, scraping off algae and stirring up the sand and rocks for the bottom-feeders, breaking up sea eggs and urchins for the small carnivores and bringing out scraps of offal for the larger ones, and now, as he swam slowly and heavily up and down the reef and through the channels that led out to deep water, his 'people' swarmed around him fearlessly and expectantly, darting at the tip of the three-pronged spear they knew only as a prodigal spoon, flirting right up to the glass of the Pirelli and even, in the case of the fearless, pugnacious demoiselles, nipping softly at his feet and legs.

Part of Major Smythe's mind took in all these brilliantly coloured little 'people', but today he had a job to do and while he greeted them in unspoken words – 'Morning, Beau Gregory' to the dark-blue demoiselle sprinkled with bright-blue spots, the 'jewel fish' that exactly resembles the starlit fashioning of a bottle of Worth's 'Vol de Nuit'; 'Sorry. Not today, sweetheart,' to a fluttering butterfly fish with false black 'eyes' on its tail and, 'You're too fat anyway, Blue Boy,' to an indigo parrot fish that must have weighed a good ten pounds – his eyes were searching for only one of his 'people' – his only enemy on the reef, the only one he killed on sight, a scorpion fish.

Scorpion fish inhabit most of the southern waters of the world, and the 'rascasse' that is the foundation of *bouillabaisse* belongs to the family. The West Indian variety runs up to only about twelve inches long and perhaps a pound in weight. It is by far the ugliest fish in the sea, as if nature were giving warning. It is a mottled brownish grey with a heavy, wedge-shaped shaggy head. It has fleshy pendulous 'eyebrows' that droop over angry red eyes and a coloration and broken silhouette that are perfect camouflage on the reef. Though a small fish, its heavily toothed mouth is so wide that it can swallow whole most of the smaller reef fishes, but its supreme weapon lies in its erectile dorsal fins, the first few of which, acting on contact like hypodermic needles, are fed by poison glands containing enough tetrodotoxin to kill a man if they merely graze him in a vulnerable spot – in an artery, for instance, or over the heart or in the groin. They constitute the only real danger to the reef swimmer, far more dangerous than barracuda or shark, because, supremely confident in their camouflage and armoury, they flee before nothing except the very close approach of a foot or actual contact. Then they flit only a few yards on wide and bizarrely striped pectorals and settle again watchfully either on the sand, where they look like a lump of overgrown coral, or amongst the rocks and seaweed, where they virtually disappear.

And Major Smythe was determined to find one, spear it and give it to his octopus to see if it would take or spurn it, see if one of the ocean's great predators would recognize the deadliness of another, know of its poison. Would the octopus consume the belly and leave the spines? Would it eat the lot and, if so, would it suffer from the poison? These were the questions Bengry at the Institute wanted answered and today, since it was going to be the beginning of the end of Major Smythe's life at Wavelets and though it might mean the end of his darling Octopussy, Major Smythe had decided to find out the answers and leave one tiny memorial to his now futile life in some dusty corner of the Institute's marine biological files.

For, only a couple of hours earlier, Major Dexter Smythe's already dismal life had changed very much for the worse. So much for the worse that he would be lucky if, in a few weeks' time – time for the sending of cables from Government House to the Colonial Office, to be relayed to the Secret Service and thence to Scotland Yard and the Public Prosecutor, and for Major Smythe's transportation to London with a police escort – he got away with a sentence of imprisonment for life.

And all this because of a man called Bond, Commander James Bond, who had turned up at ten thirty that morning in a taxi from Kingston.

The day had started normally. Major Smythe had awoken from his Secconal sleep, swallowed a couple of Panadols (his heart condition forbade him aspirin), showered and skimped his breakfast under the umbrella-shaped sea-almonds and spent an hour feeding the remains of his breakfast to the birds. He then took his prescribed doses of anti-coagulant and blood-pressure pills and killed time with the *Daily Gleaner* until he could have his elevenses which, for some months now, he had advanced to ten thirty. He had just poured himself the first of two stiff brandies and ginger ales, 'the drunkard's drink', when he heard the car coming up the drive.

Luna, his coloured housekeeper, came out into the garden and announced, 'Gemmun to see you, Major.'

'What's his name?'

'Him doan say, Major. Him say to tell you him come from Govment House.'

Major Smythe was wearing nothing but a pair of old khaki shorts and sandals. He said, 'All right, Luna. Put him in the living-room and say I won't be a moment,' and went round the back way into his bedroom and put on a white bush shirt and trousers and brushed his hair. Government House! Now what the hell?

As soon as he had walked through into the living-room and seen the tall man in the dark-blue tropical suit standing at the picture window looking out to sea, Major Smythe had somehow sensed bad news. Then, when the man had turned slowly to look at him with watchful, serious blue-grey eyes, he had known that this was officialdom,

246

and when his cheery smile was not returned, inimical officialdom. A chill had run down Major Smythe's spine. 'They' had somehow found out.

'Well, well. I'm Smythe. I gather you're from Government House. How's Sir Kenneth?'

There was somehow no question of shaking hands. The man said, 'I haven't met him. I only arrived a couple of days ago. I've been out round the island most of the time. My name's Bond, James Bond. I'm from the Ministry of Defence.'

Major Smythe remembered the hoary euphemism for the Secret Service. He said, with forced cheerfulness, 'Oh. The old firm?'

The question had been ignored. 'Is there somewhere we can talk?'

'Rather. Anywhere you like. Here or in the garden? What about a drink?' Major Smythe clinked the ice in the glass he still held in his hand. 'Rum and ginger's the local poison. I prefer the ginger by itself.' The lie came out with the automatic smoothness of the alcoholic.

'No thanks. And here would be fine.' The man leaned negligently against the wide mahogany window-sill.

Major Smythe sat down and threw a jaunty leg over the low arm of one of the comfortable planters' chairs he had had copied from an original by the local cabinet-maker. He pulled out the drink coaster from the other arm, took a deep pull at his glass and slid it, with a consciously steady hand, down into the hole in the wood. 'Well,' he said cheerily,

247

looking the other man straight in the eyes, 'what can I do for you? Somebody been up to some dirty work on the North Shore and you need a spare hand? Be glad to get into harness again. It's been a long time since those days, but I can still remember some of the old routines.'

'Do you mind if I smoke?' The man had already got his cigarette case in his hand. It was a flat gun-metal one that would hold a round fifty. Somehow this small sign of a shared weakness comforted Major Smythe.

'Of course, my dear fellow.' He made a move to get up, his lighter ready.

'It's all right, thanks.' James Bond had already lit his cigarette. 'No, it's nothing local. I want to, I've been sent out to ask you to recall your work for the Service at the end of the war.' James Bond paused and looked down at Major Smythe carefully. 'Particularly the time when you were working with the Miscellaneous Objectives Bureau.'

Major Smythe laughed sharply. He had known it. He had known it for absolutely sure. But when it came out of this man's mouth, the laugh had been forced out of Major Smythe like the scream of a hit man. 'Oh Lord, yes. Good old MOB. That was a lark all right.' He laughed again. He felt the anginal pain, brought on by the pressure of what he knew was coming, build up across his chest. He dipped his hand into his trouser pocket, tilted the little bottle into the palm of his hand and slipped the white TNT pill under his tongue.

He was amused to see the tension coil up in the other man, the way the eyes narrowed watchfully. It's all right, my dear fellow. This isn't a death pill. He said, 'You troubled with acidosis? No? It slays me when I go on a bender. Last night. Party at Jamaica Inn. One really ought to stop thinking one's always twenty-five. Anyway, let's get back to MOB Force. Not many of us left, I suppose.' He felt the pain across his chest withdraw into its lair. 'Something to do with the Official History?'

James Bond looked down at the tip of his cigarette. 'Not exactly.'

'I expect you know I wrote most of the chapter on the Force for the War Book. It's a long time ago now. Doubt if I'd have much to add today.'

'Nothing more about that operation in the Tyrol – place called Ober Aurach, about a mile east of Kitzbühel?'

One of the names he had been living with for all these years forced another harsh laugh out of Major Smythe. 'That was a piece of cake! You've never seen such a shambles. All those Gestapo toughs with their doxies. All of 'em hog-drunk. They'd kept their files all tickety-boo. Handed them over without a murmur. Hoped that'd earn 'em easy treatment, I suppose. We gave the stuff a first going-over and shipped all the bods off to the Munich camp. Last I heard of them. Most of them hanged for war crimes, I expect. We handed the bumph over to HQ at Salzburg. Then we went on up the Mittersill valley after another hideout.' Major Smythe took a good pull at his drink and lit a cigarette. He looked up. 'That's the long and the short of it.'

'You were Number 2 at the time, I think. The CO was an American, a Colonel King from Patton's army.'

'That's right. Nice fellow. Wore a moustache, which isn't like an American. Knew his way among the local wines. Quite a civilized chap.'

'In his report about the operation he wrote that he handed you all the documents for a preliminary run-through as you were the German expert with the unit. Then you gave them all back to him with your comments?' James Bond paused. 'Every single one of them?'

Major Smythe ignored the innuendo. 'That's right. Mostly lists of names. Counter-Intelligence dope. The CI people in Salzburg were very pleased with the stuff. Gave them plenty of new leads. I expect the originals are lying about somewhere. They'll have been used for the Nuremberg Trials. Yes, by Jove!' Major Smythe was reminiscent, pally. 'Those were some of the jolliest months of my life, haring around the country with MOB Force. Wine, women and song! And you can say that again!'

Here, Major Smythe was saying the whole truth. He had had a dangerous and uncomfortable war until 1945. When the Commandos were formed in 1941 he had volunteered and been seconded from the Royal Marines to Combined Operations

Headquarters under Mountbatten. There his excellent German (his mother had come from Heidelberg) had earned him the unenviable job of being advanced interrogator on Commando operations across the Channel. He had been lucky to get away from two years of this work unscathed and with the OBE (Military), which was sparingly awarded in the last war. And then, in preparation for the defeat of Germany, the Miscellaneous Objectives Bureau had been formed jointly by the Secret Service and Combined Operations, and Major Smythe had been given the temporary rank of Lieutenant-Colonel and told to form a unit whose job would be the cleaning up of Gestapo and Abwehr hideouts when the collapse of Germany came about. The OSS got to hear of the scheme and insisted on getting into the act to cope with the American wing of the front, and the result was the creation of not one but six units that went into operation in Germany and Austria on the day of surrender. They were units of twenty men, each with a light armoured car, six jeeps, a wireless truck and three lorries, and they were controlled by a joint Anglo-American headquarters in SHAEF, which also fed them with targets from the army intelligence units and from the SIS and OSS. Major Smythe had been Number 2 of 'A' Force which had been allotted the Tyrol – an area full of good hiding places with easy access to Italy and perhaps out of Europe – that was known to have been chosen as funkhole number 1 by the people MOB Force was after. And, as Major Smythe had just told Bond, they had had themselves a ball. All without firing a shot – except that is, two fired by Major Smythe.

James Bond said casually, 'Does the name of Hannes Oberhauser ring a bell?'

Major Smythe frowned, trying to remember. 'Can't say it does.' It was eighty degrees in the shade, but he shivered.

'Let me refresh your memory. On the same day as those documents were given to you to look over, you made inquiries at the Tiefenbrunner Hotel, where you were billeted, for the best mountain guide in Kitzbühel. You were referred to Oberhauser. The next day you asked your CO for a day's leave which was granted. Early next morning you went to Oberhauser's chalet, put him under close arrest and drove him away in your jeep. Does that ring a bell?'

That phrase about 'refreshing your memory'. How often had Major Smythe himself used it when he was trying to trap a German liar? Take your time! You've been ready for something like this for years. Major Smythe shook his head doubtfully. 'Can't say it does.'

'A man with greying hair and a gammy leg. Spoke some English as he'd been a ski-instructor before the war.'

Major Smythe looked candidly into the cold, clear eyes. 'Sorry. Can't help you.'

James Bond took a small blue leather notebook

out of his inside pocket and turned the leaves. He stopped turning them. He looked up. 'At that time, as side-arms, you were carrying a regulation Webley & Scott .45 with the serial number 8967/362.'

'It was certainly a Webley. Damned clumsy weapon. Hope they've got something more like the Luger or the heavy Beretta these days. But I can't say I ever took a note of the number.'

'The number's right enough,' said James Bond. 'I've got the date of its issue to you by HQ and the date when you turned it in. You signed the book both times.'

Major Smythe shrugged. 'Well then, it must have been my gun. But' – he put rather angry impatience into his voice – 'what, if I may ask, is all this in aid of?'

James Bond looked at him almost with curiosity. He said, and now his voice was not unkind, 'You know what it's all about, Smythe.' He paused and seemed to reflect. 'Tell you what. I'll go out into the garden for ten minutes or so. Give you time to think things over. Give me a hail.' He added seriously, 'It'll make things so much easier for you if you come out with the story in your own words.' He walked to the door into the garden. He turned round. 'I'm afraid it's only a question of dotting the i's and crossing the t's. You see I had a talk with the Foo brothers in Kingston yesterday.' He stepped out on to the lawn.

Something in Major Smythe was relieved. Now at least the battle of wits, the trying to invent alibis, the evasions, were over. If this man Bond had got to the Foos, to either of them, they would have spilled the beans. The last thing they wanted was to get in bad with the government, and anyway there was only about six inches of the stuff left.

Major Smythe got briskly to his feet, went to the loaded sideboard and poured himself out another brandy and ginger ale, almost fifty-fifty. He might as well live it up while there was still time! The future wouldn't hold many more of these for him. He went back to his chair and lit his twentieth cigarette of the day. He looked at his watch. It said eleven thirty. If he could be rid of the chap in an hour, he'd have plenty of time with his 'people'. He sat and drank and marshalled his thoughts. He could make the story long or short, put in the weather and the way the flowers and pines had smelled on the mountain, or he could cut it short. He would cut it short.

Up in that big double bedroom in the Tiefenbrunner, with the wads of buff and grey paper spread out on the spare bed, he hadn't been looking for anything special, just taking samples here and there and concentrating on the ones marked in red KOMMANDOSACHE, HOECHST VERTRAULICH. There weren't many of these, and they were mostly confidential reports on German top brass, intercepts of broken Allied cyphers and the whereabouts of secret dumps. Since these were the main targets of 'A' Force, Major Smythe had scanned them with particular excitement – food, explosives, guns, espionage records, files of Gestapo personnel – a tremendous haul! And then, at the bottom of the packet, there had been the single envelope sealed with red wax and the notation ONLY TO BE OPENED IN FINAL EMERGENCY. The envelope contained one single sheet of paper. It was unsigned and the few words were written in red ink. The heading said VALUTA, and beneath was written WILDE KAISER. FRANZISKANER HALT. 100 M. OESTLICH STEINHÜGEL. WAFFENKISTE. ZWEI BAR 24 KT and then a list of measurements in centimetres. Major Smythe held his hands apart as if telling a story about a fish he had caught. Each bar would be nearly as big as a couple of bricks. And one single English sovereign of only eighteen-carat was selling nowadays for two to three pounds! This was a bloody fortune! Forty, fifty thousand pounds' worth! Maybe even a hundred! He had no idea, but, quite coolly and speedily, in case anyone should come in, he put a match to the paper and the envelope, ground the ashes to powder and swilled them down the lavatory. Then he took out his large-scale Austrian Ordnance map of the area and in a moment had his finger on the Franziskaner Halt. It was marked as an uninhabited mountaineers' refuge on a saddle just below the highest of the easterly peaks of the Kaiser mountains, that awe-inspiring range of giant stone teeth that give Kitzbühel its threatening northern horizon. And the cairn of stones would be about there, his fingernail pointed, and the whole bloody lot was only ten miles and perhaps a five hours' climb away!

The beginning had been as this fellow Bond had described. He had gone to Oberhauser's chalet at four in the morning, had arrested him and had told his weeping, protesting family that he, Smythe, was taking him to an interrogation camp in Munich. If the guide's record was clean, he would be back home within a week. If the family kicked up a fuss it would only make trouble for Oberhauser. Smythe had refused to give his name and had had the forethought to shroud the numbers on his jeep. In twenty-four hours, 'A' Force would be on its way and, by the time military government got to Kitzbühel, the incident would already be buried under the morass of the occupation tangle.

Oberhauser had been a nice enough chap once he had recovered from his fright, and when Smythe talked knowingly about skiing and climbing, both of which he had done before the war, the pair, as Smythe intended, became quite pally. Their route lay along the bottom of the Kaiser range to Kufstein, and Smythe drove slowly, making admiring comments on the peaks that were now flushed with the pink of dawn. Finally, below the Peak of Gold, as he called it to himself, he slowed to a halt and pulled off the road into a grassy glade. He turned in his seat and said candidly, 'Oberhauser, you are a man after my own heart.

We share many interests together and from your talk and from the man I think you to be, I am sure you did not cooperate with the Nazis. Now I will tell you what I will do. We will spend the day climbing on the Kaiser and I will then drive you back to Kitzbühel and report to my commanding officer that you have been cleared at Munich.' He grinned cheerfully. 'Now. How about that?'

The man had been near to tears of gratitude. But could he have some kind of paper to show that he was a good citizen? Certainly. Major Smythe's signature would be quite enough. The pact was made, the jeep was driven up a track and well hidden from the road and they were off at a steady pace, climbing up through the pine-scented foot-hills.

Smythe was well dressed for the climb. He had nothing on under his bush jacket, shorts and a pair of the excellent rubber-soled boots issued to American parachutists. His only burden was the Webley & Scott and, tactfully, for Oberhauser was after all one of the enemy, Oberhauser didn't suggest that he leave it behind some conspicuous rock. Oberhauser was in his best suit and boots, but that didn't seem to bother him and he assured Major Smythe that ropes and pitons would not be needed for their climb and that there was a hut directly up above them where they could rest. It was called the Franziskaner Halt.

'Is it indeed?' said Major Smythe.

'Yes, and below it there is a small glacier. Very pretty, but we will climb round it. There are many crevasses.'

'Is that so?' said Major Smythe thoughtfully. He examined the back of Oberhauser's head, now beaded with sweat. After all, he was only a bloody Kraut, or at any rate of that ilk. What would one more or less matter? It was all going to be as easy as falling off a log. The only thing that worried Major Smythe was getting the bloody stuff down the mountain. He decided that he would somehow sling the bars across his back. After all, he could slide it most of the way in its ammunition box or whatnot.

It was a long, dreary hack up the mountain and when they were above the tree line the sun came up and it was very hot. And now it was all rock and scree, and their long zigzags sent boulders and rubble rumbling and crashing down the slope that got ever steeper as they approached the final crag, grey and menacing, that lanced away into the blue above them. They were both naked to the waist and sweating so that the sweat ran down their legs into their boots, but, despite Oberhauser's limp, they kept up a good pace, and when they stopped for a drink and a swab down at a hurtling mountain stream Oberhauser congratulated Major Smythe on his fitness. Major Smythe, his mind full of dreams, said curtly and untruthfully that all English soldiers were fit, and they went on.

The rock face wasn't difficult. Major Smythe had known that it wouldn't be or the climbers' hut couldn't have been built on the shoulder. Toe holds had been cut in the face and there were occasional iron pegs hammered into crevices. But he couldn't have found the more difficult traverses alone and he congratulated himself on deciding to bring a guide.

Once, Oberhauser's hand, testing for a grip, dislodged a great slab of rock, loosened by years of snow and frost, and sent it crashing down the mountain. Major Smythe suddenly thought about noise. 'Many people around here?' he asked as they watched the boulder hurtle down into the tree line.

'Not a soul until you get near Kufstein,' said Oberhauser. He gestured along the arid range of high peaks. 'No grazing. Little water. Only the climbers come here. And since the beginning of the war . . .' He left the phrase unfinished.

They skirted the blue-fanged glacier below the final climb to the shoulder. Major Smythe's careful eyes took in the width and depth of the crevasses. Yes, they would fit! Directly above them, perhaps a hundred feet up under the lee of the shoulder, were the weather-beaten boards of the hut. Major Smythe measured the angle of the slope. Yes, it was almost a straight dive down. Now or later? He guessed later. The line of the last traverse wasn't very clear.

They were up at the hut in five hours flat. Major

Smythe said he wanted to relieve himself and wandered casually along the shoulder to the east, paying no heed to the beautiful panoramas of Austria and Bavaria that stretched away on either side of him perhaps fifty miles into the heat haze. He counted his paces carefully. At exactly 120 there was the cairn of stones, a loving memorial, perhaps, to some long-dead climber. Major Smythe, knowing differently, longed to tear it apart there and then. Instead he took out his Webley & Scott, squinted down the barrel and twirled the cylinder. Then he walked back.

It was cold up there at ten thousand feet or more, and Oberhauser had got into the hut and was busy preparing a fire. Major Smythe controlled his horror at the sight. 'Oberhauser,' he said cheerfully, 'come out and show me some of the sights. Wonderful view up here.'

'Certainly, Major.' Oberhauser followed Major Smythe out of the hut. Outside he fished in his hip pocket and produced something wrapped in paper. He undid the paper to reveal a hard, wrinkled sausage. He offered it to the Major. 'It is only what we call a "Soldat",' he said shyly. 'Smoked meat. Very tough but good.' He smiled. 'It is like what they eat in Wild West films. What is the name?'

'"Biltong",' said the Major. Then – and later this had slightly disgusted him – he said, 'Leave it in the hut. We will share it later. Come over here. Can we see Innsbruck? Show me the view on this side.'

Oberhauser bobbed into the hut and out again. The Major fell in just behind him as he talked, pointing out this or that distant church spire or mountain peak.

They came to the point above the glacier. Major Smythe drew his revolver and, at a range of two feet, fired two bullets into the base of Hannes Oberhauser's skull. No muffing! Dead on!

The impact of the bullets knocked the guide clean off his feet and over the edge. Major Smythe craned over. The body hit twice only and then crashed on to the glacier. But not on to its fissured origin. Half-way down and on a patch of old snow! 'Hell!' said Major Smythe.

The deep boom of the two shots that had been batting to and fro among the mountains died away. Major Smythe took one last look at the black splash on the white snow and hurried off along the shoulder. First things first!

He started on the top of the cairn, working as if the devil was after him, throwing the rough, heavy stones indiscriminately down the mountain to right or left. His hands began to bleed, but he hardly noticed. Now there were only two feet or so left, and nothing! Bloody nothing! He bent to the last pile, scrabbling feverishly. And then! Yes! The edge of a metal box. A few more rocks away and there was the whole of it! A good old grey Wehrmacht ammunition box with the trace of some lettering still on it. Major Smythe gave a groan of joy. He sat down on a hard piece of rock and his mind went orbiting through Bentleys, Monte Carlo, pent-house flats, Cartier's, champagne, caviare and, incongruously, but because he loved golf, a new set of Henry Cotton irons.

Drunk with his dreams, Major Smythe sat there looking at the grey box for a full quarter of an hour. Then he glanced at his watch and got briskly to his feet. Time to get rid of the evidence. The box had a handle at each end. Major Smythe had expected it to be heavy. He had mentally compared its probable weight with the heaviest thing he had ever carried – a forty-pound salmon he had caught in Scotland just before the war – but the box was more than double that weight, and he was only just able to heave it out of its last bed of rocks on to the thin alpine grass. He slung his handkerchief through one of the handles and dragged it clumsily along the shoulder to the hut. Then he sat down on the stone doorstep, and, his eyes never leaving the box, tore at Oberhauser's smoked sausage with his strong teeth and thought about getting his fifty thousand pounds – for that was the figure he put it at – down the mountain and into a new hiding place.

Oberhauser's sausage was a real mountaineer's meal – tough, well fatted and strongly garlicked. Bits of it stuck uncomfortably between Major Smythe's teeth. He dug them out with a sliver of matchstick and spat them on the ground. Then his intelligence-wise mind came into operation and he meticulously searched among the stones and grass, picked up the scraps and swallowed them. From now on he was a criminal – as much a criminal as if he had robbed a bank and shot the guard. He was a cop turned robber. He *must* remember that! It would be death if he didn't – death instead of Cartier's. All he had to do was to take infinite pains. He would take those pains, and by God they would be infinite! Then, for ever after, he would be rich and happy. After taking ridiculously minute trouble to eradicate any sign of entry into the hut, he dragged the ammunition box to the edge of the last rock face and, aiming it away from the glacier, tipped it, with a prayer, into space.

The grey box, turning slowly in the air, hit the first steep slope below the rock face, bounded another hundred feet and landed with an iron clang in some loose scree and stopped. Major Smythe couldn't see if it had burst open. He didn't mind one way or the other. The mountain might as well do it for him!

With a last look round, he went over the edge. He took great care at each piton, tested every handhold and foothold before he put weight on them. Coming down, he was a much more valuable life than he had been climbing up. He made for the glacier and trudged across the melting snow to the black patch on the icefield. There was nothing to be done about footprints. It would only take a few days for them to be melted down by the sun. He got to the body. He had seen many corpses during the war, and the blood and broken limbs meant nothing to him.

He dragged the remains of Oberhauser to the nearest deep crevasse and toppled it in. Then he went carefully round the lip of the crevasse and kicked the snow overhang down on top of the body. Satisfied with his work, he retraced his steps, placing his feet exactly in his old footprints, and made his way on down the slope to the ammunition box.

Yes, the mountain had burst open the lid for him. Almost casually he tore away the cartridge-paper wrappings. The two great hunks of metal glittered up at him under the sun. There were the same markings on each – the swastika in a circle below an eagle, and the date, 1943 – the mint marks of the Reichsbank. Major Smythe gave a nod of approval. He replaced the paper and hammered the crooked lid half-shut with a rock. Then he tied the lanyard of his Webley round one of the handles and moved on down the mountain, dragging his clumsy burden behind him.

It was now one o'clock and the sun beat fiercely down on his naked chest, frying him in his own sweat. His reddened shoulders began to burn. So did his face. To hell with them! He stopped at the stream from the glacier, dipped his handkerchief in the water and tied it across his forehead. Then he drank deeply and went on, occasionally cursing the ammunition box as it caught up with him and banged at his heels. But these discomforts, the sunburn and the bruises, were nothing compared with what he would have to face when he got down to the valley and the going levelled out. For the time being he had gravity on his side. There would come at least a mile when he would have to carry the blasted stuff. Major Smythe winced at the thought of the havoc it would wreak on his burned back. 'Oh well,' he said to himself almost light-headedly, 'il faut souffrir pour être millionaire!'

When he got to the bottom and the time had come he sat and rested on a mossy bank under the firs. Then he spread out his bush shirt and heaved the two bars out of the box and on to its centre, tying the tails of the shirt as firmly as he could to where the sleeves sprang from the shoulders. After digging a shallow hole in the bank and burying the empty box, he knotted the two cuffs of the sleeves firmly together, knelt down and slipped his head through the rough sling, got his hands on either side of the knot to protect his neck, and staggered to his feet, crouching far forward so as not to be pulled over on his back. Then, crushed under half his own weight, his back on fire under the contact with his burden, and his breath rasping through his constricted lungs, coolie-like, he shuffled slowly off down the little path through the trees.

To this day he didn't know how he had made it to the jeep. Again and again the knots gave under the strain and the bars crashed down on the calves of his legs, and each time he had sat with his head in his hands and then started all over again. But finally, by concentrating on counting his steps and stopping for a rest at every hundredth, he got to the blessed little car and collapsed beside it.

And then there had been the business of burying his hoard in the wood, amongst a jumble of big rocks that he would be sure to find again, and of cleaning himself up as best he could and getting back to his billet by a circuitous route that avoided the Oberhauser chalet. And then it was all done and he had got drunk by himself on a bottle of cheap schnapps, eaten and gone to bed and to a stupefied sleep. The next day, MOB 'A' Force had moved off up the Mittersill valley on a fresh trail, and six months later Major Smythe was back in London and his war was over.

But not his problems. Gold is difficult stuff to smuggle, certainly in the quantity available to Major Smythe, and it was now essential to get his two bars across the Channel and into a new hiding place. So he put off his demobilization and clung to the privileges of his temporary rank, particularly to his Military Intelligence passes, and soon got himself sent back to Germany as a British representative at the Combined Interrogation Centre in Munich. There he did a scratch job for six months during which he collected his gold and stowed it away in a battered suitcase in his quarters. Then on two weekend leaves he flew to England, each time carrying one of the bars in a bulky briefcase. The walk across the tarmac at Munich and Northolt and the handling of his case as if it contained only papers required two benzedrine tablets and a will of iron; but at last he had his fortune safe in the basement of an aunt's flat in Kensington and could get on with the next phase of his plans at leisure. He resigned from the Royal Marines, got himself demobilized and married one of the many girls he had slept with at MOB Force Headquarters, a charming blonde Wren called Mary Parnell from a solid middle-class family. He got passages for them both in one of the early banana boats sailing from Avonmouth to Kingston, Jamaica, which they both agreed would be a paradise of sunshine, good food and cheap drink and a glorious haven from the gloom, restrictions and Labour Government of post-war England. Before they sailed, Major Smythe showed Mary the gold bars, from which he had chiselled away the mint marks of the Reichsbank. 'I've been clever, darling,' he said. 'I just don't trust the pound these days, so I've sold out all my securities and swapped the lot for gold. There'll be over twenty thousand pounds' worth there if I play it right. That should give us a fair slice of the good life, just cutting off a chunk now and then and selling it.'

Mary Parnell was not familiar with the ramifications of the currency laws. She knelt down and ran her hands lovingly over the gleaming bars. Then she got up and threw her arms round Major Smythe's neck and kissed him. 'You're a wonderful, wonderful man,' she said, almost in tears. 'Frightfully clever and handsome and brave and now you're rich as well. I'm the luckiest girl in the world.'

'Well anyway we're rich,' said Major Smythe. 'But

promise me you won't breathe a word or we'll have all the burglars in Jamaica round our ears. Promise?'

'Cross my heart.'

Prince's Club, in the foot-hills above Kingston, was indeed a paradise. Pleasant enough members, wonderful servants, unlimited food and cheap drink, and all in the wonderful setting of the tropics that neither of them had known before. They were a popular couple and Major Smythe's war record earned them the entrée to Government House society, after which their life was one endless round of parties, with tennis for Mary and golf (with the Henry Cotton irons!) for Major Smythe. In the evenings there was bridge for her and the high poker game for him. Yes, it was paradise all right, while, in their homeland, people munched their spam, fiddled in the black market, cursed the government and suffered the worst winter weather for thirty years.

The Smythes met all their initial expenditure from their combined cash reserves, swollen by wartime gratuities, and it took Major Smythe a full year of careful sniffing around before he decided to do business with the Messrs Foo, import and export merchants. The brothers Foo, highly respected and very rich, were the acknowledged governing junta of the flourishing Chinese community in Jamaica. Some of their trading was suspected to be devious in the Chinese tradition, but all Major Smythe's casually meticulous inquiries confirmed that they were utterly trustworthy. The Bretton Woods Convention, fixing a controlled world price for gold, had been signed and it had already become common knowledge that in Tangier and Macao – two free ports which, for different reasons, had escaped the Bretton Woods net – a price of at least one hundred dollars per ounce of gold, ninety-nine fine, could be obtained compared with the fixed world price of thirty-five dollars per ounce. And, conveniently, the Foos had just begun to trade again with a resurgent Hong Kong, already the entrepôt for gold-smuggling into the neighbouring Macao. The whole set-up was, in Major Smythe's language, tickety-boo. He had a most pleasant meeting with the Foo brothers. No questions were asked until it came to examining the bars. At this point the absence of mint marks resulted in a polite inquiry as to the original provenance of the gold.

'You see, Major,' said the older and blander of the brothers behind the big, empty, mahogany desk, 'in the bullion market the mint marks of all respectable national banks and responsible dealers are accepted without question. Such marks guarantee the fineness of the gold. But of course there are other banks and dealers whose methods of refining,' his benign smile widened a fraction, 'are perhaps not quite, shall we say, so accurate.'

'You mean the old gold brick swindle,' said Major Smythe with a twinge of anxiety. 'Hunk of lead covered with gold plating?'

Both brothers tee-heed reassuringly. 'No, no,

Major. That of course is out of the question. But,' the smiles held constant, 'if you cannot recall the provenance of these fine bars, perhaps you would have no objection if we were to undertake an assay. There are methods of determining the exact fineness of such bars. My brother and I are competent in these methods. If you would care to leave these with us and perhaps come back after lunch?'

There had been no alternative. Major Smythe had to trust the Foos utterly now. They could cook up any figure and he would just have to accept it. He went over to the Myrtle Bank and had one or two stiff drinks and a sandwich that stuck in his throat. Then he went back to the cool office of the Foos.

The setting was the same – the two smiling brothers, the two bars of gold, the briefcase, but now there was a piece of paper and a gold Parker pen in front of the elder brother.

'We have solved the problem of your fine bars, Major,' ('Fine'! Thank God, thought Major Smythe) 'and I am sure you will be interested to know their probable history.'

'Yes indeed,' said Major Smythe, with a brave show of enthusiasm.

'They are German bars, Major. Probably from the wartime Reichsbank. This we have deduced from the fact that they contain ten per cent of lead. Under the Hitler régime, it was the foolish habit of the Reichsbank to adulterate their gold in this manner. This fact became rapidly known to dealers and the price of German bars, in

270

Switzerland, for instance, where many of them found their way, was adjusted downwards accordingly. So the only result of the German foolishness was that the national bank of Germany lost a reputation for honest dealing it had earned over the centuries.' The Chinaman's smile didn't vary. 'Very bad business, Major. Very stupid.'

Major Smythe marvelled at the omniscience of these two men so far from the great commercial channels of the world, but he also cursed it. Now what? He said, 'That's very interesting, Mr Foo. But it is not very good news for me. Are these bars not "good delivery", or whatever you call it in the bullion world?'

The elder Foo made a slight throwaway gesture with his right hand. 'It is of no importance, Major. Or rather, it is of very small importance. We will sell your gold at its true mint value, let us say, eighty-nine fine. It may be re-fined by the ultimate purchaser, or it may not. That is not our business. We shall have sold a true bill of goods.'

'But at a lower price.'

'That is so, Major. But I think I have some good news for you. Have you any estimates as to the worth of these two bars?'

'I had thought around twenty thousand pounds.'

The elder Foo gave a dry chuckle. 'I think, if we sell wisely and slowly, you should receive more than one hundred thousand dollars, Major – subject, that is, to our commission, which will include shipping and incidental charges.'

'How much would that be?'

'We were thinking about a figure of ten per cent, Major. If that is satisfactory to you.'

Major Smythe had an idea that bullion brokers received a fraction of one per cent. But what the hell? He had already as good as made ten thousand pounds since lunch. He said 'Done' and got up and reached his hand across the desk.

From then on, every quarter, he would visit the office of the Foos, carrying an empty suitcase. There would be five hundred new Jamaican pounds in neat bundles on the broad desk and the two gold bars, that diminished inch by inch, together with a typed slip showing the amount sold and the price obtained in Macao. It was all very simple and friendly and highly businesslike, and Major Smythe didn't think that he was being submitted to any form of squeeze other than the duly recorded ten per cent. In any case he didn't particularly care. Two thousand net a year was good enough for him, and his only worry was that the income tax people would get after him and ask him what he was living on. He mentioned this possibility to the Foos. But they said he was not to worry and, for the next two quarters, there was only four hundred pounds instead of five on the table and no comment was made by either side. 'Squeeze' had been administered in the right quarter.

And so the lazy, sunshiny days passed by and stretched out into years. The Smythes both put on weight and Major Smythe had the first of his two coronaries and was told by his doctor to cut down on his alcohol and cigarettes and take life more easily. He was also to avoid fats and fried food. At first Mary Smythe tried to be firm with him; then, when he took to secret drinking and to a life of petty lies and evasions, she tried to back-pedal on her attempts to control his self-indulgence. But she was too late. She had already become the symbol of the janitor to Major Smythe and he took to avoiding her. She berated him with not loving her any more and, when the resultant bickering became too much for her simple nature, she became a sleeping-pill addict. Then, after one flaming, drunken row, she took an overdose 'just to show him'. It was too much of an overdose and it killed her. The suicide was hushed up, but the resultant cloud did Major Smythe no good socially and he returned to the North Shore which, although only some three miles across the island from the capital, is, even in the small society of Jamaica, a different world. And there he had settled in Wavelets and, after his second coronary, was in the process of drinking himself to death when this man called Bond arrived on the scene with an alternative death warrant in his pocket.

Major Smythe looked at his watch. It was a few minutes after twelve o'clock. He got up and poured himself another stiff brandy and ginger ale and went out on to the lawn. James Bond was sitting under the sea-almonds, gazing out to sea.

273

He didn't look up when Major Smythe pulled up another aluminium garden chair and put his drink on the grass beside him. When Major Smythe had finished telling his story, Bond said unemotionally, 'Yes, that's more or less the way I figured it.'

'Want me to write it all out and sign it?'

'You can if you like. But not for me. That'll be for the court martial. Your old Corps will be handling all that. I've got nothing to do with the legal aspects. I shall put in a report to my own Service of what you've told me and they'll pass it on to the Royal Marines. Then I suppose it'll go to the Public Prosecutor via Scotland Yard.'

'Could I ask a question?'

'Of course.'

'How did they find out?'

'It was a small glacier. Oberhauser's body came out at the bottom of it earlier this year. When the spring snows melted. Some climbers found it. All his papers and everything were intact. The family identified him. Then it was just a question of working back. The bullets clinched it.'

'But how did you get mixed up in the whole thing?'

'MOB Force was a responsibility of my, er, Service. The papers found their way to us. I happened to see the file. I had some spare time on my hands. I asked to be given the job of chasing up the man who did it.'

'Why?'

James Bond looked Major Smythe squarely in

the eyes. 'It just happened that Oberhauser was a friend of mine. He taught me to ski before the war, when I was in my teens. He was a wonderful man. He was something of a father to me at a time when I happened to need one.'

'Oh, I see.' Major Smythe looked away. 'I'm sorry.'

James Bond got to his feet. 'Well, I'll be getting back to Kingston.' He held up a hand. 'No, don't bother. I'll find my way to the car.' He looked down at the older man. He said abruptly, almost harshly – perhaps, Major Smythe thought, to hide his embarrassment – 'It'll be about a week before they send someone out to bring you home.' Then he walked off across the lawn and through the house and Major Smythe heard the iron whirr of the self-starter and the clatter of the gravel on the unkempt drive.

Major Smythe, questing for his prey along the reef, wondered what exactly those last words of the Bond man had meant. Inside the Pirelli his lips drew mirthlessly back from the stained teeth. It was obvious, really. It was just a version of the corny old act of leaving the guilty officer alone with his revolver. If the Bond man had wanted to, he could have telephoned Government House and had an officer of the Jamaica Regiment sent over to take Major Smythe into custody. Decent of him, in a way. Or was it? A suicide would be much tidier, save a lot of paperwork and tax-payers' money. Should he oblige the Bond man and be tidy? Join Mary in whatever place suicides go to? Or go through with it – the indignity, the dreary formalities, the headlines, the boredom and drabness of a life sentence that would inevitably end with his third coronary? Or should he defend himself – plead wartime, a struggle with Oberhauser on the Peak of Gold, prisoner trying to escape, Oberhauser knowing of the gold cache, the natural temptation of Smythe to make away with the bullion, he, a poor officer of the Commandos confronted with sudden wealth? Should he dramatically throw himself on the mercy of the court? Suddenly Major Smythe saw himself in the dock, a splendid, upright figure, in the fine bemedalled blue and scarlet of the ceremonial uniform which was the traditional rig for courts martial. (Had the moths got into the japanned box in the spare room at Wavelets? Had the damp? Luna would have to look to it. A day in the sunshine if the weather held. A good brushing. With the help of his corset, he could surely still get his forty-inch waist into the thirty-four-inch trousers Gieves had built for him twenty, thirty years ago.) And, down on the floor of the court, at Chatham probably, the Prisoners' Friend, some staunch fellow, at least of colonel's rank in deference to his own seniority, would be pleading his cause. And there was always the possibility of appeal to a higher court. Why, the whole affair might become a *cause célèbre*. He would sell his story to the papers, write a book . . . Major

Smythe felt the excitement mounting in him. Careful, old boy! Careful! Remember what the good old snip-cock had said! He put his feet to the ground and had a rest amidst the dancing waves of the nor'-east trades that kept the North Shore so delightfully cool until the torrid months, August, September, October, of the hurricane season. After his two pink gins, skimpy lunch and happily sodden siesta, he would have to give all this more careful thought. And then there were cocktails with the Arundels and dinner at the Shaw Park Beach Club with the Marchesis. Then some high bridge and home to his Secconal sleep. Cheered by the prospect of the familiar routine, the black shadow of Bond retreated into the background. Now then, scorp, where are you? Octopussy's waiting for her lunch! Major Smythe put his head down and, his mind freshly focused and his eyes questing, continued his leisurely swim along the shallow valley between the coral clumps that led out towards the white-fringed reef.

Almost at once he saw the two spiny antennae of a lobster, or rather of its cousin, the West Indian langouste, weaving inquisitively towards him, towards the turbulence he was creating, from a deep fissure under a nigger-head. From the thickness of the antennae it would be a big one, three or four pounds! Normally, Major Smythe would have put his feet down and delicately stirred up the sand in front of the lair to bring the lobster farther out, for they are an inquisitive family. Then he would have speared it through the head and taken it back for lunch. But today there was only one prey in his mind, one shape to concentrate on – the shaggy, irregular silhouette of a scorpion fish. And ten minutes later, he saw a clump of seaweedy rock on the white sand that just wasn't a clump of seaweedy rock. He put his feet softly down and watched the poison spines erect themselves along the back of the thing. It was a good-sized one, perhaps three-quarters of a pound. He got his three-pronged spear ready and inched forward. Now the red angry eyes of the fish were wide open and watching him. He would have to make a single quick lunge from as nearly the vertical as possible, otherwise, he knew from experience, the barbed prongs, needle sharp though they were, would almost certainly bounce off the horny head of the beast. He swung his feet up off the ground and paddled forward very slowly, using his free hand as a fin. Now! He lunged forwards and down-wards. But the scorpion fish had felt the tiny approaching shock-wave of the spear. There was a flurry of sand and it had shot up in a vertical take-off and whirred, in almost bird-like flight, under Major Smythe's belly.

Major Smythe cursed and twisted round in the water. Yes, it had done what they so often do, gone for refuge to the nearest algae-covered rock and there, confident in its superb camouflage, gone to ground on the seaweed. Major Smythe had only to swim a few feet, lunge down again, this time more accurately, and he had it, flapping and squirming on the end of his spear.

The excitement and the small exertion had caused Major Smythe to pant and he felt the old pain across his chest lurking, ready to come at him. He put his feet down and, after driving his spear all the way through the fish, held it, still flapping desperately, out of the water. Then he slowly made his way back across the lagoon on foot and walked up the sand of his beach to the wooden bench under the sea-grape. Then he dropped the spear with its jerking quarry on the sand beside him and sat down to rest.

It was perhaps five minutes later that Major Smythe felt a curious numbness more or less in the region of his solar plexus. He looked casually down and his whole body stiffened with horror and disbelief. A patch of his skin, about the size of a cricket ball, had turned white under his tan and, in the centre of the patch, there were three descending punctures topped by little beads of blood. Automatically, Major Smythe wiped away the blood. The holes were only the size of pinpricks, but Major Smythe remembered the rising flight of the scorpion fish and he said aloud, with awe in his voice, but without animosity, 'You got me, you bastard! By God, you got me!'

He sat very still, looking down at his body and remembering what it said about scorpion fish stings in the book he had borrowed from the Institute and had never returned – *Dangerous*

Marine Animals, an American publication. He delicately touched and then prodded the white area round the punctures. Yes, the skin had gone totally numb and now a pulse of pain began to throb beneath it. Very soon this would become a shooting pain. Then the pain would begin to lance all over his body and become so intense that he would throw himself on the sand, screaming and thrashing about, to rid himself of it. He would vomit and foam at the mouth and then delirium and convulsions would take over until he lost consciousness. Then, inevitably in his case, there would ensue cardiac failure and death. According to the book the whole cycle would be complete in about a quarter of an hour – that was all he had left – fifteen minutes of hideous agony! There were cures, of course – procaine, antibiotics and antihistamines – if his weak heart would stand them. But they had to be near at hand and, even if he could climb the steps up to the house and supposing Jimmy Greaves had these modern drugs, the doctor couldn't possibly get to Wavelets in under an hour.

The first jet of pain seared into Major Smythe's body and bent him over double. Then came another and another, radiating through his stomach and limbs. Now there was a dry, metallic taste in his mouth and his lips were prickling. He gave a groan and toppled off the seat on to the beach. A flapping on the sand beside his head reminded him of the scorpion fish. There came a lull in the spasms of pain. Instead his whole body felt as if it was on fire but, beneath the agony, his brain cleared. But of course! The experiment! Somehow, somehow he must get out to Octopussy and give her her lunch!

'Oh, Pussy, my Pussy, this is the last meal you'll get.'

Major Smythe mouthed the jingle to himself as he crouched on all fours, found his mask and somehow forced it over his face. Then he got hold of his spear, tipped with the still flapping fish, and, clutching his stomach with his free hand, crawled and slithered down the sand and into the water.

It was fifty yards of shallow water to the lair of the octopus in the coral cranny and Major Smythe, screaming all the while into his mask, somehow, mostly on his knees, made it. As he came to the last approach and the water became deeper, he had to get to his feet and the pain made him jiggle to and fro, as if he was a puppet manipulated by strings. Then he was there and, with a supreme effort of will, held himself steady as he dipped his head down to let some water into his mask and clear the mist of his screams from the glass. Then, blood pouring from his bitten lower lip, he bent carefully down to look into Octopussy's house. Yes! the brown mass was still there. It was stirring excitedly. Why? Major Smythe saw the dark strings of his blood curling lazily down through the water. Of course! The darling was tasting his blood. A shaft of pain hit Major Smythe and sent him reeling. He heard himself babbling deliriously into his mask. Pull yourself together, Dexter, old boy! You've got to give Pussy her lunch! He steadied himself and, holding the spear well down the shaft, lowered the fish down towards the writhing hole.

Would Pussy take the bait, the poisoned bait that was killing Major Smythe, but to which an octopus might be immune? If only Bengry could be here to watch! Three tentacles, weaving excitedly, came out of the hole and wavered round the scorpion fish. Now there was a grey mist in front of Major Smythe's eyes. He recognized it as the edge of unconsciousness and feebly shook his head to clear it. And then the tentacles leapt! But not at the fish! At Major Smythe's hand and arm. Major Smythe's torn mouth stretched in a grimace of pleasure. Now he and Pussy had shaken hands! How exciting! How truly wonderful!

But then the octopus, quietly, relentlessly, pulled downwards and terrible realization came to Major Smythe. He summoned his dregs of strength and plunged his spear down. The only effect was to push the scorpion fish into the mass of the octopus and offer more arm to the octopus. The tentacles snaked upwards and pulled more relentlessly. Too late Major Smythe scrabbled away his mask. One bottled scream burst out across the empty bay, then his head went under and down and there was an explosion of bubbles to the surface. Then Major Smythe's legs came up and the small waves washed his body to and fro while the octopus explored his right hand with its buccal orifice and took a first tentative bite at a finger with its beak-like jaws.

The body was found by two young Jamaicans spinning for needle fish from a canoe. They speared the octopus with Major Smythe's spear, killed it in the traditional fashion by turning it inside out and biting its head off, and brought the three corpses home. They turned Major Smythe's body over to the police and had the scorpion fish and the 'sea-cat' for supper. The local correspondent of the *Daily Gleaner* reported that Major Smythe had been killed by an octopus, but the paper translated this into 'found drowned' so as not to frighten the tourists.

Later, in London, James Bond, privately assuming 'suicide', wrote the same verdict of 'found drowned', together with the date, on the last page and closed the bulky file.

It is only from the notes of Dr Greaves, who performed the autopsy, that it has been possible to construct some kind of a postscript to the bizarre and pathetic end of a once valuable officer of the Secret Service.

CHAPTER 7

THE PROPERTY OF A LADY

It was, exceptionally, a hot day in early June. James Bond put down the dark grey chalk pencil that was the marker for the dockets routed to the double O Section and took off his coat. He didn't bother to hang it over the back of his chair, let alone take the trouble to get up and drape the coat over the hanger Mary Goodnight had suspended, at her own cost (damn women!), behind the Office of Works' green door of his connecting office. He dropped the coat on the floor. There was no reason to keep the coat immaculate, the creases tidy. There was no sign of any work to be done. All over the world there was quiet. The In and Out signals had, for weeks, been routine. The daily top secret SITREP, even the newspapers, yawned vacuously – in the latter case scratchings at domestic scandals for readership, for bad news, the only news that makes such sheets readable, whether top secret or on sale for pennies.

Bond hated these periods of vacuum. His eyes, his mind, were barely in focus as he turned the pages of a jaw-breaking dissertation by the Scientific Research Section on the Russian use of cyanide gas, propelled by the cheapest bulb-handled children's water pistol, for assassination. The spray, it seemed, directed at the face, took instantaneous effect. It was recommended for victims from twenty-five years upwards, on ascending stairways or inclines. The verdict would then probably be heart-failure.

The harsh burr of the red telephone sprayed into the room so suddenly that James Bond, his mind elsewhere, reached his hand automatically towards his left arm-pit in self-defence. The edges of his mouth turned down as he recognized the reflex. On the second burr he picked up the receiver.

'Sir?'

'Sir.'

He got up from his chair and picked up his coat. He put on the coat and at the same time put on his mind. He had been dozing in his bunk. Now he had to go up on the bridge. He walked through into the connecting office and resisted the impulse to ruffle up the inviting nape of Mary Goodnight's golden neck.

He told her 'M' and walked out into the close-carpeted corridor and along, between the muted whizz and zing of the Communications Section, of which his Section was a neighbour, to the lift and up to the eighth.

Miss Moneypenny's expression conveyed nothing. It usually conveyed something if she knew something – private excitement, curiosity, or, if Bond was in trouble, encouragement or even anger. Now the smile of welcome showed disinterest.

Bond registered that this was going to be some kind of a routine job, a bore, and he adjusted his entrance through that fateful door accordingly.

There was a visitor – a stranger. He sat on M's left. He only briefly glanced up as Bond came in and took his usual place across the red leather-topped desk.

M said, stiffly, 'Dr Fanshawe, I don't think you've met Commander Bond of my Research Department.'

Bond was used to these euphemisms.

He got up and held out his hand. Dr Fanshawe rose, briefly touched Bond's hand and sat quickly down as if he had touched paws with a Gila monster.

If he looked at Bond, inspected him and took him in as anything more than an anatomical silhouette, Bond thought that Dr Fanshawe's eyes must be fitted with a thousandth of a second shutter. So this was obviously some kind of an expert – a man whose interests lay in facts, things, theories – not in human beings. Bond wished that M had given him some kind of a brief, hadn't got this puckish, rather childishly malign desire to surprise – to spring the jack-in-a-box on his staff. But Bond, remembering his own boredom of ten minutes ago, and putting himself in M's place, had the intuition to realize that M himself might have been subject to the same June heat, the same oppressive vacuum in his duties, and, faced by the unexpected relief of an emergency, a small one perhaps, had decided to extract the maximum effect, the maximum drama, out of it to relieve his own tedium.

The stranger was middle-aged, rosy, well-fed, and clothed rather foppishly in the neo-Edwardian fashion – turned-up cuffs to his dark blue, four-buttoned coat, a pearl pin in a heavy silk cravat, spotless wing collar, cuff links formed of what appeared to be antique coins, pince-nez on a thick black ribbon. Bond summed him up as something literary, a critic perhaps, a bachelor – possibly with homosexual tendencies.

M said, 'Dr Fanshawe is a noted authority on antique jewellery. He is also, though this is confidential, adviser to HM Customs and to the CID on such things. He has in fact been referred to me by our friends at MI5. It is in connection with our Miss Freudenstein.'

Bond raised his eyebrows. Maria Freudenstein was a secret agent working for the Soviet KGB in the heart of the Secret Service. She was in the Communications Department, but in a watertight compartment of it that had been created especially for her, and her duties were confined to operating the Purple Cipher – a cipher which had also been created especially for her. Six times a day she was responsible for encoding and dispatching lengthy SITREPS in this cipher to the CIA in Washington. These messages were the output of Section 100 which was responsible for running double agents. They were an ingenious mixture of true fact, harmless disclosures and an occasional nugget of the grossest misinformation. Maria Freudenstein, who had been known to be a Soviet agent when she was taken into the Service, had been allowed to steal the key to the Purple Cipher with the intention that the Russians should have complete access to these SITREPS – be able to intercept and decipher them – and thus, when appropriate, be fed false information. It was a highly secret operation which needed to be handled with extreme delicacy, but it had now been running smoothly for three years and, if Maria Freudenstein also picked up a certain amount of canteen gossip at Headquarters, that was a necessary risk, and she was not attractive enough to form liaisons which could be a security risk.

M turned to Dr Fanshawe. 'Perhaps, Doctor, you would care to tell Commander Bond what it is all about.'

'Certainly, certainly.' Dr Fanshawe looked quickly at Bond and then away again. He addressed his boots. 'You see, it's like this, er, Commander. You've heard of a man called Fabergé, no doubt. Famous Russian jeweller.'

'Made fabulous Easter eggs for the Czar and Czarina before the revolution.'

'That was indeed one of his specialities. He made many other exquisite pieces of what we may broadly describe as objects of vertu. Today, in the sale rooms, the best examples fetch truly fabulous prices – £50,000 and more. And recently there entered this country the most amazing specimen

288

of all – the so-called Emerald Sphere, a work of supreme art hitherto known only from a sketch by the great man himself. This treasure arrived by registered post from Paris and it was addressed to this woman of whom you know, Miss Maria Freudenstein.'

'Nice little present. Might I ask how you learned of it, Doctor?'

'I am, as your Chief has told you, an adviser to HM Customs and Excise in matters concerning antique jewellery and similar works of art. The declared value of the package was £100,000. This was unusual. There are methods of opening such packages clandestinely. The package was opened – under a Home Office Warrant, of course – and I was called in to examine the contents and give a valuation. I immediately recognized the Emerald Sphere from the account and sketch of it given in Mr Kenneth Snowman's definitive work on Fabergé. I said that the declared price might well be on the low side. But what I found of particular interest was the accompanying document which gave, in Russian and French, the provenance of this priceless object.' Dr Fanshawe gestured towards a photostat of what appeared to be a brief family tree that lay on the desk in front of M. 'That is a copy I had made. Briefly, it states that the Sphere was commissioned by Miss Freudenstein's grandfather directly from Fabergé in 1917 – no doubt as a means of turning some of his roubles into something portable and of great value. On his death in 1918 it passed to his brother and thence, in 1950, to Miss Freudenstein's mother. She, it appears, left Russia as a child and lived in White Russian *émigré* circles in Paris. She never married, but gave birth to this girl, Maria, illegitimately. It seems that she died last year and that some friend or executor, the paper is not signed, has now forwarded the Sphere to its rightful owner, Miss Maria Freudenstein. I had no reason to question this girl, although as you can imagine my interest was most lively, until last month Sotheby's announced that they would auction the piece, described as "the property of a lady", in a week from today. On behalf of the British Museum and, er, other interested parties, I then made discreet inquiries and met the lady, who, with perfect composure, confirmed the rather unlikely story contained in the provenance. It was then that I learned that she worked for the Ministry of Defence and it crossed my rather suspicious mind that it was, it say the least of it, odd that a junior clerk, engaged presumably on sensitive duties, should suddenly receive a gift to the value of £100,000 or more from abroad. I spoke to a senior official in MI5 with whom I have some contact through my work for HM Customs and I was in due course referred to this, er, department.' Dr Fanshawe spread his hands and gave Bond a brief glance, 'And that, Commander, is all I have to tell you.'

M broke in, 'Thank you, Doctor. Just one or two final questions and I won't detain you any further. You have examined this emerald ball thing and you pronounce it genuine?'

Dr Fanshawe ceased gazing at his boots. He looked up and spoke to a point somewhere above M's left shoulder. 'Certainly. So does Mr Snowman of Wartski's, the greatest Fabergé experts and dealers in the world. It is undoubtedly the missing masterpiece of which hitherto Carl Fabergé's sketch was the only record.'

'What about the provenance? What do the experts say about that?'

'It stands up adequately. The greatest Fabergé pieces were nearly always privately commissioned. Miss Freudenstein says that her grandfather was a vastly rich man before the revolution – a porcelain manufacturer. Ninety-nine per cent of all Fabergé's output has found its way abroad. There are only a few pieces left in the Kremlin – described simply as "pre-revolutionary examples of Russian jewellery". The official Soviet view has always been that they are merely capitalist baubles. Officially they despise them as they officially despise their superb collection of French Impressionists.'

'So the Soviet still retain some examples of the work of this man Fabergé. Is it possible that this emerald affair could have lain secreted somewhere in the Kremlin through all these years?'

'Certainly. The Kremlin treasure is vast. No one

knows what they keep hidden. They have only recently put on display what they have wanted to put on display.'

M drew on his pipe. His eyes through the smoke were bland, scarcely interested, 'So that, in theory, there is no reason why this emerald ball should not have been unearthed from the Kremlin, furnished with a faked history to establish ownership, and transferred abroad as a reward to some friend of Russia for services rendered?'

'None at all. It would be an ingenious method of greatly rewarding the beneficiary without the danger of paying large sums into his, or her, bank account.'

'But the final monetary reward would of course depend on the amount realized by the sale of the object – the auction price for instance?'

'Exactly.'

'And what do you expect this object to fetch at Sotheby's?'

'Impossible to say. Wartski's will certainly bid very high. But of course they wouldn't be prepared to tell anyone just how high – either on their own account for stock, so to speak, or acting on behalf of a customer. Much would depend on how high they are forced up by an underbidder. Anyway, not less than £100,000 I'd say.'

'Hm.' M's mouth turned down at the corners. 'Expensive hunk of jewellery.'

Dr Fanshawe was aghast at this bare-faced revelation of M's philistinism. He actually looked

M straight in the face. 'My dear sir,' he expostulated, 'do you consider the stolen Goya, sold at Sotheby's for £140,000, that went to the National Gallery, just an expensive hunk, as you put it, of canvas and paint?'

M said placatingly, 'Forgive me, Dr Fanshawe. I expressed myself clumsily. I have never had the leisure to interest myself in works of art nor, on a naval officer's pay, the money to acquire any. I was just registering my dismay at the runaway prices being fetched at auction these days.'

'You are entitled to your views, sir,' said Dr Fanshawe stuffily.

Bond thought it was time to rescue M. He also wanted to get Dr Fanshawe out of the room so that they could get down to the professional aspects of this odd business. He got to his feet. He said to M, 'Well, sir, I don't think there is anything else I need to know. No doubt this will turn out to be perfectly straightforward (like hell it would!) and just a matter of one of your staff turning out to be a very lucky woman. But it's very kind of Dr Fanshawe to have gone to so much trouble.' He turned to Dr Fanshawe. 'Would you care to have a staff car to take you wherever you're going?'

'No thank you, thank you very much. It will be pleasant to walk across the park.'

Hands were shaken, goodbyes said and Bond showed the doctor out. Bond came back into the room. M had taken a bulky file, stamped with the top secret red star, out of a drawer and was already immersed in it. Bond took his seat again and waited. The room was silent save for the riffling of paper. This also stopped as M extracted a foolscap sheet of blue cardboard used for Confidential Staff Records and carefully read through the forest of close type on both sides.

Finally he slipped it back in the file and looked up. 'Yes,' he said and the blue eyes were bright with interest. 'It fits all right. The girl was born in Paris in 1935. Mother very active in the Resistance during the war. Helped run the Tulip Escape Route and got away with it. After the war, the girl went to the Sorbonne and then got a job in the Embassy, in the Naval Attaché's office, as an interpreter. You know the rest. She was compromised – some unattractive sexual business – by some of her mother's old Resistance friends who by then were working for the NKVD, and from then on she has been working under Control. She applied, no doubt on instruction, for British citizenship. Her clearance from the Embassy and her mother's Resistance record helped her to get that by 1959, and she was then recommended to us by the FO. But it was there that she made her big mistake. She asked for a year's leave before coming to us and was next reported by the Hutchinson network in the Leningrad espionage school. There she presumably received the usual training and we had to decide what to do about her. Section 100 thought up the Purple Cipher operation and you know the rest. She's been working for three years inside headquarters for the KGB and now she's getting her reward – this emerald ball thing worth £100,000. And that's interesting on two counts. First it means that the KGB is totally hooked on the Purple Cipher or they wouldn't be making this fantastic payment. That's good news. It means that we can hot up the material we're passing over – put across some Grade 3 deception material and perhaps even move up to Grade 2. Secondly, it explains something we've never been able to understand – that this girl hasn't hitherto received a single payment for her services. We were worried by that. She had an account at Glyn, Mills that only registered her monthly pay cheque of around £50. And she's consistently lived within it. Now she's getting her pay-off in one large lump sum via this bauble we've been learning about. All very satisfactory.'

M reached for the ashtray made out of a twelve-inch shell base and rapped out his pipe with the air of a man who has done a good afternoon's work.

Bond shifted in his chair. He badly needed a cigarette, but he wouldn't have dreamed of lighting one. He wanted one to help him focus his thoughts. He felt that there were some ragged edges to this problem – one particularly. He said, mildly, 'Have we ever caught up with her local Control, sir? How does she get her instructions?'

'Doesn't need to,' said M impatiently, busying himself with his pipe. 'Once she'd got hold of the

Purple Cipher all she needed to do was hold down her job. Damn it man, she's pouring the stuff into their lap six times a day. What sort of instructions would they need to give her? I doubt if the KGB men in London even know of her existence – perhaps the Resident Director does, but as you know we don't even know who he is. Give my eyes to find out.'

Bond suddenly had a flash of intuition. It was as if a camera had started grinding in his skull, grinding out a length of clear film. He said quietly, 'It might be that this business at Sotheby's could show him to us – show us who he is.'

'What the devil are you talking about, 007? Explain yourself.'

'Well, sir,' Bond's voice was calm with certainty, 'you remember what this Dr Fanshawe said about an underbidder – someone to make these Wartski merchants go to their very top price. If the Russians don't seem to know or care very much about Fabergé, as Dr Fanshawe says, they may have no very clear idea what this thing's really worth. The KGB wouldn't be likely to know about such things anyway. They may imagine it's only worth its break-up value – say ten or twenty thousand pounds for the emerald. That sort of sum would make more sense than the small fortune the girl's going to get if Dr Fanshawe's right. Well, if the Resident Director is the only man who knows about this girl, he will be the only man who knows she's been paid. So he'll be the underbidder. He'll be sent to

Sotheby's and told to push the sale through the roof. I'm certain of it. So we'll be able to identify him and we'll have enough on him to have him sent home. He just won't know what's hit him. Nor will the KGB. If I can go to the sale and bowl him out and we've got the place covered with cameras, and the auction records, we can get the FO to declare him persona non grata inside a week. And Resident Directors don't grow on trees. It may be months before the KGB can appoint a replacement.'

M said, thoughtfully, 'Perhaps you've got something there.' He swivelled his chair round and gazed out of the big window towards the jagged skyline of London. Finally he said, over his shoulder, 'All right, 007. Go and see the Chief of Staff and set the machinery up. I'll square things with Five. It's their territory, but it's our bird. There won't be any trouble. But don't go and get carried away and bid for this bit of rubbish yourself. I haven't got the money to spare.'

Bond said, 'No, sir.' He got to his feet and went quickly out of the room. He thought he had been very clever and he wanted to see if he had. He didn't want M to change his mind.

Wartski has a modest, ultra-modern frontage at 138 Regent Street. The window, with a restrained show of modern and antique jewellery, gave no hint that these were the greatest Fabergé-dealers in the world. The interior – grey carpet, walls panelled in sycamore, a few unpretentious vitrines – held none of the excitement of Cartier's, Boucheron or Van Cleef, but the group of framed Royal Warrants from Queen Mary, the Queen Mother, the Queen, King Paul of Greece and the unlikely King Frederick IX of Denmark, suggested that this was no ordinary jeweller.

James Bond asked for Mr Kenneth Snowman. A good-looking, very well-dressed man of about forty rose from a group of men sitting with their heads together at the back of the room and came forward.

Bond said quietly, 'I'm from the CID. Can we have a talk? Perhaps you'd like to check my credentials first. My name's James Bond. But you'll have to go direct to Sir Ronald Vallance or his PA. I'm not directly on the strength at Scotland Yard. Sort of liaison job.'

The intelligent, observant eyes didn't appear even to look him over. The man smiled. 'Come on downstairs. Just having a talk with some American friends – sort of correspondents really. From "Old Russia" on Fifth Avenue.'

'I know the place,' said Bond. 'Full of rich-looking icons and so on. Not far from the Pierre.'

'That's right.' Mr Snowman seemed even more reassured. He led the way down a narrow, thickly carpeted stairway into a large and glittering show-room which was obviously the real treasure house of the shop. Gold and diamonds and cut stones winked from lit cases round the walls.

298

'Have a seat. Cigarette?'

Bond took one of his own. 'It's about this Fabergé piece that's coming up at Sotheby's tomorrow – this Emerald Sphere.'

'Ah, yes.' Mr Snowman's clear brow furrowed anxiously. 'No trouble about it I hope?'

'Not from your point of view. But we're very interested in the actual sale. We know about the owner, Miss Freudenstein. We think there may be an attempt to raise the bidding artificially. We're interested in the underbidder – assuming, that is, that your firm will be leading the field, so to speak.'

'Well, er, yes,' said Mr Snowman with rather careful candour. 'We're certainly going to go after it. But it'll sell for a huge price. Between you and me, we believe the V and A are going to bid, and probably the Metropolitan. But is it some crook you're after? If so you needn't worry. This is out of their class.'

Bond said, 'No. We're not looking for a crook.' He wondered how far to go with this man. Because people are very careful with the secrets of their own business doesn't mean that they'll be careful with the secrets of yours. Bond picked up a wood and ivory plaque that lay on the table. It said:

It is naught, it is naught, saith the buyer.
But when he is gone his way, he boasteth.
—Proverbs XX, 14

299

Bond was amused. He said so. 'You can read the whole history of the bazaar, of the dealer and the customer, behind that quotation,' he said. He looked Mr Snowman straight in the eyes. 'I need that sort of nose, that sort of intuition in this case. Will you give me a hand?'

'Certainly. If you'll tell me how I can help.' He waved a hand. 'If it's secrets you're worried about, please don't worry. Jewellers are used to them. Scotland Yard will probably give my firm a clean bill in that respect. Heaven knows we've had enough to do with them over the years.'

'And if I told you that I'm from the Ministry of Defence?'

'Same thing,' said Mr Snowman. 'You can naturally rely absolutely on my discretion!'

Bond made up his mind. 'All right. Well, all this comes under the Official Secrets Act, of course. We suspect that the underbidder, presumably to you, will be a Soviet Agent. My job is to establish his identity. Can't tell you any more, I'm afraid. And you don't actually need to know any more. All I want is to go with you to Sotheby's tomorrow night and for you to help me spot the man. No medals, I'm afraid, but we'd be extremely grateful.'

Mr Kenneth Snowman's eyes glinted with enthusiasm. 'Of course. Delighted to help in any way. But,' he looked doubtful, 'you know it's not necessarily going to be all that easy. Peter Wilson, the head of Sotheby's, who'll be taking the sale,

300

would be the only person who could tell us for sure – that is, if the bidder wants to stay secret. There are dozens of ways of bidding without making any movement at all. But if the bidder fixes his method, his code so to speak, with Peter Wilson before the sale, Peter wouldn't think of letting anyone in on the code. It would give the bidder's game away to reveal his limit. And that's a close secret, as you can imagine, in the rooms. And a thousand times not if you come with me. I shall probably be setting the pace. I already know how far I'm going to go – for a client by the way – but it would make my job vastly easier if I could tell how far the underbidder's going to go. As it is, what you've told me has been a great help. I shall warn my man to put his sights even higher. If this chap of yours has got a strong nerve, he may push me very hard indeed. And there will be others in the field of course. It sounds as if this is going to be quite a night. They're putting it on television and asking all the millionaires and dukes and duchesses for the sort of gala performance Sotheby's do rather well. Wonderful publicity of course. By jove, if they knew there was cloak-and-dagger stuff mixed up with the sale, there'd be a riot! Now then, is there anything else to go into? Just spot this man and that's all?'

'That's all. How much do you think this thing will go for?'

Mr Snowman tapped his teeth with a gold pencil. 'Well now, you see that's where I have to keep quiet. I know how high I'm going to go, but that's my client's secret.' He paused and looked thoughtful, 'Let's say that if it goes for less than £100,000 we'll be surprised.'

'I see,' said Bond. 'Now then, how do I get into the sale?'

Mr Snowman produced an elegant alligator-skin notecase and extracted two engraved bits of pasteboard. He handed one over. 'That's my wife's. I'll get her one somewhere else in the rooms. B5 – well placed in the centre front. I'm B6.'

Bond took the ticket. It said:

Sotheby & Co.

Sale of

A Casket of Magnificent Jewels
and
A Unique Object of Vertu by Carl Fabergé

The Property of a Lady
Admit one to the Main Sale Room
Tuesday, 20 June, at 9.30 p.m. precisely

ENTRANCE IN ST GEORGE STREET

'It's not the old Georgian entrance in Bond Street,' commented Mr Snowman. 'They have an awning and red carpet out from their back door now that Bond Street's one-way. Now,' he got up from his chair, 'would you care to see some Fabergé? We've got some pieces here my father bought from the Kremlin around 1927. It'll give you some idea what all the fuss is about, though of course the Emerald Sphere's incomparably finer than anything I can show you by Fabergé apart from the Imperial Easter Eggs.'

Later, dazzled by the diamonds, the multi-coloured gold, the silken sheen of translucent enamels, James Bond walked up and out of the Aladdin's Cave under Regent Street and went off to spend the rest of the day in drab offices around Whitehall planning drearily minute arrangements for the identification and photographing of a man in a crowded room who did not yet possess a face or an identity but who was certainly the top Soviet spy in London.

Through the next day, Bond's excitement mounted. He found an excuse to go into the Communications Section and wander into the little room where Miss Maria Freudenstein and two assistants were working the cipher machines that handled the Purple Cipher dispatches. He picked up an *en clair* file – he had freedom of access to most material at headquarters – and ran his eye down the carefully edited paragraphs that, in half an hour or so, would be spiked, unread, by some Junior CIA clerk in Washington and, in Moscow, be handed, with reverence, to a top-ranking officer of the KGB. He joked with the two junior girls, but Maria Freudenstein only looked up from her machine to give him a polite smile and Bond's skin crawled minutely at this proximity to treachery and at the black and deadly secret locked up beneath the frilly white blouse. She was an unattractive girl with a pale, rather pimply skin, black hair and a vaguely unwashed appearance. Such a girl would be unloved, make few friends, have chips on her shoulder – more particularly in view of her illegitimacy – and a grouse against society. Perhaps her only pleasure in life was the triumphant secret she harboured in that flattish bosom – the knowledge that she was cleverer than all those around her, that she was, every day, hitting back against the world – the world that despised, or just ignored her, because of her plainness – with all her might. One day they'd be sorry! It was a common neurotic pattern – the revenge of the ugly duckling on society.

Bond wandered off down the corridor to his own office. By tonight that girl would have made a fortune, been paid her thirty pieces of silver a thousandfold. Perhaps the money would change her character, bring her happiness. She would be able to afford the best beauty specialists, the best clothes, a pretty flat. But M had said he was now going to hot up the Purple Cipher Operation, try a more dangerous level of deception. This would be dicey work. One false step, one incautious lie, an ascertainable falsehood in a message, and KGB

304

would smell a rat. One more, and they would know they were being hoaxed and probably had been ignominiously hoaxed for three years. Such a shameful revelation would bring quick revenge. It would be assumed that Maria Freudenstein had been acting as a double agent, working for the British as well as the Russians. She would inevitably and quickly be liquidated – perhaps with a cyanide pistol Bond had been reading about only the day before.

James Bond, looking out of the window across the trees in Regent's Park, shrugged. Thank God it was none of his business. The girl's fate wasn't in his hands. She was caught in the grimy machine of espionage and she would be lucky if she lived to spend a tenth of the fortune she was going to gain in a few hours in the auction rooms.

There was a line of cars and taxis blocking George Street behind Sotheby's. Bond paid off his taxi and joined the crowd filtering under the awning and up the steps. He was handed a catalogue by the uniformed commissionaire who inspected his ticket, and went up the broad stairs with the fashionable, excited crowd and along a gallery and into the main auction room that was already thronged. He found his seat next to Mr Snowman, who was writing figures on a pad on his knee, and looked round him.

The lofty room was perhaps as large as a tennis court. It had the look and the smell of age and the two large chandeliers, to fit in with the period, blazed warmly in contrast to the strip lighting along the vaulted ceiling whose glass roof was partly obscured by a blind, still half-drawn against the sun that would have been blazing down on the afternoon's sale. Miscellaneous pictures and tapestries hung on the olive green walls and batteries of television and other cameras (amongst them the MI5 cameraman with a press pass from the *Sunday Times*) were clustered with their handlers on a platform built out from the middle of a giant tapestried hunting scene. There were perhaps a hundred dealers and spectators sitting attentively on small gilt chairs. All eyes were focused on the slim, good-looking auctioneer talking quietly from the raised wooden pulpit. He was dressed in an immaculate dinner jacket with a red carnation in the buttonhole. He spoke unemphatically and without gestures.

'Fifteen thousand pounds. And sixteen,' a pause. A glance at someone in the front row. 'Against you, sir.' The flick of a catalogue being raised. 'Seventeen thousand pounds I am bid. Eighteen. Nineteen. I am bid twenty thousand pounds.' And so the quiet voice went, calmly, unhurriedly on while down among the audience the equally impassive bidders signalled their responses to the litany.

'What is he selling?' asked Bond, opening his catalogue.

'Lot 40,' said Mr Snowman. 'That diamond

rivière the porter's holding on the black velvet tray. It'll probably go for about twenty-five. An Italian is bidding against a couple of Frenchmen. Otherwise they'd have got it for twenty. I only went to fifteen. Liked to have got it. Wonderful stones. But there it is.'

Sure enough, the price stuck at twenty-five thousand and the hammer, held by its head and not by its handle, came down with soft authority. 'Yours, sir,' said Mr Peter Wilson and a sales clerk hurried down the aisle to confirm the identity of the bidder.

'I'm disappointed,' said Bond.

Mr Snowman looked up from his catalogue, 'Why is that?'

'I've never been to an auction before and I always thought the auctioneer banged his gavel three times and said going, going, gone, so as to give the bidders a last chance.'

Mr Snowman laughed. 'You might still find that operating in the Shires or in Ireland, but it hasn't been the fashion at London sale rooms since I've been attending them.'

'Pity. It adds to the drama.'

'You'll get plenty of that in a minute. This is the last lot before the curtain goes up.'

One of the porters had reverently uncoiled a glittering mass of rubies and diamonds on his black velvet tray. Bond looked at the catalogue. It said 'Lot 41' which the luscious prose described as:

A PAIR OF FINE AND IMPORTANT RUBY AND DIAMOND BRACELETS, the front of each in the form of an elliptical cluster composed of one larger and two smaller rubies within a border of cushion-shaped diamonds, the sides and back formed of simpler clusters alternating with diamond openwork scroll motifs springing from single-stone ruby centres millegriffe-set in gold, running between chains of rubies and diamonds linked alternately, the clasp also in the form of an elliptical cluster.

* According to family tradition, this lot was formerly the property of Mrs Fitzherbert (1756–1837) whose marriage to the Prince of Wales afterwards Geo. IV was definitely established when in 1905 a sealed packet deposited at Coutts Bank in 1833 and opened by Royal permission disclosed the marriage certificate and other conclusive proofs.

These bracelets were probably given by Mrs Fitzherbert to her niece, who was described by the Duke of Orleans as 'the prettiest girl in England'.

While the bidding progressed, Bond slipped out of his seat and went down the aisle to the back of the room where the overflow audience spread out into the New Gallery and the Entrance Hall to watch the sale on closed circuit television. He casually inspected the crowd, seeking any face he could recognize from the 200 members of the Soviet embassy staff whose photographs, clandestinely obtained, he had been studying during the past days. But amidst an audience that defied classification – a mixture of dealers, amateur collectors and what could be broadly classified as rich pleasure-seekers – was not a feature, let alone a face, that he could recognize except from the gossip columns. One or two sallow faces might have been Russian, but equally they might have belonged to half a dozen European races. There was a scattering of dark glasses, but dark glasses are no longer a disguise. Bond went back to his seat. Presumably the man would have to divulge himself when the bidding began.

'Fourteen thousand I am bid. And fifteen. Fifteen thousand.' The hammer came down. 'Yours, sir.'

There was a hum of excitement and a fluttering of catalogues. Mr Snowman wiped his forehead with a white silk handkerchief. He turned to Bond, 'Now I'm afraid you are more or less on your own. I've got to pay attention to the bidding and anyway for some unknown reason it's considered bad form to look over one's shoulder to see who's bidding against you – if you're in the trade that's to say – so I'll only be able to spot him if he's somewhere up front here, and I'm afraid that's unlikely. Pretty well all dealers, but you can stare around as much as you like. What you've got to do is to watch Peter Wilson's eyes and then try and see who he's looking at, or who's looking at him. If you can spot the man, which may be quite difficult, note any movement he makes, even the very smallest. Whatever the man does – scratching his head, pulling at the lobe of his ear or whatever, will be a code he's arranged with Peter Wilson. I'm afraid he won't do anything obvious like raising his catalogue. Do you get me? And don't forget that he may make absolutely no movement at all until right at the end when he's pushed me as far as he thinks I'll go, then he'll want to sign off. Mark you,' Mr Snowman smiled, 'when we get to the last lap I'll put plenty of heat on him and try and make him show his hand. That's assuming of course that we are the only two bidders left in.' He looked enigmatic. 'And I think you can take it that we shall be.'

From the man's certainty, James Bond felt pretty sure that Mr Snowman had been given instructions to get the Emerald Sphere at any cost.

A sudden hush fell as a tall pedestal draped in black velvet was brought in with ceremony and positioned in front of the auctioneer's rostrum. Then a handsome oval case of what looked like white velvet was placed on top of the pedestal and, with reverence, an elderly porter in grey uniform with wine red sleeves, collar and back belt, unlocked it and lifted out Lot 42, placed it on the black velvet and removed the case. The cricket ball of polished emerald on its exquisite base glowed with a supernatural green fire and the jewels on its surface and on the opalescent meridian winked their various colours. There was a gasp of admiration from the audience and even the clerks and experts behind the rostrum and sitting at the tall counting-house desk beside the auctioneer, accustomed to the Crown jewels of Europe parading before their eyes, leaned forward to get a better look.

James Bond turned to his catalogue. There it was, in heavy type and in prose as stickily luscious as a butter-scotch sundae:

THE TERRESTRIAL GLOBE DESIGNED IN 1917 BY CARL FABERGÉ FOR A RUSSIAN GENTLEMAN AND NOW THE PROPERTY OF HIS GRANDDAUGHTER 42 A VERY IMPORTANT FABERGÉ TERRESTRIAL GLOBE.

A sphere carved from an extraordinarily large piece of Siberian emerald matrix weighing approximately one thousand three hundred carats and of a superb colour and vivid translucence, represents a terrestrial globe supported upon an elaborate *rocaille* scroll mount finely chased in *quatre-couleur* gold and set with a profusion of rose-diamonds and small emeralds of intense colour, to form a table-clock.

Around this mount six gold *putti* disport themselves among cloud-forms which are naturalistically rendered in carved rock-crystal finished matt and veined with fine lines of tiny rose-diamonds.

The Globe itself, the surface of which is meticulously engraved with a map of the world with the principal cities indicated by brilliant diamonds embedded within gold collets, rotates mechanically on an axis controlled by a small clock-movement, by *G. Moser*, signed, which is concealed in the base, and is girdled by a fixed gold belt enamelled opalescent oyster along a reserved path in *champlevé* technique over a moiré *guillochage* with painted Roman numerals in pale sepia enamel serving as the dial of the clock, and a single triangular pigeon-blood Burma ruby of about five carats set into the surface of the orb, pointing the hour.

Height: 7½ in. *Workmaster, Henrik Wigström.* In the original double-opening white velvet, satin-lined, ovi-form case with the gold key fitted in the base.

★ The theme of this magnificent sphere is one that had inspired Fabergé some fifteen years earlier, as evidenced in the miniature terrestrial globe which forms part of the Royal Collection at Sandringham. (See plate 280 in *The Art of Carl Fabergé*, by A. Kenneth Snowman.)

After a brief and searching glance round the room, Mr Wilson banged his hammer softly. 'Lot 42 – an object of vertu by Carl Fabergé.' A pause. 'Twenty thousand pounds I am bid.'

Mr Snowman whispered to Bond, 'That means he's probably got a bid of at least fifty. This is simply to get things moving.'

Catalogues fluttered. 'And thirty, forty, fifty thousand pounds I am bid. And sixty, seventy, and eighty thousand pounds. And ninety.' A pause and then: 'One hundred thousand pounds I am bid.'

There was a rattle of applause round the room. The cameras had swivelled to a youngish man, one of three on a raised platform to the left of the auctioneer who were speaking softly into telephones. Mr Snowman commented, 'That's one of Sotheby's young men. He'll be on an open line to America. I should think that's the Metropolitan bidding, but it might be anybody. Now it's time for me to get to work.' Mr Snowman flicked up his rolled catalogue.

'And ten,' said the auctioneer. The man spoke into his telephone and nodded. 'And twenty.'

Again a flick from Mr Snowman.

'And thirty.'

The man on the telephone seemed to be speaking rather more words than before into his mouthpiece – perhaps giving his estimate of how much further the price was likely to go. He gave a slight shake of his head in the direction of the auctioneer and Peter Wilson looked away from him and round the room.

'One hundred and thirty thousand pounds I am bid,' he repeated quietly.

Mr Snowman said, softly, to Bond, 'Now you'd better watch out. America seems to have signed off. It's time for your man to start pushing me.'

James Bond slid out of his place and went and stood amongst a group of reporters in a corner to the left of the rostrum. Peter Wilson's eyes were directed towards the far right hand corner of the room. Bond could detect no movement, but the auctioneer announced, 'And forty thousand pounds.' He looked down at Mr Snowman. After a long pause Mr Snowman raised five fingers. Bond guessed that this was part of his process of putting the heat on. He was showing reluctance, hinting that he was near the end of his tether.

'One hundred and forty-five thousand.' Again the piercing glance towards the back of the room. Again no movement. But again some signal had been exchanged. 'One hundred and fifty thousand pounds.'

There was a buzz of comment and some desultory clapping. This time Mr Snowman's reaction was even slower and the auctioneer twice repeated the last bid. Finally he looked directly at Mr Snowman. 'Against you, sir.' At last Mr Snowman raised five fingers.

'One hundred and fifty-five thousand pounds.'

James Bond was beginning to sweat. He had got

absolutely nowhere and the bidding must surely be coming to an end. The auctioneer repeated the bid.

And now there was the tiniest movement. At the back of the room, a chunky-looking man in a dark suit reached up and unobtrusively took off his dark glasses. It was a smooth, nondescript face – the sort of face that might belong to a bank manager, a member of Lloyd's, or a doctor. This must have been the prearranged code with the auctioneer. So long as the man wore his dark glasses he would raise in tens of thousands. When he took them off, he had quit.

Bond shot a quick glance towards the bank of cameramen. Yes, the MI5 photographer was on his toes. He had also seen the movement. He lifted his camera deliberately and there was the quick glare of a flash. Bond got back to his seat and whispered to Snowman, 'Got him. Be in touch with you tomorrow. Thanks a lot.' Mr Snowman only nodded. His eyes remained glued on the auctioneer.

Bond slipped out of his place and walked swiftly down the aisle as the auctioneer said for the third time, 'One hundred and fifty-five thousand pounds I am bid,' and then softly brought down his hammer. 'Yours, sir.'

Bond got to the back of the room before the audience had risen, applauding, to its feet. His quarry was hemmed in amongst the gilt chairs. He had now put on his dark glasses again and Bond put on a pair of his own. He contrived to slip into the crowd and get behind the man as the chattering crowd streamed down the stairs. The hair grew low down on the back of the man's rather squat neck and the lobes of his ears were pinched in close to his head. He had a slight hump, perhaps only a bone deformation, high up on his back. Bond suddenly remembered. This was Piotr Malinowski, with the official title on the Embassy staff of 'Agricultural Attaché'. So!

Outside, the man began walking swiftly towards Conduit Street. James Bond got unhurriedly into a taxi with its engine running and its flag down. He said to the driver. 'That's him. Take it easy.'

'Yes, sir,' said the MI5 driver, pulling away from the curb.

The man picked up a taxi in Bond Street. The tail in the mixed evening traffic was easy. Bond's satisfaction mounted as the Russian's taxi turned up north of the Park and along Bayswater. It was just a question whether he would turn down the private entrance into Kensington Palace Gardens, where the first mansion on the left is the massive building of the Soviet Embassy. If he did, that would clinch matters. The two patrolling policemen, the usual Embassy guards, had been specially picked that night. It was their job just to confirm that the occupant of the leading taxi actually entered the Soviet Embassy.

Then, with the Secret Service evidence and the evidence of Bond and of the MI5 cameraman, there would be enough for the Foreign Office to declare Comrade Piotr Malinowski persona non grata on the grounds of espionage activity and send him packing. In the grim chess game that is secret service work, the Russians would have lost a queen. It would have been a very satisfactory visit to the auction rooms.

The leading taxi *did* turn in through the big iron gates.

Bond smiled with grim satisfaction. He leant forward.

'Thanks, driver. Headquarters please.'

CHAPTER 8

THE LIVING DAYLIGHTS

James Bond lay at the five-hundred-yard firing point of the famous Century Range at Bisley. The white peg in the grass beside him said 4.4 and the same number was repeated high up on the distant butt above the single six-foot-square target that, to the human eye and in the late summer dusk, looked no larger than a postage stamp. But Bond's lens, an infra-red Sniperscope fixed above his rifle, covered the whole canvas. He could even clearly distinguish the pale-blue and beige colours into which the target was divided, and the six-inch semicircular bull looked as big as the half moon that was already beginning to show low down in the darkening sky above the distant crest of Chobham Ridges.

James Bond's last shot had been an inner left – not good enough. He took another glance at the yellow-and-blue wind flags. They were streaming across range from the east rather more stiffly than when he had begun his shoot half an hour before, and he set two clicks more to the right on the wind gauge and traversed the cross-wires on the Sniperscope back to the point of

318

aim. Then he settled himself, put his trigger finger gently inside the guard and on to the curve of the trigger, shallowed his breathing and very, very softly squeezed.

The vicious crack of the shot boomed across the empty range. The target disappeared below ground and at once the 'dummy' came up in its place. Yes, the black panel was in the bottom right-hand corner this time, not in the bottom left: a bull.

'Good,' said the voice of the Chief Range Officer from behind and above him. 'Stay with it.'

The target was already up again and Bond put his cheek back to its warm patch on the chunky wooden stock and his eye to the rubber eyepiece of the 'scope. He wiped his gun hand down the side of his trousers and took the pistol grip that jutted sharply down below the trigger guard. He splayed his legs an inch more. Now there were to be five rounds rapid. It would be interesting to see if that would produce 'fade'. He guessed not. This extraordinary weapon the Armourer had somehow got his hands on gave one the feeling that a standing man at a mile would be easy meat. It was mostly a .308 calibre International Experimental Target rifle built by Winchester to help American marksmen at World Championships, and it had the usual gadgets of super-accurate target weapons – a curled aluminium 'hand' at the back of the butt that extended under the armpit and held the stock firmly into the shoulder, and an adjustable pinion below the rifle's centre of gravity to allow the stock to be 'nailed' into its grooved wooden rest. The Armourer had had the usual single-shot bolt action replaced by a five-shot magazine, and he had assured Bond that if he would allow only two seconds between shots to steady the weapon there would be no fade even at five hundred yards. For the job that Bond had to do, he guessed that two seconds might be a dangerous loss of time if he missed with his first shot. Anyway, M had said that the range would be not more than three hundred yards. Bond would cut it down to one second – almost continuous fire.

'Ready?'

'Yes.'

'I'll give you a count-down from five. Now! Five, four, three, two, one. Fire!'

The ground shuddered slightly and the air sang as the five whirling scraps of cupro-nickel spat off into the dusk. The target went down and quickly rose again decorated with four small white discs closely grouped on the bull. There was no fifth disc – not even a black one to show an inner or an outer.

'The last round was low,' said the Range Officer lowering his night-glasses. 'Thanks for the contribution. We sift the sand on those butts at the end of every year. Never get less than fifteen tons of good lead and copper scrap out of them. Good money.'

Bond had got to his feet. Corporal Menzies from the Armourers' section appeared from the pavilion of the Gun Club and knelt down to dismantle the

Winchester and its rest. He looked up at Bond. He said with a hint of criticism, 'You were taking it a bit fast, sir. Last round was bound to jump wide.'

'I know, Corporal. I wanted to see how fast I *could* take it. I'm not blaming the weapon. It's the hell of a fine job. Please tell the Armourer so from me. Now I'd better get moving. You're finding your own way back to London, aren't you?'

'Yes. Good night, sir.'

The Chief Range Officer handed Bond a record of his shoot – two sighting shots and then ten rounds at each hundred yards up to five hundred. 'Damned good firing with this visibility. You ought to come back next year and have a bash at the Queen's Prize. It's open to all comers nowadays – British Commonwealth, that is.'

'Thanks. Trouble is, I'm not all that much in England. And thanks for spotting for me.' Bond glanced at the distant Clock Tower. On either side, the red danger flag and the red signal drum were coming down to show that firing had ceased. The hands stood at nine fifteen. 'I'd like to have bought you a drink, but I've got an appointment in London. Can we hold it over until that Queen's Prize you were talking about?'

The Range Officer nodded noncommittally. He had been looking forward to finding out more about this man who had appeared out of the blue after a flurry of signals from the Ministry of Defence and had then proceeded to score well over ninety

321

per cent at all distances, and that after the range was closed for the night and visibility was poor to bad. And why had he, who only officiated at the annual July meeting, been ordered to be present? And why had he been told to see that Bond had a six-inch bull at 500 instead of the regulation fifteen-inch? And why this flummery with the danger flag and signal drum that were only used on ceremonial occasions? To put pressure on the man? To give an edge of urgency to the shoot? Bond. Commander James Bond. The NRA would surely have a record of anyone who could shoot like that. He'd remember to give them a call. Funny time to have an appointment in London. Probably a girl. The Range Officer's undistinguished face assumed a disgruntled expression. Sort of fellow who got all the girls he wanted.

The two men walked through the handsome façade of Club Row behind the range to Bond's car that stood opposite the bullet-pitted iron reproduction of Landseer's famous 'Running Deer'. 'Nice-looking job,' commented the Range Officer. 'Never seen a body like that on a Continental. Have it made specially?'

'Yes. The Sports Saloons are really only two-seaters. And damned little luggage space. So I got Mulliner's to make it into a real two-seater with plenty of boot. Selfish car, I'm afraid. Well, good night. And thanks again.' The exhaust boomed healthily and the back wheels briefly spat gravel.

The Chief Range Officer watched the ruby lights

vanish up King's Avenue towards the London road. He turned on his heel and went to find Corporal Menzies on a search for information that was to prove fruitless. The corporal remained as wooden as the big mahogany box he was in the process of loading into a khaki Land-Rover without military symbols. The Range Officer was a major. He tried pulling his rank without success. The Land-Rover hammered away in Bond's wake. The major walked moodily off to the offices of the National Rifle Association to try and find out what he wanted in the library under 'Bond, J.'.

James Bond's appointment was not with a girl. It was with a BEA flight to Hanover and Berlin. As he bit off the miles to London Airport, pushing the big car hard so as to have plenty of time for a drink, three drinks, before the take-off, only part of his mind was on the road. The rest was re-examining, for the umpteenth time, the sequence that was now leading him to an appointment with an aeroplane. But only an interim appointment. His final rendezvous on one of the next three nights in Berlin was with a man. He had to see this man and infallibly shoot him dead.

When, at around two thirty that afternoon, James Bond had gone in through the double-padded doors and had sat down opposite the turned-away profile on the other side of the big desk, he had sensed trouble. There was no greeting. M's head was sunk into his stiff turned-down collar in a

Churchillian pose of gloomy reflection, and there was a droop of bitterness at the corners of his lips. He swivelled his chair round to face Bond, gave him an appraising glance as if, Bond thought, to see that his tie was straight and his hair properly brushed, and then began speaking, fast, clipping off his sentences as if he wanted to be rid of what he was saying, and of Bond, as quickly as possible.

'Number 272. He's a good man. You won't have come across him. Simple reason that he's been holed up in Novaya Zemlya since the war. Now he's trying to get out – loaded with stuff. Atomic and rockets. And their plan for a whole new series of tests. For 1961. To put the heat on the West. Something to do with Berlin. Don't quite get the picture but the FO say if it's true it's terrific. Makes nonsense of the Geneva Conference and all this blether about nuclear disarmament the Communist bloc are putting out. He's got as far as East Berlin. But he's got practically the whole of the KGB on his tail – and the East German security forces of course. He's holed up somewhere in the city and he got one message over to us – that he'd be coming across between six and seven pm on one of the next three nights – tomorrow, next day, or the day after. He gave the crossing point. Trouble is,' the downward curve of M's lips became even more bitter, 'the courier he used was a double. Station WB bowled him out yesterday. Quite by chance. Had a lucky break with one of the KGB codes. The courier'll be flown out for trial, of course.

But that won't help. The KGB know that 272 will be making a run for it. They know when. They know where. They know just as much as we do and no more. Now, the code we cracked was a one-day-only setting on their machines. But we got the whole of that day's traffic and that was good enough. They plan to shoot him on the run. At this street crossing between East and West Berlin he gave us in his message. They're mounting quite an operation – operation "Extase" they call it. Put their best sniper on the job. All we know about him is that his code name is the Russian for "Trigger". Station WB guess he's the same man they've used before for sniper work. Long-range stuff across the frontier. He's going to be guarding this crossing every night and his job is to get 272. Of course they'd obviously prefer to do a smoother job with machine-guns and what have you. But it's quiet in Berlin at the moment and apparently the word is it's got to stay so. Anyway,' M shrugged, 'they've got confidence in this "Trigger" operator and that's the way it's going to be!'

'Where do I come in, sir?' James Bond had guessed the answer, guessed why M was showing his dislike of the whole business. This was going to be dirty work and Bond, because he belonged to the Double-O Section, had been chosen for it. Perversely, Bond wanted to force M to put it in black and white. This was going to be bad news, dirty news, and he didn't want to hear it from one of the Section officers, or even from the Chief of

Staff. This was to be murder. All right. Let M bloody well say so.

'Where do you come in, 007?' M looked coldly across the desk. 'You know where you come in. You've got to kill this sniper. And you've got to kill him before he gets 272. That's all. Is that understood?' The clear blue eyes remained cold as ice. But Bond knew that they remained so only with an effort of will. M didn't like sending any man to a killing. But, when it had to be done, he always put on this fierce, cold act of command. Bond knew why. It was to take some of the pressure, some of the guilt, off the killer's shoulders.

So now Bond, who knew these things, decided to make it easy and quick for M. He got to his feet. 'That's all right, sir. I suppose the Chief of Staff has got all the gen. I'd better go and put in some practice. It wouldn't do to miss.' He walked to the door.

M said quietly, 'Sorry to have to hand this to you. Nasty job. But it's got to be done well.'

'I'll do my best, sir.' James Bond walked out and closed the door behind him. He didn't like the job, but on the whole he'd rather have it himself than have the responsibility of ordering someone else to go and do it.

The Chief of Staff had been only a shade more sympathetic. 'Sorry you've bought this one, James,' he had said. 'But Tanqueray was definite that he hadn't got anyone good enough on his Station, and this isn't the sort of job you can ask a regular soldier to do. Plenty of top marksmen in the BAOR, but a live target needs another kind of nerve. Anyway, I've been on to Bisley and fixed a shoot for you tonight at eight fifteen when the ranges will be closed. Visibility should be about the same as you'll be getting in Berlin around an hour earlier. The Armourer's got the gun – a real target job, and he's sending it down with one of his men. You'll find your own way. Then you're booked on a midnight BEA charter flight to Berlin. Take a taxi to this address.' He handed Bond a piece of paper. 'Go up to the fourth floor and you'll find Tanqueray's Number 2 waiting for you. Then I'm afraid you'll just have to sit it out for the next three days.'

'How about the gun? Am I supposed to take it through the German customs in a golf bag or something?'

The Chief of Staff hadn't been amused. 'It'll go over in the FO bag. You'll have it by tomorrow midday.' He had reached for a signal pad. 'Well, you'd better get cracking. I'll just let Tanqueray know everything's fixed.'

James Bond glanced down at the dim blue face of the dash-board clock. Ten fifteen. With any luck by this time tomorrow it would all be finished. After all, it was the life of this man 'Trigger' against the life of 272. It wasn't *exactly* murder. Pretty near it, though. He gave a vicious blast on his triple windhorns at an inoffensive family saloon, took the roundabout in a quite unnecessary dry skid, wrenched the wheel harshly to correct it and pointed the nose of the Bentley towards the distant glow that was London Airport.

The ugly six-storey building at the corner of Kochstrasse and the Wilhelmstrasse was the only one standing in a waste of empty bombed space. Bond paid off his taxi and got a brief impression of waist-high weeds and half-tidied rubble walls stretching away to a big deserted crossroads lit by a central cluster of yellowish arc lamps, before he pushed the bell for the fourth floor and at once heard the click of the door-opener. The door closed itself behind him and he walked over the uncarpeted cement floor to the old-fashioned lift. The smell of cabbage, cheap cigar smoke and stale sweat reminded him of other apartment houses in Germany and Central Europe. Even the sigh and faint squeal of the slow lift were part of a hundred assignments when he had been fired off by M, like a projectile, at some distant target where a problem waited for his coming, waited to be solved by him. At least this time the reception committee was on his side. This time there was nothing to fear at the top of the stairs.

Number 2 of Secret Service Station WB was a lean, tense man in his early forties. He wore the uniform of his profession – well-cut, well-used, lightweight tweeds in a dark-green herringbone, a soft white silk shirt and an old school tie – in his case Wykehamist. At the sight of the tie, and while they exchanged conventional greetings in the small musty lobby of the apartment, Bond's spirits, already low, sank another degree. He knew the type: backbone of the Civil Service; over-crammed and under-loved at Winchester; a good second in PPE at Oxford; the war, staff jobs he would have done meticulously; perhaps an OBE; Allied Control Commission in Germany where he had been recruited into the I Branch and thence – because he was the ideal staff man and A1 with Security and because he thought he would find life, drama, romance, the things he had never had – into the Secret Service. A sober, careful man had been needed to chaperon Bond on this ugly business. Captain Paul Sender, late of the Welsh Guards, had been the obvious choice. He had bought it. Now, like a good Wykehamist, he concealed his distaste for the job beneath careful, trite conversation as he showed Bond the layout of the apartment and the arrangements that had been made for the executioner's preparedness and, to a modest extent, his comfort.

The flat consisted of a large double bedroom, a bathroom, and a kitchen containing tinned food, milk, butter, eggs, tea, bacon, bread and one bottle of Dimple Haig. The only odd feature in the bedroom was that one of the double beds was angled up against the curtains covering the single broad window and was piled high with three mattresses below the bedclothes.

Captain Sender said, 'Care to have a look at the field of fire? Then I can explain what the other side have in mind.'

Bond was tired. He didn't particularly want to go to sleep with the picture of the battlefield on his mind. He said, 'That'd be fine.'

Captain Sender switched off the lights. Chinks from the street light at the intersection showed round the curtains. 'Don't want to draw the curtains,' said Captain Sender. 'Unlikely, but they may be on the look-out for a covering party for 272. If you'd just lie on the bed and get your head under the curtains, I'll brief you about what you'll be looking at. Look to the left.'

It was a sash window and the bottom half was open. The mattress, by design, gave only a little and James Bond found himself more or less in the firing position he had been in on the Century Range, but now staring across broken, thickly weeded bombed ground towards the bright river of the Zimmerstrasse – the border with East Berlin. It looked about a hundred and fifty yards away. Captain Sender's voice from above him and behind the curtain began reciting. It reminded Bond of a spiritualist séance.

'That's bombed ground in front of you. Plenty of cover. A hundred and thirty yards of it up to the frontier. Then the frontier – the street – and then a big stretch of more bombed ground on the enemy side. That's why 272 chose this route. It's one of the few places in the town which is broken land – thick weeds, ruined walls, cellars – on both sides of the frontier. He will sneak through that mess on the other side and make a dash across the Zimmerstrasse for the mess on our side. Trouble is, he'll have thirty yards of brightly lit frontier to sprint across. That'll be the killing ground. Right?'

Bond said, 'Yes.' He said it softly. The scent of the enemy, the need to take care, already had him by the nerves.

'To your left, that big new ten-storey block is the Haus der Ministerien, the chief brain-centre of East Berlin. You can see the lights are still on in most of the windows. Most of those'll stay on all night. These chaps work hard – shifts all round the clock. You probably won't need to worry about the lighted ones. This "Trigger" chap'll almost certainly fire from one of the dark windows. You'll see there's a block of four together on the corner above the intersection. They've stayed dark last night and tonight. They've got the best field of fire. From here, their range varies from three hundred to three hundred and ten yards. I've got all the figures and so on when you want them. You needn't worry about much else. That street stays empty during the night – only the motorized patrols about every half an hour – light armoured car with a couple of motor-cycles as escort. Last night, which I suppose is typical, between six and seven when this thing's going to be done, there were a few people that came and went out of that side door.

Civil servant types. Before that nothing out of the ordinary – usual flow of people in and out of a busy government building – except, of all things, a whole damned women's orchestra. Made the hell of a racket in some concert hall they've got in there. Part of the block is the Ministry of Culture. Otherwise nothing – certainly none of the KGB people we know, nor any signs of preparation for a job like this. But there wouldn't be. They're careful chaps, the opposition. Anyway, have a good look. Don't forget it's darker than it will be tomorrow around six. But you can get the general picture.'

Bond got the general picture and it stayed with him long after the other man was asleep and snoring softly with a gentle regular clicking sound – a Wykehamist snore, Bond reflected irritably.

Yes, he had got the picture – the picture of a flicker of movement among the shadowy ruins on the other side of the gleaming river of light, a pause, then the wild zigzagging sprint of a man in the full glare of the arcs, the crash of gunfire and either a crumpled, sprawling heap in the middle of the wide street or the noise of his onward dash through the weeds and rubble of the Western Sector – sudden death or a home run. The true gauntlet! How much time would Bond have to spot the Russian sniper in one of those dark windows? And kill him? Five seconds? Ten? When dawn edged the curtains with gun-metal, Bond capitulated to his fretting mind. It had won. He went softly into the bathroom and surveyed the ranks of medicine bottles that a thoughtful Secret Service had provided to keep its executioner in good shape. He selected the Tuinal, chased down two of the ruby-and-blue depth-charges with a glass of water and went back to bed. Then, pole-axed, he slept.

He awoke at midday. The flat was empty. Bond drew the curtains to let in the grey Prussian day and, standing well back from the window, gazed out at the drabness of Berlin and listened to the tram noises and to the distant screeching of the U-Bahn as it took the big curve into the Zoo station. He gave a quick, reluctant glance at what he had examined the night before, noted that the weeds among the bomb rubble were much the same as the London ones – rose-bay willow-herb, dock and bracken – and then went into the kitchen. There was a note propped against a loaf of bread: 'My friend [a Secret Service euphemism which in this context meant Sender's chief] says it's all right for you to go out. But to be back by 1700 hours. Your gear [double-talk for Bond's rifle] has arrived and the batman will lay it out this pm. P. Sender.'

Bond lit the gas cooker, burned the message with a sneer at his profession, and then brewed himself a vast dish of scrambled eggs and bacon which he heaped on buttered toast and washed down with black coffee into which he had poured a liberal tot of whisky. Then he bathed and shaved, dressed in the drab, anonymous, middle-European clothes he had brought over for the purpose, looked at his disordered bed, decided to hell with it, and went down in the lift and out of the building.

James Bond had always found Berlin a glum, inimical city dry varnished on the Western side with a brittle veneer of gimcrack polish, rather like the chromium trim on American motor-cars. He walked to the Kurfürstendamm, sat in the Café Marquardt, drank an espresso and moodily watched the obedient queues of pedestrians waiting for the 'Go' sign on the traffic lights while the shiny stream of cars went through their dangerous quadrille at the busy intersection. It was cold outside and the sharp wind from the Russian steppes whipped at the girls' skirts and at the waterproofs of the impatient hurrying men each with the inevitable briefcase tucked under his arm. The infra-red wall heaters in the café glared redly down and gave a spurious glow to the faces of the café-squatters consuming their traditional 'one cup of coffee and ten glasses of water', reading the free newspapers and periodicals in their wooden racks or earnestly bent over business documents. Bond, closing his mind to the evening, debated with himself about ways to spend the afternoon. It finally came down to a choice between a visit to that respectable-looking brownstone house in the Clausewitzstrasse, known to all concierges and taxi-drivers, or a trip to the Wannsee and a strenuous walk in the Grunewald. Virtue triumphed. Bond paid for his coffee, went out into the cold and took a taxi to the Zoo station.

The pretty young trees round the long lake had already been touched by the breath of autumn and there was occasional gold amongst the green. Bond walked hard for two hours along the leafy paths, then chose a restaurant with a glassed-in veranda above the lake and greatly enjoyed a high tea consisting of a double portion of matjes herrings smothered in cream and onion rings, and two 'Molle mit Korn', the Berlin equivalent of a 'boiler-maker and his assistant' – schnapps, doubles, washed down with draught Löwenbräu. Then, feeling more encouraged, he took the S-Bahn back into the city.

Outside the apartment house, a nondescript young man was tinkering with the engine of a black Opel Kapitan. He didn't take his head out from under the bonnet when Bond passed close by him and went up to the door and pressed the bell.

Captain Sender was reassuring. It was a 'friend' – a corporal from the transport section of Station WB. He had fixed up some bad engine trouble on the Opel. Each night, from six to seven, he would be ready to produce a series of multiple back-fires when a signal on a walkie-talkie operated by Sender told him to do so. This would give some kind of cover for the noise of Bond's shooting. Otherwise the neighbourhood might alert the police and there would be a lot of untidy explaining to be done. Their hideout was in the American sector and, while their American 'friends' had given Station WB clearance for this operation, the 'friends' were naturally anxious that it should be a clean job and without repercussions.

Bond was suitably impressed by the car gimmick, as he was by the very workmanlike preparations that had been made for him in the living-room. Here, behind the head of his high bed, giving a perfect firing position, a wood and metal stand had been erected against the broad window-sill and along it lay the Winchester, the tip of its barrel just denting the curtains. The wood and all the metal parts of the rifle and Sniperscope had been painted a dull black and, laid out on the bed like sinister evening clothes, was a black velvet hood stitched to a waist-length shirt of the same material. The hood had wide slits for the eyes and mouth. It reminded Bond of old prints of the Spanish Inquisition, or of the anonymous operators on the guillotine platform during the French Revolution. There was a similar hood on Captain Sender's bed, and on his section of the window-sill there lay a pair of night-glasses and the microphone for the walkie-talkie.

Captain Sender, his face worried and tense with nerves, said there was no news at the Station, no change in the situation as they knew it. Did Bond want anything to eat? Or a cup of tea? Perhaps a tranquillizer – there were several kinds in the bathroom?

Bond stitched a cheerful, relaxed expression on his face and said no thanks, and gave a light-hearted

336

account of his day while an artery near his solar plexus began thumping gently as tension built up inside him like a watch-spring tightening. Finally his small talk petered out and he lay down on his bed with a German thriller he had bought on his wanderings, while Captain Sender moved fretfully about the flat, looking too often at his watch and chain-smoking Kent filter-tips through (he was a careful man) a Dunhill filter holder.

James Bond's choice of reading matter, prompted by a spectacular jacket of a half-naked girl strapped to a bed, turned out to have been a happy one for the occasion. It was called *Verderbt, Verdammt, Verraten*. The prefix *'ver'* signified that the girl had not only been ruined, damned and betrayed, but that she had suffered these misfortunes most thoroughly. James Bond temporarily lost himself in the tribulations of the heroine, Gräfin Liselotte Mutzenbacher, and it was with irritation that he heard Captain Sender say that it was five thirty and time to take up their positions.

Bond took off his coat and tie, put two sticks of chewing gum in his mouth and donned the hood. The lights were switched off by Captain Sender and Bond lay along the bed, got his eye to the eye-piece of the Sniperscope and gently lifted the bottom edge of the curtain back and over his shoulders.

Now dusk was approaching, but otherwise the scene, a year later to become famous as 'Checkpoint Charlie', was like a well-remembered photograph – the waste-land in front of him, the bright river of the frontier road, the farther waste-land and, on the left, the ugly square block of the Haus der Ministerien with its lit and dark windows. Bond scanned it all slowly, moving the Sniperscope, with the rifle, by means of the precision screws on the wooden base. It was all the same except that now there was a trickle of personnel leaving and entering the Ministry through the door on to the Wilhelmstrasse. Bond looked along at the four dark windows – dark again tonight – that he agreed with Sender were the enemy's firing points. The curtains were drawn back and the sash windows were wide open at the bottom. Bond's 'scope could not penetrate into the rooms, but there was no sign of movement within the four oblong, black, gaping mouths.

Now there was extra traffic in the street below. The women's orchestra came trooping down the pavement towards the entrance – twenty laughing, talking girls carrying their instruments – violin and wind instrument cases, satchels with their scores, and four of them with the drums – a gay, happy little crocodile. Bond was reflecting that some people still seemed to find life fun in the Soviet Sector, when his glasses picked out and stayed on the girl carrying the 'cello. Bond's masticating jaws stopped still and then reflectively went on with their chewing as he twisted the screw to depress the Sniperscope and keep her in its centre.

The girl was taller than the others and her long, straight, fair hair, falling to her shoulders, shone

338

like molten gold under the arcs at the intersection. She was hurrying along in a charming, excited way, carrying the 'cello case as if it were no heavier than a violin. Everything was flying – the skirt of her coat, her feet, her hair. She was vivid with movement and life and, it seemed, with gaiety and happiness as she chattered to the two girls who flanked her and laughed back at what she was saying. As she turned in at the entrance amidst her troupe, the arcs momentarily caught a beautiful, pale profile. And then she was gone and, it seemed to Bond, with her disappearance a stab of grief lanced into his heart. How odd! How very odd! This had not happened to him since he was young. And now this single girl, seen only indistinctly and far away, had caused him to suffer this sharp pang of longing, this thrill of animal magnetism! Morosely, Bond glanced down at the luminous dial of his watch. Five fifty. Only ten minutes to go. No transport arriving at the entrance. None of those anonymous black Zik saloons he had half expected. He closed as much of his mind as he could to the girl and sharpened his wits. Get on, damn you! Get back to your job!

From somewhere inside the Ministry there came the familiar sounds of an orchestra tuning up – the strings tuning their instruments to single notes on the piano, the sharp blare of individual wood-winds – then a pause and then the collective crash of melody as the whole orchestra threw itself competently, so far as Bond could judge, into the opening bars of what even to James Bond was vaguely familiar.

'The Polovtsian Dances from *Prince Igor*,' said Captain Sender succinctly. 'Anyway, six o'clock coming up,' and then, urgently, 'Hey! Right-hand bottom of the four windows! Watch out!'

Bond minutely depressed the Sniperscope. Yes, there was movement inside the black cave. Now, from the interior, a thick black object, a weapon, had slid out. It moved firmly, minutely, swivelling down and sideways so as to cover the stretch of the Zimmerstrasse between the two waste-lands of rubble. Then the unseen operator in the room behind seemed satisfied and the weapon remained still, fixed obviously to a stand such as Bond had beneath his rifle.

'What is it? What sort of gun?' Captain Sender's voice was more breathless than it should have been. Take it easy, dammit! thought Bond. It's me who's supposed to have the nerves.

He strained his eyes, taking in the squat flash eliminator at the muzzle, the telescopic sight and thick downward chunk of magazine. Yes, that would be it! Absolutely for sure – and the best they had!

'Kalashnikov,' he said curtly. 'Sub-machine-gun. Gas-operated. Thirty rounds in 7.62 millimetre. Favourite with the KGB. They're going to do a saturation job after all. Perfect for range. We'll have to get him pretty quick or 272'll end up not just dead but strawberry jam. You keep an eye out for

340

any movement over there in the rubble. I'll have to stay married to that window and the gun. He'll have to show himself to fire. Other chaps are probably spotting behind him – perhaps from all four windows. Much the sort of set-up we expected, but I didn't think they'd use a weapon that's going to make all the racket this one will. Should have known they would. A running man would be hard to get in this light with a single-shot job.'

Bond fiddled minutely with the traversing and elevating screws at his fingertips and got the fine lines of the 'scope exactly intersected, just behind where the butt of the enemy gun merged into the blackness behind. Get the chest – don't bother about the head!

Inside the hood, Bond's face began to sweat and his eye socket was slippery against the rubber of the eye-piece. That didn't matter. It was only his hands, his trigger-finger, that must stay bone dry. As the minutes ticked by, he frequently blinked his eyes to rest them, shifted his limbs to keep them supple, listened to the music to relax his mind.

The minutes slouched on leaden feet. How old would she be? Early twenties – say, twenty-three. With that poise and insouciance, the hint of authority in her long easy stride, she would come of good racy stock – one of the old Prussian families probably, or from similar remnants in Poland or even Russia. Why in hell did she have to choose the 'cello? There was something almost indecent

341

in the idea of that bulbous, ungainly instrument between her splayed thighs. Of course Suggia had managed to look elegant, and so did that girl Amaryllis somebody. But they should invent a way for women to play the damned thing side-saddle.

At his side Captain Sender said, 'Seven o'clock. Nothing's stirred on the other side. Bit of movement on our side, near a cellar close to the frontier; that'll be our reception committee – two good men from the Station. Better stay with it until they close down. Let me know when they take that gun in.'

'All right.'

It was seven thirty when the KGB sub-machine-gun was gently drawn back into the black interior. One by one the bottom sashes of the four windows were closed. The cold-hearted game was over for the night. 272 was still holed up. Two more nights to go!

Bond softly drew the curtain over his shoulders and across the muzzle of the Winchester. He got up, pulled off his cowl and went into the bathroom and stripped and had a shower. Then he had two large whiskies on the rocks in quick succession, while he waited, his ears pricked, for the now muffled sound of the orchestra to stop. When at eight o'clock it did (with the expert comment from Sender, 'Borodin's *Prince Igor*, Choral Dance Number 17, I think,') he said to Sender, who had been getting off his report in garbled language to the Head of Station, 'Just going to have another look. I've rather taken to that tall blonde with the 'cello.'

'Didn't notice her,' said Sender, uninterested. He went into the kitchen. Tea, guessed Bond. Or perhaps Horlicks. Bond donned his cowl, went back to his firing position and depressed the Sniperscope to the doorway of the Ministry. Yes, there they went, not so gay and laughing now. Tired, perhaps. And now here she came, less lively but still with that beautiful careless stride. Bond watched the blown, golden hair and the fawn rain-coat until it had vanished into the indigo dusk up the Wilhelmstrasse. Where did she live? In some miserable, flaked room in the suburbs? Or in one of the privileged apartments in the hideous, lavatory-tiled Stalinallee?

Bond drew himself back. Somewhere, within easy reach, that girl lived. Was she married? Did she have a lover? Anyway to hell with it! She was not for him.

The next day, and the next night-watch, were dupli-cates, with small variations, of the first. James Bond had two more brief rendezvous, by Sniperscope, with the girl, and the rest was a killing of time and a tightening of the tension that, by the time the third and final day came, was like a fog in the small room.

James Bond crammed the third day with an almost lunatic programme of museums, art galleries, the zoo and a film, hardly perceiving anything he looked

343

at, his mind's eye divided between the girl and those four black squares and the black tube and the unknown man behind it – the man he was now certainly going to kill tonight.

Back in the apartment punctually at five, Bond narrowly averted a row with Captain Sender, because he had poured himself a stiff whisky before putting on the hideous cowl that now stank of his sweat. Captain Sender had tried to prevent him and, when he failed, had threatened to call up Head of Station and report Bond for breaking training.

'Look, my friend,' said Bond wearily, 'I've got to commit a murder tonight. Not you. Me. So be a good chap and stuff it, would you? You can tell Tanqueray anything you like when it's over. Think I like this job? Having a Double-O number and so on? I'd be quite happy for you to get me sacked from the Double-O Section. Then I could settle down and make a snug nest of papers as an ordinary Staffer. Right?' Bond drank down his whisky, reached for his thriller, now arriving at an appalling climax, and threw himself on the bed.

Captain Sender, icily silent, went off into the kitchen to brew, from the sounds, his inevitable cuppa.

Bond felt the whisky beginning to melt the coiled nerves in his stomach. Now then, Liselotte, how in hell are you going to get out of this fix?

It was exactly six five when Sender, at his post, began talking excitedly. 'Bond, there's something moving way back over there. Now he's stopped – wait, no, he's on the move again, keeping low. There's a bit of broken wall there. He'll be out of sight of the opposition. But thick weeds, yards of them, ahead of him. Christ! He's coming through the weeds. And they're moving. Hope to God they think it's only the wind.

Now he's through and gone to ground. Any reaction?'

'No,' said Bond tensely. 'Keep on telling me. How far to the frontier?'

'He's only got about fifty yards to go.' Captain Sender's voice was harsh with excitement. 'Broken stuff, but some of it's open. Then a solid chunk of wall right up against the pavement. He'll have to get over it. They can't fail to spot him then. Now! Now he's made ten yards, and another ten. Got him clearly then. Blackened his face and hands. Get ready! Any moment now he'll make the last sprint.'

James Bond felt the sweat pouring down his face and neck. He took a chance and quickly wiped his hands down his sides and then got them back to the rifle, his finger inside the guard, just lying along the curved trigger. 'There's something moving in the room behind the gun. They must have spotted him. Get that Opel working.'

Bond heard the code word go into the microphone, heard the Opel in the street below start up, felt his pulse quicken as the engine leaped into life and a series of ear-splitting cracks came from the exhaust.

The movement in the black cave was now definite. A black arm with a black glove had reached out and under the stock.

'Now!' ejaculated Captain Sender. 'Now! He's run for the wall! He's up it! Just going to jump!'

And then, in the Sniperscope, Bond saw the head of 'Trigger' – the purity of the profile, the golden bell of hair – all laid out along the stock of the Kalashnikov! She was dead, a sitting duck! Bond's fingers flashed down to the screws, inched them round and, as yellow flame fluttered at the snout of the sub-machine-gun, squeezed the trigger.

The bullet, dead on at three hundred and ten yards, must have hit where the stock ended up the barrel, might have got her in the left hand, but the effect was to tear the gun off its mountings, smash it against the side of the window-frame and then hurl it out of the window. It turned several times on its way down and crashed into the middle of the street.

'He's over!' shouted Captain Sender. 'He's over! He's done it! My God, he's done it!'

'Get down! said Bond sharply, and threw himself sideways off the bed as the big eye of a searchlight in one of the black windows blazed on, swerving up the street towards their block and their room. Then gunfire crashed and the bullets howled into their window, ripping the curtains, smashing the woodwork, thudding into the walls.

Behind the roar and zing of the bullets, Bond heard the Opel race off down the street and, behind that again, the fragmentary whisper of the orchestra. The combination of the two background noises clicked. Of course! The orchestra had probably raised an infernal din throughout the Haus der Ministerien, having been used, like the back-firing Opel on this side, to provide some cover for a sharp burst of fire, on their side by 'Trigger'. Had she carried her weapon to and fro every day in that 'cello case? Was the whole orchestra composed of KGB women? Had the other instrument cases contained only equipment – the big drum perhaps the searchlight – while the real instruments were available in the concert hall? Too elaborate? Too fantastic? Probably. But there had been no doubt about the girl. In the Sniperscope, Bond had even been able to see one wide, heavily lashed, aiming eye. Had he hurt her? Almost certainly her left arm. There would be no chance of seeing her, seeing how she was, if she left with the orchestra. Now he would never see her again. Their window would be a death trap. To underline the fact, a stray bullet smashed into the mechanism of the Winchester, already overturned and damaged, and hot lead splashed down on Bond's hand, burning the skin. On Bond's emphatic oath, abruptly the firing stopped and silence sang in the room.

Captain Sender emerged from beside his bed, brushing glass out of his hair. They crunched across the floor and through the splintered door into the kitchen. Here, because it faced away from the street, it was safe to switch on the light.

'Any damage?' asked Bond.

'No. You all right?' Captain Sender's pale eyes were bright with the fever that comes in battle. They also, Bond noticed, held a sharp glint of accusation.

'Yes. Just get an Elastoplast for my hand. Caught a splash from one of the bullets.' Bond went into the bathroom. When he came out, Captain Sender was sitting by the walkie-talkie he had fetched from the sitting-room. He was speaking into it. Now he said into the microphone, 'That's all for now. Fine about 272. Hurry the armoured car, if you would. Be glad to get out of here, and 007 will need to write his version of what happened. Okay? Then OVER and OUT.'

Captain Sender turned to Bond. Half accusing, half embarrassed, he said, 'Afraid Head of Station needs your reasons in writing for not getting that chap. I had to tell him I'd seen you alter your aim at the last second. Gave "Trigger" time to get off a burst. Damned lucky for 272 he'd just begun his sprint. Blew chunks off the wall behind him. What was it all about?'

James Bond knew he could lie, knew he could fake a dozen reasons why. Instead he took a deep pull at the strong whisky he had poured for himself, put the glass down and looked Captain Sender straight in the eye.

'"Trigger" was a woman.'

'So what? KGB have got plenty of women agents – and women gunners. I'm not in the least surprised. The Russian women's team always does well in the World Championships. Last meeting, in Moscow, they came first, second and third against seven countries. I can even remember two of their names – Donskaya and Lomova, terrific shots. She may even have been one of them. What did she look like? Records'll probably be able to turn her up.'

'She was a blonde. She was the girl who carried the 'cello in that orchestra. Probably had her gun in the 'cello case. The orchestra was to cover up the shooting.'

'Oh!' said Captain Sender slowly, 'I see. The girl you were keen on?'

'That's right.'

'Well, I'm sorry, but I'll have to put that in my report too. You had clear orders to exterminate "Trigger".'

There came the sound of a car approaching. It pulled up somewhere below. The bell rang twice. Sender said, 'Well, let's get going. They've sent an armoured car to get us out of here.' He paused. His eyes flicked over Bond's shoulder, avoiding Bond's eyes. 'Sorry about the report. Got to do my duty, y'know. You should have killed that sniper whoever it was.'

Bond got up. He suddenly didn't want to leave the stinking little smashed-up flat, leave the place from which, for three days, he had had this long-range, one-sided romance with an unknown girl – an unknown enemy agent with much the same job in her outfit as he had in his. Poor little bitch! She would be in worse trouble now than he was! She'd certainly be court-martialled for muffing this job. Probably be kicked out of the KGB. He shrugged. At least they'd stop short of killing her – as he himself had done.

James Bond said wearily, 'Okay. With any luck it'll cost me my Double-O number. But tell Head of Station not to worry. That girl won't do any more sniping. Probably lost her left hand. Certainly broke her nerve for that kind of work. Scared the living daylights out of her. In my book, that was enough. Let's go.'

CHAPTER 9

007 IN NEW YORK

The story that follows was first published in the USA in October 1963 in the *New York Herald Tribune* under the title 'Agent 007 in New York'. Ian Fleming's original title was 'Reflections in a Carey Cadillac' and the original typescript is dated in Ian's handwriting 'Aug. 20 1963'. In 1964 it was included in the chapter on New York in the American edition of *Thrilling Cities*, which, in Ian's words, consists of 'thirteen essays on some thrilling cities of the world written for the *Sunday Times* in 1959 and 1960'.

Ian's original essay on New York begins, 'I enjoyed myself least of all in New York', and was clearly much influenced by a special issue of the weekly magazine the Nation, dated 31 October 1959, and entitled *The Shame of New York*, to which Ian devoted two pages out of the six printed in the original Cape British edition of the book. The American publishers clearly anticipated the hostile reaction of many Americans (not only New Yorkers) to the original piece and asked Ian to provide some consolation. His response was to add

'007 in New York' and the following introductory paragraph solely for the US edition of the book:

By way of a postscript I might say that I am well aware these grim feelings I have expressed for New York may shock or depress some of my readers. In fact, I would be disappointed if this were not the case. In deference to these readers, I here submit the record of another visitor to the city, a friend of mine with the dull name of James Bond, whose taste and responses are not always my own and whose recent minor adventure in New York (his profession is rather an odd one) may prove more cheerful in the reading.

Peter Janson-Smith
London, April 2001

It was around ten o'clock on a blue and golden morning at the end of September and the BOAC Monarch flight from London had come in at the same time as four other international flights. James Bond, his stomach queasy from the BOAC version of 'An English Country House Breakfast', took his place stoically in a long queue that included plenty of squalling children and in due course said that he had spent the last ten nights in London. Then to Immigration – fifteen minutes to show his passport that said he was 'David Barlow, Merchant' and that he had eyes and hair and was six feet tall; and then to the Gehenna of the Idlewild Customs that has been carefully designed, in Bond's opinion, to give visitors to the United States coronary thrombosis. Everyone, each with his stupid little trolley, looked, after a night's flight, wretched and undignified. Waiting for his suitcase to appear behind the glass of the unloading bay and then to be graciously released for him to fight for and hump over to the customs lines, all of which were overloaded while each bag or bundle (why not a spot-check?) was opened and prodded and then laborously closed, often between slaps at fretting children, by its exhausted owner. Bond glanced up at the glass-walled balcony that ran round the great hall. A man in a rainproof and Trilby, middle-aged, nondescript, was inspecting the orderly hell through a pair of folding opera-glasses. Anybody examining him or, indeed, any one else through binoculars was an object of suspicion to James Bond, but now his conspiratorial mind merely registered that this would be a good link in an efficient hotel-robbery machine. The man with the glasses would note the rich-looking woman declaring her jewellery, slip downstairs when she was released from Customs, tail her into New York, get beside her at the desk, hear her room number being called to the captain, and the rest would be up to the mechanics. Bond shrugged. At least the man didn't seem interested in him. He had his single suitcase passed by the polite man with the badge. Then, sweating with the unnecessary central heating, he carried it out through the automatic glass doors into the blessed fresh fall air. The Carey Cadillac, as a message had told him, was already waiting. James Bond always used the firm. They had fine cars and superb drivers, rigid discipline and total discretion, and they didn't smell of stale cigar smoke. Bond even wondered if Commander Carey's organization, supposing it had equated

David Barlow with James Bond, would have betrayed their standards by informing CIA. Well, no doubt the United States had to come first, and anyway, did Commander Carey know who James Bond was? The Immigration people certainly did. In the great black bible with the thickly printed yellow pages the officer had consulted when he took Bond's passport, Bond knew that there were three Bonds and that one of them was 'James, British, Passport 391354. Inform Chief Officer.' How closely did Careys work with these people? Probably only if it was police business. Anyway, James Bond felt pretty confident that he could spend twenty-four hours in New York, make the contact and get out again without embarrassing explanations having to be given to Messrs Hoover or McCone. For this was an embarrassing, unattractive business that M had sent Bond anonymously to New York to undertake. It was to warn a nice girl, who had once worked for the Secret Service, an English girl now earning her living in New York, that she was cohabiting with a Soviet agent of the KGB attached to the UN and that M knew that the FBI and the CIA were getting very close to learning her identity. It was doing the dirt on two friendly organizations, of course, and it would be highly embarrassing if Bond were found out, but the girl had been a first-class staff officer, and when he could, M looked after his own. So Bond had been instructed to make contact and swindles leered and winked. What happened to these re-sprayed crocks when the weather had finally rotted their guts? Where did they finally go to die? Mightn't they be useful if they were run into the sea to conquer coastal erosion? Take a letter to the *Herald Tribune*!

Then there was the question of lunch. Dinner with Solange would be easy – Lutèce in the sixties, one of the great restaurants of the world. But for lunch by himself? In the old days it would certainly have been the '21,' but the expense-account aristocracy had captured even that strong-hold, inflating the prices and, because they didn't know good from bad, deflating the food. But he would go there for old times' sake and have a couple of dry martinis – Beefeaters with a domestic vermouth, shaken with a twist of lemon peel – at the bar. And then what about the best meal in New York – oyster stew with cream, crackers, and Miller High Life at the Oyster Bar at Grand Central? No, he didn't want to sit up at a bar – somewhere spacious and comfortable where he could read a paper in peace. Yes. That was it! The Edwardian Room at the Plaza, a corner table. They didn't know him there, but he knew he could get what he wanted to eat – not like Chambord or Pavillon with their irritating Wine and Foodmanship and, in the case of the latter, the miasma of a hundred different women's scents to confound your palate. He would have one more dry martini at the table, then smoked salmon and the particular scrambled eggs he had once (Felix Leiter knew the head-waiter) instructed them how to make.* Yes, that sounded all right. He would have to take a chance with the smoked salmon. It used to be Scotch in the Edwardian Room, not that thickly cut, dry and tasteless Canadian stuff. But one could never tell with American food. As long as they got their steaks and sea-food right, the rest could go to hell. And everything was so long frozen, in some vast communal food-morgue presumably, that flavour had gone from all American food except the Italian. Everything tasted the same – a sort

*SCRAMBLED EGGS 'JAMES BOND.'
For four individualists:

12 fresh eggs
Salt and pepper
5–6 oz. of fresh butter

Break the eggs into a bowl. Beat thoroughly with a fork and season well. In a small copper (or heavy-bottomed saucepan) melt four oz. of the butter. When melted, pour in the eggs and cook over a very low heat, whisking continuously with a small egg whisk.

While the eggs are slightly more moist than you would wish for eating, remove pan from heat, add rest of butter and continue whisking for half a minute, adding the while finely chopped chives or fine herbs. Serve on hot buttered toast in individual copper dishes (for appearance only) with pink champagne (Taittainger) and low music.